END GAME

END GAME

MATTHEW GLASS

CORVUS

First published in the UK in 2011 by Corvus,
an imprint of Atlantic Books Ltd.

9 8 7 6 5 4 3 2 1

A CIP catalogue record for this book is available from
the British Library.

ISBN: 978-1-84887-774-0 (hardback)
ISBN: 978-1-84887-775-7 (trade paperback)

Printed in Great Britain by the MPG Books Group

Corvus
An imprint of Atlantic Books Ltd
Ormond House
26-27 Boswell Street
London WC1N 3JZ

www.corvus-books.co.uk

To claim a refund on your purchase price of *End Game*, send
your name, postal address, email address and receipt to: *End
Game* Offer, Corvus, Ormond House, 26-27 Boswell St, London
WC1N 3JZ. You should also include a short explanation of why
you do not think *End Game* is the best thriller you've read in the
last twelve months. This offer is valid for copies purchased up
until 30th April 2011.

END GAME

prologue

Masindi, Uganda
July 5, 2018

PEOPLE BEGAN ARRIVING at daybreak. They came along the dirt roads and tracks leading into the town, some on foot, some in brightly painted trucks that bounced in and out of potholes, bringing the products of the local countryside, maize, chillies, sweet potato, okra, tomatoes, onions, gourds. They spread their wares on rugs in the marketplace. Business began, as it did every Thursday. A group of policemen stood by, lazily leaning on their rifles and exchanging remarks with the traders. The colonial-era shopfronts around the market were faded and peeling, bearing handwritten signs. The Bamugisa Barber Shop. Honest Brothers General Store. The shopkeepers waited in the doorways and bantered with the country people, enticing them inside.

By four o'clock it was over. The market emptied. The people who had come into the town made their way back into the countryside. The shopkeepers watched them go.

Night fell. The bare red dirt of the streets turned inky black. Lights glowed for a while in the shops and then went out.

And then they came. Out of the scrub north of the town. Twenty-five, maybe thirty. They wore green fatigues. Some were tall, lean, in their late teens or twenties. Others were children. They carried machetes and rough wooden clubs. The older ones had Kalashnikovs.

In the Masindi Hotel, a colonial building dating from the 1920s, a few westerners were drinking in the bar. The town had nothing much of interest for tourists. Travellers who stopped in Masindi were usually on their way to the Murchison Falls, sixty miles to the northwest, or on their way back. A couple of the drinkers were aid workers from the

1

town's hospital, where an American medical charity, Health for All, supplemented the government service.

But the hotel wasn't the objective of the group that had come in from the bush, and they slipped silently past it, hugging the shadows and ignoring the lights and the sound of voices from the bar. One of them knew the town and was leading the others. They used the darkest streets, avoiding the police station. They streamed through the empty market and past the shops, now shuttered, that surrounded it. Finally they stopped.

Further along the street a naked bulb hung at the entrance to the hospital compound. Inside the fence, a row of long, barracks-like wards stood in the darkness. Beyond the wards were the living quarters of the foreign staff.

The leaders of the group exchanged words. One of them went up the street and looked and came back. There was no sign of a guard at the gate. More words were exchanged. Then the adults amongst them grabbed hold of the children, in case they should try to back off, and they moved up the street and went in.

The killing began with machetes and clubs. The screams of the patients woke the four guards who were asleep in their shack in the compound. They had pistols. Gunfire broke out. Twenty minutes later a group of police arrived in an open-top vehicle and were mown down by two of the attackers who had been left at the gate, while behind them the frenzy of killing in the compound continued. Soldiers from the regional army barracks joined the assault. They stormed the entrance, losing a number of their men in the street. Inside, they had to fight for the hospital ward by ward. Then they had to fight for the grounds. It wasn't until dawn that they took back control.

The light of morning revealed the death toll. Two hundred and eighteen bodies were found in the hospital, the living quarters and the grounds. Most had been clubbed or hacked to death. At least as many again were injured. Six attackers were taken alive with wounds of varying severity.

Word of the massacre was already being fed to the world over mobile phone. News outlets around the globe carried interviews with confused tourists who had awoken to the sound of gunfire from across the town. The district's civil governor made a statement that admitted an incident had taken place but gave no details. In the army infirmary, the captured attackers were being interrogated. Lying on blood-stained stretchers, they claimed to be fighters of the Lord's Resistance Army, making no attempt to hide their identities. The district military commander was skeptical. LRA activity had been subdued over recent months, and the group had never struck so far from the heartland of its insurgency in the far north of the country. Masindi was over a hundred miles from the jungle borderlands of Uganda, Congo and Sudan where the LRA had waged a thirty-year war of terror. It had always been safe from such attacks.

Yet the injured prisoners persisted in their story, even when their interrogators used blows to try to beat an alternative version out of them. They seemed to want to be sure the authorities knew. And the killing method and the presence of children amongst the attackers were consistent with the practices of the LRA. It seemed that the LRA had chosen to strike the town as a way of sending a message to the government that it was still in business, more dangerous than ever.

Over the next day, the bodies were identified. Of the dead, one hundred and seventeen were patients, fifty-nine were hospital staff, twenty-four were police and soldiers, and eighteen were the corpses of attackers.

Amongst the fifty-nine dead staff, thirty-two were citizens of the United States.

1

HE OPENED THE file. It wasn't the first time he had looked at it. He glanced down the lines of the first page, a summary of the known sequence of events. The following two pages were intelligence background on the LRA and the regional political situation. The next page was an outline of possible options for response from his national security advisor. After that were pictures and short biographies of each of the dead Americans, four to a page. There were eight pages of them. Another three had died of their wounds since the file had been prepared, and a number of others were in critical condition.

He looked through the pictures. Then he turned back to the page that set out the options for response. He had issued an immediate condemnation of the killings. One of the options was to leave it at that. There were several others. In the wake of the attack, the Ugandan government had called on the US to aid it in eradicating the LRA.

He read over the options, thinking through the implications.

Thomas Paxton Knowles was a tall man of fifty-eight with a jutting, square jaw and a full head of greying hair. President for eighteen months, he had spent twenty years of his life making his way towards the White House, the last four as governor of Nevada.

Like any president, Tom Knowles had inherited a ready-made complexity of foreign involvements the day he walked into the Oval Office. Seventeen years after invading Afghanistan US forces were still deployed in and around Kabul, supposedly acting as advisors and trainers to the Afghan army, and American drone aircraft were a constant feature in the skies over the Pakistan border. Five years on from the Georgia crisis the presence of US troops remained a constant irritant with the Russians, without any obvious exit strategy. Closer to home, what had started as a program of joint US and

Mexican border patrols had turned into a fortified deployment with a virtual war being fought with armed drugs gangs on both sides of the border and frequent US casualties. Colombia, Liberia, Haiti and the Philippines were all places where there were US missions of varying sizes.

That was a good long list and it posed enough challenges without requiring any additions. The Masindi Massacre was one in a litany of outrages by a longstanding, local insurgency in a distant country in which a group of Americans had happened to get involved. The charity had been warned by the State Department about sending people to serve in Uganda. It would be perfectly possible for him to do nothing beyond the condemnation he had already issued.

But thirty-two Americans – rising to thirty-five, and possibly going higher – had been killed in cold blood. And who was to say the LRA hadn't targeted the hospital compound in Masindi because they knew Americans would be there?

A good part of the Republican Party was demanding some kind of response, but Knowles didn't need political pressure to make him feel the need for action. From all he had been told in the last couple of days, the LRA was a cancer on humanity. It had no apparent program beyond the murder, rape and robbery of the local populations in a terrorized triangle of territory in northern Uganda, southern Sudan and northeast Congo. Like some kind of hideous reptile, it survived in the dark crevices created by the political tensions between the three affected states. Every time the group seemed to be dying away, it flared back into life, usually with a spectacular atrocity like the Masindi Massacre. Peace talks had brought the insurgency to the brink of cessation a number of times, only to collapse when the leaders of the group disappeared into the jungle to restart hostilities. At other times the Ugandan army had mounted a drive to eradicate it but had ground to a halt in the dense jungle of the area through inadequate manpower and lack of resolve from the other two countries where the LRA found temporary shelter before reinfiltrating its Ugandan base. And while this was happening, the ranks of the insurgents were constantly replenished by the abduction of children and their forced conversion into soldiers. There were stories of children being taken back to their villages and compelled to kill their own parents to prove their loyalty to their abductors. After thirty years of fighting this monster the Ugandan authorities felt powerless to eradicate it.

Knowles could envisage himself agreeing to the Ugandan government's request. If he gave the go-ahead, US troops could probably be on the ground in weeks. Eradicating the LRA was a clear objective, defined, contained, with a short time horizon, a willing local government, and an unambiguous case for intervention in the name of humanitarian goals. He hadn't seen a military assessment yet, but he didn't think an outfit like the LRA would pose much of a threat to the US army. His national security advisor, Gary Rose, thought likewise. The situation in Uganda had nothing in common with the awful embroilments in Afghanistan and Georgia, where military success was prevented by constant political double-dealing and corruption.

But Tom Knowles was a politician, not a crusader. As the standard bearer of the centrist wing of the Republican Party, he had taken the Republican nomination two years previously after a bruising set of primaries that narrowed down to a straight runoff with Mitch Moynihan, an Idaho senator out of the hardcore Republican right. The election he fought the following November was the first in which the recession that came out of the credit crunch of '08 and its long, lingering shock waves were beginning to seem a thing of the past. The pendulum had swung back and the country right across the political spectrum, left as well as right, responded to a rhetoric of smaller government, tax cuts and reduced federal spending. Knowles carefully kept his program moderate. He crafted a kind of reverse-Obama coalition of Republicans and centrist Democrats that swept him to power. His first eighteen months in the Oval Office had delivered economic stability and rising markets. That was the first thing the American electorate demanded of its president and would be until the trauma of the economic crisis was a lot more distant still. Rectitude and trust, as he said in just about every one of his speeches on the economy. Growth without overheating. That was the focus, a sound and stable domestic economy, and that was what he aimed to deliver. New foreign adventures weren't supposed to be on the menu.

Yet presidents aren't elected so as not to raise their eyes beyond the horizon, even presidents elected to steer a steady course away from the reef of a monumental economic trauma. Like all his predecessors, Tom Knowles took his place in history extremely seriously. He did have an international agenda, although not one that he had talked about much in the election or in the eighteen months since he had been sworn in. Together with his national security advisor and defense secretary, he felt that over the last eight years the US had led too little, had been too much interested in consensus and too little prepared to act. It was as if the country had looked at what it had done during the Bush years, saw the results, and been fearful of doing the same again, so fearful that it hadn't trusted itself to do anything on its own. It was a fearfulness that made him angry. Knowles believed that the world needed leadership now more than ever before. As China and India and Brazil rose to prominence – each with its different perspective and political culture – he felt strongly that the world needed someone to set out certain common, ineluctable principles and to be prepared to put those principles into action. Rightly or wrongly, Tom Knowles believed that only the United States could play that role.

The truth was, he couldn't have asked for a better opportunity than the one the Masindi Massacre presented. It came at the perfect time in his first term, with eighteen months of solid governance behind him to show that he was no trigger happy adventurer and enough time left ahead of him to get the whole thing done before he faced the American people again. None of the current US foreign interventions was of his making and each was bogged down in one way or another, in his view, because of compromises and poor decisions made by previous administrations. This one would be his, one that he could launch, prosecute and bring to a close on his watch, one that would allow him to show how a US military intervention should be done.

Beyond the effect of freeing the people of north Uganda from a terrorist menace, an intervention against the LRA would make a strong point. It would make the kind of statement Knowles wanted to make about American leadership in the world and about American willingness to exert that leadership when the cause was just.

Yet he knew enough history to recognize that his inclination to reach for the gun needed to be questioned. In the first flush of outrage after the massacre, the American people would support him. But it was easy to start something like this and then find, for reasons you hadn't foreseen, that it turned into a quagmire from which there was no honorable way out. And the American people wouldn't thank him for that. They wouldn't thank him in two years' time if he hadn't got it done and American boys were dying in Uganda when he was up for re-election.

He leafed through the file. He looked at the pages of faces staring out at him, young American men and women. All good people, all motivated by altruism – all dead. He paused and read a couple of the biographies beside the pictures.

He just didn't see how this could turn into a quagmire. It was so clear cut. The local political support was there, the objective was so well defined, the cause so just.

2

MARION ELLMAN LOOKED around the horseshoe-shaped table in the middle of the UN Security Council chamber. Seventeen ambassadors were seated there, including herself. Set back from the table, the spectator seats within the chamber were largely filled with African diplomats waiting to see which way the vote would go. Ellman herself had no idea.

It had taken almost two months to get here. Tom Knowles' idea of starting the operation against the LRA within a few weeks had sounded fine until the military planners got to work. The government of Uganda didn't need UN authorization to invite the US army onto its territory, but it soon became clear that the only practical way to project force into the landlocked territory of Uganda would require access across Kenya. The Kenyan government was prepared to provide air and land access and the use of a military base in the northwest of the country in exchange for a large chunk of development and military assistance, but not without domestic political cover in the form of a UN resolution calling for armed intervention in the Republic of Uganda. Suddenly the US found itself needing not only a majority on the Security Council, but the avoidance of opposition from China and Russia, the two veto-wielding members of the Council who were likely to vote down the resolution. That in turn meant weeks of negotiation and horse-trading in the corridors of the UN headquarters in Manhattan and in foreign ministries across the world.

Through the summer the State Department machine worked at getting a majority of votes behind a resolution and putting the Chinese and Russians into a position where they couldn't – or wouldn't – vote against it. They had reasons to. The Russians were always looking for leverage against the US because of the continuing American presence in Georgia. The Chinese were deeply involved in Sudan, where they ran the oil industry, and had no reason to want to see US troops across the Ugandan border, for however short a time. But for their own domestic and regional strategic reasons, neither government wanted to be seen gratuitously blocking an operation with overwhelmingly humanitarian aims. That was where they were vulnerable and Marion Ellman, the US ambassador to the UN, led the diplomatic offensive. Forty-four, an ex-assistant secretary of state for Latin American affairs and professor of international relations at Berkeley, Ellman was a tall woman, usually dressed in a pant suit, with an attractive, slightly masculine face and dark shoulder-length hair.

Now she waited for the president of the Council to open the debate.

As proposer of the resolution, Ellman spoke first. Her speech was relatively brief. Minds around the table had been made up, she knew, and nothing she said now was going to change them. The crimes of the LRA were well known. She gave a succinct overview of the LRA's murderous record and the failed attempts by the Ugandan government to eradicate it. Without naming them explicitly, she concluded with a last reminder to China and Russia of how they would be seen if they blocked the resolution.

The Russian ambassador, Evgeny Stepsin, didn't speak in the debate. The Chinese ambassador, Liu Ziyang, made remarks about the gravity of the decision and the risks attached to the internationalization of any conflict, no matter how localized it seemed. Ellman listened carefully to his words. It was always hard to read the nuances through translation, when not only the subtlety of meaning might be lost but the words were detached from the expression and body language that accompanied them. She knew Liu wasn't going to vote in favor. She tried to decipher whether he was using his apparent objection to 'internationalization', as he called it, in order to rationalize an abstention. Or was he trying to justify a veto? The Chinese ambassador was a small, energetic man with rimless spectacles. By the time he concluded Ellman still didn't know which way China was going to go.

Speaking in French, the Ivory Coast ambassador, the Council's president for the month, called for the vote.

First he asked those in favor of the resolution to raise their hands. Ellman did so and looked at the other ambassadors. She counted them off. Argentina, France, India, Ireland, Ivory Coast, Spain, Thailand, Tunisia and, sitting right beside her, the United Kingdom.

Ten votes, including hers, out of seventeen. She let out her breath. She had a majority. That was the first hurdle.

The translation of the Ivory Coast ambassador's voice came through her earpiece, calling on those voting against the resolution.

Chad, Bolivia and Serbia immediately voted no. Then Brazil. Then Malaysia.

She looked at Liu Ziyang across the stenographers' table in the middle of the horseshoe. Further around the table sat the big bulk of Evgeny Stepsin.

Neither Liu nor Stepsin made a move.

'Abstentions?' said the voice of the translator in her earphone.

Silently, the two men raised their hands.

THE SESSION BROKE up. The Ugandan ambassador, who had been watching from the spectator seats in the chamber, headed straight for her.

He grabbed her hand in both of his and wouldn't let it go. He was a large man in a grey double-breasted suit that made him look even larger, and he was genuinely choked up. He tried to tell her how much this meant to Uganda but all he managed to say was that he couldn't express how much it meant. Ellman nodded. 'We're going to do what we can,' she said. He thanked her again. There were tears in his eyes.

'We depend on you, Madam Ambassador,' he said, still holding her hand in his big, soft mitts.

'You *can* depend on us,' she said.

The Kenyan ambassador joined them. Marion managed to extricate her hand from the Ugandan ambassador's grip. They talked for a few minutes about the implications of the vote. Ellman couldn't give them a timetable for action. That would be worked out over the coming days.

Out of the corner of her eye she noticed the Sudanese ambassador deep in conversation with Liu.

China had spent a decade building up its position in Africa, and nowhere more dominantly than in Sudan. The strong opinion in the State Department was that if the US was going to do this thing, it would have to be done in coalition. France and Britain had already told her they were prepared to consider sending limited contingents. Participation from developing countries would be even more important. No matter how small the contributions, no matter how symbolic, they were needed. China would simply lose too much face if the US went in alone.

The Kenyan and Ugandan ambassadors were still speaking to her. Ellman nodded, only half listening. She looked at Liu again. The Chinese ambassador glanced at her from behind his rimless glasses and turned away.

3

THE MAN HOLDING the laser pointer was a short, barrel-chested admiral called Pete Pressler, head of the US Africa Command. In front of him in the White House Situation Room sat the president, the most senior members of the administration, the Joint Chiefs of Staff, and a dozen other military officers and presidential aides.

The red dot of the pointer moved across a map and stopped on a town called Lodwar in northern Kenya.

'That's the closest we can get to the Uganda border with a runway with the spec we need,' said Pressler. 'Gives us coverage of southern Sudan and northwest Congo if we need it as well. We'll pilot the drones out of Creech air force base in Nevada. Operations will be coordinated from the *Abraham Lincoln*, which will be my command post.'

'Offshore?'

'Exactly, Mr President. Off the Kenyan coast. We'll have the entire carrier strike group in theater. We'll refuel Lodwar by air. The storage capacity they have on the ground isn't worth jack so we'll put tanks in first thing. Operationally, our primary weapon will be unmanned aircraft. Other than that, we'll use Apaches or F-35s if we think they're needed, special forces if we've got a high value target and we decide we want to take him alive or can't get to him any other way. Otherwise, it'll be air power.'

The president stretched out in his chair and locked his hands behind his head. 'How does this work with the drones? It's jungle up there, right?'

Pressler nodded. 'Infrared, Mr President. Goes right through the tree canopy. We'll blanket the place with unmanned vehicles. Day, night. Anything moves in there, in the open, under the trees, we'll pick it up.'

'What if it's an animal?' asked Gary Rose, the national security advisor.

'It's the patterns we'll be looking for. The numbers involved, the way the groups move. If we have a single individual and we pick him up on infrared, we're not going to go after that. Could be anything, and if it's a fighter, well, this time he gets away. But when you start to see a group moving in the pattern that human groups move, then you know you're dealing with something.'

'What if they're gorillas?' asked Roberta Devlin, Knowles' chief of staff. She was a small, intense woman with probing blue-green eyes. 'Don't they move in groups?'

'I believe they do have gorillas in that area, ma'am.'

'If we blow the hell out of a clan of gorillas we'll take more flak than if we massacred a whole town of Afghans.'

'I don't believe the US military ever massacred a town of Afghans,' said Mortlock Hale, the chairman of the Joint Chiefs of Staff. He had held a number of commands in Afghanistan and didn't appreciate the insinuation.

'We can live with some dead gorillas,' said the president. 'Admiral, this doesn't sound like it's going to be a very thorough process.'

'It's not an invasion, Mr President. We're not aiming to conquer this territory, only to cleanse it.'

'Mr President, if I may,' said General Hale. 'Insurgencies normally depend on support from the local population. Not this one. The population dreads them and they run a mile if they know they're coming. Normal counter-insurgency strategy, which is about choking off support from the local population, isn't what we need. We're going to beat these guys with a two-pronged strategy: Interdict and Attrit. By using the air power Admiral Pressler has described, we interdict the enemy's routes out of the jungle to replenish their supplies and their escape routes out of Uganda into Sudan and Congo. Meanwhile, as they're bottled up, we pick them off – that's the attrition – and destroy whatever supplies they've got, which further reduces their ability to survive. At a certain point we'll see them trying to break out through our interdiction. We'll encourage defection by dropping leaflets and other communication modalities to show them they've got no chance of outlasting us. Hopefully that'll help detach the weakly committed and get them out of the jungle. The fanatics, we're going to have to kill.'

The president glanced at Gary Rose.

'Sounds about as clean as you can do it,' said the national security advisor.

'John?' said the president to the defense secretary.

'I'm good with this. It's a solid plan that makes the best of our capabilities.' John Oakley was a bear of a man, an ex-undersecretary of the army in the second Bush administration. Tom Knowles had known him all the way back when they were together at law school and highly respected him. Oakley was a strong advocate of unmanned force and had steered the defense budget into a massive expansion of unmanned technology. Uganda was an opportunity to prove the worth of his strategy in a topography unlike Afghanistan or Georgia.

'What if some of these guys manage to break out, say, to Sudan?' asked Devlin.

Oakley shrugged. 'You mean if we're in hot pursuit? We go after them. If we land a few bombs in southern Sudan, what are they going to do?'

'The UN resolution only refers to Uganda,' said the secretary of state, Bob Livingstone.

Oakley shrugged again.

'There are Chinese military in Sudan.'

'Not that they admit to. Anyway, like I said, what are they going to do? Shoot down a couple of drones. Who cares?'

'Wait a minute,' said Livingstone. 'Are you saying this is *all* going to be done with unmanned vehicles? Do we really believe that's how it's going to work?'

The president glanced at the military men.

'We think it's feasible,' said Pressler. 'Seventeen years in Afghanistan has taught us a hell of a lot about use of unmanned weaponry.'

'Not enough to get us out of there.'

'I'm not saying that's all we'll use. As I mentioned, when there is a need, we'll project manned air power. I'll have plenty of that in theater.'

'Mr President,' said the secretary of state, 'the plan that General Hale and Admiral Pressler are presenting is, if I understand it, a plan for the United States acting alone. Have we made that decision?'

'Mr Secretary,' said Hale, 'there are no other potential partners who have anywhere near our depth of experience in the use of unmanned attack vehicles, with the possible exception of the Israelis, and their experience is largely limited to urban environments. And of course this is a judgment for the president, but I don't think we would want the Israelis involved here.'

'We can do this ourselves,' said Oakley.

'I know we *can*, but–'

'We're going to learn a lot from this. We're going to extend our experience with unmanned vehicles into a whole new type of terrain. That alone would make the operation worthwhile.'

'So you can guarantee me with this plan of yours there won't be any casualties,' said the president.

'There'll be a hell of a lot of LRA casualties,' replied Pressler.

The president smiled. 'But our guys?'

Pressler was serious now. 'No one can guarantee there won't be any, sir. But I can guarantee you that the risk is low, the total number of Americans in harm's way is small, enemy arms are very unsophisticated, and whatever we can do with unmanned vehicles, we'll do. This is about the lowest risk operation I've ever had the privilege of planning. I don't aim on losing anybody.'

'How long before you can be on the ground?'

'We have a liaison team ready to go into Nairobi as soon as they get the word. We can do the setup in Lodwar in a couple of weeks as long as the Kenyans cooperate. By that time the *Lincoln* strike group will be in theater and we're ready to roll.'

'Two weeks?'

Pressler nodded.

'How long before you get results?' asked one of the other men in the room. Ed Abrahams was the president's senior political advisor and strategist, a corpulent fifty-three-year-old Californian who had been memorably described as having the brain of Einstein in the body of Moby Dick.

'We'll start to gather information immediately.'

'Results,' said Abrahams.

'Body count, Admiral,' said the president. 'I think you'll find that's what Ed means.'

'It's hard to say. As soon as we can. We find a group, we'll take them out.'

'Within weeks?'

'Definitely. I would hope so.'

Abrahams glanced at the president. His place in these meetings was more to listen than to speak, but Knowles always understood the point when he did intervene. There was nothing Ed Abrahams saw, heard or read that he didn't put through a political filter. The congressional midterm elections were on November 6, eight weeks away. Thirty-three Senate seats were up for grabs, of which four were potentially winnable by Republican candidates. Any two of those seats would give the Republicans sixty votes in the Senate, making the president's program pretty much unstoppable. A strong performance in the midterms would also go a long way to guaranteeing his unopposed renomination in two years' time.

Abrahams and the president had discussed the Uganda intervention exhaustively over the previous few days. Politically, at one level, it was a risk. Tom Knowles had had a good first two years in office, the economy was continuing to grow, and he looked set to achieve the gains he needed in Congress on that record alone. If they launched this operation and something went wrong, that could only be jeopardized. In that respect, they would be better waiting until after the midterm elections. On the other hand, launching the operation would boost his immediate popularity, and a few notable successes in the field before the elections would make him even more popular. And waiting until after the elections, after it had taken so long to get to this point, might make him look as if he was vacillating and give ammunition to his critics. The Republican right was always ready to take shots at him, midterms or no midterms, and the Democrats, who would normally be in favor of deliberation, would turn instantly into ardent supporters of action if that meant they could paint him as a procrastinator. Besides, he wanted to get going. The pressure to unleash a response suited him down to the ground.

'So you can do this in a risk-free way,' said Abrahams.

'Sir, nothing's totally risk-free,' replied Pressler.

'Ah, I think what we can say,' said General Hale, 'is that for the first period we can restrict ourselves pretty much entirely to unmanned sorties. Do you agree, Admiral Pressler?'

Pressler looked at him blankly. He was a field commander and lacked the political antennae that Hale had developed in Washington. 'That's the aim, but as the commander in theater I would–'

'Of course,' said Hale. 'But I think we could agree that for any non-emergent intervention requiring manned force, presidential approval would be required. I think that could be one of the rules of engagement, at least in the first period.'

'That sounds very sensible, General,' said Abrahams.

Hale gazed meaningfully at Pressler. The admiral may have lacked political antennae, but he knew enough to understand what that look meant. He kept quiet.

'You got a name for this operation, Admiral?' asked Walt Stephenson, the vice-president.

Pressler turned to him. 'Not yet.'

'We need a good name. That's half the battle.'

Oakley grinned. 'We've got a few ideas.'

'Okay, this is sounding pretty good,' said the president. 'Roberta, are we looking okay in Congress?'

Knowles' chief of staff nodded. Congress would be voting to authorize the intervention in the next couple of days. The numbers handily gave them the vote. There was strong support in the country and most members of Congress, so close to an election, weren't about to oppose it.

'Good. Admiral Pressler, I understand I'm going to see more detailed plans in the next few days.'

'Yes, sir. My staff–'

'Mr President,' said the secretary of state, 'I do want to come back to the question of whether we do this alone.'

'I thought we just agreed we would,' said Oakley. 'What are the Brits going to do? Give us a communications unit? Great, we could really use one.'

The president smiled. 'John, let Bob have his say. Bob, what is it?'

'We need to do this as a coalition,' said Livingstone.

He paused, glancing at Gary Rose. The national security advisor, a man of medium height with short dark hair and an elongated nose, was watching him, head tilted slightly, arms folded. Livingstone knew that Rose was a lot closer to the president than he was. It was an open secret that Rose had wanted to be secretary of state and Knowles had originally considered giving him the position, but decided that he needed to use the appointment to build support for the administration amongst right-leaning Democrats. Knowles had even privately mooted nominating a Democrat for the post until a strong backlash from the Republican congressional leadership persuaded him to shut that option down. Senator Bob Livingstone, an affable, chubby Missourian in his late sixties with silky white hair, was the next best choice. A longserving member of the Foreign Affairs Committee, he was about the most moderate Republican in the Senate, someone a person like Mitch Moynihan would hardly recognize as belonging to the same party. Livingstone accepted the nomination in the expectation that he would be the president's lead source of foreign policy. But the reality had turned out somewhat differently. Livingstone soon realized that the president had appointed him for political reasons and had appointed Rose because he actually wanted his advice. The secretary of state hadn't proven strong enough to overcome the president's reliance on the other man. Anything he sent to the president was passed directly to the national security advisor to be read.

Livingstone looked back at the president. 'We got the vote in the Security Council, but there's a lot of resistance. China's losing face. They're heavily involved in Sudan and across the entire Central African region, and now we're coming in there to do this thing and one way of reading it is that implicitly we're saying, you should have done this yourselves, you could have offered to do it, and now we're going to come and do it for you.'

'And what was to stop them?' demanded Oakley.

'The Ugandans don't want Chinese forces on their territory. They don't want them within a million miles.'

'And maybe they've got good reason. Mr President, we have thirty-nine dead Americans and that's thirty-nine good reasons for us to go in there and beat the hell out of whoever did it, UN resolution or no resolution. Well, we've got a resolution. That's great. Thanks, Bob. I don't see why we need anyone's help.'

'Because we need help on other things,' said Livingstone. Diplomatic considerations, he knew, were like water off a duck's back to John Oakley. 'The Arctic treaty, the situation in South Africa. Carbon emissions, as always. You name it. There's a thousand things and you can't just rule them out of the picture. If we're going to show leadership on those things we're going to need support.'

'Maybe we do better on those things if we show strong leadership on something else first,' said Gary Rose.

'Like this?'

'Yes. Like this. If you ask me, Bob, this is the perfect way to do it.'

Livingstone guessed that the president and Gary Rose had had extensive discussions about the message this intervention would send to the rest of the world. The president hadn't discussed it with him at all.

'I'm not sure what we're going to look like messing around for two months while we try to line up a coalition,' added Ed Abrahams pointedly.

The president glanced at him, then turned back to Livingstone.

'Bob,' he said, 'I want us to go out and do this thing because it's a good thing and we should do it. The United States should lead on this. The LRA is an evil in our world and they've been given many opportunities to lay down their arms and they haven't done that. And now they've killed a bunch of Americans and the time has come for them to feel our wrath, the anger and power of the civilized world. I don't see any person who could possibly create an argument against us doing this.'

'I'm not disputing that,' said Livingstone. 'But there are different ways we can do this. We can reach out and try to create a coalition, even reach out to China and Russia–'

Oakley snorted.

'Even reach out to them,' persisted Livingstone, 'and see if they'll join us. If you go back a little, remember, Russia joined us in Kosovo.'

'Yeah,' said Oakley, 'and do you remember the race for Pristina?'

'Sounds like it'll take for fucking ever,' muttered the vice-president.

'It will take a little time,' said Livingstone, 'that's true. But I think–'

'The eighty-odd per cent of Americans who want us to do this don't want to see us fucking around for six months trying to get two Brits and an Aussie to come join us,' said Stephenson. 'They want to see Uncle Sam go in there and get the job done!'

Knowles smiled. He had brought Walt Stephenson, a Florida senator, onto the ticket for his ability to deliver Florida's electoral college votes. Not for his tact.

'I understand that,' said Livingstone, 'but I do think that–'

'And we're not looking for hundreds of thousands of troops, right?' Stephenson looked at Hale. 'This is, what, a couple of thousand?'

'Somewhat more, sir, with the naval contingent.'

'One carrier strike force.' Stephenson threw a glance at the president and shrugged dismissively.

'Nonetheless,' said Livingstone, still trying to get the point across, 'if we want to maximize this opportunity, we should take the extra time, build the coalition, and try to keep our relationships good for all the other reasons that we need them.'

'The alternative view, Bob,' said Gary Rose, 'is that bold action, decisive action, does a lot to return us to the leadership position which, frankly, we've largely lost over the past few years. It shows the United States doing what it should do, setting out good, solid principles and leading the world in enforcing them. I'd rather see us do the other things from that position.'

'I think we're showing that leadership by what we've already done in getting the Security Council resolution,' said Livingstone.

'And I think you'll squander it by what you're suggesting,' retorted Oakley.

'Mr President,' said General Hale, 'it's not my role to offer political advice, but in military terms, we can do this much cleaner and quicker if we do it ourselves.'

Livingstone looked at Hale in irritation. They could do it with others if they had to.

There was silence.

The president thought for a moment. 'I think we can show strength in a coalition, even in this situation. Gary, I do think the United States can show leadership in that context. I don't think that's a door we should close right now. Bob, I think you should go out there and try to build a coalition for us. And in the meantime, Admiral Pressler, you should continue to develop the plan in case we have to go it alone. Let's start talking to whoever we have to talk to in Nairobi.'

'Yes, sir,' said the admiral.

There was silence again. Bob Livingstone looked around. Everyone in the room was watching him. He felt like a guy who'd just volunteered to go way, way out on a limb.

'Mr President, if I'm going to build a coalition, how long have I got?'

The president frowned. 'I don't know, Bob. Let's see how it goes.'

4

IN HER OFFICE opposite the UN building, Marion Ellman watched the screen.

The statement was being made in the East Room of the White House. Flanking the president were John Oakley, Gary Rose, Bob Livingstone and two men in military uniform. Ellman recognized Mortlock Hale, the chairman of the Joint Chiefs of Staff. She didn't recognize the other one, a short, barrel-chested man with close-cropped hair.

The notification that a statement was to be made had come through to her office only an hour earlier. All she knew was that it involved the resolution for action in Uganda.

The president spoke.

'Ladies and gentlemen, thank you for coming. I would like to announce today the United States deployment in response to Security Council resolution 2682, which, as you know, calls on willing parties to assist the government of the Republic of Uganda to combat the terrorist group known as the Lord's Resistance Army. In the three weeks since the resolution was passed Secretary Livingstone has had numerous discussions with our allies across the world and we are appreciative of the generous support they have offered. It has also become clear to us that what will best serve the interests of the situation is a rapid, active deployment to deal with this problem once and for all. In consultation with the government of Uganda, I have therefore decided to press ahead immediately with a deployment of US forces in an operation that we are calling Jungle Peace.'

Marion Ellman stared at the screen. Immediately? Was that what the president had said? Immediately?

'The objective of operation Jungle Peace will be as outlined in resolution 2682, namely, to assist the government of the Republic of Uganda to remove the Lord's Resistance Army from its territory, to apprehend, if possible, its leaders and foot soldiers and to deliver them to justice, and to re-establish conditions of peaceful life in the area previously afflicted by the LRA. In addition, the United States will be providing to the government of Uganda a significant development and aid package to assist reconstruction in the area once Jungle Peace has achieved its objectives, details of which we will release in due course.'

Ellman watched the rest of the statement. The president explained that his decision was motivated not only by the deaths of thirty-nine Americans, but by the longstanding suffering of the people of northern Uganda. It was in America's interest, he said, to alleviate injustice and oppression wherever it was, because it was in the interest of the United States to have a world that was free, prosperous and untainted by fear. He said the usual things about the grave responsibility of being commander in chief and the deep obligation this imposed to ensure that such a decision wasn't taken lightly – which it hadn't been. He thanked the government of the Republic of Kenya and its people for agreeing to facilitate access for US forces and he thanked the allies of the United States who had generously offered to consider joining the operation. Finally he introduced the commander of the operation.

Ellman watched the barrel-chested man, who the president had just named as Admiral Pete Pressler, step forward. He thanked the president for his confidence. He said that the bulk of forces were already in theater, and operations would commence within days.

Forces were *in theater*? Marion Ellman's disbelief had turned to rage long before the president had finished speaking. Now her anger went incandescent. How long had this been going on? When had American forces arrived in Uganda? When *exactly* had the president made the decision to go it alone?

She looked at the group standing with the president behind Pressler. Bob Livingstone gazed at the admiral, nodding now and again as he spoke.

*

THE FRENCH AMBASSADOR to the UN, François Dubigny, was first on the phone. The French had offered six helicopter pilots and a medical team to the coalition effort. Dubigny was an urbane Parisian who couldn't quite resist a certain male gallantry – or call it chauvinism – whenever they spoke. He chuckled gently.

'I think, Marion, you have been … how do you call it … a smokescreen, perhaps, for your president?'

Ellman was still boiling, but she wasn't going to show that to Dubigny. 'Not at all, François,' she replied crisply. 'For the last three weeks I've been saying the coalition had to be built quickly. I always said we weren't going to wait forever.'

That was the line she had to take. It was about the only line she could take without appearing a complete jackass.

'As you wish,' said Dubigny. 'If you ask me, three weeks is not forever. Perhaps your president, however, works to a different timetable, with an election marked at the end of it.'

'He wants to get things done. He's not prepared to wait around. I always said that.'

Dubigny chuckled again. '*Bon*. Still, I have seen a few smokescreens in my time, and you, Marion, today, much to my regret, very much have the appearance of one.'

She had a lot more conversations that afternoon. Sir Antony Seale, the British ambassador, was predictably indignant. The Brits had offered a contingent of drone pilots to be based at US air force base Creech with the probable intention of learning as much as they could from their American counterparts. Other ambassadors were confused, or angry, and probably secretly relieved. Whatever they really felt, she was in an invidious position. Until the previous day she had been telling these same people the US was looking for a broad coalition and cajoling them to seek a speedy commitment from their leaders.

She let her anger out when she finally spoke with Bob Livingstone. The secretary of state said he had found out about the statement only the previous evening. Marion found that a little hard to believe.

'Rose sent over a draft of the statement at 10pm last night,' said Livingstone. 'That's the first I heard of it. I spoke to him right away and then I spoke to him again first thing this morning and he said the president was going to do it and if I had any suggestions for the draft, I better get them in. That line about thanking our allies, you can thank me for that.'

'Is that the best you could do?'

'Yes, it was. There were a bunch of other lines that didn't make it. Personally, I'm just glad that one did.'

Ellman was silent. She knew as well as anyone that Livingstone had become an increasingly less important figure in the two years that the administration had been in office, but treatment like this was utter contempt. And it was visible. The details weren't important – whether the statement had been sent to him at 9pm or 10pm didn't matter – but anyone watching would know that while Livingstone had been running around trying to build a coalition, the White House had been planning something entirely different. Power in foreign affairs rests with the president. It's shared by the secretary of state only to the extent that people believe the secretary speaks with the president's voice. People had already doubted that of Bob Livingstone. Now there wasn't even a doubt.

If she knew it, Marion realized, Bob would know it even better. She understood he must be hurting. But he was a loyal servant. Even to her, privately, he was unlikely to admit how hurt he must be.

'What does he gain from this, Bob? Is this a premeditated act to cut us down? I don't understand how that serves anyone's interest.'

'The way Gary explained it to me, Marion, is that Pressler wanted complete surprise. The LRA has enough communications capability to know what's going on and he wanted them thinking we were slowly building a coalition and they had months to build up supplies and hide themselves out.'

'Did you know this?' asked Ellman incredulously.

'Not till yesterday.'

Ellman laughed.

'It's plausible,' said Livingstone.

'Sure. And they thought we couldn't keep it secret.'

'I guess they figured it might affect the way we went about talking to our allies.'

Marion shook her head. She wondered whether the secretary could possibly believe what he had just said. She liked Bob Livingstone, he was a good, decent man. But he wasn't hard enough. He gave the benefit of the doubt. He didn't fight the turf wars.

'The operation's already begun,' said Livingstone. 'Apparently we've had drones doing surveillance for two days.'

'What's the rush?'

'Come on, Marion. You know as well as me. The president wants hits before November 6.'

'And for that he's prepared to tick off just about every one of our allies?'

'Let's be fair. Most of them were all talk.'

'But there are ways to do it, Bob!'

'Yeah, I know. I just think … with the midterms coming up, he's not prepared to be seen as a president who gets a go-ahead and then messes around. He wants to be seen as decisive. Go in there, get it done. There's a lot at stake in these midterms, you know that.'

Marion didn't know whether Livingstone really thought that any of this could justify the way the president had acted or the damage he had done to the ability of the State Department – and Livingstone personally – to be effective. Maybe he did, or maybe it was a rationalization to preserve a little dignity in the demeaning situation in which he found himself.

'Marion, I'm sorry about this. I wish I could have stopped it. I know you're exposed. After me, you're probably the person most exposed by all this.'

'It's the whole department, Bob. The president's got to realize that. He's got to realize what he's done.'

'Well, he's done it.'

Ellman thought about what a fool she looked. She thought about the kinds of conversations she was going to have the next time she had to persuade other countries to join an American initiative. Much as she liked Bob Livingstone, it was a curse to work with a weak secretary of state. There was no other department where weakness at the top made everyone so vulnerable.

'Did you speak with Liu?' asked Livingstone.

'No. Do you want me to?' Ellman wasn't looking forward to her next conversation with the Chinese UN ambassador. She thought she had a reasonable working relationship with Liu, but this was going to test it. The Chinese had already lost face over the resolution. Now they were losing even more face with the US going into Uganda alone. And the president's line in his statement about America having an interest in freedom and justice everywhere was gratuitous. More than gratuitous, inflammatory. However the president meant it – and Ellman realized he had probably viewed it from the domestic perspective, as an explanation to the American people about his motivation for sending troops to a foreign country – the Chinese were going to interpret it as a shot straight at them. They were incredibly sensitive to anything that could be interpreted, however indirectly, as a criticism of their political system and human rights record.

She was about to ask Livingstone about that line, but stopped. He understood the nuances as well as she did. That line would never have come from him. It would have made it into the statement only despite his attempts to finesse it.

'Bob,' she said, 'I could talk to Liu, but I'm not sure what I'd say. Have we got a line? Have we got anything to say apart from what the president said already?'

'We could say we're going to stick to the terms of the resolution, we don't have any hidden objectives in the region.'

'I've said that to him already. I can say it again but what's the point? Anyone can see it's not what *we* say that matters.'

There was silence on the line. Ellman regretted having made that last remark.

'Yeah, maybe we should leave it,' said Livingstone eventually. 'The president's spoken. I don't know if we want to gloss it.'

'What's the gloss? It is what it is.'

'Yeah. You're right.' Livingstone paused. 'I'll talk to Haskell, see what he thinks.'

Steve Haskell was the US ambassador in Beijing.

'Sure,' said Ellman. 'Talk to Haskell. But you said it yourself, Bob. The president's spoken. If the Chinese want to say something in response, they'll find a way.'

5

WU GUOZENG WAITED for Steve Haskell to sit down. Haskell had brought one of his senior aides as interpreter and note-taker. Wu had an interpreter with him as well, although his English was just about as good as Haskell's. Between stints at the Chinese mission to the UN, four years in roles at the Washington embassy, and five years as the Chinese ambassador to the US, Wu had spent upwards of a dozen years in the States. This was his second year in the job as vice-foreign minister with responsibility for North America, and he was widely tipped as a potential future foreign minister for the People's Republic.

Haskell's diplomatic credentials were a little slimmer. He was a long-time Republican Party donor and, as Tom Knowles' appointee, had taken up his post as ambassador in Beijing just a year previously. But he had a thorough working knowledge of China and could even hold his own in Mandarin, and his appointment was widely considered to be an astute one. First as a partner with the international law firm Spearman Maybury and then with the investment bank UDB Philips, he had run offices in Hong Kong and Shanghai and otherwise been involved in China for over thirty years, and his network in the Chinese business community and amongst government financial officials was unrivalled.

Wu had a long face and thinning hair with a combover. Haskell had once been red-headed but now had a bare cranium. There wasn't enough left for a combover should he have even wanted one. The two men had met regularly since Haskell arrived at the US embassy and generally they got on pretty well. Wu had a good sense of humour and was fairly open and pragmatic. He had been around American diplomats and politicians for so long that he was realistic about what could be achieved and how best to go about it. Steve Haskell liked to think he was fairly pragmatic as well.

He knew, however, that this wasn't going to be an amicable conversation. He imagined there must have been much discussion in the Chinese government compound in Beijing, the Zhongnanhai, over the two days since the president's announcement of Jungle Peace. Whatever Wu privately felt, Haskell knew that the Chinese vice-minister had a message to deliver, and it was one that would have come from a lot higher up in the hierarchy than his vice-ministerial department. Haskell just wasn't sure how hard the message was going to be.

The president's announcement had received generally positive coverage in the American press, and the US blogosphere was largely supportive. Most Americans seemed to see the action as a disinterested mission by the US to liberate a long-suffering part of the world from a resident evil. Steve Haskell himself saw the mission in this light, but he was well aware of Chinese sensibilities on the matter. He could hardly fail to be – not from the noise being made in China, but from the silence. The Chinese media was virtually ignoring the issue and very little in the way of blogosphere comment was being allowed past the government censorship operation on the net. The Security Council vote had received only perfunctory mention and the president's announcement had passed without notice. Haskell had been around China long enough to know what that meant. When the regime felt that it had been attacked and could turn injury to its advantage, it whipped up a fury. He had been in Shanghai in the late nineties and had seen the government-sponsored demonstrations after the accidental bombing of the Chinese embassy in Belgrade. Chanting crowds had thundered past the Spearman Maybury building and he and his staff had been trapped for two days, having to spend a night in the office. But everyone knew the anger was largely manufactured and the staged demonstrations were under close government control. When there was public anger in China, you knew where you stood. Silence was something else. Silence was more ambiguous, threatening. When the Chinese government clamped down on news reporting from abroad, it usually meant it was seriously scared of losing face. That was when it was at its most dangerous.

Wu spoke in Mandarin. He had a note for the United States government from the government of the People's Republic. He handed Haskell a sealed envelope.

'This note refers to the recent commencement of hostilities by American forces in Uganda,' said Wu. 'My government wishes to ensure that we have clarity between our two governments on our expectations in this issue.'

Haskell's aide translated the words, although Haskell's Mandarin was pretty sharp. He responded in English. Normally he was comfortable conversing in Mandarin, but for certain conversations he wanted to be sure he was entirely in control of the nuances in his speech.

'I'm certain that clarity is critical and whatever we can do to achieve that will be a good thing.'

Wu nodded. 'My government, as you know, does not oppose your mission. If we oppose your mission we would have voted against resolution 2682.'

'And the US government is grateful that you didn't.'

'We will, however, oppose anything that goes beyond the provisions of the resolution.'

'We would not anticipate taking any action that goes beyond the resolution,' replied Haskell.

'The resolution refers only to Uganda.'

'And to other countries who may invite member states to assist them in bringing the actions of the LRA to an end.'

'That is correct,' said Wu. 'I am not aware of any other states who have issued such an invitation.'

'Nor am I,' said Haskell. He smiled.

Wu frowned. 'Ambassador, we will oppose any intervention in other states.'

'We have no intention of intervening in other states.'

'This will be a very delicate situation.'

Haskell didn't respond immediately. His aide had translated the word that Wu had chosen, *xianruo*, as 'delicate', but Haskell's Mandarin was good enough that he knew the word also had a strong connotation of fragility. And the tone in which the vice-minister said it left no doubt that it concealed a host of further, more worrisome meanings.

Haskell had been briefed by State. Border demarcation between Uganda, Sudan and Congo in the jungle-clad region in question was blurred, to say the least, and there were a number of areas of dispute between the countries. Steve Haskell couldn't imagine a US Apache pilot worrying too much over the niceties when in pursuit of enemy combatants on the ground. International law over hot pursuit could be interpreted to allow incursion into other states. It could also be interpreted to forbid it.

Facing an insurgency that roamed across the borders of three states, it wasn't too hard to imagine incidents that the Chinese government could use to protest against the mission if it chose to do so.

'I will read this note now, Vice-Minister, if I may, in case I need to ask you for any clarification.'

'Please,' said Wu.

Haskell opened the envelope. It was a brief note, containing little more than what the Vice-Minister had already said. It gave no greater insight into the Chinese government's intentions.

Haskell put the note away. 'We will of course provide a response as soon as my government has had time to consider this note.'

Wu nodded.

'However, I trust that your government will interpret our actions in the spirit of our mission. The Lord's Resistance Army is a truly evil group and I personally believe that removing it is something that we all should be interested in seeing done. The United States has no interest in this mission but to do that, and to do it as quickly as possible with least cost in the lives of our soldiers and the lives of civilians on the ground.'

Wu gazed at him impassively. Haskell knew the vice-minister wouldn't respond to that. This was a minuted conversation and he wasn't being tasked by his superiors with giving a moral evaluation of Jungle Peace.

'I just want you and your government to understand that,' said Haskell.

Wu smiled briefly. 'We look forward to receiving a reply from your government.'

IN THE CAR, Haskell read over the note again, then handed it to his aide.

'It's interesting they chose Wu to deliver the message,' he said.

The aide nodded, reading the note.

Haskell had expected to be called in to see the Chinese foreign minister. It was a good sign, he thought, that the Chinese government seemed to be keeping it one level lower down.

'What do you think?' said Haskell. 'I don't think they're going to make too much noise about it.'

'Doesn't look like it.'

'The media silence says to me: we're embarrassed by this. Something happens that they don't like, they're still going to be embarrassed by it. Even more so. I think the message here is, don't make us say anything on this. Don't put us in a situation where we have to say something, where we have to remind people what's going on. You have a resolution, and we can live with it, but don't go outside the terms of that resolution because then you're going to force us to make a protest, and we don't want to do that. It won't be good for either of us.'

'And that would happen if the government of Sudan started making complaints that we were in their space. They'd demand Chinese backing in public and the Chinese would feel they'd have to give it.'

'Exactly,' said Haskell. 'So the message is: stay out of Sudan.'

'On the other hand,' said his aide, 'this could be a genuine warning. If we do something they interpret as wrong they might use it as a pretext to get aggressive. They could see this note as setting a line in the sand. At the extreme, they might even want us to overstep it. They might want a pretext to show how tough they are.'

Haskell frowned. It was possible. 'I wonder where the army stands on this.'

His aide shrugged. She handed back the note. 'I'm just playing devil's advocate. If they were setting up a pretext, this wouldn't have been a private warning. It'd be on the front page of the *Renmin Ribao* and every media outlet in the world would get a press release. It only works as a pretext if everyone knows the line in the sand has been drawn. If it's done in private, it doesn't help them.'

'I guess that's true.'

'On balance, Ambassador, I think you're right. They're saying, do what you have to do in Uganda, get in and out as quick as you can, and while you're there, stay out of Sudan so we don't need to do anything.'

Haskell read over the note again. Then he folded it and put it back in its envelope. 'Yeah,' he said. 'I think that's what they're saying.'

6

THE MEETING ROOM was a small, glassed-in oblong on one side of the thirty-fourth floor of a tower in midtown Manhattan. Twenty-three people were crammed inside around a table that had been designed for ten, chairs layered two deep. In the middle of it all sat Ed Grey.

Grey was fifty-one, a big, handsome man with slicked-back hair who was the principal partner of Red River Investments. The term hedge fund had gone out of fashion, discredited by the global financial crisis and made unattractive by regulation, and Red River was technically a DIV, or Diversified Investment Vehicle, but its activities were pretty much the same. Grey had come out of one of the few operations in the hedge fund world that had bet on the collapse of the subprime market and earned staggering returns for its temerity – or perspicuity – when the financial world was imploding in the heady summer of 2008. Grey himself had established his reputation with a series of audacious bets on oil and gas prices during the downturn and had garnered enough of a client following to go out on his own and set up Red River in 2012. He named the company after the ranch in Colorado that he had bought with a fraction of the earnings of those years. The vast bulk of his profits went into the fund, together with an initial subscription of $2 billion from external investors. Six years later, he had upwards of $16 billion of client funds under management, leveraged up to close to $60 billion through bank financing.

The people around him ranged in age from mid twenties to late thirties, mostly men, a couple of women. Casual dress was the order, chinos, even one or two in jeans. There were other people in Red River – the chief operations officer, finance officer, compliance officer, a couple of marketing people, various administrative people – but these twenty-two were the heart and brain of the firm. Six of them were portfolio managers, the traders who were allocated capital from the fund and structured the deals that made Red River's money. The others were market analysts and quantitative analysts working for the portfolio managers, scouring the markets, developing ideas, doing research and running quantitative models that would enable the portfolio managers to make their trading decisions.

Ed Grey himself directly managed a portfolio of around thirty per cent of the firm's capital, mostly in commodities and developing markets, as well as acting as the CEO and chief investment officer. His most senior portfolio manager, Tony Evangelou, was a big-hitting equities trader who focused on US and European markets, and managed around a quarter of the fund. The rest of the capital was more or less evenly divided among the other managers who had expertise in bonds and foreign exchange.

Communication across the group was essential. Grey and Evangelou were focused on finding the big, event-driven opportunities that could earn forty, fifty, sixty per cent returns as one-off bets. The other managers largely worked steady, low-risk trades that earned a reliable eight to ten per cent a year and gave the DIV a baseline return. But any one of the managers might come across a one-off opportunity for extraordinary returns or be seeing trends in his or her market that might be relevant to any of the others. As a multistrategy, global DIV, the portfolio manager group had to be able to form a view of the way key economic trends around the world were heading, and structure their trades accordingly. They sat at the same desk and were always exchanging information, but Grey liked to get them together in the meeting room as well, sometimes daily. Most times he got the analysts in with them also. Discussion was open. Anyone could put forward an idea and anyone could challenge it.

Today, he had Uganda on his mind.

Tony Evangelou thought it was nothing. 'No one cares, Ed. No one sees it making a difference to anything.'

'It's a big yawn from where I sit,' said Maria Lomax, who traded foreign exchange. 'No one's seeing a scenario where it matters.'

The other portfolio managers agreed.

'Then we challenge that,' said Grey. When the market uniformly expected trends to go in one direction, the trick was to find the reason the market might be wrong, quantify the probability and structure a trade that gave a huge payout if you were right and that imposed no loss – or even made you some money – if you weren't.

But there was no trade to be done if the probability was zero.

'What makes the market care?' said Evangelou. 'Nothing. It's too small, Ed. It's not a bite on a rat's ass.'

'Say the military lose some guys in there.'

Evangelou shrugged.

'Say we get sucked in.'

'It's not Iraq. What's the spend? It's chickenfeed.'

'You want to check that?' said Ed to one of the analysts.

The analyst nodded. Through research into Defense Department spending at various levels of foreign-deployed force, he would be able to create a set of scenarios for military spending that he could run through his models. A significant rise in military spend would raise the budget deficit, which would affect the dollar, interest rates, bond prices and likely a bunch of other asset classes as well.

'What about Uganda?' said Adil Menon, one of the portfolio managers. 'Maybe Kenya. Let's think about opportunity. We have no exposure at all to those markets. It's no-lose. If this intervention gets rid of the LRA, there'll be some kind of economic payoff. If it fails, they're no worse off than they are today.'

Grey knew nothing about the Central African region and had never invested there. Adil, who mostly traded currency, was keen to develop a specialism in fourth-wave countries, as the least developed of the emerging markets were known.

'You want to get out there?' he said.

Adil nodded.

'Maybe we put a couple of hundred million into Uganda if we can find some opportunities,' said Ed. He liked the idea. He had made a heap of money in Ghana at one stage after having read a couple of articles about the country in *The Economist* and getting out there to investigate.

'Liquid opportunities,' said Evangelou. 'Don't get us stuck in some shitty trades we can't get out of, Adil.'

Menon smiled. That was Evangelou's mantra, liquidity, having a market that was deep enough with a sufficient number of counterparties so you could get out of a large position when you wanted to. You never wanted to be the last guy holding the parcel with no one to pass it to. Evangelou hated developing markets, especially fourth wave, because liquidity was always an issue.

'So apart from local effects in the region, this Uganda thing is a storm in a teacup, huh?' said Grey.

There were nods around the table.

Grey thought so himself, but he was going to continue to challenge that view as the situation developed. Markets across the world had been on a slow but steady bull run for almost three years and event-driven opportunities for outsize returns were few. He didn't think this was one of them, but he was going to keep watching. The conflict looked so trivial that if it blew up into something big and began to have a material impact, the opportunity for those who spotted the effect early was going to be substantial.

'Anything else?' he said.

There was silence for a moment.

'I have an idea.'

Ed looked along the table and two rows back to see who had spoken. Boris Malevsky was a new joiner Ed and Tony had hired out of Morgan Stanley to work as an analyst on Evangelou's team. He was the child of Russian immigrants and had a slight accent courtesy of the first eleven years of his life in Moscow. Boris was curly-headed, overweight, sweaty and, in the fortnight since he had joined Red River, rarely clean-shaven. Grey liked him. There was something about Malevsky that made Grey think he might have what it takes to be a trader, a mix of intellect, rebelliousness and contrarianism that you always find in truly great portfolio managers who are capable of backing themselves against the market to win the kind of iconic bets that he himself had won over the years. On the other hand, you often found those same qualities in truly terrible fund managers who were capable of losing more money than most people knew existed. The difference between the two was another set of qualities: the stomach to hold a position, the discipline to execute your strategy, and most importantly, the humility to accept that you were wrong when the market had turned against you and the flexibility to act on that real-ization quick enough to save yourself from a trap door that was opening under your feet. Ed Grey had no idea if Malevsky had those qualities, but he wanted to find out.

'What is it?' he said.

'We short US banks.'

There were smirks around the table. Ed Grey wondered if Malevsky was saying that just to show how contrarian he could be. The line between a contrarian and an idiot was a thin one.

'What's that got to do with Uganda?' said Evangelou.

'Nothing. I didn't say it did.'

'Then what the fuck are you talking about?'

'I'm saying we should short some banks,' said Boris, with a slight Slavic slur just detectable in his accent.

'Boris, right now banks are on a one-way ride.'

'And we're long all the way.'

'Because they're on a one-way ride.'

'And if there's a correction?'

'They're still on a one-way ride. If there's a correction, it's limited. At Red River we look at a six month to one year horizon and our investors know that. If banks correct, over that time horizon they'll come back and they'll still keep going up.'

'I agree,' said Malevsky. 'But shouldn't we make some money in the correction?'

Grey watched him with interest. 'How do you know there's going to be a correction?'

'You think this Uganda thing's going to do it?' said Maria Lomax. 'You know some banks with exposure to Uganda?'

'It's going to be good for them,' said Evangelou. 'Adil's right.'

'It's got nothing to do with Uganda,' said Malevsky.

'Boris, why the correction?' asked Grey.

'This administration is scared of a bubble. It's scared of anything that looks like a bubble.'

'We haven't got a bubble,' said Evangelou impatiently.

'No, but we're in a bull market that's run eleven consecutive quarters. You look at any public statement that's ever come from Knowles, from the Fed, from the Treasury. This administration will not allow the banks to drive a bubble.'

Evangelou rolled his eyes. 'We haven't *got* a bubble.'

'We're coming up to the midterms. If anything happens, even the slightest thing, they're going to overreact. They're going to do something, or say something, that'll haul the sector back. The Fed especially. You look at the way Strickland talks.'

Ron Strickland was chairman of the Federal Reserve, appointed by the previous administration explicitly to do what Alan Greenspan and Ben Bernanke hadn't done, burst the bubbles that inevitably develop in the financial system before they get too big to bust. When Knowles took office he affirmed that was exactly what he wanted Strickland to keep doing.

'That's his job. That's what this administration is focused on. They'll sacrifice twenty-five, fifty basis points of growth if they think they have to. They won't say that, but that's what they'll do.'

'Why now?' said Grey.

'I'm not sure it's going to be right now. I'm only saying, this is the kind of time when it might happen. Midterms coming up. Maybe there's a feeling things have been going good a little too long and we're getting to that point where you need to be watchful. The Democrats are saying this administration isn't committed to regulation. There's just a bunch of things that might make them damp down somewhat. Not do anything dramatic – just show they're in control.'

Grey considered it. The rationale was way too vague, too wishful, to back with any of the fund's capital.

'I'm not saying we short the whole sector,' said Malevsky. 'It's going to be a wobble, not a crash. But when it wobbles, there'll be some that really drop.'

'Really?' said Evangelou skeptically. 'Do you have any in mind?'

Malevsky glanced around the table, then looked back at Grey.

Grey understood. 'Okay,' he said.

BEING A TRADER for two decades had taught Ed Grey a bunch of lessons. One of them was that it's easy to be right at the wrong time. You could have the greatest trade in the world, and if you did it at the wrong time you'd lose a shitload of money. The fact that six months or a year later the market moved in the direction you predicted was zero consolation. Everyone had done it, himself included. The trick was not to do it too often.

Was a correction coming? Probably. Markets always get a little twitchy after prolonged periods of rising value and some participants decide to sell and take their profits, if for no other reason than everyone knows the party has to end some time. More and more people were talking about it, and at some point that kind of talk becomes self-fulfilling. But that wasn't stopping anyone yet. It was the typical schizophrenic behavior of the market, where investors rationally know that the good times can't last forever and yet keep acting as if they can.

The question was: when, how long and how deep was the inevitable dip going to be?

If market fears and desire for a little profit-taking were the only reasons for the correction, it would be shallow and short-lived, as Tony Evangelou expected, with a rapid return to growth. In that case, the risk-reward for trying to pick the timing of a minor correction didn't add up.

Was there any reason for it to be deeper? There was a general sense in the financial community that regulation was falling behind again. The new rules that had been introduced under Obama in the years after the crisis had been around long enough now for smart people to start finding ways around them. Everyone knew there were novel financial products and practices that could potentially – in certain circumstances – create the same kind of risks that had brought down Lehman Brothers at the height of the last financial crisis. But those circumstances didn't exist and no one believed anything like that level of risk had actually developed. No one believed the world was back to anything like the corrupted, hollow shell of a financial system that had been in place in 2008.

Globally there were the usual tensions. An implicit deal had been struck in the worst days of the financial crisis: China would increase consumption and reduce savings as a way of rebalancing the world's trade flows, and in return it would receive a greater say in global financial governance and institutions such as the IMF and G20. The deal had been breached by both sides. The old G7 powers still retained enough votes to get pretty much whatever they liked in the IMF, and the G22, as it was now, was an empty talkfest that left the western powers to do their deals in informal meetings in

Washington, London and Tokyo. China continued to maintain an artificially undervalued currency, paying lip service to its obligations with occasional tiny revaluations, and sequestered its citizens' savings in state banks instead of encouraging domestic consumption. The disturbances in China in 2014 had only entrenched the problems – making it easier for the Chinese regime to argue that it couldn't make any of the necessary changes and for the west to argue that China wasn't ready for a larger international role. Essentially, then, nothing had changed but for the added resentment on each side towards the other for having, as each side saw it, reneged on their side of the deal. Red River had some big, long-term bets placed on the way the dollar, euro and yuan would move in relation to one another, and Ed Grey was confident that eventually those bets would pay out. In the meantime, growth continued, stretching the global imbalances even more, and it was in no one's immediate interest to do anything about it.

Everything suggested that there could be a market correction but it was going to be shallow and short. It was possible, as Malevsky said, that the administration would want to show how tough it was in the next couple of months, and talk out of the Fed might make the correction a little deeper, if it happened at all. Even so, the risk-reward profile just wasn't there for Red River to take a position.

And yet there was something more than this that Malevsky was thinking of, Grey understood. Something he knew.

HE PULLED HIM into his office and asked Evangelou to come in as well.

'So who are they, Boris?' he said. 'Who are these banks?'

'I've got four in mind.'

'How have you identified them?' demanded Evangelou.

'Basic analysis. Leverage, capital ratios, loan books … I'm not saying these banks are going to fail. I'm just saying they're the most vulnerable. When Strickland feels he needs to start talking the market down, they're the ones that are going to drop.'

'How much?' said Grey.

'I'm guessing ten, fifteen per cent. Maybe twenty.'

'Why isn't everyone else shorting them?' said Evangelou.

'Because no one thinks they're the ones that are going to hurt. And no one's prepared yet to bet on a correction. But there will be one. Strickland will overreact and haul things back.'

Grey thought about it. It was the perennial paradox in the markets. If no one else was doing something, why should you? On the other hand, if you only did what everyone else did, you never made any money.

'Ed, this is all hunch,' said Evangelou.

Grey agreed. There was nothing behind this, it seemed, but some simple analysis and Malevsky's insistence that the Fed chairman would be too heavy-handed in his statements, which was pure speculation. But he was interested in seeing what Malevsky was made of as a trader. It might be worth putting twenty or thirty million into short positions to find out.

To sell short, a DIV 'borrowed' stocks for an agreed period from banks that were holding them on behalf of passive shareholders like pension funds or university endowments. That cost a fee, usually measured in thousandths of a per cent of the stock's value, for each day you borrowed them. When you got hold of the stock, you sold it for its current price and hoped you could buy it back cheaper before you had to return it to the bank that had lent it. In other words, you were betting on the stock falling. The difference in the price when you sold and the price when you bought the stock back, less the fee for borrowing the stock, was the profit. Or the loss, if the stock price rose. In the meantime, the longer you held the stock, the greater the fee you paid.

And Malevsky, of course, had no idea when this correction of his was going to happen.

'Strickland's testifying to Congress next Tuesday,' said Malevsky. 'That's his last testimony before the midterms. We could borrow for a week. Worse case, we lose the fee. What will it be for a week? Nothing. Best case, Strickland says something and we get the dip.'

'Wrong,' said Evangelou. 'Worst case, Strickland says the opposite because he thinks the president wants him to boost the markets and we get a spike. No way he's talking the market down a month before the midterms.'

'No way he's talking it up. That's not something he does and that's not what the president wants. If anything, he wants Strickland to push things down a little. Wall Street will yell and Knowles'll make polit-ical hay with his rectitude-and-trust spiel.'

'Before an election? I don't think so.'

'Why not? Doing that before the election is exactly what Knowles wants. He wants to show he's tough. The markets can't push him around. There'll be no bubble on his watch. If he has to take action to stop one developing, he will.'

Evangelou looked at Grey. 'Ed, this is all a hunch about the psychology of what Strickland's going to say. This is bullshit.'

Grey was inclined to agree. He had hoped there was something more that Malevsky knew but it looked as if he was all hot air. 'Boris,' he said, 'I don't think–'

'There's one more thing,' said Malevsky.

Grey stopped.

'I heard something when I was at Morgan. Not something in the public domain.'

Grey raised an eyebrow. *This* was it.

'I heard something about one of these banks needing to raise some capital. Something about losses they need to declare.'

Now Grey understood. Malevsky had been hoping to present his idea as the result of some great psychological insight and analytical research. In fact, there was a nugget of very valuable – and very confi-dential – information underlying it.

Malevsky shrugged.

'How much capital will they need?'

'I don't know. Enough to make people interested.'

'A couple of billion?' Grey paused. 'Five billion?'

'I don't know. I really don't. But I do know they've got losses they need to declare and they're big enough to make them come to the market for funds.'

'So that was all bullshit?' said Evangelou. 'All that stuff about Strickland and the correction and everything?'

'No, I believe it's going to happen. That's the context. Strickland's going to keep talking hard. Maybe before the election, maybe after. I'm not sure when. But when you get this bank coming to the market for more capital in that context, suddenly there'll be pressure on banks. The other ones, the other three I've identified, are the ones I think most likely to take a hit. I've done the analysis on them.'

'Would you have identified the first bank from your analysis?'

Malevsky shook his head. 'That's what's so beautiful about it. No one's going to expect it.'

Grey looked at Evangelou. 'What do you think?'

Evangelou shrugged. 'It's a little more interesting, that's for sure. It's not exactly kosher.'

Grey didn't say anything to that. Rumor was rife in every market. In most cases, unless you went about it extremely stupidly, the difference between insider information and informed speculation was almost impossible for an investigator to make out.

Malevksy watched him hopefully.

'It's chickenshit,' said Evangelou. 'Ed, what is it? What are we going to make? One bank. Who knows what the others will do? Say we put a hundred million on this one bank and it comes off ten per cent. Say twenty per cent. Twenty million? Is it worth it?'

'Maybe we take a bigger position.'

'And maybe it goes nowhere. And if we have to short a bunch of others, and they go nowhere ...'

Grey nodded. Still, it was interesting. 'I like the thinking. We have something that's pretty much a sure-fire thing, which derisks the trade, and if Strickland does his bit like Boris says, we get a bonus on the other three. I like the structure.'

Malevsky smiled.

'Which one is it, Boris, this bank of yours? Is it a serious player?'

Malevsky nodded.

'Which bank?'

'Fidelian.'

7

MARION ELLMAN PUT her points succinctly. Efforts to deal with climate change since Copenhagen had so far largely been a failure not only because the targets set at successive meetings were insufficient, but because enforcement had been nonexistent. But recognition of this problem was increasing. With recognition would come action to address the problem. The place for that was the next major round of negotiations, scheduled for Santiago in two years' time. The Santiago round had to create a global enforcement mechanism that would ensure compliance. She was confident it would do that and cited a number of reasons for believing so. One of the key foreign policy objectives of the United States in the coming two years leading up to Santiago was to provide the leadership to ensure that goal was reached.

The moderator of the panel nodded. Further along the table Marion saw Joel Ehrenreich raise an eyebrow skeptically. Joel was a short, tubby guy with receded hair and a thick moustache. He was a good friend of Marion's. Typically, when he got his chance, he proceeded to challenge her position point for point.

They had been invited to sit on the panel discussion as part of a series on global governance that was being held by the Council on Foreign Relations. Joel was a professor of international relations at Yale, but prior to that had been on the faculty at Berkeley during the time that Marion held a professorship there. Their natural ways of looking at the world were different, which always made for robust arguments.

Joel was a conceptual thinker, he looked at events in the context of long historical trends – decades, centuries – and was never happier than in an ivory tower. His academic work was on the evolution and decline of empires. Marion was more interested in the pragmatics of international relations, the dynamics between governments, the incremental year-to-year steps by which change was achieved – and being a part of it. After having provided a certain amount of foreign policy thinking to the Knowles campaign, she jumped at the opportunity when she was offered the position of UN ambassador. Joel Ehrenreich would have run a mile.

The panel was over by seven o'clock and Marion took Joel back to her apartment for dinner. They had take-in Japanese together with Marion's husband, Dave Bartok, and their nine-year-old, Ella. Marion and Dave also had a four-year-old, Benjamin, but he was in bed by the time Marion got back. She went in to see if he was awake. He was lying curled up, asleep, his face bathed yellow by a night light.

Ella had grown up around adult conversation on international affairs and took an interest that somewhat outstripped her under-standing. She wanted to know what Joel had said at the meeting.

'I argued that we haven't taken a significant step towards more effective global governance since the United Nations was set up,' replied Joel.

'Really?' said Ella seriously, holding a piece of tuna sushi between two chopsticks. 'Did you agree with that, Mom?'

'No, honey, I didn't.'

'Okay,' said Ella. 'So this is like a disagreement between you two?'

'You could say that,' said Marion. 'A healthy disagreement.'

Ella was silent, chewing her sushi thoughtfully. The adults watched her.

'I don't know what global governance is,' she said eventually.

Joel grinned. 'Don't worry, honey. There isn't any.'

'Joel, that's not true!' said Marion.

Ella looked at Dave. 'Looks like they're having another healthy disagreement,' she said conspiratorially.

Dave laughed. 'Looks like they are.'

After dinner Ella went to get ready for bed. Marion went with her. When she came back Dave had made coffee. He poured her a cup.

Dave was a lawyer with a small Wall Street firm. His career had played second fiddle to Marion's as her jobs had taken the family east and then west and then east again across the country. That was a deal they had agreed. They both had a strong sense of public service and while Marion worked in education or the administration, this was Dave's way of fulfilling it.

'Joel's got a book coming out,' she said to Dave as she took the coffee.

Joel gave him a look of mock apology. 'What else am I supposed to do with my life?'

'Don't act so coy,' said Marion. 'I heard you work it in a couple of times tonight.'

'You can't blame me for trying.'

'What's it called?' asked Dave.

'*Switch.*' Joel grinned. 'I know, I know. Catchy title, huh? *Switch: The historical imperative for the twenty-first century.* I'll send you a copy.' He glanced at Marion. 'I will, actually.'

'I'll look forward to it.'

'Read it,' said Joel. 'Not the whole thing. Chapter 1, chapter 4, chapter 6. That's enough. Of course, it's elegantly argued and beautifully written, so if you want extra punishment you can read the whole thing.'

'I'll see what I can do.'

Joel nodded. He took a sip of his coffee, then leaned back with a faint smile on his lips.

'What?' said Marion.

'Nothing.'

'I know that look, Dr Ehrenreich.'

'Okay. I'll tell you what it is. This Uganda escapade intrigues me. It's interesting.'

'Really? I think it's very straightforward.'

'You're way too smart to think that, Marion. Especially the way the president has chosen to go about it. He might think it's straightforward, but you don't.'

Marion didn't reply.

'I see we can't divulge state secrets.'

'Tell me why you think it's not straightforward.'

'Okay.' Joel hardly needed more of an invitation. 'Well, for a start, it's a sign of weakness on the part of the United States.'

Marion nodded non-committally. Typical Joel. Say something as outrageously contrarian as you can and then sit back to see what happens. Everyone saw the intervention as a show of strength. The debate within the administration – to the extent there had been any debate – had centered on whether it was the right time and place for it.

'How so?' she said. It was always entertaining to watch Joel scrambling to create a rationale for something he had thrown out for effect.

But this was obviously a view he had thought about. 'This is a challenge to China. We go into a region in which they see themselves as having established a place as the predominant power and say we're going to clean something up. But the thing we choose is so straightforward, so black and white that we corner them into a situation where they can't object. But let's face it, it's an issue that's completely trivial in respect of our own geostrategic interests. So if I'm sitting on the other side, if I'm sitting in Beijing, this doesn't say to me, hey, you know what, the US is a strong power and it's going to challenge me on issues of genuine concern. It says to me, the US is a weakening power and knows it can only challenge me on an issue that doesn't touch on my critical interests.'

Marion glanced at Dave for a moment, then back at Joel. 'That's a novel interpretation.'

'You don't think it's right?'

'No, I don't think it is right. For a start, you're looking at this through the lens of geostrategic advantage.'

'There's another one?'

'Joel, this isn't about that. When he spoke on this the president was very clear in saying that, first, the United States has a duty and obligation to protect its own citizens – thirty-nine of whom were killed in cold blood by this group, if you remember – and, second, that we have a duty and obligation to anyone in the world when they need protection and their own governments aren't able to give it to them.'

'And don't tell me that point there, right there, doesn't rile the Chinese all the way to the Great Wall and back again.'

Marion smiled knowingly. 'Come on, Joel, let's not muddy the waters. I said "aren't able", not "aren't willing". That would be a whole different doctrine. The Chinese know we're talking about a restricted, contained operation where the Ugandan government itself has invited us in. That makes all the difference. Now, I agree with you, completely confidentially between you and me and Dave, I'm not a great fan of the way the president's chosen to do it. And if you ask me does that make it harder for the Chinese, I would say, yes, it does. But that doesn't change the main thrust of what we're doing. There is absolutely no agenda underlying Jungle Peace that's about establishing some kind of strategic advantage for the United States in Central Africa. That's not what this is about and the Chinese have been reassured on that numerous times. We've made it very clear to them at every level, at every contact, at every opportunity. Me included. I've said it any number of times to Liu at the UN.'

'And what have they said?'

Marion shrugged. She had seen the content of the note that had been delivered to Steve Haskell, along with his report of the meeting with the Chinese vice-foreign minister, but she wasn't at liberty to reveal it.

Joel watched her.

'Like I said, I'm not saying China doesn't have reason to feel a little aggrieved at the way we've done it, I'm not saying that going in with a coalition wouldn't have been better.'

'Or that at least you could have been told you wouldn't have time to build one,' said Joel, who was aware, like everybody else in the international relations community, that the State Department had been hung out to dry while the Pentagon was going full steam ahead.

Marion didn't take the bait. She had no intention of revealing to Joel the full extent of her irritation with the manner in which the president had acted. 'Look, does China perceive this as a challenge? The loss of face, I accept, is an issue, and I don't mean to minimize it. But is that the question, do they see this as a bigger challenge? Joel, I can't say for certain, but my guess is that they don't. As long as we do it like we've said we will, and as long as we're not there so long that it looks like we're trying to establish some kind of permanent presence, I think they understand what we're saying.'

'Well, that's good,' said Joel, 'because we're going to need their help to get out of there.'

'Meaning what?'

'Meaning when something goes wrong, they're going to get dragged in.'

'You're assuming something's going to go wrong.'

'Show me a military operation where it hasn't. Say we end up chasing some LRA into Sudan. You've got the seeds of a confrontation right there and it can go a thousand different ways. The only one who's got any influence with Sudan is China.'

'No one can guarantee everything's going to go right,' said Marion. 'That's a risk.'

'And I'm saying we'll end up with China having to rescue us. You know, it's possible the Chinese have lured us into this whole thing.'

'Joel, that is so ridiculous …' Marion couldn't help laughing. Now she knew he was being contrarian just for the hell of it.

'I'm serious! Why do you think it's impossible?' Joel turned to Dave with a look of injured innocence, as if appealing for justice. Then he looked at Marion again, his face changing back instantly. 'You know, if you were Mao in 1960, you would have wanted to support the Vietcong just to draw us into Vietnam. Getting us into Vietnam is what led eventually to getting Nixon to China. We withheld recognition of them for twenty-four years but Vietnam changed that. So if you were Mao in 1960, you might have said, let's get the Vietcong insurgency going and let's suck the Americans in until they realize they can't pretend we don't exist any more.'

'I don't think Mao said that in 1960,' said Marion.

'Neither do I. But if he was smarter he would have. Maybe President Zhang's saying it now.'

'Joel, we already recognize China.'

'There are other things they want from us.'

'I don't think Uganda's going to be a Vietnam.'

'I agree. And I sure hope not. But the situation doesn't need to be identical for the same principles to apply. Suck us in and get us into a situation where we have no alternative but to acknowledge they're a player.'

'We already acknowledge they're a player.' Marion couldn't help smiling. 'Joel, I've got no idea whether you're serious or not.'

'I'm serious. I'm deadly serious. You know, I'm glad Knowles has done this. I mean, I don't think he's got the first idea what he's doing, but I think there's a good chance we'll end up in a situation where we're going to need China to help us out.'

'I really hope that's not going to happen.'

'No, I do. That would be a good thing. We have to share leadership with them and we should be actively looking for ways to do it. We have to switch to doing that. In fact, someone's just written an excellent book about precisely that point.' Joel paused theatrically. 'Oh!

Me. We have to switch from a stance where we sit here figuring out what we can do to bolster our position and what crumbs we have to let the Chinese have in order to keep them quiet, to one where we actively seek to create a joint leadership approach.'

Marion didn't disagree with that. She just thought it was going to take a long, long time until the US and China were anywhere near able to behave in that fashion.

'Unless we change our approach, we're going to see conflict over global issues. I'm serious, I'm talking about real conflict. The problems won't solve themselves. You know how it works, Marion. When the tensions are there, anything can act as a trigger.'

'And what's the time scale for this conflict of yours?' asked Marion half-jokingly.

'Listen,' said Joel. He sat forward, an intense expression on his face. 'Marion, I know you and I think differently. I know you think I'm the kind of historical thinker who's completely impractical when it comes to the reality of the day-to-day relationships between states.'

Marion smiled. 'I wouldn't say exactly that.'

'Not in front of me. It's okay, I know you would. And you, you're very practical. You take that knowledge you have and distil it into learning to manage real diplomacy. Practical, meaningful stuff that makes a difference from one day to the next. I'm in awe of that, really, I am. But you know, Marion, there are times when the two converge. The big historical stuff and the day-to-day. This is one of those times. Let me give you an example. South Africa. We both know the Chinese government is cosying up to the ANC dictatorship. We're seeing a world power helping a country move *away* from democracy to an alternative form of government. Think about that. We haven't seen anything like it since the height of the Cold War.'

'Joel, we're working very hard to stop it. That's high on our agenda, very high.'

'And I hope you succeed. But to me, it's the phenomenon that's important, what it means about what's happening in our world. The way power is shifting and being used.'

'You're right, Joel. We're completely different. It's not the phenomenon that's important to me. It's the reality of it. It's what it does to the people of South Africa. It's what we do about it.'

'I agree with that,' said Joel. 'I'm not being theoretical here. I apologize. That was badly expressed. What I mean is we have to start sharing leadership with them – over things like South Africa, for example – or we just won't solve the problems we have to solve and we're going to end up either with a very bad outcome or a fight. And it's not easy, because they're pissed. And they have a right to be. They didn't get any of the influence we promised them after the financial crisis.'

'What about their talk about rebalancing their economy?' said Dave.

'Exactly. They're pissed. We're pissed. So what, right? Countries have been pissed all through history. No, this is different. The nature of the problems we face doesn't allow that. We can't just stay pissed at each other and not want to cooperate. We have to cooperate, and fast. We cooperate – *seriously* cooperate – or we fight.'

'That's an extreme way of putting it,' said Marion.

Joel shrugged. 'That's what I think.'

'I don't agree with you. You're way too black and white.'

'Not as black and white as Tom Knowles.'

Marion didn't reply to that. She didn't think Knowles' thinking was generally black and white, but it seemed to have been this time. She didn't agree with Joel that China was necessarily going to have to bail the US out of there – and she was even less in agreement with his contrarian view that that would be a good thing – but she did agree that launching the intervention unilaterally in Uganda would make a bunch of things on which they needed Chinese cooperation a lot harder to achieve.

'My fear,' said Joel, 'is that Tom Knowles, even if he recognizes the need to make a switch of this magnitude, isn't big enough to do anything about it.'

'He's a competent president,' said Marion.

'We need more than a competent president. We need someone much bigger than that.'

'So we're doomed to conflict in your opinion?' Marion said it with a smile.

'I fear we are,' said Joel seriously, 'unless Tom Knowles undergoes some kind of personality change. Or the next president. We might get lucky. I don't know the time scale, but when the stresses build up like this the trigger can be anything.'

8

IN HIS OFFICE on the thirty-fourth floor, Ed Grey turned up the volume on CNBC. Tony Evangelou and Boris Malevsky were with him.

The screen showed a Senate committee room. Ron Strickland, chairman of the Federal Reserve, had already taken his seat at the table in front of the bar. A former professor of economics at Stanford, Strickland was a craggy-faced man with a head of silver hair, heavy brows, and a large wart on the left side of his chin. He was arranging his papers in front of him. A moment later the chairman of the Senate Banking Committee, Louisiana Republican Bill Givens, welcomed him, and Strickland commenced the presentation of his quarterly monetary policy report.

He started with a survey of the state of the domestic economy and global trends. He then progressed to his projections for economic activity. Overall the outlook was benign, with risks weighted to the upside. Then came his inflation projections.

Strickland was a slow-talking, methodical man. You didn't listen to his speeches for entertainment. Yet Grey, Evangelou and Malevsky were hanging on his every word.

'I now come to my view of the sustainability of market activity,' said Strickland on the screen.

Ed Grey leaned forward in his seat. This was the so-called bubble statement, an element in the chairman's report in which he gave a view of sustainability of activity in critical investment markets – stocks, bonds, commodities, housing. Veiled references to irrational exuberance were no longer thought to be enough and the statement had been introduced as one of the responses to the failure of the Greenspan–Bernanke period of chairmanship to deal with bubbles inflating across asset markets. It remained a controversial element, much hated by Wall Street.

Strickland continued in his customary monotone.

'While we see no evidence of bubble-type activity, we remain alert to the possibility that the upside view over the short- to medium-term horizon will encourage an increasing level of activity in a number of asset classes. Pricing and volume data indicate an increasing risk appetite among certain investor segments backed by rising levels of leverage. In particular, we continue to see a notable increase in the market uptake of certain collateralized derivatives, and although these are a legitimate means of diversifying portfolio risk they also carry a systemic risk through secondary and tertiary markets and, as I have reported before, we believe could exacerbate overheating should this begin to develop. We remain particularly watchful of a number of segments of the equities derivatives markets and remain vigilant to the exposure of the banking sector, which would be a key concern should overexposure develop.' Strickland paused portentously. 'We will use monetary policy if overheating appears to be taking place. We will use it rapidly, decisively, and are prepared to do so.'

Grey glanced at Malevsky. He was frowning as he gazed at the screen. Evangelou caught Grey's eye and shrugged.

When Strickland had finished his prepared remarks, the questions from the senators began. After a few questions one of the Democratic senators brought him back to the bubble statement.

'Mr Chairman, you talked about rising risk appetite and leverage. Can you be more specific about the levels of these rises?'

'If I had to characterize them, Senator, I would describe them as moderate to medium. My office can supply the data.'

'That would be helpful. But I take it you're saying you do have significant concerns at the moment.'

'It depends, Senator, what you mean by significant.'

The senator sighed impatiently. 'I think most people would understand what I mean, Mr Chairman. It sounds as if you have significant concerns that you will need to intervene.'

'Senator, let me try to be clearer. We monitor these parameters. Will the day come when we need to intervene? Logically the answer to that must be yes, because every single cycle that we have ever seen in this country has culminated in a bubble and then gone on to a bust, and part of my mandate is to ensure that we don't get to that point again. And if without intervention we would get to that point, it stands to reason that intervention at some point will be required.'

'Mr Chairman, that's a wonderful theoretical answer.'

'Thank you, sir.'

There was a ripple of laughter from the audience.

Strickland's craggy face remained serious. He had little in the way of a sense of humor and hadn't seen the irony in the senator's compliment. Since taking the post as head of the Fed his technical and ponderous communication style had been the target of much criticism.

'Mr Chairman,' said the senator in a show of exasperation, 'what point is there if you have concerns and don't make the extent of these concerns known? Surely the point of these concerns is to warn unsuspecting investors in good time to help them make informed decisions. Quarter after quarter, you come before this committee and tell us you have concerns and yet you do not tell us how strong they are. If I heard you correctly, I think you're telling us your concerns are strong. Is that correct?'

'Mr Senator, I have said repeatedly, and I think I have said it again today in the clearest terms I can, that the Federal Reserve will not hesitate to act should this be required. That is a responsibility the president has laid upon me and I take it with all seriousness. I think the unsuspecting investor, as you have described him or her, can take comfort in that.'

The senator gazed at Strickland, then shook his head in a calculated show of dissatisfaction.

Bill Givens, the Republican chair of the committee, knew what the other senator had been trying to do. The Democrats would want nothing more than to have the Fed chairman admit that a bust was imminent in his last testimony before the midterm elections. Givens wanted to make sure that impression was reversed.

'Mr Strickland,' he said, 'perhaps it would be helpful if you could tell us how close you are to taking action over these concerns. From what I heard you say, you don't actually believe there's imminent danger of a bubble, do you?'

'It depends what you mean by imminent, Senator.'

There were more smiles amongst the audience.

'You talked about taking monetary action. Would you say you're close or far from taking a further step?'

'I don't know if there's any absolute measure of that distance, Senator Givens.'

'Then a relative one,' said Givens in frustration. 'Are you closer or further than you were before? Nothing I've heard says to me you're any closer. What you've said, I think, is that in fact we're no closer to that because of the vigilance you and the rest of the administration are constantly exercising.'

Givens stopped, wishing that Strickland would just say yes. That was all he needed to say. Yes.

Strickland frowned. 'Senator, we're continually vigilant, as you say. We will not allow irrational market activity to develop without intervening to put a stop to it. We will not tolerate irrational exuberance or anything approaching it. We're very clear on our responsibilities on that point. I'm very clear on my responsibilities on that point.'

Givens shook his head. Strickland didn't know a line when he was fed it.

The questioning on the screen went on, now focusing on a detail of the inflation outlook that Strickland had presented. Eventually it came to an end and Strickland got to his feet.

Grey muted the volume and looked at the stock price data Malevsky had brought with him before Strickland started speaking. Fidelian Bank was down a couple of percentage points over the past week. The other three banks Malevesky had picked were flat. But the banking sector as a whole was up slightly, so in relative terms, they too had fallen. Yet relative falls didn't make him any money.

The previous week, Ed Grey had put an exposure of $50 million behind Malevsky's idea. Half of it was committed to shorting Fidelian, the rest distributed among the other three banks. If he closed out the trade now, he would show a minuscule gain from Fidelian's decline and nothing from the others.

Malevsky had argued that Strickland's statement would help to create a climate in which the market might correct. Now the statement had been made.

'No one's dumping banks over this,' said Evangelou.

'He was a little stronger than usual,' said Malevsky. 'That sentence – rapidly, decisively, whatever it was – that was very explicit. And he wanted to get that point across in the questions as well.'

'He's said it before. I'm telling you, no one's dumping banks over this.'

Grey agreed. He looked at Malevsky. 'So what do you think?'

Malevsky frowned.

'I'll tell you what I think,' said Evangelou impatiently. 'We're sitting on a shitload of these stocks, paying for every day we borrow them, and they're not going anywhere.'

'Fidelian's down a couple of per cent,' said Malevsky.

'That's *us*, Boris. That's us doing the selling. I don't see anyone joining us. Ed, let's close this out and forget about it. Let's go back to making money. Nice idea, Boris, but no cigar.'

Grey gazed at Malevsky. 'What do you think?' he said again.

'Tony's right, no one's dumping banks on this.'

'So you want to close it out?'

'No, I'd hold. Fidelian's coming to the market for cash. That's still there.'

'When?' demanded Evangelou.

Malevsky shrugged.

'I'm not interested in holding and hoping,' said Grey. 'We close it out unless something's going to happen.' He paused. 'By the way, Boris, I meant to tell you. This is your idea, so I'm going to give you five per cent of what we earn. That's the good news. The bad news? I'm going to sack you if this trade makes a loss.'

Evangelou smiled.

Grey wanted to see what Malevsky was made of. That was what this trade was about at least as much as the money it might make or lose. Identifying a rookie who had what it took to become a great trader was no easy task. As often as not, even someone as experienced as Ed Grey got it wrong until he saw that person act under fire. Blowing a few million in losses now was nothing if it helped you find someone who could earn you billions in the future – or if it helped you see that this same person would lose you billions instead.

Grey wanted to see whether Malevksy had the stomach to hold a serious position. There was no way to see that unless Malevsky had skin in the game. Serious skin.

'Seriously, Boris, I will sack your ass.'

Malevsky shrugged. 'I get five per cent, right?'

'You do. Now, what do you think?'

'I can always get another job.'

'Not after what I'll say about you if you fuck this up. You'll get another job, but it'll be cleaning toilets.'

Evangelou grinned. He loved seeing his boss in action. At his best, Ed Grey was a big, brash, bone-crunching bully. 'You want to see what happens to guys Ed sacks. He will hound you, Malevsky. He will hound you out of this industry.'

'Tony,' said Grey, 'you flatter me.'

Malevsky muttered something in Russian.

'Okay, Boris,' said Grey, 'let me give you a clue. If I were you, here's what I'd be asking. Why is Tony wrong?'

Evangelou raised an eyebrow.

'Why is he wrong, Boris? He's just told you no one's dumping banks over this. Why's he wrong? Give me a reason.'

'He's not wrong,' said Malevsky.

'No?'

'Not today. But tomorrow he will be. People will be looking around. They're aware. Strickland specifically mentioned banks. He mentioned overexposure. He said he was going to act rapidly, decisively. No one's dumping banks, but everyone's aware now at the first sign of trouble they're going to be in Strickland's sights.'

'You're talking yourself into this, Boris,' murmured Evangelou with amusement. 'I love it. Keep going.'

'People who think banks are a little overvalued,' said Malevsky, ignoring him, 'are going to get jittery. Maybe Strickland will push up interest rates after what he just said. If they see some bank stocks dropping, they'll decide it's time to get out.'

'That's it?' said Grey.

'No. We know for a fact one of those banks is going to come to the market for cash.'

Grey smiled. He liked the way Malevsky had said that Tony wasn't wrong – but that he was. And he was inclined to agree with Malevsky's logic, or to be interested enough to want to find out. The critical point was that people had to see bank stocks falling. Without that, Strickland's words wouldn't have any effect.

The Fed chairman's words weren't anywhere near strong enough to create a cause for bank stocks to fall – but they did create a context.

If the timing was right, if someone hit the market with a big bunch of sell orders just when the market itself was wondering whether anyone was going to react to Strickland's statement, they might inject enough uncertainty to actually start the market moving. But it would take a lot more than the $50 million he had put in to do that.

He glanced at Evangelou. His senior portfolio manager knew exactly what Grey was thinking. Evangelou didn't like this kind of trading. Intuitive stuff wasn't his style. He didn't like anything where he couldn't get an analyst to turn the rationale into a quantitative model and run two dozen scenarios on it.

'Ed, you don't want to put that much in,' he said.

'Don't I?' said Grey.

9

TOM KNOWLES GLANCED over the two stapled pages in his hand. There was nothing much in them that the uniformed officer in front of him hadn't already covered in his verbal summary. Ten days into Jungle Peace, the president was still receiving a daily briefing on the operation. The Pentagon's White House liaison officer came in each morning to present the update at the daily StratCom, the strategy and communications meeting held at 8am in the Oval Office.

The usual participants at the StratCom were White House press secretary Dean Moss, White House chief of staff Roberta Devlin, Gary Rose, Ed Abrahams, Director of the National Economic Council Marty Perez, and Sandra Ruiz-Kellerman, a pollster and political advisor who had made her name in a series of high-profile Republican campaigns. Together they represented Tom Knowles' closest and most trusted White House advisors.

Knowles put down the paper. It reported a series of drone reconnaissance sorties over northern Uganda. A pair of Chinese destroyers was shadowing the *Abraham Lincoln* strike group in international waters off Uganda, as they had done since the beginning of the operation. The LRA, which had proven to have the capability of posting messages and even video on the internet, had posted another message threatening to beat the American invaders to death and eat their brains, which was apparently supposed to scare them.

'So essentially, Colonel,' he said to the officer, 'nothing's changed since yesterday.'

'I wouldn't quite say that, sir. As I said, in the past twenty-four hours we've flown twenty-seven drone sorties and covered a number of areas that we hadn't had the opportunity to survey previously.'

'And found?'

'We've excluded significant enemy concentrations in those areas, Mr President.'

The president shook his head. 'Zip. That's what you're telling me. We found zip. How many of these guys have we actually killed?'

'We estimate in the region of four to six.'

'In two weeks?'

'Somewhat less than two weeks, Mr President.'

Knowles glanced at Gary Rose.

'Mr President,' said the colonel, 'we have significantly reduced their activity amongst the civilian population. Our assessment is they're laying low, moving between sites in small groups. That's pretty much what we expected them to do.'

'I thought we expected to find them with our drones and blow the hell out of them.'

'Well, we're hoping to do that, sir. Our strategy is interdict and attrit. This is interdiction. The attrit element takes a little longer. Right now we expect them to break up into small groups and try to lay low for a period, but that's not something they can sustain over the long term, and when it becomes unsustainable for them, that's when we will, as you say, begin to eliminate them in larger numbers.'

There was silence. Knowles looked questioningly at the others. There were no remarks.

'Alright,' he said. 'Thank you, Colonel.'

'Thank you, Mr President.'

The officer picked up his briefcase and left the room.

'Same story every day,' muttered Knowles. He looked at Rose. 'What do you think?'

The national security advisor shrugged. 'There'll be a couple of phases in this and we're still in the first. We're using a light touch approach. We don't want to send ground troops into that jungle. I think this approach will work but it does mean it's going to take more time. The alternative is putting large numbers of troops on the ground and that's an option we ruled out at the start.'

'Sandy, how long have we got on this?'

'At this stage,' said Ruiz-Kellerman, 'our polling is saying we have solid support among people who are aware of the operation. They're glad we went in.'

'They're not concerned we don't have anything to show?'

'Not yet. The whole thing changes if we take casualties.'

'That's the point of the strategy we've chosen,' said Rose.

'Gary, are you saying we're not going to get a body count before the midterms?'

'I'm saying it's possible. That's only four weeks now. It could take longer before we get a meaningful success.'

The president looked at Abrahams.

'I don't think that's necessarily a problem,' said Abrahams. 'People like the fact we've gone in, that's been a boost. Now everything stays steady and we're looking at getting the numbers we need on the Hill in the midterms. Would you agree with that, Sandy?'

Ruiz-Kellerman nodded. 'If the election was tomorrow, we'd get sixty in the Senate. Maybe sixty-one. In the House, we expand our majority ten to twenty.'

'So it's risk minimization,' said Abrahams. 'A big bunch of dead LRA gets us a little more support, a couple of Americans in body bags loses us a hell of a lot more. Risk-reward, it makes no sense to take a chance. That says we go with the strategy, like Gary says. Unmanned vehicles – no risk. We just need to start adjusting press expectations. Start talking about interdiction, safety of the civilian population, that kind of stuff. Make those the wins. Give it a humanitarian angle. Make if feel good, like we're achieving something.'

'That doesn't sound too exciting,' said Devlin.

Abrahams glanced at Moss. 'We can make it sound exciting, right, Dean?'

The press secretary smiled.

Knowles nodded. 'Okay. Sandy, you agree?'

'I do. I think that's right.'

'Okay,' said the president. They were done with that. 'Roberta, what else have we got?'

'We should talk about where we are on the Emergency Relief bill,' said Devlin. 'Senator Hotchkiss made a speech in New Orleans last night where he came out against the additional appropriations facilities we have in the bill.'

Don Hotchkiss was turning into a thorn in Knowles' flesh. The senator was a traditional, right-wing Texas conservative and short of announcing his candidacy he was doing everything he could to position himself to challenge for the Republican nomination in two years' time. The midterm election results would determine whether he would actually launch a bid. Hotchkiss was a more credible candidate than any of the conservatives Knowles had had to face in his first run, Mitch Moynihan included. Knowles didn't look forward to facing a serious challenge from within his own party.

'We've got to start going after this guy,' said Abrahams. 'I mean, seriously, we've got to go after him.'

'Hotchkiss will take another three or four senators with him on this bill,' said Devlin. 'It if was someone else, I wouldn't worry.'

Abrahams looked at the president. 'We've got to put Hotchkiss in his corner of the cage and make sure he's still sitting there in two years' time. I'm going to take a look at it.'

Knowles nodded. He glanced at his watch. 'What else? Where am I this afternoon? Alabama?'

'Colorado,' said Devlin.

Knowles smiled. He loved campaigning, and he loved it even more when his ratings were so high. There were twenty-seven days to the midterms and his schedule had him out of Washington for no less than eighteen of them. Tom Knowles was a president candidates wanted to be seen with, and there was enough at stake for him in the midterms to be prepared to put the time into helping get key candidates over the line. In Colorado, the Republicans had an impressive challenger in a tight Senate race. Knowles would be speaking on a platform with him in Denver.

'What about the first lady?' he said. 'She coming with me?'

'No, sir. I believe she'll be with you in Iowa on Saturday.'

'Okay. Josh done the speech?'

Ed Abrahams smiled. 'How much work does it need?'

Knowles laughed. He gave just about the same stump speech for every candidate he supported. First there was a brief folksy section about the candidate that his speechwriter, Josh Bentner, prepared on the basis of facts supplied by the candidate's campaign manager. The main section of the speech then focused on Knowles' record as president, which was the same on every occasion, with a drop-in set of remarks about the benefits his administration had brought to the candidate's state. Finally he came back to a brief endorsement of the candidate.

Knowles had a good story to tell and he felt good standing up to tell it. The first two years of his presidency had been reassuringly benign. No specter of a return to financial disaster. The details varied state by state, but the message of the speech was always the same. Trust. Rectitude. Stability. Scrutiny. Prosperity and growth without the fear of a crash.

'We done?'

'Almost,' said Devlin, looking at the screen of her tablet. 'Strickland gave his quarterly report yesterday. We should cover that off.'

Knowles looked at Marty Perez, his economic advisor.

'Nothing special,' said Perez. 'He talked about how he was ready to intervene.'

'That's what we want, right?'

'Yeah. He kept hammering it in the questions, possibly a little too much. You know what he's like. He can be a little tin-eared and then the press read everything he says like it's the Talmud. There's no doubt his communication's a problem.'

'You think we should reappoint him?'

There were glances around the room. Knowles had asked the question somewhat mischievously. Marty Perez, he knew, coveted the job of chairman of the Fed for himself. Strickland's term ran another two years. Tom Knowles thought Strickland was doing a pretty good job, although everyone was always talking about his communication style. Personally, he found him stiff and long-winded, and he had no great personal rapport with the man. But as long as the economy was running smoothly he could live with that.

'I just think he's never going to be a great communicator,' said Perez eventually.

'We all know that,' said Ed Abrahams. 'Look, have we got a problem from his statement yesterday or not?'

Perez shook his head. 'No. There was a little selling in the market afterwards, that's all.'

10

THE NAME STRUCK him. He had seen it on the list recently, he knew, without having expected to. And here it was again. Fidelian Bank.

Sammy Horwitz was a young staffer in the division of Bank Supervision in the New York district of the Federal Reserve. Part of his job was to look over the so-called five per cent list, a daily spreadsheet that showed the stock price movements of all bank or bank holding companies quoted on the New York Stock Exchange. The New York Fed didn't regulate investment banks like Fidelian but they were on the list as well because of the effects they could have on the banks that the Fed did regulate. Any stock that had moved five per cent or more than the average movement in the sector was highlighted, blue for up, red for down. Three days after Ron Strickland's report to the Senate Banking Committee, Fidelian was red. On the spreadsheet Horwitz could see that it gone red two days previously as well.

There was only one problem with the five per cent list. Although the excess stock price movements were clearly identified, there were no rules about what anyone was supposed to do with them. The stock price was only one of numerous indicators of a bank's health, in this case reflecting the market's view. Accordingly, a five per cent stock price movement within a day might make perfect sense given what the Fed already knew, and in that case one would have been more surprised to find that it hadn't occurred. Other times it came out of the blue, and might mean the market genuinely knew something that the regulators didn't – which was worrying. Arguably more often, it might mean the market thought it knew something that in fact it didn't – which wasn't.

Sammy Horwitz, of course, knew something about Fidelian. It was an investment bank that had undergone rapid growth out of the financial crisis with a large franchise in Asian markets. But that wasn't enough. His first job was to find out more.

First he pulled the stock price history off Bloomberg. Going back a year, it showed a fairly steady line, somewhat underperforming the banking sector as a whole, but with nothing notable until the significant falls over the past few days. He downloaded the Fidelian file off the Fed's internal system and the company's latest filings from the Securities and Exchange Commission website. He scanned them quickly. Fidelian wasn't on any watch list for at-risk banks. Its capital ratio and other key financial indicators were adequate. He rang his counterpart at the SEC and was told they weren't aware of any concerns. He hit the Fidelian website and did a search of its investor relations section for any announcements over the past couple of weeks that might have turned the market sour on it. He drew a blank. He did a press search for articles and analysis and drew another blank.

An hour after noticing its name on the list, Sammy Horwitz still had no idea why Fidelian stock was falling.

Later that day he mentioned it to his boss, Cindy Moore. She hadn't heard any rumors of problems with Fidelian.

'What are the trade volumes?' said Moore.

'Average.' Horwitz had already thought of that. If trade in the stock was unusually light, a couple of oddball trades could distort the price.

'Keep an eye on it,' said Moore.

Horwitz checked the price at the end of the day. The stock had fallen a couple of per cent further. The next day, Friday, Fidelian kept falling. By early afternoon it was down almost fifteen per cent over the week.

Horwitz took it back to his boss.

Cindy Moore put in a call to Joe Mancini, head of Market Surveillance at the New York Stock Exchange. She asked him if he knew anything about Fidelian. Mancini said he'd get back to her. He called back on Monday. Fidelian stock had opened still lower.

'We don't see anything in it,' said Mancini.

'It's down almost twenty per cent in the past week.'

'Obviously some people don't think very much of it. That's the market. What're you gonna do?'

'You don't think it's being targeted by shorts?'

'Probably is. Listen, Cindy, the whole banking sector is down a little.'

'What are you hearing?'

'Your chairman spooked the market. When he says stuff like that on Capitol Hill, what do you think's going to happen?'

'He didn't say anything. What did he say?'

'What can I tell you? You've got the whole sector down a little so naturally there's one or two under some real pressure, and apart from Mr Strickland's erudite remarks the world looks exactly the same as it did a fortnight ago. At least I haven't noticed any change.'

'Do you know who's selling?'

Mancini laughed. 'Listen, we'll keep an eye on it.'

Later, Moore had another call from Mancini to say there were rumors in the market that a couple of banks might be coming to the market for a cash call over the next few weeks and people were taking bets on who it was going to be.

'And Fidelian's one of them?' said Moore.

'I'm guessing, looking at the numbers. Their percentage of shorted stock is up. But it's a rumor, Cindy. It might be Fidelian today, it might be someone else tomorrow.'

'And you think this is all legit?'

'They're allowed to bet. That's what markets do, Cindy.'

Moore rolled her eyes. Mancini had a habit of talking about what 'markets do' as if he was instructing a child in the ways of the world. He thought everyone at the Fed was an academic who had no idea how the market really worked, and the only thing worse in his view than a man from the Fed was a woman from the Fed. Moore could almost taste the condescension every time she spoke to him.

'Joe, if something's going on here, we've got to stop it right now.'

'Something like what?'

'Is this some kind of coordinated action?'

'Like a bear raid?' Mancini chuckled. 'Look, they're being shorted, right? That doesn't mean we're looking at a bear raid.'

'I don't think this is funny. Can you tell me that for sure? Can you tell me for sure nothing's going on here?'

'I can only tell you what I can tell you.' Mancini's voice was snappy now. 'If I thought we were looking at something illegal you can bet your bottom dollar I'd be doing something about it and I wouldn't be waiting for you to tell me.'

'I hope not.'

'Of course not. But you know, I need some evidence first. Last time I looked this is still a free market. They're taking bets, Cindy. Okay? They're taking bets out there on who's going to come back to the market for cash. And people are taking profit. It's been a good year. Some people are gonna want to take a little profit and when they hear Professor Strickland saying the party's over and they see the market getting a little jittery they say it's time to do it. Strickland's paid to burst the bubble, right? They're worried that's what he's going to do.'

Cindy was silent for a moment. 'Where did you hear these rumors?'

'Jeez, Cindy! It's just something guys are hearing. You ought to get in the market a little. There are rumors out there every single day.'

'You don't know any more about it?' said Moore, ignoring the jibe.

'I don't. I swear I don't. It'll be this rumor today, it'll be something else tomorrow. We've got a little profit-taking going on, it makes it all seem a little worse.'

Moore was silent.

'Come on, Cindy. It's like a snake pit out there. You've got to sit back and let them writhe. Enjoy it. Watch them eat each other and give thanks to God you're not out there with them.'

'Yeah,' said Moore. 'Thanks.' She put the phone down. Mancini might be right, but she was paid to do more than watch the snakes writhe, as he put it. And she thought he was way too complacent. For someone paid to identify market manipulation, he was way too willing to accept that any given pattern of trades was just the regular market at work. Joe Mancini had always struck her as the kind of regulator who was invariably ready to arrive just as soon as the horse had bolted.

She wasn't going to leave it at that. She had worked at the New York Fed for the past fourteen years and that meant she had seen the events of '08 up close. She had seen Bear Stearns get sold over a weekend. She had seen Lehman go down and AIG nationalized in the course of forty-eight hair-raising hours. Once things started moving, she knew, they could move with extraordinary speed. This needed to go higher. She spoke to her boss, who spoke to his boss, Jerry Rabin, the president of the New York Fed. They both already knew that Fidelian's stock was slipping. Rabin got on the phone to Bill Custler, the CEO of Fidelian Bank.

Rabin knew Custler well. He asked him what he thought was going on with the stock price. Custler said he had no idea.

'Bill,' said Rabin, 'is there something we should know?'

'We're in compliance,' said Custler.

'I'm not saying you're not.' Rabin paused. He respected Bill Custler as a competent and honest executive. 'People are shorting you, Bill. Why are they doing that?'

'I have no idea.'

Rabin didn't know if he heard something in Custler's tone. It was a little more stiff and formal than normal.

'Bill, if you've got something to tell us, for God's sake, tell us early.'

There was silence.

Rabin waited for him to reply.

'Bill?'

'Jerry,' said Custler, 'I've got nothing to tell you.'

11

TONY EVANGELOU LAUGHED. 'Ed,' he said, 'you're insane.'

Ed Grey grinned. 'So you're telling me we close out now?'

'Yes, I'm telling you we close out now. Let's buy the stock, send it back, close out now and be thankful this blind fucking bet came good.'

Grey looked at Evangelou in mock dismay. 'Tony, I expected more from you.'

'Sure you did.'

Grey turned to Boris Malevsky. 'How much do we take if we close out now?'

'Thirty-one million.'

'How much you going to get if we do?'

'One point six,' said Malevsky. 'Five per cent, right?'

'You're rounding up!' Grey laughed. 'Why not? You ever had a one point six million bonus?'

Malevsky shook his head.

'What do you want to do? You want the one point six?'

'Double or nothing,' said Evangelou. 'Goes the wrong way, you still lose your job, Malevsky.'

'That's true,' said Grey. 'Huh, Boris? What do you think?'

Malevsky hesitated. 'I think it's got a way to go.'

'Really,' said Grey. 'Why?'

'There's a cash call coming from Fidelian. The market still doesn't know about it.'

'The market's marked them down twenty per cent for no apparent reason but Strickland's speech and our own fine leadership,' said Evangelou. 'Twenty per cent. How much capital does that say Fidelian has to raise? Have you crunched those numbers, Boris?'

'Nine billion.'

'A twenty per cent fall says they have to raise nine billion?'

'That's right.'

'That's a ridiculous amount. They're not coming to the market for that much.'

Boris shrugged.

'Ed, we have no real research behind this, we have no rationale, we have no–'

'And Boris here has just made himself one point six million. This is just starting. I take your point about the nine billion, Tony. That's way too much. But that's the point. It's not rational now. The whole sector's moving. We're on the tiger, Tony. We're riding it. When you ride the tiger, you ride it to the end. You ride her to the fucking end. It is the biggest, biggest, biggest mistake you can make to get off too early.'

'This tiger is falling flat right under us. This tiger is running out of steam. In another second it's gonna turn around and bite the hell out of our ass for still being on its back.'

'Well, that is a possibility.' Grey grinned. He was definitely of the school that said you added to your trade when your trade was doing well. Evangelou was more conservative. He was all numbers, not feel. He was very disciplined, a take-your-profit-at-your-target kind of trader and always needed pushing to stake more on his trades. But Grey respected that. He was the opposite. It was what made them such a good team when it came to managing the really big-bet trades that came along only once or twice a year.

He swung around and faced the screens on the wall of his office. One of them showed the price for the overall banking sector. The other showed Fidelian. The movement in the market over the past week had been more than he expected. 'You think we're doing that? I mean, Fidelian, maybe. But the sector, the whole fucking sector. Look at the sector. How much are we in now?'

'Two hundred,' said Evangelou.

'Two hundred,' murmured Grey. He took a slurp on his coffee. 'That's nothing.'

'Who'd you talk to?' said Evangelou knowingly.

'A couple of guys.'

You couldn't expect a market to move without the odd shot of rumor to lubricate the rails. To help build momentum, Grey had spoken to a number of other Divvies he knew closely. He certainly hadn't told them about Boris Malevsky's piece of information. That particular nugget of gold was for Red River alone. But you didn't have to reveal what you knew to start the rumors flying. You only had to be careful that those rumors – or the variants of them that were sure to develop – didn't swing back to bite you. The guys you spoke to weren't your friends, no matter how well you knew them. They were in the market, and they were in it to make money. For every dime someone makes in the market, someone else loses the same amount. There was no one you could trust. If you gave a signal and someone thought it was pointed in the wrong direction, they'd be your biggest cheerleader and then bet against you to help the market cut your throat. The more of your blood was on the carpet, the more money they'd make.

'Someone else is in,' said Grey.

Evangelou nodded. 'Two hundred's not going to move the sector like that.'

'How much? A half billion?'

'Depends. That could get it going.'

'Who would it be?' Grey thought through the likely participants in the game. How many was it likely to be? That made a difference. If there was one big player with a chunk in the game, the minute that player pulled the plug and started buying, prices would rebound and everyone else, including Red River, would get lost in the afterwash. If it was a number of players, no one individual had the power to do that. It might leave Red River, with two hundred in, as the lead player.

'Ed, this is all froth.'

'Maybe,' said Grey. The received wisdom said that short sellers couldn't move a market where investors didn't want it to go, not for any length of time. It would rapidly rebound as investors came in to buy at levels they deemed to be attractive.

'We'd have to go another two hundred minimum,' said Tony.

Grey nodded. Even that might not be enough. And if the market turned, you wouldn't be able to buy the stocks at a sensible price to close out a position that big. Liquidity, as Evangelou would have been quick to point out, would drain away. Price would overshoot as people realized someone was looking to buy every stock they could find. You could take a bath damn quick. To put any more in now, you'd need to have a strong, strong reason to believe the market had further to fall. The very act of shorting that much more would help it down, but it wouldn't stay down for long if the market as a whole didn't believe the sector should be down there. People would start buying.

He looked at Malevsky. 'What do you think, Boris? Do you take your one point six and go home?'

Malevsky shook his head.

'Really? Get this wrong, I'm still going to sack your ass.'

Boris grinned.

'Give me a reason,' said Grey. 'Give me a reason not to give you one point six million dollars.'

'I've got two. One, Strickland's talking to the National Press Club tomorrow.'

Evangelou rolled his eyes. 'This again ...'

'Two, I was sixteen the day Lehman Brothers went bust.'

'That was your birthday?' said Evangelou. 'Not like I can see what that's got to do with anything.'

'It wasn't my birthday, but I remember it like it was.'

'Who doesn't?'

'Exactly. And I wasn't even interested in finance. Back then I was going to be a doctor. But Lehman went down and everybody knew about it, even me, Boris Malevsky the doctor-to-be. I saw an interesting headline this morning. *Are we on the verge of finding the next Lehman?*'

'That's ridiculous.'

'I agree. But I also think it's the kind of talk Strickland is going to want to stop in its tracks. And I think the entire administration is going to want to make sure there's no talk like that going around. So I think Strickland is going to come out very, very bullish on the banks. He's going to say there's nothing wrong, the regulation's good, the system's strong, etc., etc.'

'Which, fundamentally, we believe it is,' said Evangelou.

'Correct. And when Strickland says that, and people are asking if we've got the next Lehman, I think Strickland's going to have exactly the opposite effect of what he wants. People are going to say, hell, the Fed's saying that, I'm getting out of banks!'

Grey laughed.

'I'm serious,' said Malevsky.

'I know you are. So why doesn't Strickland realize it? He's not dumb. You know, he might even remember Lehman as well as you, Boris.'

'So what else does he say? He's got no out. If he's lukewarm on it, it looks as if there's something wrong. If he doesn't address it, he looks complacent.'

'Then he shouldn't speak at all,' said Evangelou.

'You're right. He should cancel the talk. But it's been publicized. So what does it look like if he cancels? It's a catch 22.'

Grey frowned. 'Fundamentally, Boris, what you're saying is there's no way Strickland can calm the market.'

'Not if it wants to correct. Maybe there's a little panic out there. I'm not saying this is a crash. I still think we're in line for a correction, a small one. It'll overshoot, that's all, but if there's panic out there, it'll overshoot even more.'

Evangelou snorted. 'This is just guesswork. What Strickland's going to say, what he isn't going to say ...'

'But what Boris is saying is that whatever Strickland says, it makes things worse. That's no-risk, Tony.'

'Only if you believe everyone's ready to panic.'

Ed Grey didn't believe the market was ready to fall into a full-blown panic, but the stock movements in the past few days did make him think it was jittery. Everyone felt the market was due a correction and were wondering if this was it. If it was, it would be the first correction that both this Fed chairman and Treasury secretary had faced, which would make everyone even more nervous.

'Ed,' said Evangelou, 'you can bet on this, but you're betting blind.'

'Boris?'

'I don't know what Strickland's going to say. I just think he's got a hard job to say the right thing and he's not someone who's too slick with his communication. He's probably the last guy you want to have standing up and talking right now. But what do I know? Personally, right now, I've got one point six million. That's nothing compared with what I'll have if it goes our way. If it doesn't, I lose one point six I never even had and a job I've had for two months.' He shrugged and said something in Russian.

'What does that mean?'

'Fuck it!'

Grey laughed. Malevsky reminded him of himself.

Ed Grey contemplated the screens on the wall. He had no research or quantitative rationale to back this. But out on the floor he had a bunch of portfolio managers doing exactly those kind of trades, grinding out the steady, low-margin business that brought the fund a reliable eight or ten per cent per annum. The big trades, the ones that took the returns up into the stratosphere, always had an element of hunch about them.

But not as much as this. Normally there was more research and a better rationale behind it. This really was betting blind, as Evangelou had said. Or almost blind. They did have one solid fact – that Fidelian was coming to the market for cash. But the fall in stock price had already factored in a capital raising of nine billion, which was more than Fidelian could possibly be expecting to raise. The rest was emotion.

But emotion could make you a lot of money, as long as you didn't make the mistake of feeling it yourself.

Say they took their exposure up to half a billion, thought Grey. Say the market turned against them and prices climbed, say by five per cent before they could close out. That gave them a loss of twenty-five million. On the other hand, say Fidelian and the others they had shorted went down another twenty per cent.

The risk-reward ratio wasn't great. It wasn't as high as he would normally demand for a bet like this. But the rest of the fund was strong. The analysts ran scenarios across the entire portfolio on a daily basis. They were up thirty-six per cent for the year, almost double the target return he submitted to his investors. The scenario modeling showed that it would take a coordinated, significant downturn across numerous asset classes and markets to really hurt him. In that context, a loss of twenty-five million, or even a worst-case loss of fifty, was nothing.

'If we were going to do this,' said Grey eventually, 'we'd have to increase our positions before Strickland speaks.'

Malevsky nodded. 'That's tomorrow.'

12

THE CROWD IN the ballroom was bigger than usual. National Press Club lunches are typically affairs for the connoisseur, arranged far in advance, long on theory, history or nostalgia but rarely aligned with the twenty-four-hour news cycle. For that to happen, the Club needs an extraordinary stroke of luck.

Ron Strickland's speech had been scheduled months previously to mark his second anniversary in the post. He took his place at the podium after being introduced by the Club president, Claire Weissman. Behind him was the familiar blue background with the name of the club in white lettering repeated across it. He looked around the room and saw just about every economic journalist of national stature in the audience.

'I'm very grateful to the National Press Club for the opportunity to speak to you today. As it turns out, it probably saves me quite a number of interviews.'

There was a smattering of laughter, more at the sight of Ron Strickland trying to open with a joke than at the quality of the witticism.

'Speaking as an economist, an economy of scale, if you will.'

There was a little more laughter. But the wooden jokes, if Strickland had calculated them to lighten the atmosphere, only heightened the sense of expectation in the room. After the reaction in the markets to his comments before Congress the previous week, the journalists had come with high anticipation. Claire Weissman looked around the audience. People were standing at the back. It was the stuff her dreams were made of.

Strickland cleared his throat.

'I was asked to become chairman of the Federal Reserve somewhat over two years ago,' he read from his prepared remarks, 'and I can honestly say this has been the most important and fulfilling two years in my career. No chairman of the Fed deals with exactly the same run of economic events that any other chairman faces and therefore probably the single most important quality in being able to do this job properly is flexibility both in terms of policy goals and use of the instruments the Fed has at its disposal. When I look back over these two years I have to say I think it has been a pretty benign period, which is a credit to the single-minded leadership of my predecessor, Jeff Kohler, who I think was a truly outstanding Fed chairman. If Jeff was still with us I'm pretty sure I wouldn't be the one standing in front of you today.' Strickland paused, and there were a few polite nods in the audience. 'So, let me tell you some of the things that I think are most important in what we've done over the past couple of years.'

He continued reading. The first nine-tenths of the speech was the exact one that he and his staff had prepared prior to the latest events in the markets. Strickland was puzzled at the apparent effect of his report to Congress, which he had expected to be the exact opposite. He knew the White House wanted him to take a firm line with the markets and use his public announcements to give that message. He still didn't know how, but perhaps he had overdone it slightly. Strickland didn't believe there were any exceptional problems in the market that were going to require his intervention any time soon, and he certainly didn't believe there were any fundamental problems with the banking system. He was determined to use this occasion to reassure the markets that the Fed was on the ball and that the banking system in the US was as safe and well regulated as it had ever been. More so, in fact.

Eventually he got to it.

'Now, I don't mean to ignore the gorilla in the room. The outlook for the economy is extremely favorable and we see healthy growth continuing both in the short and medium terms, as I outlined in my testimony to Congress last week. And as far as I can tell, nothing has changed since then, although we have seen some volatility in certain sectors of our markets. But within a growth trajectory such as I have described inevitably we are going to see market volatility of varying degrees and in my opinion that's an absolutely normal part of the market's own self-correcting process and is nothing to cause alarm. When that volatility impacts the financial sector, however, and in particular the banking sector, then understandably people start to become a little more nervous and I guess it's natural for people to cast their minds back to events of ten years ago and ask themselves whether our system is about to go into a similar crisis. And you'll be relieved to know the answer is no.'

Strickland paused, expecting at least a little laughter. There was silence.

'Well, this is when the supervisory role of the Fed and the things I talked about earlier become paramount. And that goes as well for the other authorities that are responsible for regulating banks and financial institutions that don't fall under the Fed's jurisdiction. So naturally we're looking at every institution to assess its compliance and its financial soundness and if there's any doubt over any of them then we have mechanisms in place, as you know, to ensure compliance and to use our policy tools to relieve any pressures, if there are any, and even to take control of the deposit-taking banks through the Federal Deposit Insurance Corporation and protect depositors if that's required. I think that's what people are concerned to know, that no matter what the stock price happens to be on a given day our banks are sound and deposits are safe and there hasn't been a return to the risky practices that led to 2008. When I say that we'll take action if necessary, that's preventive action. It's not action that happens after there's been a crisis, but action to prevent one, so we never get left in a situation again where we're picking up the pieces. That's the reassurance that I can categorically give today and which I think is the reassurance that people are looking for from the Federal Reserve. We have a good, solid, sound banking system that is in no way comparable to the corroded situation that existed in 2008. Ten years ago, our banking system and just about the entire international banking system was a disaster waiting to happen and had been for a couple of years. There is no disaster waiting to happen today. What we have is a system that is strong, solid and tightly overseen and regulated by ourselves and the other responsible bodies.'

Strickland paused again. The silence coming back at him felt stony. He didn't feel he was getting through. Ron Strickland had no idea how wooden and predictable he sounded to those listening to him. As far as he was concerned, what he was saying was so self-evidently true that he wondered how anyone could fail to get it. For a split second he wondered whether he should go off the cuff, but decided to stick to the script. All he had left were his concluding remarks. A minute later he was done.

Clare Weissman asked if he would take questions.

'Sure,' he said. 'I'll take a couple.'

The hand of just about every financial journalist in the room went up. The lead business correspondent of the *Wall Street Journal* was first.

'Mr Chairman, I'm very interested in your comments about the gorilla in the room, as you call it. I'm not quite clear what you've been saying to us. Are you saying the movements that we've seen in the stock prices in the banking sector over the past few days aren't of any concern to you?'

'No, I'm not saying they're of no concern,' said Strickland. 'Clearly we watch this very carefully.'

'Then of how much concern are they?'

'They're not of *concern* ...' Strickland stopped. 'Let me rephrase that. The market makes its own assessment of the value of any given institution. I don't need to tell you that it does that on the basis of a whole range of factors, the strength of the balance sheet, the growth prospects, the quality of the management team. A whole bunch of things. Those assessments change on a continuous basis. Our role is to make sure that the underlying institution, the thing the market is valuing, is sound, that it has the correct capital reserves, that it's compliant in its practices, that it's not getting up to the kind of mischief we saw in 2008, that depositors can be sure their money is being well managed, that shareholders and bondholders know they're dealing with an honest institution. If we're satisfied with that, then the market's valuation is the market's valuation, and that's a matter for the market.'

'So are there any banks where you're not satisfied in those terms?'

'As you know, we have a watch list and we always have some institutions that are under a higher degree of scrutiny. That's absolutely normal. That's part of our role, to make sure that if there's any potential problems we know about them early and we can work with the bank in question – if that's needed, and most often it isn't – to help get them through.'

He took another question.

'Mr Chairman, I'd like to pursue the first question. How many banks are you working with right now in the way you described?'

Strickland shook his head. He looked around the room. The journalists gazed back.

'You know I can't comment on that,' he said.

'Mr Chairman, this has implications. Some of these banks are not going to be able to raise funds if their stocks drop below a certain level. Other banks are not going to lend to them if they think that's going to happen.'

'Well, the Fed is there to relieve those pressures through its liquidity operations and other measures I described earlier.'

'Was the Fed there in 2008?'

'Yes. I would argue that it was. I would argue, and I don't think any fair person would disagree, that without the Fed in 2008 and the release of liquidity and the other support it gave we probably would have seen the complete collapse of our banking system and potentially the international banking system. Now, what happened back then wasn't pretty, but it wasn't as bad as that.'

Strickland paused. He found himself getting a little angry. These journalists were experienced financial commentators. They understood this stuff as well as he did. He didn't know why he was getting these questions.

He cleared his throat and pointed at another.

'Mr Chairman, do you think it's short sellers who are driving the market?'

'I wouldn't know,' he replied curtly. 'That's a question for the folks at the Stock Exchange and the Securities and Exchange Commission.'

'Would it worry you if they were?'

'What would worry me is if people believed we had some kind of a problem when we don't.' He pointed at another journalist. 'Yes?'

'Mr Chairman, you referred to your report to Congress last week and I wonder whether you think in any way that your comments have actually helped to create uncertainty in the market.'

Strickland shook his head. 'How would that have helped to create uncertainty?'

'Well, you talked about certain asset classes that you felt were overvalued and more or less threatened to … clamp down in some way on activity around those. When you say you won't tolerate irrational exuberance or anything approaching it people immediately think we're looking at monetary tightening. I just wonder whether you think that kind of talk may actually have been counterproductive and whether you may regret having said that.'

Strickland felt his irritation rising again. 'Look, first, when you talk about my remarks, let's get them accurate. I did not say that any asset classes were overvalued. I said that price and volume data showed increasing activity in certain classes of equity derivatives and we were watching that and we would intervene as appropriate. That doesn't mean we're going to intervene. It just means we have the weapons.'

'Mr Chairman, you've just said you had price data, surely that's saying they're overvalued.'

'It's not saying they're overvalued. It's not my role to say whether they're overvalued. I'm simply saying that we look at the activity levels.'

He glanced at Weissman, who was standing a few yards to the side. But the president of the National Press Club had no intention of ending the questioning. The coverage of this, she knew, was going to be fantastic.

'I'll take one more,' said Strickland. He pointed.

Bernard Tobin of the *Economic Review* took the microphone. 'Mr Chairman, can you comment on Fidelian Bank?'

'No, Bernard,' he replied impatiently. 'I can't comment on Fidelian Bank. I can't comment on any individual bank and I think you know that.' Strickland hadn't been pointing at Tobin, but at the woman behind him. Tobin had a huge bee under his bonnet about the banking failures in the last financial crisis, having lost a personal investment of some hundreds of thousands in Bear Stearns stock. Everyone knew he was always looking for an excuse to slam the Fed, which he held responsible. 'Bernard, I was actually pointing at–'

'Okay, so here's my question. Let's say I've got a thousand dollars to invest and I'm thinking maybe I should be putting it into Fidelian Bank. And let's say with all the scrutiny you've been talking about you know that Fidelian Bank is *this f*ar away from being bankrupt. Don't you think you ought to tell me before I put my thousand bucks in?'

'Bernard, I said I was pointing at–'

'Is that a question you don't want to answer, Mr Chairman?'

'Of course I'll answer it,' retorted Strickland angrily. 'Let's just get everything very clear. I'm not saying Fidelian Bank is near being bankrupt. In fact, although I don't comment on individual banks, I can tell you that as far as I'm aware Fidelian Bank is nowhere near being bankrupt. And by the way, you couldn't put a thousand dollars in there, because it's not a deposit-taking bank. It's an investment bank with investment bank activities.'

'Then let's say it was another bank.'

'Well, if there was a bank like that – and I'm not saying there is – if I came out and said it was close to bankruptcy, effectively that would make it bankrupt, wouldn't it? You know that perfectly well.'

'And if I put my thousand bucks in, and it goes bankrupt tomorrow, I lose it.'

'No, you don't, because it's FDIC protected.'

'Say I put my thousand bucks into its stock.'

'Well, all I can say is that's your choice. In that case you choose to take a risk. If you don't want to take a risk, deposit your money into a bank. It's FDIC protected. It's a hundred per cent safe.'

'But what I'm saying is–'

'Bernard, I think you've had more than a couple of questions.'

'But I'm just saying–'

'What? What are you saying?'

'I'm just saying you have some knowledge that I don't have, and which may make quite a big difference to a lot of people's lives, taxpayers, and you're a publicly paid figure, so don't you think you should give that knowledge to the people who pay your salary? You know, you've mentioned 2008 quite a lot, and one of the things about 2008 is a lot of people lost a lot of money because no one was telling them until it was way too late what kind of institutions they were investing in. And I'm not talking about rich people here. I'm not talking about the guys who took the bonuses. I'm talking about retirement savings. I'm talking about people who are living in poverty today because of what Mr Greenspan and Mr Bernanke allowed to happen back then. So all I'm saying is, you're standing here in front of the National Press Club. You've got a huge economy of scale here, like you said yourself. You must know there are certain banks in trouble, it's clear the market thinks there are, but we don't know who they are and that uncertainty is bringing the whole market down, the good with the bad. So here's your chance to clear it up. Mr Chairman, tell us straight. Who's in trouble?'

Ron Strickland stared at him. Bernard Tobin made him sick. Tobin wasn't living in poverty and all that stuff about people who were was just so much showboating. The question put him in an impossible position and Tobin knew it. He couldn't have given an answer even if he wanted to. The banks on his watch list were the same ones that had been there two, three months ago. He had no idea why the market had taken fright. For all he knew it might have been a bunch of short sellers placing bets, as the press themselves seemed to think. He still couldn't believe that his report to Congress had anything to do with it. If anything, he thought, the situation would have been worse without it.

The room waited for his response.

Strickland shook his head. 'I can't make a comment on that.'

13

ED ABRAHAMS TOOK the call. He was in the car with the president, who had just come out of a lunch for major Republican donors in Miami with Florida governor Rick Martinez. In forty-five minutes Knowles was due at a town hall meeting in Fort Lauderdale with Senator Jeff Logan, before going on to Gainesville to give a speech that evening at the University of Florida. Both Martinez and Logan were fighting tight midterm races against strong Democratic challengers.

It was Roberta Devlin on the phone. Abrahams listened to what she had to say as the president looked over the Q&As Josh Bentner had prepared for him for the town hall meeting. Then Abrahams put his phone down and logged onto the screen in the back of the limo. He got up the *Economic Review* website and clicked on a headline.

Fed chairman refuses to name failing banks

'Tom, you'd better have a look at this,' said Abrahams.
Knowles looked up from his Q&As.

Federal Reserve Chairman Ronald J Strickland today refused to name failing banks within the American banking system.

In a speech at the National Press Club, Strickland confirmed that a number of banks were under close scrutiny by the Fed, and did not rule out the possibility that takeovers by the Federal Deposit Insurance Commission would be required. Drawing a number of direct parallels with 2008, Strickland remarked that similar action would be taken if required.

Referring to Fidelian Bank, which has recently seen sharp falls in its stock price, Strickland remarked that he was unaware of any immediate threat of bankruptcy. However, in response to a direct request to name the banks in question, Strickland refused, thereby adding to the uncertainty rocking the financial markets.

'What's this?' murmured Knowles.

Abrahams was busy with his tablet getting the latest Dow Jones figures. The index was down two per cent.

Knowles glanced at him. 'Did he really say that stuff?'

'He must have said something.' Abrahams gazed at the screen again. 'I'll get Dean on the line.'

A moment later the voice of Dean Moss, the White House press secretary, was on the speakerphone.

'Looks like we got a mini crisis going here.'

'What the hell did Strickland say?' demanded the president.

'I'm still waiting on the transcript. From what I understand, he's been taken out of context. Some journalist from the *Economic Review* pushed him to name the banks the Fed thinks are weak and he obviously refused and they've taken that and built this so-called story. I think he got into some kind of a shouting match, which didn't help.'

'But this is bullshit?' said Abrahams.

'Absolutely. This journalist has a thing about the Fed. The others are hyping it to see where it'll go. It's election fever. What can you say? Anything for a headline.'

'You still haven't got the transcript?'

'I'm waiting on it, Ed.'

'Well, get it down to us as soon as you've got it.'

'Sure. And in terms of what we're going to say …?'

'We'll get back to you,' said Abrahams, and cut the line.

Knowles looked at him. 'What do you think?'

Abrahams frowned. 'Not sure.'

'Do we ignore it or do we try to nip it in the bud?'

'That's the question.'

Knowles glanced out the window at the view of north Miami rushing by. 'Is this the kind of thing Strickland thinks is helpful? He's supposed to provide reassurance, not start a panic three weeks before the midterms.'

Abrahams was silent.

'What the *hell* has he been saying?'

'I'm sure we'll find he put forward a very sensible position. His problem is he's an academic. The guy doesn't see what people are doing to him until he reads it in the papers the next day.'

Knowles thought about the speech he was giving just about every day now in support of one Republican candidate or another. Trust. Rectitude. Stability. Scrutiny. Prosperity and growth without the fear of a crash.

'Before we overreact,' said Abrahams, 'let's find out whether there's anything going on. Let's talk to Strickland. And the Treasury secretary. I'll set up a call. You go in and do your town hall with Logan. Chances are no one in there will have heard about this.'

'They've got cell phones. The Democrat plants will know all about it.'

Abrahams smiled. 'Then do the presidential thing you do so well.'

'And then?'

'Then,' said Abrahams, 'I'll have figured out whether we should ignore it or not.'

AIR FORCE ONE was on the tarmac at Jacksonville, having flown the president from the Fort Lauderdale meeting. Marine One, the presidential helicopter, waited to take the president the sixty-mile hop to the University of Florida at Gainesville for his next speech. It should have left twenty minutes previously, but the president still hadn't emerged from the plane.

He sat in his office on Air Force One with Ed Abrahams and Josh Bentner. On the line from various places in Washington were Ron Strickland and Treasury Secretary Susan Opitz as well as the president's senior aides.

By now Knowles had seen footage of the key parts of Strickland's remarks, including his exchange with the *Economic Review* journalist. The Fed chairman hadn't said anything wrong in itself, but it had been a hamfisted performance. He could have handled the questions with a lot more grace and sophistication. Instead, he had looked tetchy, impatient and uncomfortable, and in the end had almost blown his top. He had handed anyone who wanted to distort his remarks a choice selection of lines.

The Dow had closed three per cent down. First off, Knowles wanted to be sure there was no genuine crisis underlying what was happening in the markets.

Opitz and Strickland were both confident. Neither of them knew anything to suggest that a crash was coming.

'I think the market's just saying things have been a bit too good for a bit too long,' said Strickland, 'and we've got a modest correction going on.'

'Mr Chairman,' said Abrahams, 'it doesn't feel modest.'

'They never do when they start. There's always the fear of how far they're going to go.'

'And you're saying this isn't going to go far,' said the president.

'There's no reason for it to.'

Knowles glanced at Abrahams, who rolled his eyes. 'Well, Ron,' said the president, 'I think we all need to use language that's a little more respectful of people's fears.'

'There's nothing to fear,' said Strickland. 'Hand on heart, Mr President, I'm telling you that I know of nothing out there that's comparable. Unless someone's hiding something, and hiding it well, we don't have a Bear Stearns, we don't have a Lehman.'

'Can you be sure?'

'I don't see one. And even if there is something, we don't have the level of insane systemic risk exposure that we had in '08. We just don't have it.'

'Well, let's be sensitive in the way we say that,' said Knowles. 'If journalists are going to bait you, Ron, you're going to have to deal with it.'

'Alright,' said Strickland. 'Okay. Fine. I don't mean to cause any problems.'

There was silence for a moment 'Marty,' said the president. 'You there?'

'Yes, sir,' said Marty Perez, his economic advisor.

'You agree with Ron and Susan?'

'Yes, I do. The market's ripe for a minor correction. It's October. This is the month when it always happens. A few people are taking profits. Once they've done that they'll come back in and buy the stocks back. In a few weeks it's going to look a lot less bad than it feels now.'

Knowles glanced at Abrahams. There was only one date that concerned him, November 6. It wasn't possible for this correction, as everyone kept calling it, to have happened at a worse time.

'What about that bank? What's it called, that bank I keep hearing about?'

'Fidelian,' said Abrahams.

'It's getting slammed,' said Strickland. 'There's no doubt about that. You get that in any correction. Rumors go round and a couple of companies get it in the neck. As far as we know, Fidelian's okay. It's not great, but it's okay.'

'Has anyone talked to them?'

'The New York Fed talked to them a couple of days back. The CEO's a guy by the name of Bill Custler. Jerry Rabin knows him. He's a good guy. He'd tell us if there was anything we needed to know.'

'Maybe you should talk to him yourself.'

'I could.'

'What about you, Susan?'

'I'm planning to,' said the Treasury secretary.

'Okay.' Knowles paused. 'We have to get control of this.' He looked at Abrahams. 'I don't care if it's October or whatever the heck it is. We're not having a panic now.'

'I don't think we should ignore this,' said Abrahams. 'Whatever the *Economic Review* would like us to believe, there's no story here. It'll blow itself out, but so close to the midterms we can't take the chance that it blows up first. We need to put this to bed. I think you should use your speech tonight to make a strong statement.'

'Anyone disagree with that?'

There was silence.

'Okay, let's go back to the start. I want to be a hundred per cent clear on this. First of all, Susan, Ron and Marty, you're all saying we don't have a significant concern?'

'That's right, Mr President,' said Opitz. 'We have the normal range of activity and no systemic risk beyond what we would expect to see.'

'Ron, you comfortable with that statement as well?'

'Yes, sir.'

'You got that, Josh?' said Knowles to his speechwriter, who was sitting on the other side of the Air Force One office.

Bentner nodded.

'So I'm going to say my number one priority is the stability and growth of our economy, that all my administration's policies are geared towards that.' He glanced at Bentner, who was taking notes. 'Josh, can we fill that out with some examples?'

Bentner nodded again.

'Then given the recent movements in the markets, I've asked the Treasury secretary and the chairman of the Fed to undertake a thorough review of the financial system and they ...'

'Sir,' said Abrahams, 'I would say you have today had discussions with the Treasury secretary and the chairman of the Fed to discuss in depth the financial system and you're satisfied that they're exercising strong supervision ... no, they have assured you that the system remains in sound health and there's no risk of disruption such as we saw in 2008.'

'You think we get it out there like that? 2008? Ron did that and look what happened.'

'With due respect to the chairman,' said Abrahams, 'it'll be the president who's speaking. I would take 2008 head on. I would show the seriousness and gravity with which you're addressing this.'

Knowles glanced at Bentner. 'You got that?'

Bentner nodded

'Then I would say something about continuing scrutiny so we're ready to take action at the first sign of any need ...' Abrahams paused. 'No, actually, I wouldn't say that. It sounds like you think there is a problem.'

'I think we should recognize that people are concerned about volatility,' said Marty Perez. 'They're concerned about stock prices going down. I think we need some words about that because that's what's really worrying people. Let's address it and not minimize it.'

'So what does the president say?' said Bentner. 'That he recognizes it's happening and he understands the anxiety it causes but the fundamentals are sound?'

'Something like that,' said Perez.

'Look,' said the president, 'basically I want to say there's no underlying problem, but in case there is one, I'm here, and if there is, we'll deal with it right away, but there isn't one.' The president paused.

'Something like that. Josh, figure out how to say it. That's what you do, right?'

Bentner grinned. He got up. 'I'll go get started.'

He left the room.

'Okay,' said Knowles, 'do we need to do anything else about this? Apart from making statements, I mean.'

'I don't know what else we can do,' said Opitz. 'It's the market. If it's correcting, we have to let it correct. It's not our role to try to prop it up in any way.' She paused. 'I guess we could talk about coming down on the short sellers.'

'They banned them in 2008 and there's no evidence it made a difference,' said Perez.

'Can it hurt?' asked the president.

'It's interfering with the market. In principle, that's something we don't want to. Wall Street will go postal.'

'Not everyone on Wall Street,' said Opitz pointedly.

'Might make us look like we're doing something,' said the president.

'Let me talk to Mike O'Brien,' said Opitz. O'Brien was the head of the Securities and Exchange Commission. 'I'll see what he thinks. I don't think we want to ban them, not right now, but maybe I'll drop a hint. Put the shorts on notice.'

'How?'

'There are ways.'

'Okay, Susan, I'll leave that to you. So that's it now? We don't believe there's anything else we need to be doing? Ron?'

'No, sir.'

'I think that's enough,' said Opitz. 'At this stage I don't think it looks political. If you make your statement tonight, Mr President, and–'

'Hold up.' Knowles frowned. What did you just say, Susan? This doesn't look political? How could it be political?'

'There is one thing about Fidelian. You look at its major shareholders, and around a quarter of its stock – twenty-six per cent to be exact – is held by something called the People's Investment Corporation. That's a sovereign investment fund owned by the Chinese state.'

'So you're saying the Chinese state owns a quarter of this bank?'

'Well, the Chinese state owns the PIC, and the PIC owns a quarter of Fidelian, so effectively, yes. It's possible they own more. The PIC is a very non-transparent organization, even for a sovereign wealth fund. It has hundreds of subsidiaries, if not thousands, registered in offshore jurisdictions and there are numerous tiers of ownership before you get back to the PIC as the ultimate owner. So what we can say is that they own at least twenty-six per cent. Also, there's ownership by a Russian sovereign wealth fund and a Qatari one, each of which holds in the region of five to seven per cent.'

'Is this abnormal?' asked Abrahams.

'No. It's a high level of ownership, but not abnormal. We had a massive influx of sovereign wealth fund capital in the aftermath of the financial crisis and it's been going on ever since. I'm not saying this is necessarily significant, but it's a fact we should be aware of that the company leading the rout in the markets right now has a high owner-ship by foreign state funds. If you add up the foreign government interests in Fidelian – that's the Chinese, Russian and Qatari stakes – you're in the region of forty per cent. In reality, the PIC stake alone is so large that this company couldn't do anything against the PIC's approval. You can't go against a twenty-five per cent shareholder.'

'But if they were driving the price down in some way,' said the president, 'that would go against their own interest as an investor.'

'Absolutely. Even if you want to divest stock, you don't just dump it on the market.'

'Mr President,' said Perez, 'we should be clear that sovereign investment funds claim to act purely as investors like any other investor in the market. Every government says it's a hands-off rela-tionship, and that would include China, Russia and Qatar.'

The frown was still on the president's face. There was something deeply unsettling about what Opitz had just told him. 'Susan, we don't have any evidence that one of these funds is doing anything that would influence this, do we?'

'No, sir. As I said, I don't think there's anything to suggest that. I'm just raising the ownership issue so we've got it on the table.'

'They may be using state money, but they're shareholders like anyone else,' said Perez. 'As long as they're acting as true investors without any other agenda, they'll hurt as much as anyone.'

The conditional in Marty Perez's statement rang loud.

'We wouldn't tolerate it if they weren't acting in any way but true investors, would we?'

'Absolutely not,' said Opitz. 'That would be market manipulation.'

There was a knock on the door. The president's personal aide came in to say that the pilot of Marine One had informed him that if they didn't leave within the next couple of minutes they would be behind schedule for the speech. The preliminary cocktail reception with university dignitaries had already been canceled.

Still the president sat. If you didn't take the opportunity to think about a problem when you had the opportunity, he had learned in his time at the White House, chances were you'd never get back to it. He pondered Opitz's remarks further. It was only her judgment that the apparent attack on Fidelian wasn't political. She didn't *know* it.

The obvious political reason for doing it would be to influence the midterms. If a foreign state was doing that through an investment fund that it owned, or even thinking of doing that, it was unacceptable.

'I wonder,' he said eventually, 'whether we need to give someone a message.'

14

BOB LIVINGSTONE USHERED the Chinese ambassador in. Zhu Hongwei was a thin man with a fastidious air and a tendency to turn combative. He was close to President Zhang and was less emollient than previous Chinese ambassadors to the US. Zhang had put him in place and presumably wanted him to exercise that style in Washington, which he was well known for doing.

The two men each had an aide who would act as interpreter if required. In addition, one of the commissioners of the Securities and Exchange Commission, Michelle Morris, was in the room.

Livingstone did the introductions. When they were settled he told the ambassador that the United States had a specific concern it wanted to raise with the Chinese government.

'Indeed,' said Zhu in English. He looked at the secretary of state with a humorless smile.

'That's why I asked Commissioner Morris along. We would like to be sure that the government of the People's Republic understands how the securities markets work in this country.'

'I'm sure my government is aware of this, Mr Secretary,' said the ambassador.

'We'd like to be sure that all agencies of your government are aware of it.'

'Do you have any agencies specifically in mind?'

'Well, I guess we would be talking about the agencies that might be involved in the securities markets in this country. In particular your sovereign investment funds.'

Zhu raised an eyebrow. 'The managers of our investment funds are very experienced people in the financial area, I believe. I would not be surprised if many of them have worked for American corporations at some point in their careers. I myself am not aware of all the regulations governing the securities markets in the United States, but I have no reason to think that they would not be.'

'We're not pointing the finger at any one individual, Ambassador.'

'Is this in relation to the recent turmoil in your markets?'

'Why don't I ask Commissioner Morris to take this further at this point,' said Livingstone. The secretary of state himself didn't know much more about the SEC's concerns. He had received a call from Marty Perez asking him to set up a meeting with the Chinese ambassador so that one of the SEC commissioners could talk to him, and the briefing paper he had received from Perez spoke vaguely about concerns over recent market activity and the behavior of Chinese state investment funds.

'Thank you, Mr Secretary,' said Morris. 'Ambassador, just to make sure we get off on the right foot, we don't use the term turmoil when we talk about our markets. That term suggests that the markets are not orderly and the securities markets in the United States certainly are orderly, sir.'

Zhu smiled slightly. 'Forgive me. Slip of the tongue. I think my language is not as careful as yours, Commissioner.'

'No, your language is excellent, sir. I don't mean to offend.'

'No offence.'

Livingstone laughed. 'You wouldn't want to see us trying this in Mandarin, Ambassador.'

Zhu smiled politely.

'Sir,' said Morris, 'we have at the SEC a division called Trading and Markets. Perhaps you've heard of it?'

Zhu shook his head.

'Amongst the SEC commissioners I have oversight of that division. Its role is to maintain fair, orderly and efficient markets. It takes action where there is good reason to believe that participants in the market are acting in such a way as to subvert the operation of the markets so as to render them unfair, disorderly or inefficient. I'm sure you appreciate the importance of this.'

'Naturally.'

'Now we're aware that some of the companies most heavily affected by recent activity in the securities markets have a high degree of ownership by investment funds owned by your government. Any shareholder who has a significant holding in a company owes a particular duty to ensure that its activities are in keeping with SEC regulations and that its activities in general must not only be above board but be seen to be above board.'

'But surely they are above board,' said Zhu.

'We would like to be sure that's the case,' said Morris.

'But if it is not the case, the market would not be orderly, and you have just told me, Commissioner, that the market is orderly.'

Morris looked back at him coldly. She wasn't amused by his show of schoolboy logic. 'Regulation of our markets is not a laughing matter, sir.'

'Apologies,' said Zhu. 'I do not mean to imply that it is. I agree, Commissioner, this is a serious matter. That is why I am anxious to understand precisely what you are accusing my government of.'

Morris pulled a set of booklets out of her briefcase. 'These documents summarize a number of key areas of SEC guidelines and the regulations relevant to shareholders in the trading of securities. The full regulations are available on our website but I thought it might be a good idea to leave you with copies of the summaries.' The commissioner leaned forward and put them on the table in front of Zhu. 'Mr Ambassador, we take these issues with the utmost seriousness in the United States. We do not tolerate insider trading, the making of a false market, or market manipulation in any shape or form. The penalties we will apply to market participants who indulge in those behaviors are severe. They're outlined in the booklets and they do not stop short of criminal liability.'

Zhu was silent for a moment. 'Again, I must ask, what exactly are you accusing my government of?'

'I'm not making an accusation, Ambassador. I am simply taking the opportunity to …' Morris paused, seeking the right words, 'provide a timely reminder of the obligations of an investor in our securities.'

'And you think my government needs this reminder?'

'It's possible, sir, that some of your investment funds may need this reminder. And since your government is the ultimate owner of these investment funds, its shareholder, if you will, it seems appropriate to speak to the owner.'

'And the accusation is …?'

'Ambassador, there is no accusation. It simply seems a timely moment to make sure everyone knows what their obligations are. I'm sure I don't need to explain why this is a timely moment.'

'I see,' said Zhu. He picked up one of the booklets and glanced through it, his lip curled superciliously. Then he put it down. 'So I am to take it this is a general lesson you have chosen to give me at this timely moment about the obligations of investors in American securities and the excellence of your regulatory system.' The ambassador looked at Livingstone. 'Is that how I understand this, Mr Secretary? Out of the goodness of your heart you and the Commissioner have decided to give me a lesson in your regulatory affairs. Well, it is a very useful lesson.'

'Dr Zhu,' said Livingstone, 'I wouldn't take it like that. I think we're just trying to make sure there are no grounds for misunderstanding or misinterpretation in what's turning out to be quite a challenging time in our markets. I think you can understand why we might think it's a good idea to do that.'

Zhu nodded. He turned to Morris. 'Commissioner, I think you are … how would you say it? On a fishing expedition.'

'Sir, we're not fishing for anything. As I said, I'm not making any accusations.'

'I wonder why not.'

'I would think of this more as cautionary,' said Livingstone.

'Cautionary of what?' Zhu waited a moment, then looked at Morris. 'Thank you for these books.' He gathered them up. 'I'll make sure they're sent to the appropriate people.'

'And they can download them from our website.'

'Of course. From the website.'

'Ambassador,' said Livingstone. 'Please make sure your government understands our concern. We expect your investment funds to act responsibly. Commissioner, am I right in saying we haven't seen them do anything other than that in the past?'

'Yes, Mr Secretary, I think that's fair. But at this particular time–'

'Yes.' Livingstone smiled, cutting across her. 'See, Ambassador Zhu, this is simply a point check, if you will, to make sure responsible behavior continues. That's our message. If you can take that message to your government, we would be grateful.' Livingstone glanced at Morris. 'Is that a fair summary, Commissioner?'

'Yes, sir. But I do want–'

'Then I think we should leave it at that.'

Zhu watched them, waiting to see if Morris was going to say anything else.

She was silent.

'Good,' said Zhu eventually. 'That is very clear.'

AFTER THE AMBASSADOR had gone, Morris looked at Livingstone with a bemused expression. 'Is he always like that?'

Livingstone shrugged ruefully. 'Dr Zhu's a prickly character. Show him a high horse and he's never too slow to get up on it. Hardly seems worthwhile getting you down here for that. I could have done it myself.'

'No, sir. I think it was important the ambassador saw how seriously we're taking this.'

'Are we really saying we think we've got manipulation going on?'

'At this stage, Mr Secretary, we can't prove it. But they own at least a quarter of Fidelian Bank, which has tanked for no apparent reason. You own that much of a company and you can do pretty much anything with its stock price until people realize what you're doing.'

'And then?'

'Then we throw the book at you.'

Bob Livingstone laughed.

'Mr Secretary, if I may, I am a little concerned that the way ... with respect, the way you pitched the message at the end was a little more moderate than perhaps the way it might have been done. I realize it may not be my place to say this, and I realize you know the ambassador and I don't know him at all, and you were trying to get through to him, and he was on a high horse, as you say, but ... I don't know if we were hard enough with him at the end.'

'How so?'

'If they really are doing anything, then at this stage in our political cycle, with the midterms only a couple of weeks away, this isn't just a financial issue, this is interference in our domestic political process.'

'I presume you were about to make that point when I cut you off, Commissioner.'

'Yes, sir. As I said, it may not be my place to say this.'

Livingstone smiled. 'The point had occurred to me, but I thought it would be better not to raise it. I'll tell you why. We don't actually know that this Chinese investment fund is engaged in any kind of manipulation, do we?'

Morris shook her head.

'No. Well, if they're engaged in it, they know perfectly well what they're doing. The Chinese government is very well aware of our electoral cycle, Commissioner, and its implications. They don't need to be told that we would regard any attempt to influence it with the utmost seriousness. Giving them a reminder about our rules is enough. In case they're doing anything, it lets them know we're on to them. Ambassador Zhu and President Zhang will know perfectly well what we're saying.'

'Then why not say it?'

'Because, as you said, we don't know if they *are* doing anything. What if they're not? What if they're not engaged in any kind of manipulation and their fund is simply acting as an honest shareholder?'

'I don't get it, sir,' said Morris. 'What's the concern?'

'How much anxiety about our domestic political process do we want to reveal? Just how vulnerable do we want to show them that we feel?'

'It's a serious issue. I don't know how much more serious it can be.'

'I agree. It doesn't get more serious. But you say they may not actually have done anything.'

'So what's the concern?'

'That we might just have put an idea into their heads.'

15

MARION ELLMAN DIDN'T know that Bob Livingstone was meeting with the Chinese ambassador in Washington. She had her own meeting arranged with a different ambassador from Beijing.

It was her idea to have lunch with Liu. She had met the Chinese ambassador to the UN numerous times, both formally and in informal encounters in the UN corridors, but in the nineteen months since she had taken up her post she had never sat down with him for a private, open-ended discussion. By all accounts he was an affable character and most people who knew him liked him. Prior to the Uganda resolution their dealings had been cordial. Marion thought it was probably a good idea to make sure they were still on that footing.

Besides, there was an issue she wanted to talk to him about.

They had lunch in one of the rooms of the US mission in New York. The aide who organized it had arranged for Tex Mex to be served. According to their information, that was the Chinese ambassador's favorite.

Liu was a short, dapper man. Ellman towered over him as she greeted him.

'I thought we could just talk over some stuff,' she said after they sat down. 'In a personal capacity.'

'Yes,' said Liu. 'That sounds like a good idea.'

Ellman smiled. There was a knock on the door and two serving staff came in. Liu watched as a dish of chilli con carne was set down and chicken fajitas were placed on the table.

'I see your intelligence services have been at work, Ambassador,' he remarked wryly.

Ellman laughed. 'I hope they got it right, otherwise I'm going to feel an awful fool.'

'No, they've done a very good job.'

One of the waiters put a Coke in front of the ambassador.

'A very good job. I appreciate this, Ambassador. My only reservation in coming here was the thought that I would have to eat a Chinese banquet.'

'Call me Marion, please.'

'Yes. And call me Simon.'

'Simon. Good.'

The waiters left.

'Start, please.' Ellman herself took a taco to get things going.

Liu took a fajita. 'I love these,' he said. 'Just like Peking duck.'

Ellman smiled.

'There is no Peking duck in Beijing. Only in the west.'

'Really? There's no chilli con carne in Mexico either. Only in Texas.'

'Strange how we attribute to others the things we wish they had,' said Liu, and took a bite of his fajita.

Ellman nodded. She had heard that Liu could be somewhat of a philosopher when the mood took him.

'Is it okay? My kids love this stuff.'

'And you don't?' Liu looked at her in dismay. 'Please don't tell me I'm forcing you to eat this because of me.'

Ellman laughed. 'No, I like it too. But my kids love it. Their father feeds it to them all the time. I've got two, Ella and Ben. They're nine and four.'

'I have one,' said Liu. 'I would have liked to have another. He is now in the Ministry of Security.'

'Really?'

Liu raised an eyebrow rogueishly. 'I cannot tell you anything of what he does, in case that is why you have asked me here.'

'I'll let you off this time,' said Ellman.

Liu laughed. 'Very good.'

They ate. There was a little more small talk. Liu was proving just as charming as everyone said he was. But he was waiting, Ellman knew, for what this really was about.

'Let's talk about South Africa,' she said.

Liu nodded, taking another bite out of his fajita.

'What are we going to do?'

The Chinese ambassador frowned. He raised his napkin and dabbed at his lips, then put the napkin down again.

In June of that year, South Africa's ANC government had imposed a state of emergency when it became convinced that it was going to lose the upcoming election. Citing unrest in KwaZulu Natal as a pretext, it invoked the clause of the post-apartheid constitution allowing for a state of emergency in event of insurrection and clamped down hard. Now, four months later, the date for the elections had come and gone, police brutality was turning the unrest in KwaZulu Natal into something approaching the insurrection that the government had originally pretended was taking place, and with every passing week it looked as if the ANC seizure of the state was going from temporary to permanent.

In the early days after the announcement of the state of emergency the Security Council had managed to get unanimous agreement on a non-binding resolution 'expressing the hope' that South Africa would 'speedily' resume its normal constitutional path and that free and fair elections would be held on the scheduled date. That had about as much effect as most Security Council resolutions. Continuing to remain silent now would be tantamount to a tacit acceptance of the status quo and a virtual imprimatur from the international community for the transition of South Africa to one-party autocracy. The British government was pushing the case for a new, hard-hitting resolution demanding the immediate restoration of constitutional rule and holding of free, internationally monitored elections within three months, proposed under Chapter VII of the Security Council, which would open the path to sanctions if the ANC refused to agree. The US and France were backing it. Whether such a resolution would pass without a veto from Russia or China was extremely doubtful. Both countries had invoked constitutionally sanctioned states of emergency in various parts of their countries in recent years. And China, of course, was a one-party autocracy, which was what the ANC was in the process of creating. Russia was just about one, hidden behind a thin veil of spasmodic democracy.

The British push for a resolution was intensifying. Sir Antony Seale, their UN ambassador, had been on the phone to Marion three times in the past week, and had twice cornered her after meetings. Ellman was aware that there was domestic pressure in the UK, which had been active in leading the anti-apartheid movement thirty years earlier, to see concrete steps taken. The British labor prime minister was coming under attack from within his own party. He had to be seen to be acting.

Marion wanted action as well. What was happening in South Africa broke her heart. At sixteen years old, a schoolgirl in Philadelphia, she had watched pictures of Mandela walking free and would never forget the emotion of that day. Four years later, in her junior year at Georgetown, she had watched pictures of the queues of people lining up to vote in the first free election in South Africa's history and her heart had filled with emotion once more. Now she didn't know whether she'd ever see such pictures from South Africa again.

And yet the resolution the Brits had drafted had about as much chance of success as had her attempts to build a coalition for Uganda. They had circulated the draft to all the members of the Security Council. Nothing had come back from the Russians or the Chinese. The French ambassador had told her that his government believed they should push ahead anyway, despite the certainty of defeat, if nothing else at least to preserve the moral authority of the Council, or at least of themselves. But the moral authority of a few members of the Security Council, however well preserved, wasn't going to bring democracy back to South Africa.

It put her in despair. The longer the state of emergency went on, Marion knew, the more fixed it would become. Reversal would be increasingly difficult. She could see the dark path ahead unless something could be done to prevent it, years of rhetoric and sporadic pressure from outside the country, violence and suppression within it. It made her wonder what she was doing here at the UN, what any of them were doing here, if they couldn't stop it.

Liu cleared his throat.

'This is a difficult situation in South Africa,' he said. 'China does not feel that it should impose a political system on any other country. You know our principle of non-interference. That has always been our position. We ourselves ask to be left alone, and therefore how can we say that others should not be left alone? I think that is maybe a difference between us.'

'But South Africa already has a system,' said Ellman. 'We're not trying to impose it. What you've got is a group within that country who are subverting it.'

'That's true.'

'All we're saying to them is, respect your system. Put your system back in place.'

'The old revolutionaries would say, systems sometimes must change.' Liu smiled his mischievous smile and took a bite out of his fajita.

Marion smiled as well. That line would get a laugh even in China. Then she was serious again. 'We have to do something. This isn't like … with respect, Simon, this isn't the same as China. By doing something about this we're not saying anything about China.'

Liu frowned. But she could see he was listening as he ate.

'There's no comparison with China. The South African government isn't one that has done a great job for its country and has boosted its living standards and has developed its potential as a power on the world stage. Or even as a regional power. Speaking completely personally, if it was the Singapore of Africa you might say, okay, maybe the one-party thing might work. For a time. But it isn't like that. The ANC is a corrupt party, it's increasingly brutal, and it's taken all the huge potential of South Africa and turned it into a basket case. And that's when it *had*, theoretically, the risk of being kicked out in democratic elections. How much worse is it going to be when it doesn't face that risk?'

'So you're saying there's none of your American ideology behind what you're suggesting.'

Marion shrugged. 'Sure there is. Of course there is. I think personally, and all of America thinks everyone has the right to democracy. But I'm saying, in this case, we can make an argument on pragmatic grounds even without that. And I'm saying if we all stick to the pragmatic argument, if we say, this is not a party that has served South Africa well, this is not a party that should govern unquestioned, then I think we can all come together with a demand that this party should face the people and the people should have a right to find someone to do things better. We can make this a pragmatic argument, Simon, not an ideological one, and by doing that, if we stick strictly to that and stay away from the ideology, we can all work together to restore South Africa to its own constitution.'

Marion took a bite of a taco as she waited for Liu to respond.

'Pragmatics have ideological implications,' he said eventually.

'But it is a pragmatic argument, isn't it? They're a terrible government. South Africa deserves better.'

Liu smiled. 'That's true. They are a terrible government.'

'So let's help put that poor country out of its misery. We stood by for years while Zimbabwe was almost done to death by a one-party dictator. Surely we're not going to do it again.'

Liu was silent for a moment. 'We don't want this either. That's why we supported the first resolution. We don't think this is good for South Africa. We don't think it's good for China.'

'So you would support the kind of resolution Britain is proposing?'

Liu grimaced a little.

'Have you looked at the British text?'

'Marion, the text is ridiculous.'

'Then work with us on an alternative. Join us in a resolution that mandates sanctions. Let's do it ourselves. Forget the British. We could word it so it's not ideological. Simon, I don't think the Council can be silent on this. I don't think the United States can do nothing, or at least not try to do something.'

'China does not think a resolution is the best way.'

'Then what is?'

'Give us some time to work with the government of South Africa.'

'What does that mean?'

'We have influence there.'

Marion watched him. China's penetration of the South African economy was extensive. It had funded widespread mineral exploration through partnerships with South African businesses, many connected with corrupt officials high in the ANC. According to intelligence reports that Marion had seen, the Chinese government was now trying to broker the political crisis in South Africa by persuading the ANC to bring a token opposition presence into a national unity government that in effect would keep the ANC in power. Then there would be some kind of rigged election that would return the ANC and they would be able to say the constitution had been reinstated. The Chinese saw it as their chance to establish themselves as the ANC's protector, which would guarantee them preferred access to the country's mineral resources. Liu's plea for time sounded as if it was designed to allow them to finish the job.

'The British are nothing but an old colonial power,' said Liu. 'What they say carries no weight. In fact, it has the opposite effect. By associating yourselves with the British, you lose credibility in South Africa. Only economic clout carries weight. Give us some time to work with the South Africa government. Talk to the British and tell them to slow down. Put some pressure on them.'

'I don't think that's going to work,' said Marion.

Liu nodded. He smiled for a moment. 'What is happening in Uganda?' he asked.

Marion looked at him carefully. Was he trying to draw a connection between the two issues? What was he suggesting? That China would trade one for the other? Or was he just being polite, changing the subject when it seemed they were at an impasse that threatened the congenial spirit in which they had sat down together?

'It's going fine, to the best of my knowledge.'

'Good.'

There was silence.

'Why don't you join us?' said Marion suddenly.

Liu looked at her uncomprehendingly.

'In Uganda. Why don't you come be part of the operation?'

Liu smiled. 'This is not your government speaking. This, I'm sure, is you speaking personally, Marion.'

'Why don't you? Put some of your guys in with ours. Let's make it a joint mission. Why don't we talk about it? What can be controversial about getting rid of the LRA?'

Liu laughed.

'You think it's a crazy idea?'

'Personally, I think it's wonderful. If you and I could agree it in this room, Marion ...' he clicked his fingers, 'I would do it now.'

'Just think about what the effect would be. Just think what a statement it would make.'

'I think it's too big a statement for your government.'

'I don't know. Sound some people out. Unofficially. I'm serious, Simon. Sound some people out in Beijing.'

'I think also in Beijing we would have opposition.' Liu laughed again. 'I think you should sound some people out in Washington.'

'There'd be opposition there, I grant you.'

'I would like to see what Dr Rose would say.'

'There'd be some support as well. You might be surprised.'

'Not enough. There would not be enough people who would want us to be involved. I think your president is very happy to do it by himself. You had your chance to do it with others. You would not do this now.'

'Then make us.' Ellman paused. She hadn't even thought about this before blurting it out. The idea had just occurred to her. And she had gone way beyond what she should say, even in a personal capacity. But what the hell! She had said it now. May as well take it all the way. 'Make us an offer we can't refuse. In public. It wouldn't be that hard.'

Liu looked at her, then he shook his head, smiling.

Marion sat back. It was depressing when an idea like that couldn't even make it out of the room. She liked it. Instead of allowing Uganda to divide them, why not use it to unite them? She imagined what it would be like to hear President Knowles and President Zhang announcing that Chinese forces would join American troops in Uganda. It would have a huge impact, coming out of the blue. Like Sadat going to Jerusalem. Like Mandela walking free from Robben Island. A game-changer. It had come to her impulsively, almost as a joke, but it seemed to be the smartest thing she had thought of since the day she started at the UN.

But Liu was right. The way things were, it was in no one's interest, not in Washington nor in Beijing.

'How *is* it going in the jungle?' said Liu.

'It's going according to plan.'

'It seems slow.'

'There's a lot of improvement in the humanitarian situation.'

'I look forward to hearing about that when you make your report back to the Security Council.'

'You can bet on it.'

'I thought your president would like to have a big result to help with the elections,' said Liu with a twinkle in his eye.

Ellman shook her head, smiling. 'Nice try.'

'You know we won't be able to stand by if anything happens in Sudan.'

'You know we have no intention of doing anything in Sudan. I told you that weeks ago.'

'Good. Marion, I agree with you, the LRA is an evil thing. Personally, I hope you can get rid of it without any complications between us.'

'The best way to make sure of that is to do it together.'

Liu politely ignored the invitation to reconsider Marion's suggestion.

There was a lull. Marion thought about going back to the subject of South Africa but she didn't think they were going to get any further on that score.

'What do you think of what's happening in your markets?' said Liu. Marion looked at him.

'Your stock market. There's some uncertainty. I'm surprised. I can't see what has happened.'

'I can't either. I guess markets get jittery sometimes.'

'So you don't think we need to worry that the mighty United States markets are going to collapse again.'

Marion smiled. 'I'm not a financial expert, but I don't think so.'

'That would be a problem. Last time we had so much of our reserves tied up in your bonds and stocks.'

'I know.'

'Now we have even more.'

16

THE CHINESE AMBASSADOR in Washington, Zhu Hongwei, had direct access to President Zhang. It was up to him to decide when to use it. Consequently his report of the meeting with Bob Livingstone and the SEC commissioner, which might have spent a week circulating in the foreign ministry and gone no higher than the foreign minister, was on Zhang's desk the morning after it happened.

Zhang Yong was a sixty-four-year-old lifelong party bureaucrat who had been minister for internal security when the Chinese recession of 2014 hit the country. Suddenly China's enormous unresolved tensions – the chronic financial insecurity and alienation of hundreds of millions of urban migrants, the grievances of the countryside – which were previously held in check by economic growth, ignited in flame. Unemployment and bankruptcy fed civil unrest, which spread in some places until it amounted to insurrection and the rule of the party itself was threatened. Tibetans, Uighurs and other repressed minorities, always looking for the opportunity to assert themselves, seized the moment to rise in revolt. As internal security minister, Zhang had cracked down hard, using the internal security forces and bringing in the army ruthlessly to reimpose control. In some central and western areas of the country cities had had to be retaken as if in a war. For a number of months over the summer and fall of 2014 China teetered on the brink of anarchy. The party itself fractured and fought. Out of this turmoil Zhang had risen to power as president while two other men, defense minister Xu Changjiang and head of the army General Fan Keming, emerged in positions of strength with the backing of various parts of the armed forces. Zhang had been unable to dislodge either of them in the years that followed.

In power, Zhang had proved more sophisticated than foreign observers anticipated. Despite his background in the security services, he quickly grasped that it was not military strength that would keep the party in control in the long term, but economic prosperity. He understood that rebuilding the areas that had suffered most in the disturbances could provide a great stimulus to growth, and that recapturing business lost to competitor countries was key to recovery. Parts of China's gigantic manufacturing capacity in the south and east of the country had been shut down by the disturbances, while other parts were functioning as normal. Brutally repressing any hint of dissent, Zhang moved rapidly to bring all of it back into operation, loosening residency laws to entice rural workers to return to the cities, forcing banks to lend for reconstruction, and offering huge state subsidies – illegal under international law – to attract foreign customers that had taken their business elsewhere. The west wanted to believe – needed to believe – that China was back in business, and didn't question its methods. The effect was swifter than anyone could have imagined. Within a year Chinese output was back to where it had been before the disturbances. Two years later it was eight per cent higher.

Every decision Zhang made was calculated to strengthen China's economy. No economist himself, he relied on a group of fiercely loyal technocrats whom he quickly promoted through the finance ministry. The most senior member of this group was the finance minister, Bai Shaochun. Under Zhang's tutelage he was developing political skills and the president was grooming him as his successor.

Zhang was well aware of the fact that US banks were suffering a fall and was receiving daily reports on the impact on Chinese markets, which so far had been small in scale. But he had no knowledge of individual companies listed in New York. He passed the report from the ambassador in Washington to his closest personal advisor on US affairs, an ex-Shanghainese banker called Qin Jiwei who had spent a number of years working in New York. Qin made some inquiries. That afternoon, in his day villa in the Zhongnanhai, Zhang and Qin met with Foreign Minister Yang, Finance Minister Bai, and Hu Liren, a senior vice-minister of finance who was head of the People's Investment Corporation, the fund that held twenty-six per cent of Fidelian stock.

As Bob Livingstone anticipated, the note of the meeting that had been sent by Ambassador Zhu interpreted the encounter as an accusation that China was manipulating stock prices in order to influence the outcome of the US midterm elections. Zhang had ordered no such action to be taken. The first thing he wanted to know was whether someone else had done so.

Hu Liren shook his head. 'We are not doing this, President Zhang.'

'No one has ordered this?'

Again Hu shook his head. 'No, President Zhang.'

'Could you do it?'

'That is an interesting question, President Zhang.'

'We have studied scenarios,' said Bai. 'It is true that with a concentrated activity we could create significant movements in the market. Our holdings are sufficient in volume and diversity. But this would be against our own interests, since it would diminish the value of our holdings.'

Hu nodded, keeping quiet. Bai could have said more. Their scenarios had shown that if they did choose to use their market power to drive a fall, they could benefit enormously by having sold stocks short before engineering the panic. They could benefit a second time by buying additional stocks at the new lower prices, confident that the market would eventually recover. A fund such as the People's Investment Corporation operated with a time frame of decades. Against investors whose time horizons were measured in years, or months, or weeks, or even days, that could give them an enormous advantage. And with a fund of half a trillion dollars at Hu's disposal, the financial gains to be made from exercising this advantage could be staggering.

'These are only scenarios, President Zhang,' said Bai.

Zhang nodded. He looked at Hu. 'So what are you doing with this bank, Vice-Minister?'

'The president is referring to Fidelian Bank,' said Qin.

'We have sold a small amount of our stock recently as the price has fallen. Two per cent of our holding.'

'Why not more?'

'If we sold more we would collapse the price. It is not in our interest to do this. Also, we have two seats on the board and therefore we cannot be seen to be selling. We can only sell through other companies that are not directly connected with the PIC.'

'But you are selling, Vice-Minister. That means you think it is not a good investment.'

'It has problems, President Zhang. We are aware of this because of our seats on the board. We know certain things the market does not know.'

'What things?'

'It needs cash. It must go to the market for money.'

'Then you have made a bad investment, Vice-Minister,' said Zhang pointedly.

Hu bowed his head.

'What will happen when the market finds out about this?'

'That remains to be seen,' said Bai. 'The CEO of the bank wants us to put in the money.'

'Could we?'

'Of course.'

'What did you tell him?'

'Vice-Minister Hu led him to believe we would not do it.'

'So what will happen?'

'The money must come from somewhere else.'

'What if there is no one?'

'The American government will not let that happen,' said Qin.

'Is that what they said?'

'They do not know about it yet. It is an investment bank of a significant size.' Qin had been in New York in '08 and was deeply influenced by what he had seen there. 'They saw the effect ten years ago when they let such a bank collapse and they are scared of seeing that again. A president who allowed such a thing would take a hard blow.'

'To be technical, President Zhang,' said Hu, 'it would not collapse. There is a process for winding up such a bank. This is a new thing that was brought in after the events Minister Qin is describing.'

'But they will not want that either,' said Qin. 'It would be very complicated. If necessary, they will seek other banks to buy this one.'

'But the price will be very low,' said Zhang.

'Not so low if they are scared to wind it up.'

Bai agreed. 'And for us, there are certain other things we can do. If the price of this bank goes down, the price of other banks will go down too. We can recover our investment by using this fact. We can use this fact to increase our investment.'

Hu glanced at him, staying silent.

'All of this is normal investment activity,' continued Bai. 'The Americans can have no argument with this. Their own institutions will do the same.'

'Their own institutions do not have the power in the market that we have,' observed Yang, the foreign minister. 'Isn't that true?'

'That is true,' said Bai.

'Perhaps the Americans are asking for our help.'

Zhang looked at him.

'Perhaps Ambassador Zhu has misinterpreted. Perhaps they are not saying they are blaming us for it, perhaps they are saying, help us stop this decline.'

'Then *that* would be asking us to manipulate the market,' said Bai.

'Yet maybe that is what they are saying.'

'Ambassador Zhu says they are accusing us,' said Bai, who had seen Zhu's note of the Washington conversation.

'That is Zhu,' replied Yang darkly. As foreign minister, he was irritated by the relationship the ambassador had with the president and the frequency with which Zhu went over his head. 'He is like the boy who has stolen a dumpling. Wherever he looks he sees an accusation.'

Zhang looked at the foreign minister coldly.

'He might be wrong,' said Yang.

'Then that is a request to manipulate the market, as Bai says.'

'Maybe it is a request to understand their situation, President Zhang. They are fearful. There are elections in three weeks.'

'It is not my responsibility to make sure President Knowles gets what he wants in these elections,' said Zhang curtly. 'In Uganda, he is trying to show that America is strong. Better for us that at home he is weak.'

'That is true. Therefore he suspects that we are hurting the market.'

Qin laughed. 'Minister Yang, a minute ago you said he is asking us to help!'

Yang shot a glance at him. 'It could be either.'

'Why would I give him any help?' said Zhang. 'What help does he give us? And now he comes with this accusation.'

'If there is a collapse in their market,' said Yang, 'that will be bad for us.'

'There will not be a collapse,' said Bai quickly. He knew that a successful appeal to that fear with the president was certain to win him over.

'How do you know?' demanded Yang.

'There will not be a collapse. The situation is not one of collapse.'

'Maybe if you do the things to recover your investments it will be,' said Yang, who understood better than the president that Bai was talking about letting Hu make big bets on stocks falling, which in itself was likely to drive them down.

'That is ridiculous,' snapped Bai. 'You do not understand finance.'

'You do not understand diplomacy.'

'Enough!' said Zhang.

There was silence around him. Zhang considered what he had heard. He was no democrat himself, but he understood the sensitivity of an American president to events taking place within weeks of an election. And yet if his officials told him that the events were not of their making, what complaint could his counterpart have? And what right did he have to make accusations?

'Should we reply to this message?' he said eventually.

'Ambassador Zhu should go back and say the People's Investment Corporation is acting as an investor seeking value,' said Bai. 'It has always acted as an investor seeking value, nothing else. That is enough.'

'We should say we understand the concern of President Knowles and will act responsibly,' said Yang.

'We act as an investor seeking value,' said Bai. 'That is what it is to act responsibly.'

'Then we do not have an argument, do we?' said Zhang.

Bai and Yang glanced at each other. They certainly did have an argument.

'He should not think we will help him with this bank,' said Zhang. 'When has he helped us? Let him stop the resolution on South Africa.'

'But if there is a threat of a collapse,' said Yang, 'we would help.'

'There is no threat of a collapse,' said Bai.

17

ED GREY HAD one of the screens in his office tuned to CNBC constantly. It was around eleven o'clock when he noticed Jim Rosario doing a piece. On the bottom of the screen a headline said *Threat to Short Sellers*.

Ed turned the volume up. Rosario was saying that he had heard a rumor that the SEC would be prepared to consider a temporary ban on short selling if it felt that the market was being disproportionately driven down by short activity. He couldn't report on the truth of it but he had reason to believe it emanated from reliable sources within the administration, demonstrating the government's determination to keep US markets safe and orderly.

Everyone knew that Jim Rosario was close to Treasury. When he started talking about reliable sources in the administration, that was the department that he meant. In fact, it probably meant that Treasury had asked him to say it.

Ban short selling? At first it made Ed laugh. Then it made him angry. It made him want to go out and short a bunch more stocks just to show Treasury what he thought of it.

And that, when he considered it, was the thing that made him worry.

Grey knew that if his reaction to the statement was to show what a dumbass idea it was, that would probably be the reaction of just about every other DIV on the street. And if Rosario really was reporting something a Treasury official had told him, Ed Grey doubted that was the reaction the official was hoping to achieve. Somehow he was pretty sure Treasury didn't want every DIV in the city going out and shorting a bunch of stocks just to thumb their nose at them. Not to mention all the DIVs who were thinking, just in case the rumor was true, they should go and out and short a bunch more stocks while they still had the time. Discounting the possibility that that was what Treasury was hoping for – and the chance of that, Ed figured, was about as high as the chance that every DIV in the city would cease and desist right away – this statement was an error. A very, very bad miscalculation.

In fact, it could get a lot worse. If people really thought Treasury was serious about this, they'd jump to one conclusion: Treasury must know about something coming down the line that was a lot worse than anything the market knew. It must be getting ready for that thing to hit them. When the administration gave that impression, anything could happen.

That really worried Ed Grey. It could have pleased him. If this dumbass threat or a fear of something Treasury knew drove the banking sector even further down, he'd have a load more profit. He had north of half a billion exposure through shorted bank stocks now, and if he bought those stocks and closed out the positions he'd be over a hundred fifty million up. But Red River also had a bunch of positions in other sectors of the market, positions that pre-existed the correction in banking stocks, and they were betting on stock prices going up. Already, the fall in the banking sector was beginning to contaminate other stocks. The contagion was seeping out. From stocks it might seep into commodities. Correlations rippled across asset classes. Ed Grey didn't want to see a collapsing market. He didn't want a rout. He wanted the banking sector to go down, bottom, and go back up once Fidelian had announced its cash call and everyone heaved a sigh of relief. If the rest of the market dropped like the banks had dropped, Red River wouldn't be a hundred fifty million up. It would be up to its knees in blood.

Grey wanted this to be contained. The president's statement a few days previously in Florida had been perfect, it had had the right tone, the right pitch. But this rumor – if it did come from Treasury – made it seem as if the administration feared losing control. It had the whiff of panic.

Tony Evangelou put his head around the door. 'You seen what Rosario just said?'

Grey nodded.

'What the fuck are they doing?'

'I have no idea.'

'I just shorted another twenty million of Fidelian.'

All over the city, Grey figured, exactly the same thing was happening.

'Tony, come in and take a seat for a second. You think we should go short some other stuff?'

'I'm tempted,' said Evangelou, grabbing a chair. 'Treasury keeps saying stuff like this, we're going to make more money than we did in 2015.'

'Yeah, but we're long. Overall we're long the market.'

'But this is bullshit, Ed. If we've got a three to six month horizon, I'm comfortable. Let's make some hay but it won't last. We started it, remember? How much could Fidelian need to raise? Five billion? Ten? It's just one bank. There's nothing in this. A little overvaluation, but the market's already gone past that. It has to come back. The fundamentals are fine.'

'Maybe they're not.'

'You heard something?'

'No, but maybe they're not. Maybe Treasury knows something.'

'Yeah. I think they're bluffing. I think they just want to pull us back ahead of the midterms.' Evangelou laughed. 'Hell of a way to try to do it.'

Grey frowned. 'Maybe we didn't start this. Maybe we just thought we did. Maybe we opened something up and now it's going to run. And if it runs … If it runs, if it's a general collapse, that's a whole different story.'

Tony watched him.

'Construction, retail, mining. All the cyclicals, they're going to go.'

'They'll come back. We'll wait it out.'

Grey shook his head. Red River was heavily leveraged, more heavily than at any time in the fund's six-year history. The more successful the fund had been, the more debt he had taken on. If the markets fell, he wouldn't be able to sit it out. The banks would be after him with margin calls on their loans. That would mean he would have to sell assets to raise the cash. He would be selling those assets into a falling market. Everyone else would be in the same position, all trying to sell assets to raise cash for their banks, all driving prices even further down.

'Get the guys to do a stress test, Tony. I mean a real worst case. Let's assume we have a twenty per cent fall in equities across the board for a start.'

'We should do forty if you want to make it a real worst case.'

Grey nodded. 'Get one of the quants to run the correlations. Maybe we should take out an option to hedge the Dow.'

'Too late. We'll be paying way too much.'

'You think?'

Evangelou nodded.

'What if we short another billion?'

'Across a bunch of sectors?'

'If we can get the stock.'

'Let me get some work done on this.'

Grey nodded. 'I'm going to make some calls.'

Over the next couple of hours, Ed Grey spoke to a half dozen other Divvies. The general reaction was exactly the one that he had expected. If Treasury was going to start making threats – whether they knew something or were just talking tough – the market would show what it could really do when it set to work.

As he talked, screens on Grey's wall showed the result. He watched the markets moving down all morning. Margin calls would be coming in all over the Street, he knew. People would be selling because of that. Prices would fall further.

There was money to be made out there. There always was. But Grey had a lot of bets stacked on the market going the other way. He did some rough calculations on a notepad while he waited for Tony's scenarios. He didn't need too much detail to figure out which way they pointed.

He gazed at the figures on the notepad. Then he picked up the phone to his assistant.

'Zoe, can you get me through to the US Treasury, please?'

'In Washington, Mr Grey?'

'That's right. See if you can get me through to the office of the Treasury secretary. Her name's Susan Opitz. Ask her assistant to let her know that Ed Grey would like to speak with her.'

*

SHE RANG HIM back that evening. Grey had known Susan Opitz for twenty-plus years. They had been associates together at the New York office of McKinsey, the management consulting firm, when they were fresh out of business school. Grey had stayed there only a couple of years before moving into funds, and Opitz had stayed barely any longer before moving into the utilities industry, where her stellar career had taken her to the CEO post at GrandWest Pacific before joining Tom Knowles' cabinet. In those couple of years they had spent ten months together on the same assignment. Ten months of eighteen-hour days creates a bond you don't readily forget.

'Ed,' said Opitz, 'I should tell you right away I've got a note-taker on the line. I don't mean to imply anything but I think it's appropriate in the circumstances.'

'Sure, Susan,' said Grey. 'I understand. Hello note-taker.'

There was no response.

'What can I do for you, Ed?'

'Susan, I appreciate you calling me back.'

'Yeah. How're you doing, anyway?'

'Good. You?'

'Good. Listen, I haven't got a lot of time. I'm sorry about that.'

'No problem. You know, Jim Rosario, on CNBC today, said something about a rumor that you guys might ban short selling.'

'Yeah, I heard about that.' Opitz didn't say anything else. Rosario had been briefed by her own communications director.

'Stop me if I'm saying something I shouldn't, Susan, but if that came from one of your officials, I'm not sure what effect he thought he was going to have, but if he thought he was going to be helpful, well, we had about all the help we can take. I assume you know what happened on the markets today.'

Opitz knew. 'Ed,' she said, glancing at the aide who was taking notes, 'I'm going to have to be careful here. You'll clearly have an interest in which way the markets go and I'm going to assume you're not trying to influence me in any way.'

'Susan, I can make money whether the markets go up or down. That's not what this is about.'

In her office, Opitz raised an eyebrow. She had liked Ed Grey in the time they worked together. He was one of those big, energetic guys who treated the world like a playground created for his personal amusement. He could be a lot of fun. But she had had glimpses of another side of him, a raw, egocentric brutality when it came to looking after number one. He was attractive but dangerous, the kind of guy you could enjoy working with but wouldn't want to get too close to. And now he ran a DIV, one of the biggest in the market. She didn't trust a word he said.

'What worries me,' said Grey, 'I think what worries all of us, is if it looks like you guys don't know what you're doing. Now, I'm assuming this was some relatively junior guy who got it into his head to float some kind of balloon with Rosario under the misguided impression that was going to calm the markets. Am I right?'

Opitz didn't reply. She avoided her aide's gaze.

'Well, I don't expect you to tell me. There's only one justification for letting out a threat like that, and that's if you know something really bad.' Ed paused, listening. His primary reason for making the call was to get the message across that a veiled threat to ban shorts – or anything like it, in case Treasury had plans for anything else as stupid – would achieve the exact opposite effect they wanted. But if Treasury did know something he didn't, and he could find out about it, it certainly wouldn't hurt.

'Ed, I couldn't possibly tell you what we know and don't know.'

'Sure. Well, if this did come from your department, and if whoever said it was trying to put a leash on the shorts, he's had the opposite effect.'

'Why do you think that is?' asked Opitz carefully.

'Susan, it's the market. It's the psychology. If you're going to come out hard against us, you've got to do it right away. Threats don't work. It looks weak. You show weakness and we're going to rip your throat out just for the hell of it.'

'Is that what's happened?'

'Partly. You guys have shown fear. Loss of control. Then like I said, some other people are going to be thinking, if this is actually serious, what do they know that we don't? Better get in quick. I think that's driven a wave of short selling through the market today that wouldn't have been there if no one had said anything. Obviously I have no figures, so it's just my assessment from looking at the way the market's gone and from our own trading interactions. You know, I think if you guys want to put a floor under this you just sit back and let the market do what it does.'

Opitz frowned. No one in her department had suggested the market would react like that. They had all managed to persuade themselves that the markets would see it as an indication of their resolve. Maybe there were other reasons for what had happened today. One thing she knew for certain was that Ed Grey wouldn't be saying this if it didn't serve his own financial interests.

'Ed, I can't talk about any interventions we may or may not be thinking about.'

'I know that, Susan. And I guess it must be politically difficult for the president to let this ride with the midterms coming up. I thought his statement was good, but this thing has undone that and then some. Look, my take is that what's been happening here for the past couple of weeks is just the market doing what it does. It's no big deal. It's just some people who have obviously decided there's a little froth in there right now and so maybe it's time to take that away.'

'So you don't think there's anything fundamentally wrong underlying it?'

'I'm not sure,' said Grey. 'What do you think?'

Ed listened for Opitz's answer, still hoping to find out if the Treasury knew something he didn't.

Opitz glanced at her aide, thinking.

Suddenly she turned back to the speakerphone. 'Have you been shorting Fidelian?'

Grey laughed. 'Wow. That's direct.'

'Ed, have you? Who's lending the stock? Ed, who's lending Fidelian stock out there?'

'Even if I had been shorting Fidelian, what difference does it make?'

'I'd like to know where the stock's coming from.'

'Does it matter?'

'Yes. It does.'

Grey was silent. This was interesting. Why did it matter where the stock came from? Normally, all that mattered was how much stock was being shorted, not who was lending it.

'Ed. I want to ask you something. It's not about what you've been doing, okay? It's just about what you've seen.'

'About Fidelian?'

'In general. Is anything odd going on?'

'Odd? Susan, I don't think I get you.'

Opitz hesitated. She had a meeting scheduled with the CEO of Fidelian and the president of the New York Fed for the following day and she hoped to find out what, if anything, was going on inside that bank. Right now, she had to be exceptionally careful in what she said. She couldn't take the risk that Ed Grey would put some kind of rumor into circulation that would send another wave of selling through the market. Nor could she say anything that could later be interpreted as having given him an unfair advantage through insight into the thinking or concerns of the administration. It was safer, she thought, to say nothing.

And yet Grey was in the market in a way that none of her officials or the officials at the Fed or SEC was. He would be hearing things that would never come anywhere near their ears.

'Susan, do you want to tell me what you mean?'

'Ed, is this just a bunch of Divvies trying to make a buck?'

Grey laughed. 'You tell me.'

'Do you think so?'

'Susan, come on, it's never just the Divvies. That's a myth. The market doesn't move like this unless everyone's in.'

'When you say everyone …?'

'The banks, the funds. Mom and Pop.'

'Okay. Ed, what I'm really asking …' Opitz paused again. She glanced at her aide, who was frowning. 'You know, let's say you're borrowing shares to short the market. Who's lending?'

'I don't know. Who always lends?'

'You haven't noticed any …' Opitz was stumped. She wanted to say it. She wanted to come right out and say it: are you aware of any politically motivated sellers? Are you aware of any action taken by sovereign investment funds, and in particular the PIC? But she couldn't be that explicit. Do that, and if Grey wanted to, if it served his interests, he'd let fly rumors about who the Treasury thought was driving this and they would be ripping through the markets by the time they opened again tomorrow morning.

Grey listened to the silence. Opitz obviously had something in mind. He wondered what it was. He wondered how it would affect the way the market was moving.

'So you haven't noticed anything strange?' said Opitz eventually.

'Can you be more specific?' said Grey.

'No, it's just a general question.'

Grey waited, hoping Opitz would say more.

There was silence.

Eventually Grey spoke. 'No, Susan. I haven't noticed anything strange. I called because I wanted to tell you what I thought about Rosario's report. I thought you should know what it looked like from out here.'

'I appreciate it.'

'Susan, my sense is everyone's nervous. Everyone's wondering whether we're seeing something big here. Now, you and I will have our own opinions about that. But anything anyone says in the administration – you, the Fed, anyone – it has to be incredibly careful.'

'We're always careful.'

'I know that. But I mean really careful. I'm in this market. I'm telling you, Susan, it feels like it's tinder out there. Someone else says the wrong thing – it's going to go up.'

'What would help stop that?'

Grey thought quickly. He was ready to close out his Fidelian position and take his profit. The way the market was moving was making him nervous. There was way too much uncertainty now. He wanted something to reduce that – and there was one thing that might do it.

'Get Fidelian to preannounce their last quarter's earning,' he said. 'That's what everyone would like to see. They're not due to announce until next month. Get them to bring it forward.'

18

SUSAN OPITZ HAD met Bill Custler previously but she didn't really know him. As an ex-executive from the utilities industry, she didn't know the Wall Street coterie like Jerry Rabin, the president of the New York Fed, who had spent all of his adult life either working with them or regulating them.

She glanced at her watch. 'Let's get to the point, Mr Custler. What's the situation?'

They were sitting in Rabin's office. Rabin was a tall, dark-headed man with slouching shoulders who always looked to be weighed down by the thankless task of regulating Wall Street. Opposite them sat Custler, a slim man of medium height with thinning grey hair and blue eyes.

'You've got our filings,' said Custler. 'We're compliant. Our capital ratio's adequate.'

'Just.'

'Just is enough, ma'am.'

'Let's be frank. There's a rumor you'll be coming to the market for cash.'

'I can't confirm rumors.'

'I think you'd better start. Or else you'd better be able to deny them.'

There was silence. Custler glanced around uncomfortably.

'We've been reviewing our loan book,' he said eventually.

Opitz leaned forward. 'Mr Custler, what's in it?'

'As I said, we're reviewing it.'

Opitz glanced at Rabin, then looked back at the Fidelian CEO. 'Mr Custler, I think you're probably in a situation where you want to level with us here.'

'Bill,' said Rabin, 'you really do need to tell us what's going on.'

Custler hesitated.

'Mr Custler, you need to understand some realities. We're ten days away from an election and the president needs to get this dealt with. It's time to talk. You're sitting in the last chance saloon.'

'I'm way past the last chance saloon,' said Custler.

Opitz looked at him sharply. 'What does that mean?'

Custler took a deep breath. 'There are some loans in the portfolio … A big chunk of loans. We've got some developing markets business that was a little bullish when it was written. As you know, this bank grew very, very quickly out of the financial crisis. The management back then had a philosophy to go very aggressive to get market share, especially to build its Asian business. Part of the reason I was brought in was because that was getting a little too much. That's left a legacy. Some of the decisions back then weren't great.'

'How not great?'

'Not great.'

'You're going to write stuff down?'

Custler nodded.

'A lot?' said Rabin. 'Don't you think that's something you should have shared with us? I talked to you, Bill. For God's sake, I talked to you two weeks ago.'

Custler looked at him apologetically. 'Jerry, I'm guided by our chief compliance officer.'

'Sounds like someone needs to have a word with your chief compliance officer,' said Opitz.

'When's this writedown going to happen?' asked Rabin

'We don't file our quarterly results for another month. I've been trying to set up a bond issue.'

'Who with?'

'Morgan Stanley's the lead. The plan was to announce the issue at the quarterly at the same time as we announce the writedown.'

'And?'

'That was before our stock price headed south. The shorts are killing us. They're just killing us. Now Morgan's telling us they can't underwrite us at these prices.'

'Bill, how much capital are you hoping to raise?'

'Twenty-three billion.'

Opitz and Rabin stared at him.

'Bill …' said Rabin.

'Twenty-three billion, Jerry. That's what it is.'

Susan Opitz sat back and took a deep breath. Rabin shook his head as if testing whether he was really awake.

'Bill,' he said, 'you want to get all of this through a bond issue?'

Custler nodded.

'What about a rights issue?'

'Our shareholders … I mean our major shareholders are not supportive of that idea.'

'What about for a part of it?'

Custler shook his head.

'Will they take up a portion of the bond issue?'

'At this stage, I don't believe they will.'

'Mr Custler,' said Opitz. 'I'm afraid I have to agree with Morgans. I can't see you having a hope in hell of going to the market for twenty-three billion dollars with your share price down forty per cent in the last month and when your own major shareholders aren't prepared to provide some kind of support as a portion of that requirement.'

'Madam Secretary, I'm not disputing it. I can tell you I've had a few sleepless nights.'

'Bill,' said Rabin, 'how bad is this? How much of this twenty-three billion do you absolutely have to have? What's the minimum?'

'That is the minimum, Ron. That just keeps us adequate.'

'Jesus Christ,' murmured Rabin.

Bill Custler took a deep breath, as if relieved to have it off his chest.

'And this is all from a bunch of developing market loans?' said Rabin.

'And some other stuff. There were a lot of bad decisions.'

'Like what?' demanded Opitz.

'A whole series of things.'

'Really? Like things that have miraculously reappeared on the balance sheet?'

'Not like that. Not to my knowledge.'

'Not to your knowledge?'

'Look, Madam Secretary, I wasn't CEO when those decisions were made. This goes back five, six years. I didn't find out about the true state of this part of the business until long after I took over, and I've tried to deal with it in a way that doesn't destabilize the bank. And I could do it. We can trade through this if we can raise the capital, and until the damn shorts came along we were going to be able to raise the capital and it was all going to be okay.'

'Twenty-three billion?'

'Morgans said they thought they could do it. But now we've got the shorts on us and these rumors are going around and I don't know where they're coming from–'

'Does it matter?' demanded Rabin. 'Bill, none of the rumors are as bad as the truth.'

'Well, we were going to raise it, Jerry. It was going to be okay. Frankly, I don't know where the drop in the share price came from because as far as I know there weren't any rumors on the street until it started happening.'

'Well, someone knew something.'

'That's right. It's either from us or Morgans. I haven't heard any realistic numbers mentioned so I don't know how much anyone really knows but … yeah, someone knows something and they've been shorting us like hell.'

'And you're going to announce all this at your quarterlies?' said Rabin.

'I was going to. Now I don't think we can hold out that long.'

'I was going to say …'

'We're running out of cash. The rumor mill is killing us. Money's flowing out the door. I got margin calls and I've got guys on the repo desk telling me they can't roll our paper. You want to know what a nightmare is, you should come sit in on our credit meeting this afternoon.'

'Bill, when you say you're running out of cash, what are we talking about? Weeks?'

'Days.'

'Days?' demanded Opitz. 'You've got days left and you're not talking to us.'

'Yesterday I thought I had weeks.'

'How many days?' said Rabin.

'Three. Four maybe, depending on how it plays out.'

Opitz and Rabin stared at the CEO. His face was creased in misery.

'I'm going to have to make a statement. I can't keep holding out.

Every damn analyst out there is demanding that I preannounce our earnings.'

'A statement?' said Rabin. 'Bill, what the fuck are you gonna say?'

There was silence.

Going into this meeting, Susan Opitz had hoped that whatever was going on at Fidelian, it could at least be held back and the bank kept stable until after the election, which was ten days away. But this wasn't going to keep that long. Even if he could withstand the pressure from the analysts to say something, if Custler believed he wasn't going to be able to raise the money, he had a fiduciary duty to inform the market. This wasn't going to keep until the election. It was barely going to keep until tomorrow.

'I can't believe you haven't come to me earlier,' said Rabin.

'What can I say?' said Custler. 'Only yesterday, the day before, it didn't look that bad. The shorts have been hammering us, absolutely hammering us.' He looked up hopefully. 'Why don't you ban them like you said you would?'

'That's not going to save you, Bill.'

'No.' Custler shook his head a number of times, eyes gazing blankly at the floor.

'If you make that statement, Mr Custler, that's the end. No one's going to deal with you.'

Custler looked at Opitz helplessly. She wasn't telling him anything he didn't know already.

'Mr Custler, you need someone to put in a big slug of cash or you need to sell this bank to someone who'll take on the liability. Have you considered that?'

Custler gazed at her.

'Bill,' said Rabin, 'have you been talking to anyone?'

'I'm not authorized to do it.'

Rabin looked at him doubtfully. Wall Street CEOs didn't necessarily like each other, but they knew each other. They all knew which firms they would consider partnering with if they ever got into trouble and which deals would be a non-starter. They also knew which major investment funds might be looking for an opportunity at any given time. If things were as bad with Fidelian as Custler said, Rabin would have been extremely surprised if he hadn't been talking to a number of parties.

'What do you mean you're not authorized?' he said.

'It means I'm not authorized. My board has told me not to.'

'Your board has *what*?' said Opitz.

'Bill, do they know the situation?' said Rabin. 'Up to date? What you've just told us?'

Custler nodded.

'Well, I don't know about your board, Mr Custler, but you need a buyer. Before you make a statement to the market you need to have a buyer for this bank.'

'I agree with the secretary,' said Rabin. He didn't much care about the political timing, but he cared about the chaos that would ensue if an investment bank of Fidelian's stature announced, effectively, that it was bankrupt without any rescue plan in place. 'We need to have a buyer. Bill, I hate to say this, because I know you've got your job at stake as well, but if your shareholders really aren't going to put the cash in we're going to need to find a buyer who'll take it on, whether they like it or not.'

'Mr Custler, your shareholders are going to have to make a decision. Either they put the money up or they get the hell out of the way and let someone else do it for them.'

Custler didn't speak.

'Someone saves this bank,' said Opitz. 'Someone saves it in the next week. So it's either your guys or someone else. This bank does not go down. You do not make that statement until we have a buyer.'

'Bill, we'll let you hold off on the statement until we've got someone. Until then, we'll keep you alive if we have to. We can't let you fail. There'll be way too much effect on other banks to let that happen. That mistake was made once already, and once was enough.'

'We're not going there again,' said Opitz. 'This administration is not even *thinking* of going there. And not now. No way. We need to get this fixed right now. Mr Custler, you need to get that very clear. You need to sell this bank.'

Custler smiled ruefully.

'What?'

'Secretary Opitz. I don't think you understand. You're talking to me as if I own this bank. I only run it.'

19

THE PRESIDENT HAD just come out of a meeting with the Syrian prime minister and was supposed to be debriefing with Bob Livingstone and his chief Middle East negotiator. Instead, he found himself listening incredulously to what Susan Opitz was telling him on the phone from New York.

'I don't even think I want to save these bastards,' he said.

'Mr President, we have no choice. You let a bank like Fidelian go, and the losses ripple all the way through the system. It's going to be bad.'

'How bad?'

'It's not 2008, but the whole sector will take a hit. Lending between banks is going to slow if not stop completely. The banks won't know who they can trust so they won't trust anyone. The actual value here isn't enormous, Mr President, it's the effect on confidence. We've said for the past two years, ever since we took office, that the sector is back on track. We've made a big play of keeping a tight grip on it, and if something like Fidelian falls over at the first wobble then in terms of confidence we're back to square one.'

'I think what the secretary is trying to say,' said Abrahams, 'and if you'll excuse the French, sir, is we'll be screwed.'

The president glanced briefly at Abrahams and shook his head in disbelief. Roberta Devlin had made sure that Marty Perez was in the room as well. Ron Strickland, who had already been briefed by Opitz and Rabin, was on a line from the Fed.

'There are two immediate steps we need to take,' said Strickland. 'First, we need to make sure this bank can survive until the situation's resolved. We're putting together a short-term special liquidity facility they can access at commercial rates. They deposit assets in exchange and we're first cab off the rank if they go bust so the taxpayer's protected. Other banks will be able to access the facility on the same terms if we deem it necessary. Now, the second step, Mr President, is resolving the situation. The liquidity facility keeps Fidelian going in the short term, but once they announce their writedowns, they're finished. So we need a buyer. In order to get a–'

'Mr Chairman,' interrupted Abrahams, 'when you say the short term, how long are we talking about here? Days? Weeks?'

'Days,' said Jerry Rabin.

'What makes that the time scale?'

'There are too many rumors now. No one's prepared to lend them any money, and anyone who's got money in there is trying to get it out. They're literally bleeding to death. They need to make a statement and any statement they make is only going to confirm what the market has already guessed. If they don't make a statement – it's just as bad. In this situation, silence is guilt.'

'And to be absolutely clear,' said Abrahams, 'they'll be at this point, where they're forced to make this statement, within days?'

'They're there now. They can hold off a little longer as long as we're giving them liquidity. Without that, they're dead.'

There was silence.

'By announcing the liquidity facility we also help stem the panic in the market,' said Rabin. 'Everyone knows the Fed's there if they need us. We don't have to say who's using it.'

'And Jerry,' said the president, 'let me understand this. You're saying we can get a deal done for someone to buy this bank in a time frame of days. Is that right?'

'If we get right on it. It's going to take a hell of a lot of work from us and possibly some pressure from you.'

'Can't we wind them up?' Knowles glanced at Marty Perez as he was speaking. 'Wasn't that part of the package Obama brought in about winding up bankrupt investment banks in an orderly manner?'

'This'll be the first time,' said Rabin.

'Well, there's a first time for everything.'

'It won't appease the market. This isn't like a retail bank that goes bust where the FDIC takes it over and it keeps running. These guys shift billions in short-term finance each day and they're a counterparty in trades to just about every other bank on the Street. No matter how you do it, the so-called orderly wind-up is going to be damn messy. In the meantime, every other investment bank is going to be looking around to figure out who'll be hurt most by Fidelian's failure until the wind-up's complete. Then they don't lend to *them*. Then they're under pressure, and so on. It's a bunch of dominoes. The only way to stop Fidelian falling against the next one is either to get the cash from its shareholders or sell it so everyone's happy they're covered.'

'And we don't think we're going to get the cash from the share-holders?'

'Doesn't look like it,' said Rabin. 'And there's no way they'll get it from the market, so we have to sell it to someone who'll put that money in.'

The president calculated. The midterms were on Tuesday week, November 6. That gave him twelve days. 'Realistically, at the quickest, how long does it take to do a deal?'

'It's been done overnight, Mr President, if you've got the buyer. That's what you need. You don't have a sale if you don't have a buyer.'

'Do we?'

'Not yet. We haven't started asking. The Fidelian board has told the CEO, Bill Custler, not to go looking for one yet, but he's going back to talk to them. In the meantime, we're going to start looking anyway. Apparently Goldman was interested in Fidelian's fixed income business a while back. At one point Barclays was looking at their brokerage. Ideally I'd like to be able to sell this thing as one piece but it may be we have to break it up. We're just going to have to figure it out as quick as we can.'

'What if no one wants it?'

'I'm hoping they'll see it's in their own interest to make a sale happen. You only have to mention Lehman.'

'And is there no possibility that their shareholders might agree to bail them out?' asked Abramans.

'I wouldn't bank on it, but when they're actually faced with the prospect of having to sell, they might find the money. As I said, Custler's going back to talk to them.'

'And don't forget,' said Marty Perez, 'those same shareholders will have got the message Bob Livingstone gave them.'

The president nodded. He didn't know how much good that had done. All that had come back from the Chinese government was a combative statement about the PIC only ever having acted as a value-driven investor.

He looked around. 'Okay. And we're going to try to keep this quiet. Is that right?'

'At least until we have a buyer,' said Opitz.

'The worse things seem to be,' said Rabin, 'the more the value drops to a buyer. We've got a much better chance of selling this bank if it's still doing some business.'

'Well, that's fine. We're going to have a buyer tomorrow, right? Overnight, isn't that what you said?'

'I don't think it'll be quite overnight, Mr President.'

'I don't need to remind you about what's happening in twelve days,' said Knowles.

'No, sir.'

'Okay, thank you. Keep me informed.'

He cut the line.

'Stay here,' he said to the others in the Oval Office. He put his head out the door and asked his personal secretary to get Gary Rose.

ED ABRAHAMS GAVE Rose a summary. The president stretched back with his hands behind his head. 'What do you think?' he said.

The national security advisor considered for a moment. 'There are a number of ways to interpret it.'

'Give me the best.'

'The best? It's a market event. Simple as that. We've got a bank with a bunch of bad loans, the market sniffs a bad smell, that infects the rest and … we have what we have.'

'Give me the worst.'

'I'm not a finance expert, but I'd say … the Chinese are killing this bank on purpose.'

The president looked at Perez. 'Is that possible?'

'Sure. Technically, yes, it's possible. If you refuse to do what's necessary to stop a bankruptcy or to sell the company then obviously you're killing it. Would they be doing it? What's the rationale?' Perez shrugged. 'An entity like the PIC has enormous numbers of investments. Theoretically, they could have a whole bunch of bets placed on the market going down and they're using this one company to help make it happen. They sacrifice the value at stake in Fidelian for the money they make out of everything else. Is that possible? Yes, absolutely, it is.'

'That couldn't be legal,' said Devlin.

'No. It would be market manipulation on an absolutely massive scale.'

'You know, Gary,' said the president, 'I don't think that's the worst case.'

'That they're doing it on purpose? You don't think that's the worst case?'

'No, not that they're not doing it on purpose, but that they're not doing it for money.'

'That's true. But that was part of the message we gave them, right? If they're doing this to influence our political process, they'd better stop.'

'Why would they be trying to influence the midterms?' said Abrahams. 'Why now? Why these ones?'

'There's any number of reasons,' said Rose. 'Uganda. South Africa. A general desire to throw their weight around.'

'Because they can, is that what you're saying?'

'Maybe. Like those aircraft carriers they've built over the last few years. What are they going to use them for? Why do they need a blue ocean navy? But they want to have them. And they want us to know they have them.'

'This isn't aircraft carriers,' said Abrahams. 'This is our economy.'

'And maybe they want us to know what they can do to it.'

'But it's their economy as well,' said Devlin. 'We hurt – they hurt. You think Zhang would take a risk like this? He's all about stability, right?'

'Absolutely.'

'Then if it is political, and if they got the message, they'll stop. They've made their point. I guess … What will they do?'

'They'll find the cash for Fidelian,' said Perez.

'Let's say it's not the worst case,' said the president, 'and actually we've got this Chinese investment fund acting like a genuine investor and they don't want to throw good money after bad. Let's say that's what the issue is.'

'Then Susan needs to find a buyer.'

'Can we really do it in the time? We've got twelve days.'

'We need it done *way* quicker than twelve days,' said Abrahams. 'We're not waking up the day before the election with this still going on.'

'Half of Wall Street got sold in '08 and it took about twenty minutes,' said Perez. 'You can do it if you've got a buyer.'

'What gets us a buyer?'

'Greed,' replied Perez. 'The chance to pick up a rival operation in a fire sale.'

'What if the operation's too bad for that? What if a fire sale price isn't even cheap?'

'Fear. Fear by other bankers that their own businesses will be hit. You get them afraid enough of that, they'll buy it in an hour.' Perez smiled. 'Those are the only two emotions bankers know, fear and greed. Build up one or the other and they'll do whatever you want.'

Knowles thought about it. 'Okay. Even if we get this sale done, it's not going to look like good news, no matter how we sell it. At best, it's going to look like less-than-bad-news. We need some good news. Every damn day it's the markets. Dean can't get hold of the agenda.'

Tom Knowles' approval rating had fallen with the markets over the last couple of weeks. He was down to around fifty per cent, the lowest point in his presidency. Every Republican in a tight race was taking a hit on the president's behalf. Some had asked the president to cancel trips to speak with them. They were finding they did better in the polls if they weren't identified with him.

'What we need is a foreign policy crisis,' said Rose, only half-jokingly. 'We should talk to the Pakistanis.'

'*Good* news,' said the president irritably. 'For Christ's sake, Gary, I said good news, not some explosion in outer fucking Waziristan.' Knowles drummed his fingers impatiently on his chair. He could feel time ticking towards the midterms, day by day. And cancellations by Republican candidates were embarrassing. His crowded campaign schedule had been the subject of public discussion and suddenly there was a bunch of gaps that had to be accounted for without admitting that Republican candidates didn't want to be seen with him. 'What about Jungle Peace?' he said suddenly. 'What the hell's happening with Jungle Peace?'

Abrahams nodded. 'Score a big hit. Get that on the front pages.'

'It's about time we had some kind of a win over there.' Knowles looked at Rose. 'They must have enough intelligence by now.'

'I'm sure if we tell them to do something they can make it happen.'

'I don't want to interfere with the operational stuff but Pressler's acting like he's got years to do this. It was meant to be quick. Bam! Let's get rid of these evil guys.'

'I'll talk to the defense secretary.'

'I don't want John to think this is about publicity or anything, but we've got to start doing something. When are we meeting on this again with the military guys?'

'I'll check.'

'Make it tomorrow. And see if they can bring some ideas for things they can do.'

'And otherwise, we wait to find out,' said Abrahams.

The president looked at him. 'What?'

'Whether it's the best case or the worst case. Custler's going back to talk to the shareholders, right?'

20

ED GREY SCANNED the screens on his wall, looking at the data from the trading session that was under way in New York. He ran down row after row of numbers, searching for an answer.

Was it time to close out? The Fed's notification of short-term liquidity support had been sent out Friday morning. Stocks were largely flat through Friday trading, including Fidelian. Now it was Monday. Overnight, Asian markets had been quiet, waiting to see what Wall Street would do. The European markets had opened tentatively, holding fire until they saw what direction the Street would take. Along with hundreds of other fund owners and mangers, Grey was one of the people who would decide.

The decision wasn't straightforward.

Right now, he was a quarter billion up on Fidelian alone. Red River was another two hundred million up – or close to it – on a number of other bank stocks that Boris Malevsky had been shorting, together with additional bets that Tony Evangelou had laid in other sectors. Set against that were paper losses approaching three-quarters of a billion in a bunch of pre-existing long positions Red River had been holding on the assumption that the market was going up. Things had gone way, way further than Grey had anticipated. He had thought he was setting the cats among the banking pigeons and would make a little money in the sector – instead, the whole market was correcting. Yet Grey still believed there would be a fairly swift recovery. He was pretty sure that in six months from now, or a year at the outside, the Dow would have recovered its losses of the past four weeks and then some. So the trick, which was always the trick in running a DIV during a period of volatility, was to know when to take the gains as the market swung one way and then to take them again as it went the other way. Sell at the high, buy at the low. Or in other words, know when the top's the top, and the bottom's the bottom.

Until that moment, until you closed out your positions – until you bought back the stocks you had shorted, or sold the stocks you were holding – you had no profit. It was all on paper. And what was on paper, no matter how solid it looked, could disappear in a puff of smoke.

If he closed out his short positions now, buying stock to return the stock he had borrowed, it was copper-bottomed profit. Four hundred fifty million or thereabouts, a little over half from Fidelian. If he waited, and the market bounced, that profit could be gone. On the other hand, if the market plunged further, that profit could be doubled in a day. To Ed Grey, who was worth a couple of billion in his own right, the thrill was in making enormous, staggeringly outsize profits. A few tens of millions did nothing for him. Four hundred was nice. But eight hundred, say, or a nice round billion, that was something different. There was something special in being able to say you had made a figure with nine zeroes on the end.

Grey had another reason to have those short positions intact if the market plunged. It wasn't just the thrill of the kill. If the market dropped, he would need that extra profit to offset the additional paper losses he would make on the long positions he held. If he didn't have that offset, the losses would start to reach a size when the banks that had lent money to Red River would come knocking. They held his stocks as collateral and marked his positions to market – which meant that they calculated the value of his positions against market prices – on a daily basis. That was how they assessed the value of the collateral they held. It didn't matter that losses were notional unless he actually sold the stocks – as long as he held them, the banks treated them as if they were worth their market value on any given day. If his notional losses reached a certain level they would demand additional cash on the margin he had borrowed. If he couldn't provide it, they would sell his stocks from under him until they had what they wanted.

In a word, his short positions had turned into a hedge against the notional losses he had incurred from the very same market correction that had notionally made him so much money.

Yet if the market bounced, and he hadn't closed out those same short positions, the four hundred fifty million he had on paper would be gone forever, the market would be back where it started and the entire exercise would have yielded nothing.

He scanned the screens, gazed at the sporadically flickering numbers. Were they going to rise or fall? He was reaching into the void, into the great collective unknown that was the market, straining to find a direction.

That was what everyone was doing, he knew. He could almost feel it, smell it. People were waiting. Prices were drifting in narrow ranges. Volumes were low.

Was it a lull, or had the Fed put a floor under the market? Was the market sitting temporarily on a shelf on the way down, catching its breath before the slide continued, or was it about to get a grip, turn around and start climbing?

Ed Grey believed the banking system was fundamentally sound. He believed stock prices had been somewhat overvalued but were now heavily oversold. Both of those beliefs argued for a bounce. But timing, as always, was everything.

Fidelian was the one that was worrying him. It accounted for a quarter billion of his paper profit. How much lower could it go? There were rumors that credit lines to Fidelian were being rapidly shut down and that investors were pulling anything they could get out. Grey didn't know how Bill Custler was resisting the demands for him to release a statement. By now the rumor that Fidelian would need to come to the market for cash was all over the Street. People were saying crazy things. Eight billion. Ten billion. One wild rumor even talked about fifteen billion. When people started saying things like that, the reality never turned out to be as bad. If that was the case, when Custler finally broke his silence, the stock would bounce. After the hit it had taken it would bounce big. If that happened, a good part of that quarter billion in paper profit would go up in smoke right in front of his eyes.

Ed Grey had heard another rumor that there was interest from a number of parties in buying Fidelian. That gave him additional confidence in his hunch that the stock had been oversold. Buyers come in when they can sniff a bargain. If that was what was attracting them, they had detected a floor and would likely pay above the current price.

He watched the numbers on the screens a little longer. Then he called Evangelou and Malevsky into his office.

'What do you think?' he said.

'We're going to bounce,' said Evangelou.

'And then? We coming down again?'

'Depends on what else is out there.'

'What else *is* out there?'

Evangelou shrugged. 'Who the fuck knows?'

Grey glanced at Malevsky. 'What do you think?'

'We could bounce.'

'How much?'

'Some. Not all the way back.'

'How much is your cut now?'

'Twenty-two million.'

'That's money. Huh, Boris?' said Evangelou. 'You want to take it? Go and retire in Florida.'

Malevsky laughed.

'So you're saying we close out?' said Grey. 'Is that it?'

Evangelou nodded. Malevsky nodded as well.

'You're both wimps.'

'Ed, you want to keep going? You're fucking crazy! You want to do that, I'll bet you a thousand to the mil on our position we go up. What do you say?'

'Tempting.'

'I thought you had a pair of cojones.'

Ed Grey grinned. Then he was serious again. 'Alright. What about Fidelian? What do we think?'

'Oversold,' said Evangelou. 'Largely because of us.'

'The whole market's spooked on it now.'

'Where's the money they need going to come from?' asked Grey.

'I heard there's a buyer.'

'What if there isn't?'

'Depends how much they need.'

'Who's going to buy those bonds? Look at their stock price. Who'd put anything into that company?'

Evangelou shrugged. 'Their shareholders will put in.'

Malevsky nodded.

'They're fucked if they don't.'

'So what if they're fucked?'

'No way they're fucked. The Chinese own, what? Twenty-five per cent. Plus who knows what else. They're not going to watch that investment go down the tube. Pulling out five, ten billion's not going to be an issue for them. The other shareholders get diluted but if they want they can put in as well. If you're the Chinese, what's your alternative? Less is better than nothing, right?'

Grey leaned back in his chair. 'So we're done?'

'Aggressively,' said Malevsky, 'let's assume Fidelian needs to raise ten billion. If it's ten billion, and nothing else has changed from six weeks ago, that values them around seven per cent above where they are today. The rest of the downside is noise.'

'As soon as things calm down a little, those are the figures everyone's going to do,' added Evangelou.

Grey nodded. In about a thousand offices all over the city, those were probably the exact figures that were being crunched already. Provided everyone felt some kind of a floor had been put under the sector by the Fed's actions. If not, the noise would get louder and the downward pressure would continue.

'Okay,' said Grey, 'let's pretend like we're smart for a second. Everyone's saying the same thing. At a cash requirement of ten billion, Fidelian's seven per cent undervalued so we close out our short positions now and say thank you very much. What if we're wrong?'

'That's an aggressive case,' said Malevsky. 'If the cash requirement is less, the undershoot is even greater.'

'What if the cash requirement is more?'

'Off the top of my head, if the requirement is thirteen billion, they roughly come into line with today's price.'

'Let's take the extreme. What if they can't get it?'

'Then they get sold. From what I've heard, they probably get sold anyway and the Chinese don't have to put in anything.'

'What if they don't? What if they fail?'

'If they fail, everyone's fucked,' said Evangelou. 'The government's wind-up powers are bullshit. We're in 2008. But what's the probability, Ed?'

Grey nodded. 'I agree, but we make our money on getting the low probability events right.'

'But we lose it on getting the high probability events wrong. Look, if there weren't any dominant shareholders involved here, I'd say this is a chance we might consider taking. But the risk-reward isn't there. You've got the PIC with twenty-five per cent of the stock and effectively an unlimited cash supply from the Chinese government. If Fidelian can't raise the cash anywhere else, that's where they'll get it.'

Grey agreed. He looked at Malevsky. 'What do you think?'

'It's not a low probability event. It's a zero probability event.'

Grey laughed. 'Nothing's a zero probability event. Stick around in the business for a while.'

Malevsky shrugged. 'In the final analysis, the government can't let this bank fail. We're a week away from an election. We can create whatever scenarios we like about how much cash they need, and what the shareholders will or won't do, or whether there'll be a buyer or not, but in the end there's no scenario in which it will fail because it can't be allowed to happen.'

Grey agreed with that.

'He wants his twenty-two million,' said Evangelou.

'I wouldn't say no,' quipped Malevsky.

Grey didn't respond. Unusually, he found himself undecided. Normally he had a clear sense when a trade had run as far as it was going to run and it was time to get out. In this instance, he just wasn't sure. His trading style was always to pile more capital into a trade that was going well, and that was what he had done in this case. That was one of the first lessons he had learned in the business, that it was almost impossible to overestimate how far a move could go. When a trade hit your target, it didn't mean it was over. Often the move had just begun.

All of that argued in keeping the Fidelian position open, even increasing it. But you had to temper zeal with rationality. At some point you did have to close out. Gery didn't believe the fundamentals were there to justify a further fall either in the banking sector or across the market generally. Other than rumor and panic, it was hard to see how it had even come this far. And that argued to get out. To take four hundred fifty million out of a market that should never have given him anything like that and be damn happy he had done it.

'So what we're saying,' he said, 'is that even on an aggressive case, Fidelian's undervalued already. We've got two fifty in the bag and even on the aggressive case if we don't act we lose it. On the other hand there's a failure scenario where they can't either recapitalize or sell this bank and we get a huge blowout, but we're saying the probability's virtually zero. And we believe the fundamentals of the sector are strong, so that says we're going to bounce. And all of that says we close out. Now.'

Evangelou nodded. So did Malevsky.

'And that means we lose the hedge against our long positions. And that means that if the market really crashes, the banks come knocking.'

'But that's the zero probability event,' said Evangelou.

'The *virtually* zero probability event – which wipes us out.'

'No, it doesn't,' said Evangelou. 'We close out Fidelian and we have the cash to meet the margin calls if that happens. Ed, it's the perfect scenario. We take our profit. In the low probability event that the market keeps falling – and it's probably no more than a one to five per cent probability – that cash covers the margins and we can hold the stocks until they recover. I've had one of the quants running the numbers with the market falling another twenty per cent from here. Worst comes to the worst, we survive the short term with the Fidelian cash.'

'What if the market goes down fifty per cent?'

'Now you're not even talking about a one per cent chance. You know me, Ed. I'm a numbers guy. But this market's going up. It's corrected. It's overcorrected. And if it hasn't, we have the cash to cover any realistic scenario.'

It was decision time. This was how Ed Grey earned his money, making decisions. If you weren't prepared to do that, you'd never get your profits off paper and back into your fund.

He agreed with every word Tony said. The difficulty was the fact that this trade had turned into a massive hedge. He was way down on long positions that assumed a rise in the market, and would be down even more if the market kept falling.

But if he closed out, the cash was in the fund. Not on paper. And that would cover his margins if the market kept falling. It was only if the government stood by while Fidelian failed to raise the capital it needed, or failed to find a buyer, that the cash would be insufficient to cover him. And even then, only if the market fell to an almost unprecedented degree. The probability of all of that happening was vanishingly small.

Still, Ed Grey knew that even with those odds, it was a bet.

21

JERRY RABIN SLAMMED his fist down on the table. The president of the New York Fed was generally slow to anger, but right now he was incandescent with rage.

'What do you think is going to happen, Bill? What in God's name do you *think* is going to happen?'

Bill Custler shook his head. He didn't know what else to say. His throat was dry.

'You asked me for two more days for your board to decide. I gave that to you. Then another day. Then another day.'

'I didn't guarantee–'

'And now you come back and tell me they won't put any capital in, and they won't sell? Is that what you're telling me? They won't do one and they won't do the other!'

Custler raised his hands helplessly and let them drop. Rabin stared at him. The situation was inconceivable. For a week he and Susan Opitz had struggled to find a party that would make an offer for the remains of the shambles that was Fidelian Bank, haranguing, cajoling, holding off rumors swirling in the market and now, on Friday morning, when they had just about managed to find a buyer, Bill Custler had come to them with the news that the problem was the one thing Rabin couldn't do anything about, couldn't ever have seriously believed would be the obstacle – not that they didn't have a buyer, but that they didn't have a seller.

'You're only alive because of me, Bill! You're only alive because of the liquidity we're providing.' By now, Rabin knew the details of Fidelian's operation just about as well as Custler did himself. For the past week there had been a team of regulators from the Fed and the SEC installed in a set of meeting rooms in Fidelian's headquarters monitoring their cash requirements virtually on an hourly basis.

'Technically, Mr Rabin, the board will agree to a sale,' said one of the executives who had come with Custler, Fidelian's chief financial officer, Dick Overbrook. 'But for full market value.'

'And what do they define as full market value?' demanded Rabin.

Overbrook took a piece of paper out of the file he was holding and slid it across the table.

'That's not in any way a contractually binding acceptance, sir,' said the Fidelian general counsel, who was the other executive who had come with Custler. 'It's an estimate of the board's definition of the full market value.'

Rabin peered at the paper. So did the other two Fed officials who were with him in the meeting.

Bill Custler watched them, wincing slightly.

Rabin pushed the paper back across the table. 'That's a joke, Mr Overbrook. That's a joke and not a very funny one.'

One of Rabin's officials cleared his throat. 'We've been talking to a number of parties who might possibly have been interested in acquiring … ah … the whole or parts of Fidelian Bank. We have … ah … one party–'

'We have a buyer,' said Rabin impatiently. 'But your figure is a joke!'

'Yes,' said the official. 'We have one buyer who is potentially prepared to acquire the entire enterprise and we have … ah … a number who would be interested in various parts of the operation.' He took a page out of his briefcase and pushed it across the table. 'Naturally these are all indicative numbers and subject to due diligence but I … ah … believe they are all genuine expressions of interest and actionable within a very short period of time.'

'Immediately,' snapped Rabin. 'We need to get this done today. We need to get this done, signed, sealed and announced as soon as the markets close for the weekend.'

Custler looked at the page. Privately he thought the offers were good, even generous, but he couldn't say that. 'You know they're going to game us, Jerry.'

'That's not going to happen.'

'Of course it is. They're going to turn around when we're five minutes from signing and say they've found something in the due diligence and they're going to halve it.'

'They're not. I guarantee you they're not.'

'Then they just want to see our books so they can figure out how to protect themselves and make some money against us when we go down.'

'Bill, these are real offers. They know the situation. Understand me? They know.'

Custler understood. That meant all of Wall Street would soon know the details. This could only be kept quiet for so long.

Custler stared at the page. If it was up to him, he would have jumped at it. He sighed. 'Well, it ain't happening, Jerry. That number Dick showed you, that's what we need.'

'That number's ridiculous.'

'And those are fire sale prices,' said Overbrook, pointing at the Fed's paper.

'Well, it may have escaped your attention, Mr Overbrook, but you're in a fire. Bill, I've got you a buyer. Personally I'd take that route, but if you don't like that one, there are others who'll take it in pieces. You need to start talking to these guys. You need to start doing a deal.'

Custler shrugged. 'Jerry, it ain't happening. I don't know how else I can say it. That's the number I need. Otherwise, I'm just going to have to make my announcement. I can't keep holding off.'

'Don't you try to blackmail me!'

'I'm not trying to blackmail anyone,' said Custler wearily. 'Jerry, I'm just telling you the facts.'

Rabin stood up. He paced around the room, shaking his head in exasperation. Suddenly he stopped and turned on Custler. 'Bill, what are you doing here? You want to turn Fidelian into some kind of Lehman? Is that what you want to be, the next Lehman?'

Custler shook his head.

'You want to be the next Dick Fuld?' demanded Rabin, his voice rising. 'Is that how you want to be remembered, Bill? Like Dick Fuld?'

'No!' retorted Custler, the pain and humiliation of his position bursting out of him. 'What the fuck do you think I want? Jesus Christ,

Jerry! I've been thirty-four years in the industry and you think I want to end it like this?'

'Then how the fuck do you want to end it?' yelled Rabin.

'How the fuck do you think?' Custler yelled back.

There was silence. Both men were breathing heavily.

Rabin sat down again.

'I don't own this bank,' said Custler quietly. 'Why can't you understand that? These aren't my decisions. These are decisions for my board, and they are not leaving it to me.' He looked down at the page with the figures Fidelian's rivals were prepared to pay for its operations. 'I can tell you they won't sell for that kind of money. Nowhere near it. If you can get people to triple those numbers, maybe we've got something to talk about.'

'There's maybe ten per cent flexibility in there,' said Rabin.

'Jerry, what if they really believe we're going to go bust? What if they really, truly believe that unless they cough up this money, we're going bust with all that means for all of them?'

'They do believe it.'

'They'll lose way more money if we go bust than they're prepared to pay on these figures.'

'Trust me, Bill, they believe it.'

Custler pushed the paper back across the table. 'They couldn't.'

Rabin pushed Custler's paper back in the opposite direction. 'Your shareholders are in dreamland.'

Custler sighed heavily. 'Look at it from their perspective. What's in it for them if they agree to the kind of sale you're suggesting? For that money, they may as well let the thing go bust.' Custler pulled back Rabin's paper. 'I mean, you've got an offer here of fifty million for our Eurobonds trading operation.'

'Your Eurobonds operation isn't exactly a market leader.'

'That's your opinion.'

'Look, I agree, some parties are fishing for what they can get. Look at the other bids. You've got some very respectable offers for other parts of the business. And you've got a very acceptable unified bid for the whole enterprise which comes with the twenty-three billion of capital your operation needs to keep going.'

Overbrook snorted. 'Acceptable to who?'

Rabin ignored him. 'Bill, if your shareholders aren't prepared to back their own bank with more cash themselves, that's what you're going to get left with. They're creating the problem for themselves. Why won't they put more in?'

'I don't know. I don't know their cash position. Maybe they don't have it.'

'No one's going to believe that.'

'Mr Custler,' said one of the Fed officials, 'have you been encouraged to undertake risky activity at Fidelian?'

Custler looked at him in disbelief.

'Do you think your shareholders have directed the bank's activity in a way that is inconsistent, say, with other banks where you've worked?'

'No.' Custler looked back at Rabin. 'What is this, Jerry?'

'We're just trying to work out what's going on.'

'I've told you what I know. I've told you where we are.'

Rabin glanced at his officials. Suddenly he turned back to Custler. 'How much do they control?'

'Who?'

'The Chinese government.'

'The People's Investment Corporation has twenty-five per cent, give or take,' said Overbrook.

'We've seen the numbers.'

'Then you know that.'

'How much else?'

Overbrook was silent. He glanced at Custler.

'How much?'

'We think they're probably around forty,' said Overbrook quietly.

'But you don't know?'

'We have no way of identifying the links between our shareholders, sir. My understanding of the PIC is probably no better than yours, in fact it's probably a lot worse, but I believe they have literally hundreds of subsidiaries.'

'So where does the forty per cent number come from?'

Overbrook was silent.

'I've been told,' said Custler.

Rabin stared at him. 'You've been told outright?'

'PIC officials I've dealt with have indicated that's the proportion of votes they can control. I haven't got anything on paper.'

'You realize,' said one of Rabin's officials, 'if that's the case, and they haven't declared that, they're committing a federal felony.'

'With respect, sir, I don't think Mr Hu at the PIC is too worried about threats of a federal felony.'

'Well, he should be.'

'Al,' said Rabin to his official, 'let's not get hung up on the legalities. A three-year court case isn't going to solve our problem today.'

'That's right,' said Overbrook pointedly. 'Open that can of worms and you'll find half of Wall Street in there.'

There was silence. Facing a shareholding of that magnitude, none of the other shareholders could do anything without the PIC giving a lead.

Rabin looked at the three men seated opposite him. 'So what are we going to do?'

There was no reply.

'Bill, can you talk to them again?'

'And do what, Jerry? Threaten them with a court case?'

Rabin put his finger on the paper with the offers. 'There's money on the table.'

'It's not enough.'

'It's a start. I can go back and see if I can get some more. I'm prepared to do that if you're prepared to go back on your side and see if they'll be realistic.'

Custler shrugged.

'Will you talk to them?'

'I'll talk to them,' said Custler fatalistically. 'Of course I'll talk to them. Until I'm hoarse. I'll do anything I can to save this bank and the jobs of the people who work there. I'm just telling you I don't think that going back to my board with this is going to get us anywhere.'

'Bill, that's just not acceptable. This is coming from the president. He gave us a deadline of today. Now I'm going to have to go back and tell him we missed it.'

Custler was silent.

Rabin threw himself back in his chair. He shook his head, imagining the president's reaction. The time had ticked away. They had started with twelve days – now there were only four. Friday today. The midterm elections were on Tuesday. That left Monday to announce a deal. He tried to think how the White House might present it. Bold action taken by the administration to prevent a collapse that could have sparked another financial crisis. On the day before the midterms? He shook his head again.

Even without the election, the deal still needed to be done. The market had been holding fire too long and wasn't going to wait much longer. It had only waited this long because of the rumors that a deal would be announced before the end of the week. If the Fidelian situation wasn't clarified over the weekend, if there wasn't a definitive statement before the markets opened again, there was going to be the mother of all sell-offs on Monday.

'We need a deal,' he said. 'There's no alternative, Bill. Your share-holders need to understand that.'

'And I've told you I've told them that already and I'll talk to them again but–'

'No. Listen to what I'm telling you. We need a deal by the time the markets open Monday morning. This is it. There's no more time. They have to say yes.'

Custler looked at him pointedly. 'Then maybe someone else should give them that message.'

22

'NO, I DON'T understand!' said Knowles. 'You told me you could do it overnight. Then you told me you were going to get a deal done today at the outside.'

Jerry Rabin, speaking from New York, had just given a rundown of his conversation with Bill Custler. Susan Opitz and Ron Strickland were patched in. The president's senior aides were with him in the Oval Office.

'This isn't seriously going to happen, is it?' said Knowles. 'You're not telling me there's any serious risk this bank is going down?'

There was another silence on the line before Opitz responded. 'They know we need a deal done by the end of the weekend, Mr President.'

Tom Knowles closed his eyes. He had a bad, bad feeling about this. Rabin and Opitz had had all week to cut a deal. Now they were hoping to get it done over the weekend. Even if they did, announcing something like this the day before the election would be a horrendously risky thing to do.

'Can we push it out past Tuesday?' he asked.

'The market's demanding something. Custler's under incredible pressure to announce. We risk a total bloodbath.'

'Didn't their share price rise a little?' Knowles glanced for confirmation at Marty Perez, who nodded.

'Sir, that's because of the rumors,' said Rabin. 'People think there must be political pressure to get a deal ahead of the election so they're buying shares in hopes that pressure forces the price higher.'

Knowles shook his head in disbelief. He didn't know much about the financial markets but the more he saw of them the sicker they made him. Rumors building on rumors, and everyone trying to make money on the back of them, like vultures hovering over a carcass.

'No one's trading with Fidelian. No one's lending them money, no one's doing business with them. Right now this is a zombie bank and it's only the Fed that's keeping it alive.'

'What if we continue to negotiate through Tuesday?' said Ed Abrahams.

'We'll have the mother of all sell-offs on Monday. If Custler doesn't say anything, the markets will think he's under political pressure to stay quiet because of the election. They'll know the news is bad. They can put two and two together.'

There was silence.

'This is a mess,' said the president. 'This is just one hell of a mess.'

No one said anything. That was an understatement.

'Susan, how bad is this if it happens? Let's forget about the election. If there was no election, would we be trying to do anything about this? How bad is it economically?'

'Bad. This has pretty much come out of nowhere. A month ago, this wasn't even on the horizon. So the first thing the market's going to do is look at this and say, okay, who else? Who's next? Even if there isn't one, they're going to be looking.'

'We don't think there is a next one, by the way,' said Strickland.

'But you can't be sure,' said Abrahams. 'You didn't see this one, right?'

'That's exactly the problem right there,' said Opitz. 'That's what everyone's going to be saying, including other banks. Fidelian goes down, there's going to be a scramble for safety. First up, anything to do with Fidelian – any loan, any asset, anything – gets sold, for whatever anyone can get for it. That hits other banks who are holding Fidelian assets. That puts those other banks in danger. That makes other banks want to stop trading with *them*. When the effects start to ripple out then other institutions that are sound but don't have … let's say they don't have a lot of slack to play with, suddenly they're in trouble as well.'

'This sounds like 2008.'

'It's not 2008,' said Strickland. 'With a little short-term support, other banks aren't going to fall over. The system is fundamentally sound.'

'I agree with that,' said Opitz. 'But the shock will be huge. There's going to be overreaction. Mr President, everyone's going to say exactly what you said, this is 2008, even though it isn't. It's going to take time for them to realize that. And in that time, things are going to look very ugly.'

'Can't we force this bank to do something?' said the president. 'What about … can we take them over?'

'You mean nationalize it?'

'I don't know. Is that what I mean?'

'We have the powers to wind them up,' said Opitz, 'but that doesn't solve the problem of the impact on the market.'

'Well, can we force them to sell?'

'No, sir.'

'Are we sure about that? Have we checked all this stuff?'

'We've explored all the options.'

'I don't think we ever conceived of a situation where someone would knock back a reasonable offer when they were staring at bankruptcy,' said Ron Strickland.

'Not for commercial reasons,' murmured Ed Abrahams.

Knowles looked at him.

'Mr President,' said Rabin, 'they could be bluffing us. It may be this is a way of trying to push up the price. They may be taking us to the wire.'

'But it's possible they're not.'

'Yes, sir. My suggestion is, the only thing we can do here is exert maximum pressure. I'll be meeting with the heads of other banks I think I can get to come to the party. Will you speak to them if necessary?'

'Do I need to do that?'

'I think that may be needed, sir.'

'I'll check with counsel to see if that's okay,' said Roberta Devlin. The president nodded.

'The other thing,' said Opitz, 'is we need pressure on the other side. We need pressure on the PIC. They've either got to put up a good portion of the twenty-three billion or sell this company for a realistic price.'

'We already tried putting pressure on them,' said Abrahams.

'Then we need to do it better.'

'How do you suggest we do that?'

'They're an arm of the Chinese government.'

'We spoke to their ambassador.'

'Then we need to go higher.'

All eyes were on the president. He knew exactly what Opitz meant.

Knowles frowned for a moment. He turned to the Treasury secretary. 'I'm not talking to anyone until I have something to say.'

23

AT NINE O'CLOCK on Saturday morning, Wall Street's most powerful CEOs were gathered in a conference room at the New York Fed at 33 Liberty Street. Jerry Rabin had exercised the ultimate prerogative of his office – the ability to call the leaders of America's financial community out of their weekend homes and off their golf courses to meet in crisis conclave.

Rabin, Susan Opitz and Mike O'Brien, head of the SEC, walked into the room, accompanied by a number of their aides. The pleasantries were brief. Rabin had had his assistant organize the meeting without telling the CEOs the purpose, but they had all guessed what it was about. As instructed, they had come into the building via the back garage entrance to avoid journalists who might be waiting at the front. Each had brought a number of his top executives, but only the eight CEOs themselves sat in the room. The others cooled their heels outside.

Individually, most of the CEOs had been involved in conversations about Fidelian earlier in the week. Now Rabin laid out the latest situation, going through the details of Fidelian's upcoming losses, the cash the bank would require, and other key points to make sure the issues were fresh in everyone's mind. Matters that would normally have been the subject of the highest confidence from competitors were laid bare. The eight men listened silently, showing no outward reaction when the numbers were mentioned, exchanging, at most, a glance with one another.

Rabin didn't know exactly what to expect from them. These men knew each other well. They met at any number of events and found themselves on the same or opposite sides of any number of deals. And traditionally Wall Street bosses pulled together to save one of their brethren's skin when their own skins were threatened. But they were each king of the hill in their own organization, and they were fierce competitors. A good number of personal antagonisms had walked into that room together with those eight men. Years of poaching each other's clients, talking each other's businesses down, stealing each other's high performing executives, left plenty to be sore about. Some of them took it philosophically and remained amicable, others never let go. Jim Perlman, CEO of Goldman Sachs, and Bob Aspin of Deutsche BoA literally hated each other, the malice going back to a deal two decades earlier from which each had walked away accusing the other of dishonesty. They had been known to have stand-up shouting matches when fate put them in the same room.

Rabin didn't mention the price Bill Custler had asked for. He didn't want the bankers walking out before they even considered his request. What he did say was they had to find a way to provide a fair price for the assets of the business. They shouldn't be here if they were looking for absurdly priced bargains.

'I shouldn't be here at all,' muttered Aspin.

Perlman shrugged. 'I don't think any of us would be too disappointed if you left.'

Rabin ignored the asides. Bob Aspin had made his name as a ruthless costcutter when he brought Deutsche's US operations together with Bank of America. He hadn't been too helpful in the earlier conversations about Fidelian but Deutsche BoA was cashed up, largely as a result of Aspin's activities, and Rabin knew they were in a position to help if they chose to.

'Jerry,' said Hamish Harvey-Wills, an expatriate Brit who ran Morgan Stanley, 'it doesn't seem to me the gentlemen at Fidelian are in a particularly strong position to bargain on this one.'

'That's what you'd imagine,' said Rabin. 'In fact, don't assume that. They think they are.'

Harvey-Wills raised an eyebrow.

'They won't sell if they consider they're being exploited. They'd prefer to go bankrupt.'

'Then let 'em,' Perlman said. 'Who cares? The strong survive, the weak feed 'em.'

'Jim,' said Rabin, 'that's not a scenario we want to consider.'

'But it's a scenario they want to consider. So let's consider.' Perlman got up. 'When they're ready to consider something real, give me a call.'

'Here we go,' muttered Aspin.

'Jim, come on, sit down,' said Sonny Mello of JP Morgan Suisse. Mello was a tall, thin man with silver hair and a taste for Savile Row suits which he had flown in from London. He was more of a conciliator than the average banking chief executive and over the years had come to adopt the unofficial role of mediator to this bickering tribe when they were brought together.

Perlman looked around the room. He sat. Jim Perlman enjoyed putting on a show. He wasn't really angry. Not yet.

'Jerry,' said Ed Loeffler, the CEO of Citigroup, who had planned to be at a nephew's wedding in California this weekend but had put his flight on hold, 'I don't know about everyone else here, but I already put forward an offer for certain parts of the Fidelian business. What's the response? I assume the reason you've got us sitting here today on a Saturday morning is because they weren't prepared to accept it. Have they named a price?'

Rabin shook his head. 'They want what they call fair value. I don't know if that's a price as such.'

Loeffler watched the chairman of the Fed knowingly. 'Jerr, have they given you a number?'

'There's no binding number.'

'Jesus Christ, Jerry,' said Perlman. 'Have they or have they not given you a number?'

Rabin glanced at one of his aides.

'We have seen a number, Mr Perlman, which we do not consider realistic. It's not fixed. We don't consider it a floor.'

'To hell with what you consider it. What do *they* consider it?'

'We've told them it's unrealistic. They know it. Bill Custler is talking to his shareholders as we speak.'

'This is bullshit,' said Aspin. 'Jerry, you're asking us to buy this shitty excuse for a bank from a bunch of owners who don't accept the position they're in. Excuse me, but I never saw a deal done like that.'

Rabin didn't respond.

'Let's step back from the price for a second,' said Harvey-Wills.

'How do we know the writedowns are limited to the numbers you've mentioned? There could be massive exposure here that none of us is aware of. Not to mention that you're asking us to agree to this … When?'

'We need to announce a deal before the markets open Monday morning,' said Susan Opitz.

'Not sure that we're *quite* going to get the due diligence done.'

'Sounds like a political agenda to me,' muttered Aspin.

'You've all got your own idea of what you think Fidelian's worth,' said Rabin. 'At least you've all got a good idea of what you think some parts are worth. Bob, you wanted to buy part of its operation a year back.'

'That was then,' said Aspin. 'Half the guys we wanted have gone now.'

'Yeah,' said Perlman, 'because you poached them.'

'You got a problem with that, Jim?'

'Yeah, I got a problem with it. I got a problem with the way you fucking poached my forex team right off my floor.'

'Well, if you can't keep 'em, Jim …'

'You telling me what I can do? You wanna tell me what I can do?'

'Looks like someone has to. Ask me, someone ought to take a good long look at what you're doing over there with what was once a fine firm.'

'What *I'm* doing? If we're gonna start talking about looking at what someone's doing, I'd say we start with–'

'Gentlemen!' said Rabin. 'Enough, huh?'

Perlman stopped. He and Aspin glared at each other. The rest of the CEOs watched, disappointed that the Fed president had stopped what was shaping up to be a memorable spat between the legendary pair.

'Let's get back to what we're here for,' said Rabin. 'Here's what we're proposing. You don't need to do this by yourselves. The federal government is going to give you whatever help it can. Now, there's twenty-three billion of capital that you're going to have to put in. That's there. Factor that into your figures, assume it's going to happen and tell us what you need to be able to cover that. We're prepared to make funds available on a long-term basis. We can talk about the commercials. Next, we'll guarantee you cover for any additional writedowns Fidelian has to make over the next twelve months.'

'Who's we?' said Perlman.

'The government,' replied Opitz. 'We don't want you to have any nasty surprises. Beyond the twenty-three billion, you take only the first two billion of anything else you find. We'll carry the cost of anything else you find up to a total of twenty billion. The federal government will guarantee that.'

Jerry Rabin nodded.

There was silence in the room. Opitz could see the men calculating.

'Is that eighteen or twenty billion you'll guarantee?' asked Loeffler.

'That's eighteen. Up to a total of twenty. You take the first two, then if we're needed, we're there for up to another eighteen. We think that's an extremely generous proposition.'

'Who cares?' said Aspin impatiently. 'I don't want anything to do with this. I don't want federal money. It's poison. I don't want it and I don't need it.'

'What level of scrutiny are you going to require?' asked Harvey-Wills.

'We would need to assure ourselves,' said Rabin, 'that any additional writedowns are genuinely coming out of Fidelian business.'

'Yeah, and before you know it you'll be looking at pay and bonuses and we'll be up in front of Congress explaining why we have to pay some trader what we already agreed to pay him.' Aspin snorted and looked around at the others. 'We've seen this before. You guys, you want to get involved in that stuff, be my guest. I have no interest in it. I don't need Congress looking into my bank and I sure as hell don't need the press talking about me like I've taken some kind of money off the taxpayer.'

'Bob,' said Rabin. 'It's only a guarantee.'

'Looks the same from the outside.'

'You don't have to take it,' said Opitz.

'Yeah, right. And expose myself to an unquantified level of risk because you're asking me to do a deal in six hours. Madam Secretary, I didn't get to where I am today by being the baby people steal the candy from.'

Opitz took a deep breath. 'Mr Aspin, I think we should remember where we all come from.' She looked around the room. 'Every one of you took money from the government in '08. Every one of your institutions. To me, that means not one of you would be here today if the government, if the American taxpayer, hadn't been prepared to hold out a big bag of cash to you when it mattered. Let's just remember that. Now, what I think the American taxpayer is saying, is that it's time you guys did something in return.'

Aspin smiled incredulously. 'This is blackmail.' He looked at Rabin. 'Do you agree with what the secretary just said, Jerry? Because if you do, this is straight-out blackmail.'

'Mr Aspin, this is not blackmail,' said Opitz coolly. 'Blackmail is when someone says they're going to do something bad to you if you don't do a certain thing they desire. I am not saying that. The bad thing that will happen, you'll be doing to yourselves, because if this bank goes down, there's not one of you that won't suffer. You know that better than me. So I'm saying we have a need here, all of us, to get this settled. And I'm saying the federal government will do its bit by offering to help so you can do your bit. We're asking you to make a commercial decision in your own interest which we will support. We're not asking you to put anything at risk. We're going to take the risk away from you.'

'You're asking us to be the agents of a federal government intervention. Well, Madam Secretary, go intervene yourselves.'

'You know we can't do that.'

'And there's a good reason for that. It's called the market. The market makes the call.'

'Let's hold up,' said Rabin. 'You guys all know what happens if this bank goes down.'

'It goes down,' said Aspin.

'Bob,' said Rabin, 'I believe that's what people said the weekend before Lehman went down.'

'Fidelian ain't no Lehman.'

'It's big enough. We can't allow that to happen. Neither can you. I assume each of you has already figured out the likely hit you'll take if Fidelian falls over.'

'As I said,' said Aspin, 'Fidelian ain't no Lehman. Not for Deutsche

BoA, anyway. I think what we have here is political calculation masquerading as economics.'

'No we do not!' retorted Opitz. 'Have you calculated the cost of the systemic economic effects we're going to see if this happens? We have.'

'Blackmail,' said Aspin.

'Bob, I don't think we should use that word,' said Sonny Mello. 'I don't think that's appropriate.'

Aspin gave a disgruntled shrug.

Jerry Rabin glanced at Opitz. She nodded slightly. He looked back at the bankers. 'This is a very serious situation. The president would like to speak to you.'

One of Rabin's aides reached into his briefcase and produced a secure phone.

It took a couple of minutes to get through the White House switchboard to the president. The bankers waited silently. Aspin sat, arms folded across his chest, face set, as the president encouraged them – made it clear that he expected them – to find a way to do a deal.

'Well,' said Aspin when the president had finished. 'Now it's blackmail with icing on top.' He stood up. 'Mr Chairman, Madam Secretary, Deutsche BoA does not believe there's a deal to be done here. You said at the beginning of this meeting that everything that takes place in this room will remain confidential. I assume you will honor that undertaking.'

Rabin nodded.

'Goodbye, then.'

Aspin walked out. Perlman muttered something to himself.

There was silence.

'Okay,' said Sonny Mello. 'Here's what this deal needs to look like. There's a bunch of loans in this business that no one's going to want. We separate them out, the rest is maybe doable at a couple of bucks a share plus the money the Fed's making available. That means we're going to have to put something in to create an entity that can take those loans away. So in the words of one of my illustrious predecessors, let's make it simple. How much would each of us put in to save Fidelian?' He glanced for a moment at a piece of paper on which he had made some calculations. 'From what I've heard, and taking account of the guarantees the government's providing, I'd say ballpark we're looking at three-quarters of a billion each. Who'd agree to put that in?'

No one responded. Rabin looked around the room. The bankers avoided his gaze.

Suddenly he was afraid the rescue operation was going to stop right there.

'We can do the deal any number of ways,' he said quickly. 'Get your teams in. Do the due diligence. We've got the whole weekend.'

TOM KNOWLES SPENT the weekend at the White House. The campaigning engagements that had been organized for him had been canceled. Final polls were coming in from all over the country ahead of the elections on Tuesday. The president spent hours analyzing them with his aides. The chance of getting sixty seats in the Senate was gone. Knowles was just hoping now that the Republicans could hold the numbers they had. The discussions taking place at the New York Fed would have a big bearing on that. Failure to get a deal was too awful to contemplate.

The implications of getting a deal weren't unalloyed joy either. Ed Abrahams had been extremely wary of offering a federal guarantee, but Knowles had been convinced by Rabin and Opitz that there was no way they'd get a deal without it. But it wasn't going to look good, he knew that, and he was going to come under plenty of fire when it came out. Opitz had told him they might be able to keep the details in the public domain vague for a day or two, long enough for the true magnitude of the federal commitment to remain unclear until after the election. But even that wasn't certain. One thing that definitely was certain was that there was no more government money on offer to sweeten the deal. Eighteen billion was the max. Economic implications aside, if the sum got too big, saving the bank would be as bad for him politically as letting it fail.

Opitz updated the president through Saturday. Negotiations continued and the Treasury secretary didn't know which way things would go. The bankers had their teams working overnight but when Opitz rang on Sunday morning there was still no deal. At lunchtime

Opitz called to say that two more of the CEOs had taken their teams and walked out, and it looked as if Ed Loeffler was about to go as well, which would probably be the end of the ballgame. The president got back on the line and managed to keep Loeffler in the room. At seven in the evening Opitz rang again to say there was still no deal and she couldn't say if there would be. Knowles spoke to her at eleven and she said she still couldn't say.

He went to bed not knowing what to expect when he woke up. A call with the Chinese president had been scheduled for early the next morning before the markets opened, in the hope that there would be an offer for Fidelian that Knowles could put to him.

Normally Tom Knowles was pretty good at putting problems aside for the night. But that night he got very little sleep.

When he woke at six o'clock a message from the Treasury secretary was waiting.

24

THE DEAL HAD been finalized around 4am on Sunday. Three banks were in, breaking Fidelian into pieces and spinning off its most toxic loans into a jointly owned entity created for the purpose. The price, although higher than the previous offer that Custler had rejected, still wasn't big. It was nowhere near the number Custler had said his board would require.

At least that gave Knowles something to say. His call with the Chinese president had been scheduled for 7am in Washington, 8pm in Beijing. Gary Rose, Ed Abrahams and Roberta Devlin were in the Oval Office to listen in, together with a Mandarin speaker from the National Security Council staff.

Knowles had met Zhang on four occasions and couldn't say he liked him. His conversations with his Chinese counterpart had confirmed what he had been told to expect of him in briefings. Zhang was unfailingly formal, with a tense and controlled air, and didn't seem to warm up even in private conversation. His demeanor befitted his reputation for ruthlessness and austerity, and he was utterly obdurate in his focus on economic growth. Nothing in any of his conversations ever suggested a softening over democracy, human rights or environmental sustainability. Under Zhang, China had proven as hungry for natural resources and as deaf to demands for meaningful compromise over climate change as under any of his predecessors.

But Zhang's obsession with economic growth was at least an advantage in this circumstance. There was no benefit for the Chinese president in seeing the disruption in the American financial system that the failure of Fidelian could create. China had avoided the worst of '08 and '09 because of the extraordinary domestic stimulus it had injected, but the effect came back to haunt it six years later with inflation, a debt-riddled banking system and spiraling unemployment that had led the regime to the brink of collapse. There was no reason to suppose that Zhang would allow anything that would open the door, even fractionally, for such conditions to recur.

Yet by the same token, Knowles didn't understand why Zhang hadn't done something to save Fidelian already. For all the lip service Chinese officials paid to the transparency of their financial system, it was still an economy where, if the government told a bank to lend, it would lend. If it told its own investment fund to put money into an entity that it owned, or accept a sale, it would do so. The Chinese president couldn't possibly be unaware of the crisis that was unfolding on the American markets. Markets around the world had fallen in synch. Tom Knowles had had calls from a whole clutch of national leaders asking anxiously whether he thought the US was on the brink of significant economic problems, and Susan Opitz had had calls from an even larger number of finance ministers. The whole world was watching.

Maybe Zhang didn't know. Or maybe he didn't know the role his own investment fund was playing. Or maybe he was being told that the offer would keep getting better the longer he waited. The purpose of the call was to make sure he knew the truth about these things. To make absolutely sure the Chinese president knew that the PIC held the cards in this particular deal, that the offer the PIC was about to receive was the last best offer they would get, and to confront him with the prospect that if his investment fund wasn't prepared either to support Fidelian or to sell it, it would set off an economic storm that would quickly find its way across the Pacific from one shore to the other.

THEY EXCHANGED INTRODUCTORY pleasantries through their interpreters. Zhang's tone was as formal as ever.

Trying to strike a positive note from the start, Knowles initiated a brief discussion of the nuclear decontamination mission in the former North Korea, in which the US and China were participating side by side as members of the UN oversight panel. Bob Livingstone, informed of the possibility of an upcoming call to Zhang, had given Knowles a list of other issues to raise with the Chinese president and a series of talking points on each one, but Gary Rose, after vetting them, had ruled them out. Almost all involved some degree of conflict between the two countries and discussing them would have set the wrong tone for the conversation, or given Zhang the impression that Knowles was proposing a trade on one of them in exchange for help with Fidelian.

'Mr President,' said Knowles after a couple of minutes, 'I would like to turn to a matter in which I think there may be an opportunity for further cooperation between us.'

'Perhaps we should discuss the situation in South Africa,' came back the reply. 'We must find a more effective way of encouraging a restoration of the constitutional position in the country without being seen to impose our wills as foreign powers.'

'That's true, President Zhang, we must not impose our will. On the other hand the people of South Africa have a constitution and they deserve to be able to live under its terms.'

'There are different ways to do this,' said Zhang.

Knowles glanced at Rose. The national security advisor shook his head.

'There is another issue which I would like to discuss with you,' said Knowles. 'An urgent matter. This relates to a bank in the United States that is currently in a position of some trouble.'

'Yes. I have heard of it. That is Fidelian Bank, isn't it?'

'That's right. When I say it's an American bank, it has global operations.'

'Yes,' said Zhang. 'I am aware of this. I believe it has a banking license in China.'

Knowles raised an eyebrow. Not only had Zhang been briefed, he was happy to let Knowles know it.

'There is a very large ownership in this bank by one of your state investment funds,' said Knowles.

'Our investment funds have many holdings.'

'I would like to be completely frank with you, President Zhang. This is a very confidential and delicate matter. Fidelian Bank is on the verge of bankruptcy. My understanding is that its shareholders, led by your investment fund, are unwilling to put more money into the bank.'

'This would be a commercial decision,' said Zhang. 'I have no knowledge of the commercial decisions made by any of our state funds.'

'I understand that. Our understanding is that this fund is not willing to put more capital into the bank – which is its legitimate commercial decision, as you say – but is also not prepared to receive a reasonable price from other parties who are prepared to take on the business with its liabilities and run it in an orderly fashion.'

'I have no knowledge of the commercial decisions you are describing.'

'I'm not suggesting–'

'If they have not accepted the price–' Zhang's interpreter paused. The two interpreters had talked over each other.

'Please, go ahead, Mr President,' said Knowles.

The Chinese leader invited Knowles to speak.

'No, please go ahead,' said Knowles again.

There was silence. Knowles waited impatiently. He disliked these four-way phone conversations with two principals and two interpreters. Half the time you either had two people speaking together or no one saying anything.

'I was saying that if they have not accepted the price,' began Zhang again, 'then I must assume there is a good reason for this which I would not question. The managers for our state funds are very competent people. The funds are mandated to make the best investments on behalf of the Chinese people. That is their obligation. President Knowles, let me assure you there is nothing else that we ask them to do.'

'I understand that,' said Knowles. 'It is possible, however, that managing this fund from such a distance means they do not see all of the issues and implications of their decisions. The decision they seem to be making over Fidelian Bank has a number of very significant implications. These go far beyond the normal implications of such a decision.'

'I repeat, President Knowles, this would be a commercial decision.'

Knowles paused for a moment. He knew this was the line the Chinese president would take, but he wondered if he was getting through at all.

'President Zhang,' he said, 'I want you to know there is an offer to buy Fidelian Bank. Mr Rabin, who is the head of our Federal Reserve Bank in New York, has helped put together a deal from three other banks to buy the operation. This deal was put together last night and I believe it has not yet been put to the management of Fidelian Bank, but will be within the next hour. Fidelian Bank is aware that an offer will be coming and the CEO has arranged to speak with members of the board. I would strongly urge Fidelian Bank's board to accept it.'

'I am sure they will consider it.'

'President Zhang, it is not as much as they have asked for. In fact, it's quite a lot lower. In our view what they have asked for, to be perfectly honest, is unrealistic. What this deal offers is the very, very best that they will get. I personally intervened to make sure that this offer was at the very top of the range. Above it, in fact. When anyone looks at this deal, they should be aware it isn't a bargaining position. It's the full and final offer and there's nothing more available.'

'President Knowles, thank you for this information.'

There was silence. Knowles looked at Rose. Rose shrugged slightly.

'President Zhang, can I ask you to pass that message on to the responsible people within the investment fund? I believe they have two seats on the board. This is an urgent need. The deal will be communicated within the hour. Fidelian Bank is required to make an announcement about its position. This deal must be done before the announcement is made. It needs to be done this morning, before the market opens here in New York.'

'I understand from what you say that the offer will be communicated through the normal channels of the bank. If this is a final offer I would encourage your officials to make sure that Fidelian Bank understands this,' replied Zhang.

'They will do that, but I am concerned that the officials within your investment funds will not see this offer for what it is. I am very concerned that they understand how important it is to treat this offer seriously. This is a final offer. Mr President, would it be possible for you to ensure that they understand this?'

Knowles waited, listening closely. Everyone in the room gazed at the speakerphone.

'President Knowles, I do not interfere with the commercial decisions of the state funds.'

Knowles closed his eyes.

'However, the state funds must consider the realities of the world.'

Knowles glanced at Rose and Abrahams. They were both frowning, trying to decipher what Zhang meant.

'Mr President,' said Knowles, 'that is very helpful. There are important realities to consider. Let me say this as clearly as I can. The failure of this bank will lead to considerable uncertainty and disruption within not only our markets, but in global markets. I think this would have a severe effect not only on America but on China as well. We are all interconnected.'

'We are interconnected. That's true.'

'I am concerned that this might be the start of a serious loss of confidence and we only have to look back a few years to see where that got us.'

There was silence. Knowles suddenly wondered whether Zhang thought he was referring to the Chinese troubles of 2014. He had meant 2008.

'As I said,' said Zhang, 'we must all consider the realities.'

What exactly did Zhang mean by that? What was he referring to? Did he want to come back to the discussion about South Africa? Knowles glanced at Rose. The national security advisor shook his head.

Knowles decided to pretend he didn't apprehend anything but the most obvious inference. 'Again, I can only stress that both our countries will suffer badly if the board of Fidelian Bank doesn't accept this offer. Much of the progress we have made in the last few years will be reversed. Can I take it, Mr President, that you will make sure your officials understand the seriousness of the offer?'

'They will understand.'

'And can I stress the urgency of this?'

'The urgency is understood.'

'And the fact that this is a final offer. There will not be another opportunity. This is the last one.'

'I understand.'

'Thank you, Mr President.'

'President Knowles, is there anything else you wish to talk about?'

'Not today, President Zhang. Is there anything else you wish to talk about?'

'This phone call was at your request.'

Knowles was silent for a moment, wondering whether he had done enough. This was his last chance. But he had said what he had meant to say. Saying it again wouldn't help.

'Thank you, President Zhang. Thank you for your time. I hope that you will be able to help in this matter. It's important to talk when we can help each other.'

'I agree. I look forward to talking with you again soon.'

'Thank you, President Zhang. Good night.'

'And good morning to you, President Knowles.'

Knowles put down the phone.

He looked around. Ed Abrahams took a deep breath and blew it out slowly.

'Well, that's done,' said Knowles. 'I hope he understood that this was the absolute, final offer.'

'You told him,' said Abrahams. 'What else can you do?'

'What happens now?'

'I'll call Susan and let her know you had the conversation,' said Roberta Devlin. 'She'll call Custler to release the offer.'

'And then?'

'The Stock Exchange knows there's an announcement coming. We've vetted the statements the three banks are going to release. Josh is working on a last draft of your statement.'

'When do I make it?'

'As soon as we know Fidelian accepts.'

25

PRESIDENT ZHANG PUT down the phone. His advisor, Qin Jiwei, who had been present at the conversation, looked over his notes as the interpreter left the room.

'President Knowles is a worried man,' said Zhang.

'Yes,' said Qin. 'The question is, what is he really worried about?'

Zhang nodded. 'Go and get Bai.'

Qin got up to get the finance minister, who was waiting in an adjacent office.

Zhang waited, going over the conversation in his mind. He had no desire to help President Knowles with any domestic political difficulties he might be having. The way the American leader had unilaterally launched his initiative in Uganda had angered him, and for that reason alone he would not have been predisposed to help. Then there was the situation in South Africa, which was an issue of wholly different magnitude. In South Africa, if China was able to get its way, it would show its ability to step into disputes outside its own region as the Americans had done for so long, the mark of a true world power. Internationally, this would create a new context for negotiations on the great global issues of the world, a context in which China would have immeasurably more weight, the kind of influence that had been promised after the western downturn of 2008 and '09 but which had never materialized. At home, it would show that the true source of China's strength in the world was its economic influence – the reason the South African government was listening to China – and not its military force.

This was important to Zhang. Four years on from the disturbances of 2014, the three men who emerged in power retained their positions. Zhang himself had the loyalty of the internal security forces that he had led during the crackdown. Much of the army, Zhang knew, would side with General Fan if it came to a showdown. Defense Minister Xu drew support from parts of the military that did not back Fan, in particular elite units within the air force and certain naval elements. In this triangle, Xu was the waverer. The weakest of the three, the defense minister had no prospect of overcoming the other two, but could swing the outcome decisively one way or the other depending on where he chose to place his support. For four years he had played a game of sitting on the fence, holding on to his own position by keeping the two other men competing for his backing.

This couldn't go on. For the first couple of years after the disturbances it had been possible. But by now, Zhang was thinking about the group of leaders who would succeed him, and so was Fan. To put their own men in place and give them time to prepare for power, they must first have undivided power themselves. It was obvious that Fan was no more ready to tolerate the situation than he was. The attitude of Fan's loyalists in the army was becoming almost unbearably arrogant. Incidents took place when they confronted men from the security forces. The struggle was coming to a head.

Each man was battling for loyalty from groups in the regime outside their own core of supporters. Fan had no concept of China's strategy to offer but the idea of greater and greater military strength. For Zhang, the failure of Fidelian Bank came at a fortuitous time. The supplication of the US president to save the bank gave him another way – like the South Africa situation – of showing that his way was the more promising, that economic strength gave China the ability to exercise power, even against the United States, in a way that military force could never match. But this opportunity created its own pressure. If Zhang gave in now to the American president and did as he asked, Fan would use the episode to show that China's economic power was illusory or that he, Zhang, was too weak to wield it.

But he would not put China's economic stability at risk. If it was necessary to help the American president in order to protect China's economy, he would do it. He would have to find a way to deal with whatever Fan threw at him.

Qin came back with Bai.

'There will be an offer,' Zhang said to the finance minister.

Bai nodded.

'It will not be as much as Hu asked for.'

'How much will it be?'

'Lower,' said Qin. 'Much lower.'

'President Knowles said there will not be a higher offer,' added Zhang. 'This is the final offer.'

'Minister Bai,' said Qin, 'would you believe that?'

'I did not hear the conversation,' said Bai pointedly. He had wanted to sit in on the call.

Qin shrugged. 'Knowles is so concerned that he rings himself, and yet he cannot find a few more billions to meet our request? President Zhang, put yourself in his place. Would you call and have nothing in reserve? If he is really so worried, he will still find a way. As long as he gives them enough money, the Wall Street banks will do what he says. He will sit them down and they will come up with a deal. It is in their own interest.'

Zhang frowned. His understanding of the way the economy functioned in the United States was almost non-existent. He had worked in the security apparatus for his entire career. If it had not been for the 2014 disturbances, a man such as him would never have become president. He relied almost totally on Qin and Ambassador Zhu for his understanding of the United States.

'The more worried he is, the more certain it is,' said Qin. 'If he had *not* called you, then I would say he has no alternative. If we give in to him now, all we are doing is saving his face with Wall Street. We lose the extra money that Wall Street would pay.'

The money at stake wasn't the issue, as all three men knew.

'So we should say no?' said Zhang.

'Of course. Let him go back to Wall Street and lose his face there.'

'How does that help us?'

'Then he is weaker. He will rescue the bank at a high price and everyone will say he has spent money to save his friends on Wall Street. This will not help him in the elections. He is weaker if the Republicans do badly.'

Zhang nodded.

'And everyone will see,' added Qin. 'Fan and Xu and all their people.'

'What do you think?' Zhang asked Bai.

'I am not so sure as Minister Qin that the president will save this bank if we reject the offer.'

'Bai, look what happened the last time!' said Qin.

'If he said it is a final offer, perhaps it is a final offer. He may not be able to offer more. But if it is, that is because if the bank fails, he does not think it will lead to a collapse. Otherwise, I would agree with Minister Qin, he would save it.'

'So are we saying something different?' said Qin.

Bai shook his head. 'I think we are saying the same thing for different reasons. This is political. It is entirely political. It's about the elections. Why else do a deal so quickly? Why be in such a rush to announce?'

'The bank must make an announcement,' said Zhang. 'He said it must make it before the American markets open today.'

'And tomorrow is their election. If he doesn't have a deal, when the market opens in New York, it will fall. If the market falls, he will do badly in the election. Therefore Knowles wants an announcement of a deal. Well, if he wants an announcement, I agree with Minister Qin. Let him make Wall Street pay the top price and let him put money into the deal and let the world see what he has paid.'

'But if it is his final offer?' said Zhang.

'What is the effect of such a bankruptcy? On the election, considerable. But beyond that?' Bai shrugged. 'For a few days there will be panic. But this is not like 2008. The Federal Reserve keeps saying the system is fundamentally sound, and that also is our view. After a few days, the panic will stop. There will be no great impact. It is because it is these few days when they have their election that Knowles is so worried. If it was next week, he would not call you.'

'If there is a great impact, we too will suffer.'

'There will not be.'

'Understand me, Bai,' said Zhang, 'I do not want to create a collapse in the United States. I do not want any such thing. If there is a risk of such a thing, I will take this offer.'

'I understand, President Zhang. President Knowles does not want a collapse either. That is why he will not let this bank fail.'

'I thought you said if this bank fails there will not be a collapse,' said Zhang, pouncing on the apparent contradiction in Bai's remarks.

'Correct, there will not. There will be a panic. A few days. That will have no impact on us. And that is if Knowles does not save it. But I agree with Minister Qin. He will probably save it because this panic will make his party lose the election.'

'See?' said Qin.

'The difference is, what I am saying, is that if he does not save it, we have a small panic, but not a collapse.' Bai smiled. 'A panic, President Zhang. A short panic during his election.'

Zhang glanced at Qin. The other man nodded.

A phone vibrated in Bai's pocket. He took it out and read the message.

'This is from Vice-Minister Hu,' he said. 'He has received the offer.'

'What is it?' said Zhang.

Bai gave him the number.

There was silence.

'What time do the American markets open?' asked Zhang.

Bai told him. Zhang looked at his watch.

Zhang Yong liked to make his decisions alone. He asked both men to leave the room and wait outside.

Qin seemed sure that Knowles could get other banks to pay the sum that Hu demanded. Zhang himself was not so certain. Knowles' words on the phone had not sounded like those of a man who had an alternative. But even if he did not save the bank, Bai said there would be no collapse. A short panic, but not a collapse. That would be enough to explain the tone of seriousness, if not desperation, that had been in Knowles' voice. He feared a big loss at his election. But there was nothing for China to fear in this, or in a short panic. And why should the American president expect his assistance? It was one thing to deliberately set out to harm someone, another merely to decline to help. He had not set out to harm. The circumstances had arisen fortuitously. And helping, it turned out, would harm Zhang himself. It would give ammunition to Fan. Whereas declining to help would show Xu and those who were undecided that China's real strength lay in its economic power, not in the missiles that Fan kept building.

But even Bai could be wrong. That was the one thing that worried him. A panic could turn into a collapse. There was a risk.

Zhang was not a great gambler. He preferred a certainty to a risk.

Yet it was also a certainty that he would have to find a way, soon, to deal with General Fan.

And Bai had seemed very sure.

Zhang thought about it.

He looked at his watch.

He had to make a decision, he knew. Time was passing. The American markets would soon be open.

26

THE ANNOUNCEMENT CAME just after eight-thirty. Ed Grey was on the phone to a client in Paris, feet up on his desk, gazing out the window at the office block opposite. Tony Evangelou opened his door and looked in. Ed turned and shooed him away. Tony pointed to one of the screens on Ed's wall. Ed looked. The sound was muted, but a headline on the screen told him all he needed to know.

He stared.

His client was talking, but Ed wasn't listening. 'Gilles,' he said, 'I'm going to have to call you back. Gilles, I'm sorry, I'll get back to you.'

The headline was still there at the bottom of the screen.

FIDELIAN BANK FILES FOR BANKRUPTCY.

Evangelou was watching him.

Grey sat. He was numb. All he could think about was that he had closed out his short positions a week earlier. For a moment, the knowledge of what he had done completely froze his brain.

He got up and left his office.

A tense, eerie stillness hung over the funds desk. The managers and analysts were staring at a screen high up on the wall above the room. An interview was going on between an anchor and a reporter on a street somewhere in the financial district. A minute later it cut to a pundit in the studio.

'Anyone said why they're doing this?' asked Grey.

'Writedowns on developing markets businesses,' said Maria Lomax. 'And a bunch of other stuff. They can't raise the capital to cover it.'

'Twenty-three billion,' said Boris Malevsky. He was pale.

Grey looked at him. '*Twenty-three?*'

'The Chinese should be giving it to them,' said Malevsky. 'I don't understand this.'

The chairman of the Fed was on the screen. Ron Strickland looked worn out, haggard.

'This is a serious development that will doubtless have short-term consequences for our banking system. But the point is, we have a fundamentally sound system, we have a wind-up facility in place to deal with this bank in an orderly fashion, and we stand ready to put liquidity into the market to ensure that the effects of the failure of this one bank are contained and that we don't have a credit squeeze as a result. This is one bank. Let me repeat that, this is one bank. This is not a repeat of 2008. We do not have a string of other banks where we're going to be seeing problems. I'm very confident of that and the safeguards, in any case, are all in place. We've learned an awful lot–'

'Shut the fuck up!' yelled Evangelou. He tore off a shoe and threw it at the screen. 'Who the fuck's gonna believe a word you say?'

Grey's mind tried to process what he was hearing. How could the Fed not have known what was going to happen? This was the first bankruptcy of a major investment bank since Lehman Brothers in 2008. It had become an article of faith that that would never be allowed to happen again. The fatal error with Lehman was that the government had refused to provide support to ensure that a rescue could be arranged. When Wall Street had refused to rescue Lehman without it, the government had stepped back and let it fail. The unwritten rule was that would never happen again.

Grey looked at one of the screens on the desk showing stock prices. One by one, like bubbles popping, the numbers were turning red.

Suddenly he was conscious of all the eyes in the room looking in his direction.

They were in the realm of a vanishingly low probability event. Anything could happen. His mind began to race. The Fed was almost certainly going to drop interest rates, probably that morning. Bond prices would rise. The dollar would fall. This was going to affect just about every asset class they owned, in developed and developing markets, in equities, in bonds, in currency, in derivatives of all kinds.

'You,' he said to a couple of analysts. 'Work the model. Assume rates go down twenty-five basis points, fifty, a hundred. Take the Dow down ten per cent, twenty, fifty. Get the correlations.'

He thought a moment longer. Whatever happened longer term – and right now, that meant days – just about every market in the world except bonds was going to fall over the next few hours. Anything you could offload now, you'd be able to buy back cheaper tomorrow.

Every manager in the room was watching him. The three guys who worked the trading desk, executing trades as the managers instructed them, were waiting, phones in hand.

'Whatever you've got,' said Grey, 'sell.'

But he wasn't the only one who was saying it. Out of thousands of offices just like Red River's, from thousands of portfolio managers, a tsunami-sized wave of sell orders was roaring towards the market.

ED GREY SPENT the next couple of hours on the phone, talking to whoever he could talk to, trying to find out what he could discover. So was everyone else. No one knew anything. No one could understand why a bailout hadn't been arranged. Rumors were flying through the market about the full extent of Fidelian's losses and other banks that were under threat. A number of banks had been forced to issue statements denying that they faced a liquidity crunch, which did about as much as it always did to reassure the markets. Their stocks were down fifteen, twenty per cent and falling. As he spoke, Grey kept one eye on the prices on the screens in his office. He watched them plunging. Even with only half a mind on the numbers, he figured he would have been a billion to the good if he hadn't closed out his short positions the previous week. Now he was almost exclusively long in a market that was falling faster than a brick. He thought of the four hundred fifty million in cash he had realized from the closure of the Fidelian trade and could almost visualize it, in his mind, draining away, like sand out of an hourglass, when the banks began calling the margins. Any minute now the calls were going to start coming in. His chief financial officer was in and out of his office a half dozen times as he tracked the positions.

And then came the second shock of the morning, another headline on a screen.

FIDELIAN BAILOUT REJECTED CLAIMS ANONYMOUS SOURCE.

Grey got off the phone and turned up the volume.

'... but it certainly seems that way,' a female reporter was saying. 'The claim was apparently made by an anonymous source on Wall

Street who claims to have had access to individuals personally involved in the negotiation, Dick.'

The picture cut back to the studio anchor. 'And when was this, Andrea?'

'Over the weekend. Apparently a meeting took place here in New York at the Fed headquarters involving Fed officials and Wall Street's most powerful CEOs and a conclusion was reached in the early hours this morning. Sounds like a classic Wall Street rescue operation, Dick.'

'Which didn't come off?'

'Apparently not. According to this source, considerable pressure was placed on the bankers to come up with an acceptable solution and the offer that eventuated is said to have been quite generous, given the state of Fidelian's finances. We believe there was involvement on the administration side at the very highest level. And yet despite–'

'Andrea, sorry, I don't mean to interrupt. When you say the very highest level, are you saying the president was involved in this?'

'It doesn't get any higher, Dick.'

'But are we saying that happened? Andrea, is that what this source is telling us?'

'We don't have a confirmation or denial of that from the White House. But it does seem that there was significant political involvement in this and that would hardly be surprising given the timing of this event. The midterms are tomorrow and it's impossible to imagine there won't be a huge impact from this, Dick.'

'We'll look at the political ramifications later, but is there anything more you can tell us right now about the way this evolved?'

'The package was apparently rejected by Fidelian Bank shortly before it filed for bankruptcy this morning.'

Ed Grey watched with a kind of horrified fascination. He had known there must have been a rescue effort. It was impossible to imagine the Fed hadn't had any inkling of what was about to happen and that the administration wouldn't have tried to rescue the situation. And yet the rescue deal had been rejected.

'Have we had any word from Fidelian Bank about this, Andrea?'

'No, Dick, we haven't. CEO William Custler has been keeping a low profile today.'

'More of an invisible profile as I understand it, Andrea.'

'I don't believe anyone's had the opportunity to speak with him. We had the bankruptcy announcement from the Fidelian head of communications earlier today and that's about all as far as I'm aware. There's been no response from Fidelian to this latest allegation, although we certainly hope to be able to get that as soon as we can, Dick.'

'And is the Fed telling us anything, Andrea?'

'Not as yet, Dick.'

Grey surfed the channels. It was the same on all of them. He put the screen on mute and thought about what he had heard, watching a reporter silently mouthing his remarks. If this was to be believed, the CEO of Fidelian Bank had turned down a rescue offer in favor of filing for bankruptcy. Yet he and his board had a fiduciary duty to get the best deal for his shareholders. Grey frowned. How low was the offer if they were better off taking bankruptcy? That didn't make sense. Surely the administration wouldn't have allowed an offer that low to go forward. Not if they wanted to see a rescue done. Not on the day before the midterms. Every Republican candidate in the country would pay for it.

Anyway, this was a bank. An investment bank. A significant one. It couldn't be allowed to go bust. A deal had to be done.

Something didn't add up. Assuming the offer wasn't insultingly low, who would have rejected it?

Suddenly Ed Grey remembered Susan Opitz's words on the phone when they had spoken. 'Who's lending the stock?' she had asked. 'Who's lending it, Ed?'

Grey felt a tingle down his spine. He knew who the major shareholder in Fidelian Bank was.

He called in Tony Evangelou.

'What's happening?' he asked.

Evangelou shook his head. 'If you can find me a buyer out there I'd like to know about it.'

'Listen, I want you to get a couple of analysts on something. Take our US stocks and get them to give me a list of every one that has significant shareholdings by sovereign investment funds.'

'That'll probably be just about all of them.'

'Let's find out if it is. And how much they own. And Tony, make sure we find out which ones are owned by the Chinese.'

27

TOM KNOWLES HAD never known an election day like it. A vote held within hours of a major crisis breaking, without enough time for anyone to sit back and ask what it really meant, how serious it really was, how bad it was going to get. An election in the grip of panic. The headlines that morning had been unbelievable. Markets were falling. The press was hysterical.

Knowles spent the day in meetings with his economic advisors and senior Republican politicians and on the phone to foreign leaders. Markets were taking a hit around the globe and the confidence laboriously reconstructed in the wake of the Chinese disturbances of 2014 was evaporating as if it had never returned. He gave the same message to all the foreign leaders he spoke to. Fidelian was an isolated instance. The system was sound. Once the markets saw that, the decline would be arrested. He needed them to give that message to their own countries. The more united they could be in rejecting the idea that this was another 2008, the sooner this crisis would start to resolve.

But that would do nothing to halt the bloodbath that was being perpetrated in voting booths across the nation that day. The polls from the last week were meaningless now. Only night would tell how bad it was.

In New York, Marion Ellman was scheduled to give her first report to the Security Council on the progress of Jungle Peace. She read the words that had emerged from the tortuous joint drafting process by the Pentagon and the State Department. Progress was steady, interdiction was solid. A number of combatants had emerged from the jungle and surrendered, and were being held in Ugandan detention camps while their cases were assessed. Depredations against the civilian population in the surrounding areas had declined markedly. She gave figures to prove it. The Security Council ambassadors listened quietly. There were few questions. It was as if everyone in the room was aware that the great events of the day were taking place outside the building, in the trading rooms on Wall Street, in voting booths in school halls and municipal buildings and community centers across the country.

Sixteen Manhattan blocks away, Ed Grey spent the day trying to staunch the hemorrhage in his funds. His traders struggled to push money out of stocks into bonds, the prices of which were rocketing as investors fled equities. He worked the phones to his major clients, one after the other, dissuading them from redeeming their investments, reminding them that Red River always took a six to twelve month view of the market, telling them they would merely realize losses they could avoid if they redeemed now instead of holding on for the market to recover. He tried to keep the desperation out of his voice. He spoke to the banks throughout the day, beseeching them to hold off on margin calls that would force him to sell even more assets into a falling market. There were amazing buying opportunities as the markets marked down good stocks along with bad in their general panic but Grey was in no position to take advantage of them. He watched them floating by in front of his eyes, as if on a river of blood, unable to touch them.

THAT NIGHT, TOM KNOWLES was due as guest of honor at a dinner for Republican Party grandees. When the event had first been arranged, in the days when the Republicans had looked to be cruising to their first sixty-plus majority in the Senate since 2004, it had been conceived as an election-night celebration. Instead, it was going to be a wake. Many of the attendees had voted in their home states that morning and were flying in to be at the dinner with the prospect of a loss that appeared likely to put the number of Republican senators down towards fifty. There was even an outside chance the party would lose its majority.

At six o'clock that evening, Tom Knowles sat down in the Oval Office with Josh Bentner, his chief speechwriter, and Ed Abrahams to look over the speech he would be giving.

Bentner had spent just about the whole day on it. The speech was meant to be only about fifteen minutes long but even for a speechwriter as talented as him it was a challenge. He had shown Abrahams five drafts during the day and each time it wasn't right. Knowles had considered canceling his attendance, but Ed Abrahams was dead set against that. He thought it would be seen as an act of cowardice that would seriously damage him within the party. But how much responsibility should he take? How much blame should he volunteer to shoulder? The truth was, Knowles felt that his responsibility for the implosion of Fidelian and the collapse it had inflicted on the markets over the last couple of days was minimal, if there was any responsibility there at all. There was no failure of regulation, no executive dereliction. He didn't feel there was much more he could have done. No one could control the markets, not even the president. But the people who would be sitting in the room that night wouldn't be just any audience. Their opinions, their attitudes, the willingness to put their personal prestige, political networks, time and money behind alternative candidates would play a big part in determining the kind of challenge he would face for the nomination in two years' time. If this night had delivered sixty Senate seats, he would likely have got the nomination unopposed, a slam dunk, as Ed Abrahams liked to say. It wasn't going to be a slam dunk now.

They needed to see humility. It takes a lot to turn a party against an incumbent president, but perceived arrogance in the face of defeat is one of the things that will do it. They also needed to see that he envisaged a way out. If a movement wasn't going to start right now at the highest level of the party to put forward an alternative candidate for the nomination, they needed to feel strongly that in six months' time the turmoil on the markets was going to look like a transient blip, not the turning point that ended eleven successive quarters of economic growth. Acknowledge some level of responsibility without tainting yourself as an electoral liability. Give a strong, positive view of the future without trivializing what had had happened that very day.

He picked up the latest draft of the speech and began to work on it with Abrahams and Bentner.

At six o'clock, Marion Ellman was at the traditional Election Day cocktail party given by the American UN representative for foreign ambassadors. She mingled dutifully, feeling like she needed the task of hosting the event about as much as she needed a trip to the dentist.

François Dubigny engaged her in one of his flirtatious disquisitions. She excused herself to go talk to the new Saudi Arabian ambassador. Out of the corner of her eye she saw a huddle of Latin American ambassadors. She thought a couple of them were smirking at her. The party was a trial, to say the least.

Across town, Ed Grey was still in his office, still on the phone, and would be for hours. Red-eyed, exhausted, for him, election day was a battle for survival.

28

TOM KNOWLES RODE back to the White House with Sarah, who had been with him at the dinner.

The president's relationship with his wife was pretty much a working relationship, had been for years. There had been infidelities, thankfully with women who turned out to be discreet even when the affairs were over. But Sarah had found out about them. At one point they had considered divorce, come right to the brink. Fortunately they stepped back. It wasn't impossible that he might have become governor of Nevada as a single, divorced man with a history of infidelity, but it was inconceivable that he would have made it anywhere near the White House. Sarah herself had causes she cared for, and being first lady of Nevada, and then of the country, gave her opportunities she wouldn't have had otherwise. She worked tirelessly on behalf of returned war veterans. She campaigned for rehabilitation programs for convicted drug offenders. Tom respected her for her work. He respected her for lots of things. It was possible that after they left the White House they would get divorced. On the other hand, they might not. They had settled into a mutually convenient coexistence that sometimes, not often, flared into something warmer.

'I thought your speech was good,' she said. 'You hit the right notes.'

Knowles smiled ruefully. The mood at the dinner had been more wake than post-mortem, but that would come soon enough. People hadn't said what they were thinking – not to his face, anyway. Over the next few days Ed Abrahams would work his networks to gauge the way reaction in the party was really developing.

They went separate ways at the White House, Sarah to the residence floor, Knowles to the West Wing, where he found Abrahams, Ruiz-Kellerman and Devlin all sitting in Roberta's office, watching the results coming in. The remains of pizzas and sodas and coffees were all over the room.

He settled into a chair.

'Where are we?' he said.

'Logan's conceded in Florida,' said Devlin.

'What about Morrison?'

'He's not going to win. Buckley's safe.'

'Ogden?'

Devlin shook her head.

'Looks like Anders in Ohio is safe,' said Ruiz-Kellerman.

'Were we worried about Anders?'

'After yesterday, we were.'

'Jesus Christ. What about the House?'

'That's borderline. The networks are calling it four to five seats either way. From the polls I've seen, I agree. It's too close to call.'

Knowles let out a long breath. He looked at Abrahams. 'This is bad.'

Abrahams nodded. 'This is fucking bad.'

The president watched a bunch of pundits on the screen equivocating over who was going to control the House of Representatives.

Abrahams had spoken to Jack Harris, national chairman of the Republican Party.

'What did he say?' asked Knowles.

'Nothing. What could he say? He'll call you tomorrow.'

There was silence. The atmosphere in the room was grim.

'Well, who needs sixty seats in the Senate?' said Abrahams. 'It'd just give Hotchkiss another lever to pull. He'd threaten to vote against us and pull his little band of acolytes every time he thought it would do him good.'

'He already does that,' said Devlin.

Abrahams smiled. 'True.'

'He's going to love this. He's going to fucking love this.'

'I think we should assume his campaign starts today.'

'So does ours,' said Abrahams. 'We've got two years to put this right. As far as Hotchkiss is concerned, we paint him as a rebel. Disloyal. He'll go overboard. That's what he's like. Every time he makes trouble, we slam him.'

'Ed,' said Devlin, 'his constituency wants him to be a rebel. That's what they like about him. All those redneck anti-abortion gunslinging evangelical bigots don't have any problem at all with him bringing our programs down.'

Abrahams laughed. 'Roberta, you're talking about the soul of our party! Look, when we had fifty-eight in the Senate he could play his games and it didn't make a difference one way or the other. Now he does that and our programs fail. He does that, he's got to pay a price. In their gut, Republicans hate disloyalty. His constituency might like it but everyone else won't. Now, if he was a Democrat, they'd all love him for it. Not us. That's how we get him.'

Tom Knowles stared disconsolately at the screen. 'We got any good news about Uganda?' he said suddenly. 'Every day I get these reports and nothing's happening. Weren't we going to get some good news?'

'Just as well we didn't. Anything we got would have got lost in the noise of the last couple of days.'

'We could use some now.' Knowles looked at Abrahams. 'Can we do something about that?'

'I'll talk to Gary.'

The pundits on the screen kept pontificating. There were four of them from various parts of the country on a split screen and the anchor was trying to keep control of the discussion.

'Did anyone talk to Custler to find out why they didn't take the offer?' asked Knowles.

'Susan's talking to him. It's obvious though, isn't it? The markets worked it out. The Chinese let it fail. You look at what the market did today. Anything they could find with big Chinese government owner-ship, they dumped.'

'Is that what happened?'

Devlin nodded. 'Serves the Chinese right. Crashes the value of their holdings.'

'What happened in Shanghai?'

'Their market was down four per cent.'

'Their investment funds will be buying to keep prices up,' said Abrahams. 'It's an unwritten law. Shanghai never falls by more than four per cent in a day.'

Knowles still couldn't understand why the Chinese president had

refused to step in. Having to stem the fall in Shanghai by state intervention, however he tried to conceal it, did him no favors.

'Zhang could definitely have made the PIC do what he wanted,
right? Hell, I got the toughest bankers on Wall Street to make an offer
for a bank none of them wanted to touch. And I told him what would
happen. I told him there was no more. You heard me tell him.'

'Maybe he's trying to send a message,' said Devlin.

'What's the message? Don't call me up? Don't disturb me after
9pm?' Knowles paused. He found that suddenly he was fuming. 'That
guy, I tell you, I just hate dealing with that guy. If there's one leader
I'd like to send an exploding cigar to, it's Zhang. Anyone ever seen
Zhang laugh? It's like they've botoxed him round the mouth.'

Ed Abrahams chuckled.

'Probably wouldn't smoke the damn thing anyway even if I did
send him one,' muttered Knowles.

Abrahams laughed out loud.

'I wish you were the guy who had to talk to him, Ed. I'd hand it
over to you gladly.'

'I don't think President Zhang would appreciate that.'

'I don't think he would either. I don't think he appreciates
anything.' Knowles looked at the screen, which was showing a
schematic of the projected seats in the House of Representatives with
a surge of blue and the shrinking Republican majority in red.
Knowles stabbed his finger at it. 'You know, you're forced to the
conclusion that this was a deliberate, carefully planned conspiracy to
make that happen.'

'It's an interference with our democratic process,' said Abrahams,
utterly serious now.

'It is. It's outrageous.'

'Outrageous.'

'What are we going to do about it?'

'That's something we need to figure out.'

There was silence.

'Do we have any idea who leaked about Fidelian refusing the
offer?' asked Ruiz-Kellerman.

'It was always going to come out,' said Abrahams. 'Enough people
knew about it and the Street would have figured out there must have

been a rescue attempt. The really damaging leak would be if they knew we'd spoken to Zhang. That would make us look bad. First, we have to go calling a foreign leader for help, then he refuses to give it.'

Knowles nodded. If that came out, it would make him look terrible.

29

ON THE MORNING after the election, with the sense of political turmoil growing by the hour, Marion Ellman was pulled out of her regular staff meeting for a conference call with Bob Livingstone, who was on a visit to the Philippines. Doug Havering, the deputy secretary of state, was on the phone from Washington, together with Steve Haskell in Beijing. A National Security Council meeting had been scheduled for Friday to discuss the events leading up to the Fidelian bankruptcy and Bob Livingstone wanted to put a State Department paper to the president ahead of the meeting.

Marion didn't know why a matter like that would be an issue for the National Security Council or why State should be called on to give a view. Within the State Department, only Livingstone and the deputy secretary knew what had taken place between Tom Knowles and the Chinese president in the hours before Fidelian failed. Five minutes after the call started, when Livingstone had given his summary of events, Marion knew as well.

By the time she got home that night, having been waylaid by the British and Dutch ambassadors in a corridor of the UN building for an impromptu meeting on the South Africa resolution, Daniel was asleep and Ella was just about ready for bed. Marion read to her a little before she went to sleep. Then she checked her email and found a draft paper for the president in her inbox. She wouldn't get any other time to look at it so she sat down to work on it right away with a warmed-up dinner at her desk. By the time she was done another couple of hours had gone by.

Dave was in bed, reading a book.

He looked up as she came in. 'You done?'

She nodded and sat down on the bed. 'I'm beat.'

'You know our net worth fell another ten per cent today.'

'Really?'

'Yeah. That makes us around twenty-five per cent down on the week. Not bad. I thought your boss might want to know. What's his name again?' Dave clicked his fingers. 'Knowles? Somebody Knowles.'

'I'll be sure to tell him,' said Marion.

'You know, you should read this.' Dave closed the book and tossed it across to her.

It was Joel Ehrenreich's book, which had arrived a couple of days earlier. Marion had left it on her desk, fully intending to look at it, but hadn't had a moment.

'It's good,' said Dave.

'Have you read it?'

'Parts. You should read chapter 5.'

'Is that one of the ones Joel mentioned?'

Dave shook his head. 'Trust me, you should read it.'

She got ready and came back to bed. Dave had turned on the TV and was watching it with the volume low. Joel's book was still on the bed. She was tired but picked it up anyway. She'd at least glance at it, she thought, before she went to sleep.

The next time she looked up, Dave was lying asleep, mouth open, and the TV was showing the closing credits of the *Late Show*.

Chapter 5 was one of a number in which Joel dissected the strands of global enmeshment, as he called them. It dealt with what he called the corporate strand. It was customary, Joel argued, to think that the sphere of corporate transnational companies was the one most free of national influence. It was efficiency-maximizing and nation-neutral, stretching across political boundaries in search of the lowest costs and highest profits. Yet in reality, on one critical criterion, this wasn't the case. An analysis of a hundred publicly owned US-originated transnational corporations across all economic sectors, none of which had any US government ownership, showed that fewer than twenty were entirely free of known ownership by foreign national investment funds, and over thirty had ownership exceeding twenty per cent – enough, in most instances, for those owners to exert a prime if not controlling interest over the company. The chapter went on to outline the evolution of this situation: the avid acquisition of basement-priced stock by sovereign investment funds in the aftermath of the financial crisis; the provision of capital to enterprises hungry for funding as the upturn started; the continuing incremental accumulation of stakes in key corporations as the recovery gathered pace and surpluses built in oil-producing countries like the Gulf states and manufacturer-exporters such as China; and the tacit acquiescence by western governments in this program of acquisition in exchange for sales of the huge volumes of government bonds that were issued in the years during and after the recession.

In effect, Ehrenreich argued, the last decade had seen a massive recycling of the profits from western consumption obtained by the world's oil producers and manufacturer-exporters into ownership of the west's major businesses by state-owned funds, creating a situation in which the main economic engines and wealth creators of the free markets of the developed world were, to an unprecedented degree, government-owned. What the US government had never wanted to have – state ownership of private enterprise within the United States – had been achieved by the governments of Saudi Arabia, Abu Dhabi, China, Russia, Singapore and Kuwait. In benign conditions, this was unlikely to be an issue. But who could tell how these governments might use these holdings in conditions of stress? The world had sleep-walked into a situation in which the politics of global enmeshment, with all its tensions and potential flashpoints, was embedded deep inside the world's major transnational corporations.

Ehrenreich's point wasn't that this shouldn't have happened, or that it should be reversed. The reality of free markets was that in order to function as markets they had to be free. His point was that this situation would create an inevitable series of tensions so long as the world's global governance was unaligned with this and other thickening strands of global enmeshment. Every one of these strands was like a fault line. Sooner or later, if governance didn't come into line with them, the tension in one of these faults would cause a quake.

Dave looked around sleepily. 'You still reading?'

'I'm done,' said Marion. She closed the book and put it on her bedside table.

Dave turned off the TV. 'What do you think? I'm not sure if he's made a point of incredible insight or if he's talking out of his ass.'

'I think if I hadn't seen what I've seen over the last few days, I'd say it's … interesting.'

'Interesting?'

'Joel-interesting. Thought-provoking. Paradigm-challenging. Rich in historical context.'

'But about as likely to happen as me becoming a supreme court justice?'

Marion smiled.

'And now?'

'It gives me goose bumps.'

Dave looked at her in surprise.

'There's a little more to what's been happening than most people know.'

Dave waited.

'TS.' That was their code. TS, Top Secret, for anything she knew she shouldn't be telling him. 'I only found out today. Before Fidelian crashed, apparently we tried to get the Chinese to stop it.'

'We …?'

'Tom Knowles spoke to Zhang.'

Dave took a deep breath.

'Yeah,' said Marion. 'I know.'

30

TWO DAYS AFTER the election, pressure on the administration continued to build. The right-wing press was lacerating the president, using the results of the midterms as proof that the future of the Republican Party lay to the right. The liberal press was crowing, using the midterms as proof that the future of the country lay to the left. From within the party shots were being taken across the spectrum, with senior figures who should have known better, or who were positioning themselves for the race in two years' time, making grave statements about the implications for the president's ability to govern. There is nothing like electoral defeat to expose the fault lines in a political party. Tom Knowles had made a statement acknowledging the results of the midterms and affirming his determination to work with the new Congress to carry through his program, expressing optimism that events in the markets would prove to be temporary and contained. The markets had stopped falling but now they drifted, jittery, agitated by rumor, waiting for something to show them direction.

In the White House press briefing room, Dean Moss faced a pounding at the daily press conference. He had known a few tough days as President Knowles' press secretary but there was nothing in his experience that equated to this. Every presidency has its defining moment, a crisis that takes it by the scruff of the neck and hurls it across the room followed by a braying press corps breathless to see how the administration will pick itself up and recover, hoping to sink a few kicks into its ribs while it's down. After two relatively placid years in which Tom Knowles seemed to have lucked in for an easy ride, this was it. The pack hadn't been impressed by the president's statement and Moss bore the brunt of their dissatisfaction. They wanted more.

They wanted to know what programs Knowles would be prepared to compromise on now that he had lost control of Congress. They wanted to know whether he had been involved in trying to broker a deal over Fidelian and, if so, why it had failed. They wanted to know whether there were going to be any cabinet changes, changes at the Fed, changes in the White House. Then someone put up a hand and wanted to know if the president had spoken to President Zhang.

There was pin-drop silence in the room. Everyone who heard the question immediately understood the implication if it was true that the president had spoken to Zhang. So did Dean Moss. Only the most senior figures at the Fed, the Treasury, the State Department and the White House were supposed to be aware of it.

'You're asking me if the president spoke to President Zhang?' said Moss, playing for time. 'Is that what you're asking?'

'Yes, sir.'

'The president speaks to numerous world leaders on a regular basis. That's an important part of his job.'

'Then let me repeat the question as specifically as I can. Is it true, Mr Moss, that President Knowles spoke to President Zhang on the night before Fidelian filed for bankruptcy and asked for his help in making sure a deal was done?'

Moss hesitated. Technically he could answer no to this. The president had spoken to Zhang on the morning of Fidelian's failure.

Impulse got the better of him. 'No,' he said.

'So he didn't speak to him before Fidelian failed about the need to rescue the bank?'

'Margaret, you know I can't give a list of every conversation the president has.'

He took other questions, but the journalists kept probing on the point of a conversation between Knowles and Zhang, sensing an evasiveness in Moss's answer and homing in on it with the instinct of sharks for blood. Moss refused to answer the question again, or any variant of it, citing his principle of answering any given question only once. He didn't know if this was convincing anyone. He could feel himself sweating. He was a man of middle height with a shaven head and he knew that when he sweated, his head glistened. The reporters could probably see it.

Then he got a different question.

'How's the president holding up?'

'He's fine,' said Moss guardedly.

'Really? He's just come through what has undoubtedly been the worst midterm results for a governing party since Clinton in 1994. He's got the biggest financial crisis on his hands since Bush in '08. He's suffering the biggest general attack on him since Obama over health care. Half of his own party is casting doubt on his suitability for the nomination at the next general election and the other half is damning him, if you will, by faint praise. It's clear now he'll face a credible bid by Senator Hotchkiss to take that nomination away from him.' The journalist smiled. 'So I just wondered, how's he doing?'

Moss saw smiles around the press room. He hesitated for a moment, wondering whether he should refute those points one by one. Then he decided it wasn't worth gracing a question like that with anything more than a rebuttal.

'He's fine. Thanks for asking. The president has a strong constitution and he's upstairs in the Oval Office right now doing what needs to be done for this country. But I'll be sure to tell him you inquired. And I wouldn't go blowing things up too much. I know you guys like to do that, but this president and this administration are firmly in control. Okay, one more. Owen?'

'I don't know if we're blowing things up,' said the journalist Moss had picked out. 'Let me ask you this. We're hearing a large number of rumors circulating right now, that the Fed put a deal together, that the deal was rejected, that the people who rejected it were the Chinese government, and just now we've heard that the president was on the phone to President Zhang about precisely this thing hours before they did that. And it appears that you are not able to confirm or deny any one of these rumors. Now, I'm not asking you again, because I know you're just going to tell me you don't address rumors or you've answered that question already or whatever. So what I'm going to ask you is, Dean, what do you want me to report?'

Moss stared at him. 'That's your call, Owen.'

'So it is. But I'm giving you a chance to help me out here. Because right now, from what I've heard, all I can say is that the White House refuses to deny that any of those things happened.'

Dean Moss could feel the eyes of the entire corps on him. His mind raced, searching for a response.

'What I would like you to report, what I suggest you would report – because you've asked me, and because it's the most important thing, a lot more important than rumors of what might or might not have happened prior to Fidelian Bank filing for bankruptcy – is what's happening now. What's going to happen over the next few days. The president is working with his advisors to understand the implications of these events and what further action, if any, needs to be taken to ensure that the economy – which is strong and still has a lot of growth in it according to the Treasury Department and projections from just about every respected commentator – the president is working to make sure we stay on track to get that growth and make sure it reaches into every corner of this country. And let me also say, there's a lot of other things the president and this administration are doing. You guys tend to focus on one thing at a time, and that's understandable, but that's not how the presidency works. There are other things going on, important things, that we shouldn't lose sight of as well.'

The reporter looked at him skeptically.

'Take Jungle Peace. That's an important intervention that America's engaged in to change the lives of hundreds of thousands of people in Uganda and free them from a scourge that's blighted them for thirty years. Have we stopped that because of this? No, sir, we haven't.'

'Where are the results? When you went in there you told us there were going to be results.'

'Watch.' Moss looked at the reporters around the room. 'Just watch.'

FOUR MILES AWAY, in the Pentagon, Gary Rose was meeting with Defense Secretary John Oakley and Mortlock Hale, chairman of the Joint Chiefs of Staff. Pete Pressler was on the line from the *Abraham Lincoln* off the coast of Kenya.

Rose didn't beat around the bush. He wanted to know what was happening. A few days earlier, Pressler had reported that surveillance had revealed what appeared to be an extensive LRA camp in dense jungle a few miles south of Uganda's border with Sudan. Further surveillance had confirmed the finding and suggested that the encampment most likely included some of the senior leadership of the LRA, possibly including Joseph Koni, if he was alive. The founder of the LRA hadn't been sighted for years and there were conflicting reports if he was alive and, if so, whether he still exerted command over the group. The camp was clearly significant. Yet nothing had been done.

The problem, according to Pressler, was operational. Using drones in a jungle environment was proving to be a steep learning curve. In the almost treeless mountains of Afghanistan, visibility was unimpeded and a strike could be launched from a mile away under direct vision from the cameras on the unmanned planes. Over jungle, the drones had to fly low and slow in order for infrared detection to operate, which alerted the targets to their arrival. When they heard the drones the LRA men ran, as Pressler put it, like rats out of a sack. To hit them then would require widespread devastation, which was beyond the firepower carried by unmanned vehicles. The second problem was that once the drones did start firing, the infrared was pretty much useless as the whole detection field exploded with heat. In retrospect, this was something they should have anticipated but the operational implications only sank in after drone pilots had fired during a few early sorties. Once they let their first missile fly, the men piloting the drones back in Creech air force base in Nevada had a whiteout on their screen and from that point on were firing blind.

That left two options. They could put a force of Apaches over the area and attack with devastating power, but the helicopter pilots wouldn't have a great view of what they were shooting at. They would be more effective than unmanned aircraft, but if they failed to take out a significant number of the enemy in the first moments of the attack it was likely that the majority would get away under the jungle canopy. Alternatively they could put men on the ground, but they would be sending them against a military camp that presumably had been fortified and whose defenders were expecting an assault, with no visual reconnaissance and little prior intelligence on the nature of the resistance they would face. While this would be the most effective way of clearing the area, it carried obvious risks that the president, Pressler understood, was unwilling to entertain.

'Or Pete could continue to do what he's doing now,' added Hale. 'Harassment and interdiction. If we look at the bigger picture, we are getting individuals coming out, not a lot maybe but a couple every day, walking out of the jungle and surrendering. Now, sure, these aren't the hardline guys, mostly they're kids who were stolen from some village. Also there have been a couple of unpleasant occurrences when local people got hold of some of these kids who'd come out. It wasn't too pretty. We're trying to do something about that because it doesn't do much to encourage the others to give up. Anyway, the thing is, we could continue, and in many ways that's the least risky option.'

'But the longest,' said Rose.

'Yes, sir.'

'Admiral Pressler, how long would all this take, do you think, if that's all we did?'

'Until we've got rid of the whole LRA?' came back Pressler's voice over the phone. 'To be honest, Dr Rose, I don't think anyone can say. This group's survived in that jungle for thirty years. On the other hand, its pattern has been to regularly come out for food and medical supplies and fresh recruits. So we're not looking at a self-sufficient force and we're not looking at a force that can extract what it needs from its local population because there ain't no population in that jungle to extract it from. Probably depends on what their stores are like. We must have degraded them to some degree but, again, we can't say how much.'

'So it could be a year,' said Rose.

'I wouldn't want to put a time on it.'

'General?'

Hale shrugged.

It could be two, thought Rose. That was what that shrug meant. Gary Rose didn't know how General Hale had the barefaced cheek to sit there and tell him these things. In the discussions prior to the launch of the operation, he could distinctly remember Hale saying they'd get hits just about as soon as Pressler's force was deployed.

Rose glanced at Oakley. The defense secretary was committed to a strategy of unmanned vehicles both in the air and on land as the leading edge of the US military, and wanted Uganda to be a showcase. He wanted to see the big successes achieved by drones to help him push his case. But if unmanned force wasn't going to be enough, it wasn't going to be enough. The defense secretary knew the president wanted to see results. He wasn't going to wait two years on it.

'Let's come back to this camp,' said Rose. 'Admiral, sounds like you've got a way to make this happen.'

'Even if we just bomb the hell out of it and don't kill too many of the enemy,' said Pressler, 'that's got to hurt them. We could do that with a bunch of cruise missiles. They must have supplies in there, infrastructure. If they lose that it's got to hurt.'

Rose glanced at Oakley and shook his head slightly. That wasn't going to be enough. He could imagine the reports in a press that was already lashing the president with everything it had. This was the first significant LRA camp they had found and an attack on it that didn't kill a substantial number of combatants was going to look like a failure, no matter how many coconuts they blew up. It would look as if the LRA had outsmarted them. In the current media environment, the fact that a bloodless attack might contribute to a long-term strategy of attrition was a subtlety that wouldn't survive the press's appetite for something else they could use to beat up on the president.

'Let's think a little more aggressively,' said Oakley.

'I take it you're not referring to putting men on the ground,' said the general.

'No,' said Rose. The president didn't want American servicemen in harm's way.

'Then he wants to do it with Apaches? Pete, where are you on that?'

'We could do it. We've done the planning.'

'And the LRA, they have the wherewithal to take out any of these machines?'

'We don't think so, sir.'

Hale looked back at Gary Rose. 'There you go.'

'Well, Admiral Pressler's the operational commander,' said Rose. 'I don't want him to think there's any kind of political pressure. I hope that's clear. Admiral, this is obviously your decision.'

'Pete, how quick could you do it?'

'The planning's done,' said Pressler. 'We could do it tomorrow. We'd go in at dusk, to maximize their difficulty in regrouping after the attack's done. We just need the go-ahead.'

'Well, I think what Dr Rose is saying,' said Oakley, watching Rose's face as he spoke, 'is that if you say you can do it with Apaches and get a significantly better result than with drones, the president will okay it. Is that right, Gary?'

The national security advisor nodded. 'I would think that's right.'

31

THE FULL NATIONAL Security Council was in attendance, both its civilian and military representatives. Ed Abrahams and a number of key White House aides were seated around the room as observers. The president's objective was to understand what lay behind President Zhang's behavior and what he should do about it.

He asked Susan Opitz to kick off by giving a summary of the events leading up to the failure of Fidelian Bank and the financial aftermath in the four days that had followed. Her account was succinct – it made for pretty grim listening, and the brevity didn't lighten it. The last three days had been the three worst on the markets since Knowles took office. Tuesday, the day of the midterms, had seen the steepest fall in a single day since 2014. Interbank lending was almost at a standstill and a number of banks remained solvent only because of the cash available under the extraordinary liquidity facility that the Federal Reserve was providing.

The president then asked Ryan Ferris, the director of national intelligence, to provide his assessment of the rationale for Zhang's behavior. There was nothing to be gleaned from Chinese media and blogosphere sources, Ferris said. As far as could be gleaned from contacts within the regime, the balance of power remained as it had been. There had been no policy change, as far as they were aware, in relation to the US.

He asked if anyone else had preliminary remarks. John Oakley wanted to know what effect the rumors about the president's call to Zhang were having on the markets.

'They inject uncertainty,' said Opitz. 'Uncertainty creates volatility.'

'When you analyze the timing of the market movements over the course of the week,' said Marty Perez, 'what's clear is that it wasn't the

Fidelian bankruptcy alone that pushed the markets through the floor. It was the rumor that a deal was rejected that really crashed them. Then when the rumor came out about the president having spoken to Zhang, there was no resistance left.'

'Don't we think the market's overreacting?' said the vice-president skeptically. 'Does the Fed really need to be doing all this stuff?'

'Yes, sir. It does.'

'Feels like you can create a panic just by doing too much.'

Marty Perez didn't think much of the vice-president's grasp of economic policy. 'The Fed's doing exactly what it needs to be doing,' he said. 'If anything, it needs to be doing more.'

The vice-president raised an eyebrow. It was his usual gesture when he didn't believe something but was so far out of his depth that he couldn't think of even a half-sensible way to challenge it. His raised eyebrows were a standard joke amongst White House staff.

Knowles gazed at the notes he had jotted down while Opitz was speaking. 'So the fear driving what's happening now, if I understand what's been said – and particularly to your point, Marty, about the timing of the stock falls – is that the Chinese government purposely pushed Fidelian into bankruptcy. Is that correct?'

'Yes, sir,' said Perez. 'The question everyone's asking now, is who else are they going to do that to?'

'How large is that risk? Do we have any idea?'

'We don't have exact numbers. We estimate China to be holding between one and a half and two trillion dollars in foreign reserves. The funds available to their three largest sovereign investment funds is in the region of another one to one and a half trillion. You can add another one and a half to two trillion in the wealth funds of Saudi Arabia and the Gulf States and three, four hundred billion in Russian wealth funds if you want to look at other countries that have significant stakes in our markets.'

The numbers were ridiculous. Tom Knowles had no idea where to even start with them. How did they ever get into that situation?

'Marty, you're not saying all of that money is in US stocks,' said Rose.

'No. I don't believe anyone has done an analysis of that. But whatever the number, it's large. If that concentration is used in a purposeful fashion, is it enough to move our markets? Absolutely.'

'Well, can we at least get the number?' said the president. 'Can we at least have one or two facts?'

Perez nodded.

'Okay. Now, I told Zhang exactly what was happening. So on the face of it – unless we believe he couldn't influence the PIC, which I don't think anyone believes – he's done this in full knowledge. Before we assume that, have we got *any* evidence that says he didn't?'

There was silence.

Ryan Ferris shook his head.

'They've never behaved like this before,' said Perez eventually. 'That's the best I can say. All these are funds set up by countries running huge surpluses – some of which, at least, like the oil-exporters, can't expect those surpluses to last forever – and it makes perfect sense that they want to put that money to work. The line has always been that these are commercial investments made for commercial profit. That's always been China's line as well and as far as we're aware their behavior in the past has always supported that.'

'And they would have lost a hell of a lot of money on Fidelian,' said Opitz. 'That argues against it as well, but then we know they could have made that up in any number of ways.'

'Anything else?'

No one replied.

'Mr President,' said Bob Livingstone. 'It's clear that President Zhang could have stopped this and didn't. If that's the case, the question is whether he anticipated what's happened.'

'What the hell else would he have anticipated?' growled John Oakley.

'He may not have expected things to go as they did.'

'You think he's some kind of idiot?'

'No, John,' said Livingstone, 'I don't think he's some kind of idiot.'

'Sounds like you do.'

Livingstone clenched his jaw. He hated dealing with Oakley. The defense secretary was a bully and was particularly aggressive towards him. Gary Rose, at least, would engage in a more or less civilized debate. Livingstone didn't know why the president valued Oakley's opinion so much.

'Mr President,' he said, ignoring Oakley, 'I've had my people do some thinking on this. I hope you've had time to look at the paper I sent over.'

'I looked at it,' said Gary Rose. 'I don't think you can interpret Zhang's actions as anything other than a purposeful decision to let this bank fail.'

'I agree. What I'm saying is that he may not have anticipated the level of impact it's created. His advisors may not have led him to expect it.'

'But I told him,' said the president.

'And he may have thought you wouldn't let it fail.'

'I told him it was a final offer.'

'Sir, we know he let it fail. The question is, did he do it *in order* to create the problems that he created, or did he do it thinking that whatever would happen, would happen, and it wouldn't be too bad? That's a subtle distinction but it's an important one.'

'Is it?' demanded Oakley. 'Even if it means screwing around with our election? Give me a break! He knew exactly what he was doing.'

'Bob, what are you saying?' said the vice-president. 'This is some kind of *Fuck You* message from Zhang? The president of the United States gets on the line to ask for help and he's saying *Fuck You* to him, whatever will happen will happen? That's what you think he's doing?'

Those weren't exactly the words Livingstone would have used. 'You could put it like that.'

'Hell.' Stephenson glanced at the president. 'What the fuck does he think he's doing?'

'If it's a *Fuck You* message,' said the president, 'what's it about?'

'The usual things,' said Livingstone. 'Plus now there's Uganda. Personally I think it may be South Africa. They've been asking us to give them time to work things out with the ANC but it's pretty clear the Brits are going to push their resolution and we're not doing anything to stop them.'

'I'm not going to stop them now.'

'Like we'd let them tie up South Africa's resources for the next thirty years,' said Rose.

'Exactly. Like I'm going to let him get what he wants after all this.'

'The other possibility,' said Livingstone, 'is that this is playing to some kind of internal, domestic agenda of Zhang's we're not aware of. I've covered some possibilities in the paper.'

'Why now?' said Gary Rose.

'Something many have happened.'

'Do you know of anything?' asked the president.

'Not specifically.'

'Ryan?'

The director of national intelligence shook his head. 'As I said, we haven't got any information about a change from the status quo. It's all stable as far as we're aware. Zhang, Fan, Xu. It's the usual setup.'

'What if this is part of some kind of power struggle between them?'

'What difference would it make?' said Rose. 'Even if Zhang is playing to an internal agenda, or if Fan's constraining him, what they've done amounts to interference in our political process and a huge disruption to our economy. We can't allow other leaders to do stuff like that for their own domestic purposes. And remember, Mr President, you talked to him. It wasn't like he had no idea.'

'With respect, sir, the motives matter,' said Livingstone.

'Not from where I sit,' said Opitz. 'Whether he purposely wanted to crash our markets, or whether he was saying *Fuck You* for the hell of it, or whether he was doing some internal maneuvering for whatever reason, the market's made up its mind. All they care about is the fact that the Chinese government made a choice to let Fidelian fail. With a bailout on the table, they interpret that as a financially irrational decision, therefore it must be political. If the market thinks it's political, it *is* political. Which means we need to deal with this politically. And right now it doesn't matter what we say. We won't be believed. There's only one person who can put this thing to rest. The markets are not going to settle until they hear from Zhang's own lips that he's not going to mess with them again.'

There was silence.

Knowles looked around the room. 'Do we agree with that?'

'I think we do want to understand what he was trying to do,' said Livingstone.

'I'm not saying we don't,' said Opitz. 'But that's secondary, Bob. The primary thing now is we have a bunch of markets that, frankly, are as skittish as a cat on a hot tin roof and there's only one thing that's going to calm them down.'

Tom Knowles drummed his fingers on the table. He had already been dependent on Zhang once and look where that had got him. He didn't feel much like giving him a chance to say *Fuck You* again.

'How do we go about doing this?' he said curtly. 'Do I have to talk to Zhang again?'

'Sir, Zhang already knows your concerns on this,' said Rose. 'Possibly we may have more effect if he gets some advice coming to him from another direction.'

'I could talk to the Chinese finance minister,' said Opitz.

'I think this should come from State,' said Livingstone.

'Mr President,' said Rose. 'It's really a financial issue. I think advice coming from the finance minister would be a better idea.'

'I know Bai,' said Opitz. 'I can talk to him. Zhang depends on him for his economic advice. If Bai tells him it's important to say it, there's a good chance he will.'

'I think they'd expect it to come from State.'

'We can't have two of you talking to them,' said Knowles impatiently. 'Susan, you do it. See what happens. That alright with you, Bob?'

'I do really think this should be something that comes out of State.'

'Well, get coordinated. Susan, you talk to their finance guy. Bob, make sure Susan knows what she has to know from State. What we're looking for is a statement from Zhang that they had nothing to do with the bankruptcy of Fidelian. Something like that? Is that what we want?'

'Something like that, sir,' said Opitz. 'Something about not doing anything in the future. We'll figure it out.'

The president shook his head. 'I don't like going to them like this. I don't like it one little bit. Anyone think there's another way? John, what do you think?'

Oakley shrugged. 'We can ask him, but I wouldn't bet too much on the chances that he'll help us. Still, it's useful to the extent that it'll flush him out. I don't know what you're going to say to him, Susan, but whatever it is, let's not leave any room for him to miscalculate. Then if he makes the statement, fine. If he doesn't, we know what he's really doing, and all this stuff Bob's been saying about Zhang miscalculating, we know it's wrong. But we've got to do this quiet. Hell knows what it's going to look like if some reporter gets hold of this and says we went begging to Beijing for Zhang to say it ain't so.'

Knowles nodded. 'Can we do something about these damn leaks?' He glanced impatiently at his chief of staff. 'Roberta? Huh? Can we do something about it?'

'We're looking into it.'

'This stays quiet,' said Knowles, looking around the table. 'This stays dead quiet. Bob, you work on this directly with Susan. I don't even want your staffs involved. And Susan, be careful the way you talk to the Chinese. Let's not look like we're begging. If we get into a situation where we have to release a statement of what you said, let's make sure it looks strong. We need to make it look like we're giving them a chance to say no.'

'Like we're doing them a favor,' said Oakley. 'Which we are, because after what they've done, they don't even deserve that.'

The president nodded. 'So Bob's going to work with Susan and she's going to talk to whoever it is ...'

'Bai, sir.'

'Susan's going to talk to Bai and get something out of that bunch of fraudsters in Beijing to say they didn't set this up. Is that right? And if they don't say anything, then like John said, we know they did.' Knowles paused. 'Okay. Anything else? Thank you.'

He got up. Ed Abrahams walked out by his side.

'This is a godawful situation,' he muttered when they got in the elevator. 'Just a godawful damn mess.'

'I think we're on the way to getting it under control,' said Abrahams.

'I hope we are.'

He marched back to the Oval Office. About five minutes after he sat down there was a knock on the door and his personal secretary came in. Oakley and General Hale, who had both been at the National Security Council meeting, were outside.

'I just left them,' said Knowles.

'They say it's urgent.'

'How long have I got?'

'Your next meeting's not for another ten minutes, sir.'

'Okay, send them in.'

Knowles waited. John Oakley and Mortlock Hale came in.

'I thought we dealt with everything,' said Knowles. 'Is there something else you want to say?'

'It's not about that,' said Oakley. 'There's some news from Uganda.'

Knowles smiled. 'About time. We need something to knock this stuff off the front page.'

'Actually, sir,' said General Hale, 'it's not so good.'

32

THE HELICOPTERS HAD gone in at dusk in Uganda, 10am in Washington. An attack force of nine Apaches flew in low over the LRA base that had been identified in the jungle south of the Sudan border. What happened in the ensuing engagement was still confused and military debriefers were trying to put together the sequence of events. What was clear was that two of the Apaches were down and their four crew members were down with them.

'This happened five hours ago?' demanded Knowles incredulously. 'Five hours and no one *told* me?'

'I only just found out after the meeting, sir,' said Oakley.

'What the hell? What–' The president stopped. He looked at Hale. '*When* did you find out, General?'

'I've been aware since last night that the operation was imminent. This was the operation you authorized yesterday, Mr President.'

'And were you aware that this had turned into this ... I don't know what you'd call it. This goddamn fuck-up! Is that what you'd call it?'

'I think it's a fair description, sir. We've been trying to recover our pilots.'

'Can we find out what the situation is? Can we at least get that?'

Hale nodded. 'I'll get Admiral Pressler.'

They waited while Hale made some calls. Finally a call came back on the president's phone.

'Admiral,' said Hale into the speakerphone, 'I'm here with the president and Secretary Oakley.'

Pete Pressler was on the line from the command room of the *Abraham Lincoln* and there was a kind of low, whirring sound in the background.

'Admiral,' said Knowles, 'can you tell me what's going on?'

'We have two Apaches down, sir.' The admiral's voice was terse. 'The circumstances aren't clear yet. We believe one of them hit the tree canopy and brought the other one down. On the plus side, we believe we killed upwards of fifty LRA fighters possibly including some of their senior leadership. From that perspective it was a high-impact mission but we have four men down. We believe one of them died on impact.'

'Pete, do we know that for certain now?' said Hale.

'I believe we now have the body, sir.'

'Do we have men on the ground?' asked the president.

'Yes, sir. We do. We've secured the downed Apaches but there's no sight of our guys or any of their fighters. Just a bunch of LRA bodies in pieces. We didn't have men on the ground at the time of the incident. It was a purely aerial assault in keeping with your wishes, sir.'

'Admiral Pressler,' said Oakley, 'operational decisions are yours, as you know. The president doesn't intervene.'

'Yes, sir,' said Pressler brusquely. 'Anyway, I've got three of my guys still alive down there in enemy hands and right now that's all I'm worried about. Hold on, please.'

They heard something being said in the background and the admiral replied sharply. Then he came back on the line.

'Admiral,' said Oakley, 'how long after the incident did you get men on the ground?'

'As soon as we could. We're in darkness here now. We have drone surveillance in operation but at this point it's all infrared and the jungle comes alive at night. There's a lot of noise. We think we're tracking a number of groups that headed out in different directions after the attack. Which of them have our men is impossible to say. There's nothing I'd like to do more than take them out but if we go after them from the air we risk killing our own guys.'

There was silence. The whirring noise from the *Abraham Lincoln* filled the room.

'Admiral,' said the president, 'what's your plan?'

'At this stage we'll continue tracking them. At sunrise the guys on the ground will do a wider surveillance. With the drones, if we can get sight of the groups and if our guys aren't with them, we'll take them out. If we can locate our men I've got Chinooks ready to scramble out of Lodwar.'

'Any chance of our men on the ground getting taken?'

'There's always a chance of some kind of firefight.'

'We can't have any more casualties,' said the president.

"I don't want them any more than you do, sir. But we've taken this action, now we've got to clear it up. Our men may not be far off, especially if they're injured. They may have been dumped.'

The president glanced at Hale and nodded.

'Pete, anything else?'

'No, sir.'

'Okay. Thank you.'

The line went dead.

Tom Knowles threw himself down on one of the sofas in front of his desk.

'So far,' he said, 'no one knows about this?'

Hale shook his head. 'Not from our side, but the LRA can get to the outside world if it wants to. We know they can get messages onto the net. Taking out even one American soldier is going to be a victory for them. We should assume that right now they're trying to get the message out. It's only a matter of time.'

'And we haven't heard that they want anything for our guys?'

'Not yet. Again, that might be a matter of time.'

John Oakley doubted it. 'They're not that kind of operation. They're basically killers. They have no program.'

'There must be something,' said Knowles. 'Prisoner swaps? Supplies?'

'We've said our mission is to eliminate them. Look at it from their side. Unless we say that's not the case any more, what's the point of anything we could give them?'

'Could be that some of them might see the end's coming and might want to use our guys to cut a deal for themselves.'

Oakley looked at the general. 'Any indication of that?'

'No, sir. But it's very early.'

'Would we do it?' said the president.

'Cut a deal with them if they want to come in?'

The president nodded.

'I'd rather kill 'em,' said Oakley.

'If we have to,' said Knowles impatiently.

Oakley shrugged. 'We'd have to say they'd have to stand trial. I guess we could guarantee they won't get the death penalty. We could send them to the Hague. They don't do the death penalty there.'

The president looked at Hale. 'Are we going to need a negotiating team?'

'We're pulling one together in case we do. The longer we can keep this quiet, the better. Gives us the maximum freedom of action.'

'You just said we have to assume the LRA's going to publicize it.'

'That's true, Mr President. I'd assume they'll do it as quick as they can. They'll minimize their casualties and talk up our losses.'

'I'm no press secretary,' said Oakley, 'but we don't want to be chasing that story. We want to be in front.'

'So we need to get some kind of a statement out?' The president grimaced. 'This is going to look bad. This is going to look like one hell of a fuck-up. This is like Clinton in Somalia.'

'We've had a success here, Mr President. Let's not forget that.'

'Doesn't sound like it.'

'Fifty-plus enemy dead against four of our men.'

'There shouldn't have been *one* of our men, General. These guys are stone age.'

'I'll release a statement,' said Oakley.

'Do we acknowledge we've got a man dead and three men captured?'

'I wouldn't,' said Hale. 'Operationally the less we say about what's going on there until this is over, the better. I'd like to say we've had a successful operation, fifty enemy dead, and we've got men on the ground in the area. That gets our facts out there. That establishes how many of the enemy got killed before they get their version out. Then let's see what they come up with.'

Knowles frowned. 'I need to talk to Ed and Dean about this. John, hold off with a statement until I do.' He looked at Hale. 'General, I want to know exactly what's happening, whenever it happens. I don't care what time of night it might be. We get any information on our men, I want to know.'

'Yes, sir.'

The president stood. The others stood as well.

There was a knock on the door.

Dean Moss was standing there, ashen-faced.

'Mr President, there's a video on the net.'

THEY SAT AROUND the screen in the Oval Office. The president's key aides had joined him. Moss pulled up a website plastered with anti-American slogans. He paused with his hand on the remote.

'This is um ...' He took a deep breath. 'If anyone's squeamish, I've got to warn you, this is the time to leave.'

'Run the clip,' said the president quietly.

'Yes, sir.'

It started with someone ranting incomprehensibly in the glare of a spotlight in a shack. The picture, which must have been uploaded via a satellite connection, faded in and out a couple of times. Then the camera and the light turned and there was an American airman surrounded by five men. His face was bloodied and one eye was badly puffed, and he stood hunched, in pain, held up by the men around him. They didn't wear masks or make any effort to conceal their identities. One of them held up the dog tags they had ripped off their prisoner and shook them defiantly at the camera. One of them yelled at him. Then two of them pushed him to his knees.

Tom Knowles knew he didn't want to see what was about to come next.

It started.

'Oh, my ...' whispered Roberta Devlin, and she turned away.

'That's their style,' said Hale. 'They like to do it with clubs.'

Gary Rose got to his feet and stumbled out, hand pressed against his mouth.

The body of the airman lay on the ground now. Its legs twitched.

One of the men smashed the broken skull again, and again.

The president closed his eyes. His mind was numb.

33

TOM KNOWLES HAD never seen a man killed before, not for real, not by any method. What he knew of killing came from what he had seen in films.

He couldn't get the images out of his head. Especially the legs, the twitching legs. They were still twitching at the end. Somehow that was almost worse than the bloody, pulped skull. The convulsive twitch of those legs, like the kicking of some animal.

Normally, the senior staff in the West Wing were a kind of surrogate family for the president. Ed Abrahams, Roberta Devlin and Gary Rose understood that on nights when the chief didn't have any engagements the job often involved staying on and watching football with him in his study or a film in the White House cinema. It was semi-work as well. They talked about stuff and that often helped him come to decisions. Taking issues out of their usual context could help you see them in a different way.

But he didn't feel like company tonight. He went up to the residence floor and ate dinner alone in his study. He looked over some papers he had taken up with him. He couldn't concentrate. He turned on the TV but couldn't find anything to watch. He left it on, surfing channels, watching the images moving on the screen. They couldn't take away the images in his head.

He felt stunningly lonely. He truly felt there was no one who could share this burden. As commander in chief, he had sent that poor man to his terrible death. Jungle Peace was his and his alone. And he had wanted that raid, he had wanted it done quick. He thought of his own son, Steve, his only child. Steve and his wife and twin daughters were occasional visitors to the White House. He was hoping to see them in another couple of weeks for Thanksgiving. Last year the twins had stood alongside him as he pardoned the traditional Thanksgiving turkey in the Rose Garden until the bird turned its head and gobbled at them and the two little girls took off and ran like hell.

He smiled for a moment, thinking about it, then the smile faded off his lips.

He got up and went into the hall. He had given the room traditionally used as the president's bedroom to Sarah, and used the west bedroom as his own. He knocked on her door and opened it. She wasn't there. He looked in her study. Empty.

'Tom,' said Sarah.

He turned. She was in the hall behind him. He could see from her face that she had heard.

'I've just got back,' she said. 'I had … It doesn't matter. I had to give a speech.'

He nodded.

'You okay?'

'Sure.'

'You want to talk?'

He smiled. He didn't hear that from her very often.

'Do you?'

He shook his head. 'It's okay.'

She took his hand. 'Come on,' she said. She took him into her study.

He followed, letting her lead him.

'You want a drink?'

He nodded.

'Bourbon?'

He nodded again.

She went out and got him one.

'You're not having anything?' he said.

'No.' She shook her head and sat down on the sofa beside him. She was in a blue pant suit with a mauve shirt. Her hair was honey blonde. When he first met her it had been that color naturally. Now it needed a little help. She looked good. Sometimes he forgot what a good-looking woman she was.

She watched him.

He took a sip of the bourbon and closed his eyes.

'You didn't see that video, I hope,' he said.

'No.'

'Don't watch it. It's a horrible thing.' He looked at her. 'They're evil, Sarah. I know it's an old-fashioned word, but I don't know another one for it. You don't have to believe in God to know they're going straight to hell.' He sighed. 'I'm only trying to do what's right out there. I've got no other motive.'

'It's a good thing you're doing there, Tom.'

'I don't know if that's going to make much difference to that poor man's family. I don't know what I'm going to say when I speak to them.'

'You'll find the words.'

'There aren't any.'

'You'll find them, Tom.'

He took another sip of his bourbon. 'Harley Gauss was his name. Twenty-six years old. Captain Harley Gauss.' He was silent for a moment. 'You know, there are some things that ... Something like this changes everything.'

Sarah watched him.

He leaned back and shook his head. 'You know, this presidency ...' He smiled ruefully. 'Suddenly I feel like I don't know what I'm doing.'

'Tom, an atrocity like this ... it looms a lot bigger than it is. Right now it seems like the worst thing that's ever happened.'

'I know that. I realize that.' He paused, frowning. 'I was thinking before. It's hardly more than a month since we launched Jungle Peace. You can't believe it. You think back and ...' He stopped again, smiling disbelievingly. 'It's like a different age. We were launching a simple mission to root out a bunch of evil guys. The country backed me seventy per cent. The economy looked strong, the markets were sound. I was looking at a sixty-seat majority in the Senate and an unchallenged renomination. And now...' He laughed bitterly. 'God, Sarah, it's like it's all in ruins. In a month. One lousy month. I don't know how the hell it happened.'

She watched him.

'I've got no idea. And it's not over. They've still got two of our guys. We could have two more videos. Or it could turn into some kind of drawn-out hostage situation.'

'It won't.'

'Won't it? Neither you nor I nor anyone knows that. I don't think our people have the first idea about how to find them. And we've got men on the ground now. In the jungle. We could lose more. What happens then? Those damn military guys told me it was going to be done clean, from the air, and the first time I ask them to do something we've got two Apaches down and two dead and more missing. I can just see it getting dirtier and dirtier on the ground now. It was never meant to be like that.'

'Tom, you're imagining the worst scenario. It'll come back under control. What's to say the military don't get them back and finish the job like they said they'd do?'

'Yeah, maybe.' He worked at his temples with his fingertips. He took a deep breath and let it out slow. 'Then there's the markets and the banks and who knows what the Chinese are doing?'

Sarah looked at him uncomprehendingly. She didn't know the truth about the rumored approach to Zhang that he had made the morning Fidelian failed.

'Who knows what the hell to do? I've got Strickland and Opitz running around doing all kinds of things but I can't say I really understand if it's going to work and I don't think they do either. Looks to me like they think up one thing after the next to deal with whatever happens to come up that particular day. You know, there hasn't been a day until this last week when I wondered what I was doing here. I don't think I've ever told you this, but when I won the election, I thought I was going to feel like an impostor. Like a fraud. When I first started, I mean. I thought I'd arrive at the White House after the inauguration and the next morning I'd sit down to work in the Oval Office and I'd be thinking, I shouldn't be here. It should be Dwight Eisenhower or Ronald Reagan, not me.'

Sarah smiled.

'But I didn't, Sarah. What I'm saying is I didn't feel like that. By the time I got here, after the transition, I felt fine. I felt like this was my place. And I've felt like it every single day until this last week. And now I'm not sure. I don't know if I belong here. It sure doesn't feel like it. Feels like the country deserves something better.'

'Tom,' said Sarah. She took his hand.

'And now I've got the Veterans' Day speech on Sunday. What a time for it, huh?' He shook his head. 'You know, George W Bush said some of the nights in this office are long and lonely. That was about the only thing I ever heard him say that I thought would be worth remembering. And after two years, I thought I knew what he meant. But actually I don't think I did. Not until this week. I've had a few of those nights in the last week. I think tonight's going to be another one. I think tonight's going to be the worst one yet.'

He gazed at her. Sarah smiled. Whatever they had been through, whatever had become of their marriage, there was still an understanding, a certain deep familiarity that they shared that neither of them shared with anyone else. Sarah herself didn't know why she was still with him. She shouldn't have been, but she was. It wasn't as simple as it looked to some people who presumed to comment from the outside.

She drew him to her. She held him for a moment, and then leaned back and looked him in the eyes.

'You're a good president, Tom Knowles.'

He shook his head. 'The jury's out on that.'

'No, it's not. You wouldn't be human if you didn't have doubts. You're a good president. You'll do the right things. You'll get us through this. I believe it. The country believes it. Listen to me. You're a good president.'

'But not a good husband, huh?'

Sarah looked at him sadly. 'Oh, Tom,' she said.

34

THAT VETERANS' DAY weekend, the country was in a kind of shock. The markets, of course, were closed. For a brief respite of forty-eight hours, the financial catastrophe wasn't the thing on everyone's mind. Instead, it was the horrendous death of one man called Harley Gauss – one man who suddenly seemed to be everyone's son, or father, or brother.

Tom Knowles had spoken to the families of fallen soldiers before. He had met them, had stood beside them at funerals with flag-draped coffins. As Nevada governor and as president. Men who had died in Afghanistan, Pakistan, Colombia, the Philippines. But not one of them had died like Harley Gauss.

He spoke to them on Saturday morning, less than twenty-four hours after the events. First there was a call to a pair of grieving parents in Roseville, California, the mother and father of Jack Duffey, the pilot who had died on impact in Uganda. He assured them their son had died in a good cause. He expressed his admiration for his bravery, commitment, loyalty and patriotism. He gave thanks on behalf of the entire country for his sacrifice. He told them it was only fine young men and women like their son who kept safe the freedom and liberty that other Americans enjoyed. He listened to them say the things they needed to say, listened as the pain came out. They talked. Those were the easy calls, he had learned, the ones where the relatives talked. The hard ones were the calls where the relatives were silent, and you found yourself talking into a vacuum, sounding more grotesque and platitudinous with each word you uttered. He told the parents he would bring their boy back and there was a place for him in Arlington, among heroes, if that was where they wanted him to rest. They thanked him at the end. That always got him, the way people thanked him at the end.

Then there was the second call. This one was to a young widow in Jacksonville, North Carolina.

The words were harder to say. As he spoke he kept seeing that video, seeing those twitching legs. He wondered if she had seen it too but didn't dare to ask. He could only hope that she hadn't. She didn't speak, just emitted a flat, toneless, 'yes, sir'. Nothing else came back, nothing but a sense of great emptiness, a great, disbelieving emptiness on the other end of the phone.

'Mrs Gauss, Cindy, we will get the people who did this thing. Ma'am, we will bring these people to justice.' He had tears in his eyes.

He didn't know what to say next. That her husband had died quick? He hadn't. That he had served his country well and honorably? He had said that already. That no one deserved to be clubbed to death in the middle of the jungle by a gang of barbarian killers? Yes, but what kind of comfort was that?

'Ma'am, we will bring him back to Arlington. We will bring him back to Arlington and lay him to rest.'

'Yes, sir.'

He didn't know what else to say. But it wasn't enough.

'Cindy, have you got people looking after you? They taking care of you?'

'Yes, sir.'

'I'm going to get my private secretary to give you a number. You need to speak to me, you call that number. You call me direct.'

'Yes, sir.'

'We're going to bring him back, Cindy.'

'Yes, sir. Thank you, sir.'

AFTER THE CALLS, Knowles held a Saturday StratCom in the Oval Office. There was general agreement that they had to go on the offensive. The week that had started with an apparent deal to save Fidelian on the eve of the election had turned into an unalloyed catastrophe – financially, politically, and now militarily. Through the week their tone had become defensive. They had to change that or there would be a collapse of confidence in the administration. If the president was seen to be acting calmly and strongly on each of these fronts, with robust purpose and clear intent, the American people would come back in behind him. Horrible as it was, the killing of Harley Gauss gave him an opportunity to do that. The crisis in the markets looked like incompetence. The Midterm Massacre, as the press had termed the November 6 elections, looked like fragility. But a bare four days after the election, the killing of Harley Gauss had made that term unusable. With the brutal murder of a disarmed airman, America felt itself under attack. When the country was under attack, people wanted to support their president. They didn't want to hear partisan bickering and watch people taking shots at the commander in chief. Ed Abrahams argued that they could stretch that support to include the president's handling of the financial crisis if they could craft the right lines. But they had to seize the moment. It was time to lead.

Ruiz-Kellerman, with results of polling from the previous day – this was even before the Harley Gauss video appeared – said there was a strong appetite to see the president taking more direct control. People were sick of seeing Ron Strickland and Susan Opitz. They hadn't voted for either of those two people. They had voted for Thomas Paxton Knowles. They wanted to see the man they had put in the White House.

Knowles spoke to Jack Harris, the chairman of the Republican Party, and to the congressional majority leaders. They gave him the same message.

The Veterans' Day speech that he would be giving the following day gave him the perfect platform. It would need to be completely rewritten. Through the day, Josh Bentner and another speechwriter worked on the address. They struggled to combine references to the president's handling of the financial crisis with the almost sacred solemnity required on this tragic Veterans' Day. At around 2pm Bentner showed a first draft to Ed Abrahams.

'What are you doing?' demanded Abrahams. 'He doesn't need to say a word about the markets. All he needs to do is show that he's a statesman. He needs to show that he can feel our pain and lift us up. For Christ's sake, Josh! What's wrong with you? Poetry, not prose! He's the commander in fucking chief, not an economics professor! Make him look like it.'

The next morning Knowles flew to New York for the Veterans' Day event. Sarah accompanied him. This year, the hundredth anniversary of the original Armistice Day in 1918 when the guns of World War One fell silent, he had chosen to make his speech at the docks in New York City from which so many of the two million Americans who sailed to Europe in the last year of that conflict, and of the hundred thousand who never returned, embarked on their voyage. It was a bright November Sunday in Manhattan, and the sun glinted on the medals of the veterans sitting in front of him, medals from Georgia, Iraq, Afghanistan, Vietnam, even a few on the chests of snowy-headed veterans of World War Two, the dwindling remnant of their generation. As Knowles read the speech, with the events of the previous two days present in everyone's mind, and the knowledge that two American servicemen were at that moment in the custody of the same people who had already killed one of their comrades, the poignancy was almost unbearable. On more than one occasion there was a hoarseness in his throat. In the audience he could see old men putting handkerchiefs to their eyes. And young men too.

The final words were too sentimental perhaps. At another time, he would have had Bentner tone them down. But this time, he felt they were right. He really felt they were true. So did everyone who worked on the speech. When the time came to speak to them, the emotion in his voice was real.

'Each year, on this day, we remember. And when we remember, the pain of loss – whether it is a day ago, or a century ago – reminds us why we are here. The hurt we feel lights the path through the shadow to what we must do. America is never stronger, never brighter, never more of a beacon to the world than when the darkness in the world tries to snuff that beacon out. It will never be extinguished. We burn the more strongly and more passionately. We rise up to do the good work.' He paused. 'God bless this country. God bless America.'

35

AT THE WHITE HOUSE that night, after flying back from New York, Knowles watched the Sunday night football game with Ed Abrahams over a beer. The St Louis Rams were playing the Philadelphia Eagles. He ordered up a couple of pizzas.

St Louis was having it easy. 23 to 6 in the third quarter. The Eagles defense was a shambles.

He glanced at Ed. 'We hear anything from Susan about when she's talking to that Chinese finance minister?'

It felt that it was long ago that they had made the decision to have the Treasury secretary talk to her Chinese counterpart, but it was only two days previously.

'Tomorrow,' said Abrahams. 'First thing.'

'You think they'll make a statement?'

'They'll probably hold on a few days. I wouldn't expect it right away. By the way, Gary tells me it might be Liang, the Chinese premier, who makes it. Zhang uses him to say things he'd rather not say himself. Doesn't matter anyway. Everyone knows he's Zhang's mouthpiece so the effect would be the same. Once they say something, we can draw a line under it. They can say it was a commercial decision. They can say they didn't interfere one way or the other. Whatever lie they like. The markets will know they've got the message.'

'They'd better say something.'

'Zhang's made his point now, whatever the hell that was. He doesn't want to see the markets in a real crisis any more than we do.'

Knowles took a sip on his beer and swallowed it thoughtfully, reflecting on the last couple of days. The reaction to his speech today had been just what he wanted. The commentators were saying it was strong, statesmanlike, leaderly. Dean Moss had been briefing hard to talk that angle up.

He turned to Abrahams. 'You know, Ed, I agree with your strategy. This is the time to stop being defensive, be strong, show our own agenda. But that's just talk. Stuff's got to happen. If we don't get our guys back soon, it's going to be hard.' Knowles paused. 'We're going to have hell if we don't have them back for Thanksgiving.'

Abrahams grimaced. 'Let's not set any deadlines. We'll crucify ourselves.'

'You think we should replace Pressler?'

Abrahams looked at Knowles in surprise. 'Replacing a commander in the field isn't a small thing. The military'll go postal.'

'Yeah. Hale is just as fucking bad. Maybe I should replace him as well.' Knowles watched the screen. St Louis threw another touchdown pass. 'You see that? You ever seen a defense like that? It's a Swiss cheese it's got so many holes.'

'Tom. This is okay. You're at the halfway point of your first term. You have plenty of time to deal with this stuff.'

Knowles looked at him.

'Plenty of time.'

'You think I should cancel the CSS?'

'And do what?' said Abrahams.

The Caribbean Storm Summit was a meeting of the thirty-four Caribbean countries due to take place the following week to discuss action on hurricane activity, which was getting steadily more severe with climate change. Ostensibly its objective was to develop provisions for mutual emergency help. In reality it was a forum at which everyone else extracted funds from the US for storm recovery projects.

'Walt could go,' said Knowles. 'I'm not sure I should be out of Washington.'

'That doesn't fit with the image you presented today.'

'That image said I was going to deal with the problems here, not go off to Cancun to hand out a couple of billion dollars to our wonderful neighbors.'

'I disagree. That image said I'm the president and I'm still leading this country and damn anyone who doesn't think so, I'm still in charge. The CSS is part of being president.' Abrahams sat his big bulk forward. 'Tom, we get this stuff dealt with, we put it behind us. In two years, all people will remember is the way you *dealt* with it. Picked up the ball, ran with it, slam dunk.' Abrahams slapped one hand against the other. 'Every president has to do this. You have to show you can deal with it. That's what makes you the Chief. That's what makes you the man. It makes you more re-electable, not less.'

Knowles was silent for a moment. 'Ed, you don't feel the responsibility like I do. You weren't the one who sent those guys into Uganda.'

'Tom, I know that.'

Knowles gazed into his beer. 'Nothing else I've done haunts me like that.' He looked at Abrahams. 'I feel sick just thinking about it. It was like watching some kind of animal being killed. Who'd even kill an animal like that? What kind of people would even kill an animal like that?'

'That's why what we're doing is right.'

'I know that. Doesn't make it easier. And now we've got hostages. I think hostages, I think Jimmy Carter. I think one-term president and you spend the rest of your life fucking monitoring elections.'

'Tom, it's all about how you handle it. It's not hostages as such, it's how you deal with it. Look at the history. The Teheran hostages killed Carter, but the Beirut hostages didn't touch Ronald Reagan. Right? And why did it kill Carter? Because he let it define him. Because he locked himself away in the Oval Office and turned into a hostage himself. Ronald Reagan just kept on smiling and taking his afternoon naps and allowed the most unscrupulous things to happen to get our people back. Now, canceling the CSS, sitting here in the White House worrying about it – because God knows there's nothing more you can do – *that's* how you turn yourself into Jimmy Carter.'

Knowles took another swig of his beer, thinking about it.

'Tom, I'm not saying the stuff that's happened in the last week is good. We sure could use more than forty-nine senators. But it's happened. In a four-year term some bad things are bound to happen. True, we could have had better timing. But the one thing you do have now is the chance to show you're a strong president. And that's a good thing. So out of this very bad stuff comes at least one thing that's good.' Abrahams paused, watching the president. 'Tom, this right now is the defining week of your presidency. When historians look back on your first term, they're going to see that this was the moment you showed what you were made of. You looked right into Zhang's eyes and you faced him down. You gave comfort to the nation after the brutal killing of one of its soldiers and made sure the others were returned. You dealt with a financial crisis and turned it into a platform for growth. This is the week. A week from now, Zhang's made his statement, the markets are settled, Fidelian turns out to be just one bad bank, with a bit of luck we'll have our two guys back, and you're the hero.'

'Just like that?'

Abrahams smiled. 'Why not? Who could have said how bad this week was going to be?'

Knowles laughed.

'Just don't expect anything from Zhang right away.'

SUSAN OPITZ SPOKE to the Chinese finance minister the following morning. There was no statement from the Chinese president or his deputy that day. Or the day after. The markets remained uncertain, volatile, prey to disinformation and rumor that sent stocks of individual companies down and up and down again. The whereabouts of the missing airmen remained unknown. On Wednesday the president went to the CSS and pledged annual storm relief funds of two billion for the region. The press attacked him for the sum being either too much or too little.

There was still no statement from Zhang, but there was news from another source. Defense intelligence had received a report, of uncertain reliability, that the two missing Apache airmen were alive and had been transported across the Ugandan border into Sudan.

No one outside the highest levels of the Pentagon and the White House was being informed until the report was checked further. Everyone else was outside the loop, including the State Department.

36

MARION ELLMAN GAZED out the window at the towering rectangular face of the UN building across the street from her office as she listened to Bob Livingstone on the phone. Deputy Secretary of State Doug Havering was sitting with Livingstone in Washington. Steve Haskell was in Beijing, and Tomasina Rollins, the US ambassador to South Africa, was on the line in Johannesburg.

Livingstone wanted to form a view of the next step in dealing with the South African seizure of power by the ANC, given that the British appeared determined to introduce a Security Council resolution calling for sanctions before the end of the year. He spent the first minutes of the call outlining what he knew of the latest developments from the White House. Susan Opitz had made the call to her Chinese counterpart, he told them, and a statement from Zhang or another high official in the Chinese regime was awaited. In the mind of the White House, there was no connection between that demand and the South Africa question. He personally doubted that the Chinese government agreed.

He asked for Rollins' view of what was happening in South Africa.

Tomasina Rollins was a hugely experienced ex-assistant secretary of state for Africa, one of the few US ambassadors who knew her country as well as anyone in the State Department or CIA. Her view was that the South African president, Membathi Mthwesa, had been assured by China that they would veto the British resolution. The conundrum for the US would follow from that. The British, she had heard, were planning to pull their embassy out of South Africa and impose their own sanctions if the resolution failed. The US would have to decide whether they were going to do the same.

'If we use sanctions they'll really have to hurt. Cosmetic stuff will just feed into the South Africa-as-victim line that Mthwesa's pushing, which will boost his position. Are we prepared to get really tough? And will it work even if we are? Frankly I think our friends in Beijing will happily take any exports from South Africa that we don't want. We'd be handing Mthwesa something to hit us with in return for virtually zero impact on the ground.'

The shape of the arrangement being proposed by the Chinese, as far as Rollins was aware, was a restoration of the constitution with elections engineered so as to guarantee the ANC's victory, after which China would use its diplomatic efforts to support the government in saying that the elections had been free and fair and the constitution had genuinely been restored. Tied up with that was a big Chinese trade and aid package and an understanding that if the west didn't accept the arrangement and treated the ANC government as a pariah, China would make good any economic impact that resulted.

Within the ANC itself there were a number of groupings that opposed the Chinese arrangement. One faction didn't want to see South Africa as a one-party state and would prefer to see the ANC contest elections even if they might lose them. This was the smallest group since most of the activists who thought like this had been driven out of the party over the last couple of years. A somewhat larger group feared that an arrangement with the Chinese would make President Mthwesa untouchable within the party. They wanted the ANC to rule but they didn't want Mthwesa as president for life. And finally, the largest opposition group within the ANC had nothing against seeing the country become a one-party state, even if Mthwesa would be there for the next twenty years, but as a matter of pragmatism they didn't want to see South Africa as some kind of pariah client state of China. They saw that as a poisoned chalice, and if that was the only alternative, they would take their chances with elections. They also saw a serious risk of significant disturbances if Mthwesa got his way. Rollins believed that if the ANC went for the China protector arrangement, with the ANC installed as the only party of government, and if KwaZulu Natal refused to accept it, then something approaching a civil war really could break out. It wasn't clear that the top leadership of the ANC was prepared to fight such a conflict and this was likely the only thing still holding Mthwesa's key supporters back from agreeing to the deal.

'That's our best lever,' Rollins said. 'Hollow gestures like cosmetic sanctions that actually strengthen Mthwesa's position internally are not in our interest. Breaking off relations and taking ourselves out of the picture … if that's even under consideration, that would be insane. Our best shot is to help strengthen the prag-matic group in the ANC and try to help them find a way out. A statement of concern in the Security Council will be fine. A vetoed resolution that amounts to an ultimatum would be a disaster. I would judge that it will strengthen Mthwesa enough for him to say yes to the Chinese.'

'We need to get the Brits to hold back on this resolution,' said Marion, who had already come to this conclusion after speaking to Rollins a couple of days earlier.

Havering laughed.

'Doug, it's poorly timed and it's going to fail. If we've got people in the ANC who are on our side, like Tomasina says, we need to do what we can to strengthen their position. We need to be very firm that we're not going to accept this situation but equally firm that we're going to help South Africa find its own way out of it.'

'Mthwesa's never going to go for that,' said Havering.

Ellman tried to suppress her frustration. The Chinese wanted time to craft a deal that enough of the ANC would accept. The US could use that same time to make sure that didn't happen, working to craft a different deal. In the first instance it might take the shape of some kind of power-sharing arrangement with the opposition rather than elections, which would stand as an interim solution for a year or two. The US could offer a support package to sweeten it.

'Doug,' she said, 'this isn't for Mthwesa. This is to give something for the internal opposition within the ANC. This just needs a little patience. We need to give them a weapon and give them enough strength to use it.'

'I don't see us going to the president and saying the Brits are putting down this resolution and we're going to abstain.'

'I didn't say we abstain. We need to get the Brits to hold fire. Bob, do you agree with that? Let's try to get them to hold fire or put down something that's less confrontational, and let's work on an approach that might give the ANC opposition a way out.'

'This president is not going to abstain on a resolution that is so clear cut about democracy,' said Havering before Livingstone could reply.

'Doug,' said Marion in exasperation, 'what I just said is we talk to the Brits and try to get them to hold off.'

'The president won't want you to do that. He's expecting a resolution. And right now, he's not in any mood to try to stop it. In fact, he wants it.'

Ellman frowned, trying to understand. 'What are you telling me?'

'He's seen a paper.'

'When?'

'Rose asked for one.'

'And you've already *given* him one?'

'The president's not happy with China right now. Do you understand, Marion? He's not happy.'

'And this is going to make them behave more congenially?'

'Marion,' said Livingstone, 'there's nothing to stop us putting down an alternative strategy.'

Nothing, thought Marion. And nothing to stop them trying to get the president to consider it after they had apparently given him an opposite strategy already.

There was silence on the phone. Ellman didn't trust Doug Havering. He had obviously made up his mind that Bob Livingstone was a living husk and now it seemed that he was openly working around him with the White House. And Bob was just as much at fault for letting him.

'Look,' said Livingstone, 'let's find out how serious the Brits are about this and what they're planning to do when the resolution fails. I'll talk to London.' He waited, listening to hear if anyone had anything else to say. 'That's a first step.'

'Mr Secretary,' said Marion, 'can I have two minutes with you after this call?'

SHE WAITED UNTIL the others called off.

'Marion, go ahead,' said Livingstone.

'Bob, this isn't going to work.'

'What isn't?'

'This. This idea of supporting a resolution the Chinese are going to veto and then getting left in a position where we have to decide what to do when the Brits pull out of South Africa.'

Livingstone sighed. 'Marion, I thought you feel strongly about the South Africa situation. I thought you wanted a resolution.'

'I want a result. I want to see South Africa restored to democracy. If a resolution doesn't get us there, forget it. We need to work with forces in the ANC regime who want a restoration. We need to strengthen them against Mthwesa. Does a resolution do that? It doesn't. All it does is strengthen Mthwesa and make things worse. And it gets the Chinese pissed. We haven't even got a statement from them over Fidelian yet. Do you think this is how we're going to get it? We can't keep slapping them in the face.'

Livingstone was silent for a moment.

'Marion, it would be very bad if they didn't say anything. The consensus at the National Security Council last week was that we would understand that as an admission of guilt on Zhang's part.'

'That would be a poor interpretation without something else to evidence it.'

'I agree.'

'Bob, is that what Opitz said to their finance minister? That we'd interpret it as an admission of guilt if they didn't make a statement?'

'I don't know. I gave my input to the draft of what she was going to say. She was getting input from the White House as well. I wasn't there when she spoke.'

'Have you seen a transcript?'

'No.'

'You know, Bob, if they think that's our attitude, they won't do it.'

'That's what I told them. I said it to Susan. If there's any way, shape or form they can interpret this request as a threat, you can forget it. Better not to speak to them at all.'

Marion frowned. The notion of getting a Chinese statement on Fidelian seemed a forlorn hope.

'What's happened to our two guys who were captured in Uganda?' she asked suddenly. 'Have you heard anything?'

'No,' said Livingstone. 'What's that got to do with this?'

'Nothing. I just wondered.' Marion paused. 'You know, there's a good chance Zhang won't make a statement. Why should he? It makes him lose face. Effectively we're asking him to say he miscalculated on this one. He would have to be extremely well disposed towards us to say that.'

'He can find a form of words.'

'He'd have to be extremely well disposed to say it in any form. If we want any chance of getting that statement, we need to tell the Chinese we're not in support of the British resolution.'

'I can't do that.'

'I'll tell Liu.'

'No! Marion, you will not speak to Liu about this. Not without the president's approval.'

She didn't reply.

'Marion?'

'I heard you, Bob.'

There was silence on the phone.

'Marion, how important do you think this South Africa thing is to Zhang?'

She wasn't sure. The first resolution condemning the suspension of the South African constitution had sailed through the Security Council. But it was no ultimatum, and carried no threat of sanctions. It was hard to imagine even such a gentle statement getting through today. 'It's becoming important, I think. Let me ask you a question, Bob. Do you really think Zhang miscalculated on Fidelian?'

'Probably. I can't see why he'd want to bring this down on himself.'

'Bob, do you know Joel Ehrenreich?'

'I know the name.'

'He's published a new book. You should read it.'

'Send me a copy. Look, Marion, I've got to go. Is there anything else?'

'Maybe we should work with the Chinese on this. Maybe we should offer to sit down, China, us, South Africa, a tripartite thing, and see if we can figure out a solution.'

'That's a not a bad idea. Unfortunately, I don't think the president would agree.'

'Then he'd be wrong. Bob, he's wrong on this. If we back the

British we gain nothing more than satisfying our own sense of moral righteousness. We give up the ability to exert any influence. We win a very minor battle and lose the war.'

Livingstone sighed. 'Marion, I'm not saying you're wrong, but for this president, this is a very easy decision. It's a question of do you stand up for democracy or don't you?'

'I'm not saying we don't stand up for democracy. Of course we do. But there are ways–'

'And the president likes this one.'

'Then the president's wrong and you need to tell him.'

'Marion,' retorted Livingstone angrily, 'I don't just *tell* the president anything! I'm sorry. I'm not Gary Rose. I'm not John Oakley. In this administration that's not how it works.'

37

FOUR DAYS AFTER the initial report of the two US airmen being moved to Sudan, there was now near certainty that the men were there. The CIA had a sighting from a reliable source to add to the first source of information. Monitoring of Sudanese security communications had uncovered electronic traffic that, beneath the thin veil of a few childish code names, almost certainly referred to the Apache pilots.

There had been no statement from the Chinese government. A week had passed since Susan Opitz spoke with Finance Minister Bai.

The markets had paused, ready to jump but not sure in which direction. One day saw small rises and claims that the worst was over, the next day would see the rises reversed and claims that the worst was yet to come. Interbank lending activity was still virtually nonexistent as uncertainty continued over the viability of individual banks whose stock prices bounced around as one rumor replaced another. The Fed continued to provide liquidity, which was keeping the system afloat. Market analysts and media commentators seemed to be expecting something to come out of China, although no one knew that Opitz had made an approach. It was a temporary position. The logic of the panic was still there, if not the urgency. Until there was some clarification of how Fidelian had been allowed to fail two weeks previously, the logic would remain.

The National Security Council convened at 1pm. Opitz told the group that in her view there was potential for another significant fall across the markets, and it wouldn't take much. In circumstances such as these, even an event that at first sight looked trivial could act as a trigger.

Gary Rose spoke briefly to inform the members of the council that the two surviving airmen, Captains Pete Dewy and Phil Montez, were believed to have been in Sudan for the past four days.

Bob Livingstone looked at the president in incredulity. Four days? Four days and he hadn't been told? He opened his mouth to speak but stopped himself. He was aware of the way other people at the table were looking at him, the way you look at the chump who's the last guy to find out what everyone already knows.

He hoped the president realized that balancing his demand for a Chinese statement on Fidelian with his agreement to give US support for a resolution on South Africa had just got a whole lot more complicated.

In Uganda itself, Mortlock Hale reported, an intense onslaught of drone attacks had accounted for up to an estimated hundred enemy casualties since the attack in which Jack Duffey and Harley Gauss had died. That assault seemed to have scattered a large number of LRA fighters and some had turned up in areas of lighter cover where drones could operate more effectively.

'What about Gauss?' demanded the president. 'Did we find his body?'

'No, sir.'

'Any idea where it is?'

'We won't find it until we capture some of their guys and get the chance to question them. At the moment, given that we're restricting ourselves to unmanned vehicles, that's unlikely to happen.'

'We've got to get that body,' muttered the president.

'Frankly, Mr President, by now I don't know what will be left of it.'

'We've got to get it, General. You tell that to Pressler.'

Hale nodded. He outlined what was known about the current location of the two missing airmen. Defense intelligence had them in the southern third of Sudan, with the last reliable sighting outside the town of Rumbek, two hundred miles from the Ugandan border. The area was under constant satellite surveillance. As long as the men were still in that southern region, they could be reached by American forces operating out of their Kenyan base at Lodwar.

'Who will we be fighting?' asked Gary Rose. 'LRA or Sudanese?'

'Could be either. Could be both.'

'We should also be aware that China has military advisors in the country,' said Ryan Ferris, the director of national intelligence. China took almost all Sudan's oil and it was a widely known fact in the intelligence community that, without admitting it, China had significant numbers of military advisors helping the regime maintain itself against long-running insurgencies in the west and south.

'Advisors or troops?' said Livingstone.

'It's a fine line, Mr Secretary. If you're asking whether the Chinese in there can strap on a gun, the answer's yes. We think Dewy and Montez have probably been handed over to the Sudanese, although at this point we can't definitively say. The question is somewhat moot, anyway. We know the Sudan government knows about them from our electronic surveillance. If the LRA's still got them, it's because at this stage it suits the Sudanese to let them keep them.'

'So we're planning on going in if we think we can get them?' said Opitz.

'You bet,' said Oakley. 'They hold our guys, we go in.' He threw a glance in Bob Livingstone's direction. 'They don't need a UN resolution to know that.'

'I think we'll locate them,' said Ferris. 'Sudan isn't Beirut.'

'If they've handed them over to the Sudanese,' said Livingstone, 'what are they getting for them?'

'Guns. Possibly more sophisticated weapons. They're probably looking for ground to air capability.'

'And the Sudan government?' said the president. 'Why the hell do they want in to this?'

Rose answered. 'We have half their government still under indictment for crimes against humanity. We have a supposed no-fly zone over Darfur that's been in a place for a decade. We have sanctions against any kind of financial dealings with their regime and it's basically only China and its friends who deal with them.'

'And they think we're going to drop our sanctions over two hostages?'

'They might. They might just be dumb enough to believe that.'

'Jesus, let's hope not.'

'Mr President,' said Bob Livingstone, 'in the event that we don't find Dewy and Montez, someone's going to have to put pressure on the Sudan government.' He hated to say it, but someone had to. It was as if he had been assigned the role of party-pooper in chief and was condemned to play it at one meeting after the other. 'We all know who that's going to have to be. Something's going to have to give.'

The president gazed at him for a moment. 'What do you suggest?'

Livingstone explained that by persuading the British to hold off on their resolution, or at least not backing it, they would appear to be giving something to the Chinese, which might persuade them to be helpful over Fidelian and over the men in Sudan.

'That's like paying a kidnapper,' said Oakley.

'It's not. It gives us time to help strengthen a coalition within the ANC against the Chinese arrangement. It works in our favor even though it looks like it works in theirs.'

'Exactly. It looks like it works in theirs.'

'That's not the reality.'

'Reality is we go in and get our guys ourselves.'

'Reality is,' said Livingstone, feeling his heart pounding with anger, 'that's all very well but the *reality* is that General Hale here doesn't actually know where they are, or am I mistaken, General? No. So if that stays the same, we're going to need China's help to get them out. John, you can shake your head as much as you like but that's how it is. And we still want them to give a statement about Fidelian, and you're saying we still want them to support a sanctions threat over South Africa. Plus a whole bunch of other things that are coming up in the next year over the Arctic, climate change, you name it. Just think about how much we want from them.'

'We'll get our guys,' said Oakley. 'Ask me to trust the US army or Zhang and his cronies in Beijing, and I know who I'd trust.'

Livingstone almost thumped the table. What kind of an argument was that?

'Bob,' said the president, 'you can go ahead and talk to these elements in the ANC who you say are on our side.'

'And the resolution?'

'That's separate. If the Brits bring it, we back it.'

'Then we need to ask them not to bring it.'

'The British prime minister's spoken to me. He needs to bring it and I've said we'll back him.'

'And that's exactly what China wants us to do. It plays into their hands. They'll veto it and all we'll achieve is to undermine the people we want to strengthen in South Africa. It strengthens Mthwesa and drives him into China's arms.'

'I've said we'll back it.' The president's tone was curt. 'I can't tell Zhang I'm not going to back democracy in South Africa to get our two guys back. That's the deal you're proposing.'

'With respect, sir, it's not. What I'm saying is we're actually more likely to get democracy in South Africa if we don't have a resolution. Let's give the Chinese the time they think they want, and we'll use that ourselves for our own purposes.'

'Well, I'm sorry but that doesn't work because it would look like a deal. John's right, it would look like we're paying a kidnapper. Perception's the reality. You pay once, you pay again. That's not the kind of relationship I'm prepared to have with Zhang.'

'Mr President, that's not–'

'Bob, write a paper.'

Oakley grinned.

Livingstone opened his mouth to speak, then stopped, seeing the way the president was watching him. Beneath the table, his hands were shaking. He felt ill, almost nauseated. Marion Ellman's words at the end of their last conversation had stung him and he had pushed harder in this meeting than he generally did. He loosened the knot of his tie, feeling clammy and breathless. He wasn't a confrontational man and going head to head with John Oakley was something he dreaded. And even having done it, he felt that he had been ineffectual.

The president was speaking again. 'I'm assuming at this stage we keep it quiet about our guys being in Sudan.'

Hale nodded.

'Sudan needs to know that we know they've got our people and we expect them back,' said Oakley. 'We need to tell those bastards we'll go in and take our guys if they don't give them back right now.'

'Bob, you want to make sure they get that message?'

Livingstone looked up and nodded.

'I'll give you a draft,' said Rose.

'General,' said the president, 'Admiral Pressler is ready to move, I assume?'

'We can go at a moment's notice. As soon as we have a location, it'll be your call.'

The president nodded. Thanksgiving was three days away. He wondered if there was a chance the two pilots would be back.

'Okay,' he said. 'Let's do that. Now, the other thing I want to know is, what's going on with Zhang? Anyone hear anything? Is there going to be a statement or not?'

No one knew.

'Mr President,' said Susan Opitz, 'I understand Congress is going to be calling Bill Custler to testify after Thanksgiving.'

Knowles closed his eyes for a moment. That was great. That was just what they needed.

'If Custler knows some kind of detail about what was going on in the Chinese government and testifies to that effect, it might make a statement by the Chinese irrelevant anyway.'

'When's he being called?'

'Next Monday.'

Knowles sat back in his chair and let out a long breath. It was possible that Zhang was waiting to see what Custler would say. The Chinese president wouldn't want to make a statement and then have the CEO of Fidelian contradict him. That would mean another week without a word from the Chinese side.

'I've spoken to Custler once since it happened,' said Opitz. 'He refused to divulge anything that went on between him and his board. I believe he does have the right to stay silent on that before the committee. If he chooses not to, if he wants to drop some kind of bombshell, I don't know what it's going to be.'

'Don't you think we should find out?'

'Mr President?' It was the president's counsel. 'I think it would be extremely unwise for any official of the administration to approach Mr Custler at this point, now that he's been called by Congress. From the outside it could easily be construed as an attempt to interfere with his testimony. If the secretary or anyone else chooses to go that route they'd need to have counsel at that meeting and be prepared to provide a verbatim transcript of the conversation.'

The president smiled incredulously.

'I'm serious, sir.'

'That sounds pretty strong.'

The lawyer nodded.

The president looked at Opitz. 'You've really got no idea what he's going to say?'

The Treasury secretary shook her head.

38

'MR CUSTLER, CAN you tell me how you would describe your objectives as Chief Executive Officer of Fidelian Bank?'

Bill Custler returned the gaze of Henry Westheim, a small, snub-nosed Philadelphia Democrat who sat second left from center at the bar of the Senate Banking Committee.

'Senator, I believe it was in keeping with the objectives of just about any CEO of a major investment bank. I was never asked to do anything different than I was asked to do in my previous jobs.'

'How would you describe those objectives?'

Custler thought for a moment. 'To manage the affairs of the bank in a manner most conducive to creating value for its shareholders, to deliver a great service for its customers, to provide a conducive and secure environment for its employees. To be a good member of the corporate and financial community. And also, of course, complying with all the relevant regulation.'

'And do you think that is what you achieved?'

'Within the constraints of the cards that were dealt to me, I believe that I did. Yes, sir.'

'What were these "cards", as you call them?' Westheim said it with a sneer.

'It's no secret now that there were huge issues at the bank and I'm not trying to unduly exonerate myself, Senator, but those issues largely predate my time at Fidelian and I guess they're the cards I'm talking about. So within those constraints, sir, I believe that I did manage to achieve my objectives as I understood them to be.'

'To be a good member of the … how did you put it? The corporate and financial community?'

'Yes, sir.'

'To provide a conducive and secure environment for your employees? The large majority of whom, I would imagine now, are no longer employees. They might be interested to hear that you believe you managed to do that for them. Mr Custler, your attitude seems awfully complacent for someone who has just presided over the … well, I think the *New York Times* can probably say it more eloquently than me.' Westheim made a show of holding up a tablet computer showing a recent article from the newspaper. 'I quote: … over the most egregious example of banking ineptitude that we have seen since Dick Fuld led Lehman Brothers to oblivion ten years ago.'

'Congressman, I don't quite see it that way.'

'No, sir, but the American people does.'

Bill Custler didn't respond to that. He knew that a lot of what he would face in this congressional committee room would amount to grandstanding for the television cameras that were positioned around the chamber. There was going to be as much lecturing as questioning, as much grasping at soundbites as probing into the facts. His lawyer, who was sitting beside him, had advised Custler to respond sparsely to those things, if at all. It would be no-win for him if he tried to mollify the worked-up outrage. It wasn't there to be mollified. It was there to be seen.

Senator Givens, the chair of the committee, turned to another senator, Republican Nancy della Rovere from Arizona.

Della Rovere spent at least half of her allotted fifteen minutes with a set of opening remarks attacking the rules on banking regulation that had been brought in under the Democratic – she emphasized this around a dozen times – Obama administration. Finally she got to her questions. 'Mr Custler,' she said, 'I would like to understand better the evolution of this event. You referred to issues at your bank and clearly there were issues. That may be somewhat of an understatement, if you'll allow me to say so. Can I ask you when you first became aware of the problems that led to the bankruptcy of Fidelian Bank?'

'Senator, I'll need to be a little precise in the way I answer this, so I'll ask you to bear with me. The problems, that is the … losses, in our developing markets businesses, which were the core of the problems that contaminated everything else, as I've already explained … they'd been clear for some period of time. The decisions which were responsible for those losses go back a lot further, in most instance many years.'

'Mr Custler, I asked you when you became aware of them.'

'Yes, ma'am, that's what I'm getting to. I had been aware of them for some months, but I believed that we would be able to manage the impact of these losses in the normal way. What I mean by that,' he added quickly, seeing the senator opening her mouth to ask a question, 'is by going to the market for a capital raising in order to replenish our balance sheet once we wrote those losses down. Senator, I've raised capital on the markets on a number of occasions, with other institutions and in fact with Fidelian Bank as well. This was a rather large sum that we needed, that's true, but in principle I had no reason to imagine the exercise would be different to any of the others.'

'So you thought you were going to be able to raise twenty-three billion dollars?'

'Yes, ma'am. So did Morgan Stanley, incidentally, which was going to be the lead underwriter on the bond issue. It was a large sum, as I've just said, but our judgment was that we could do it.'

'But it turned out that you couldn't?'

'No, ma'am.'

'When did you become aware of that?'

'It was only in the weeks leading up to our bankruptcy. Largely it was a function of the stock price. Our stock price, as you know, fell considerably, and as that happened it became clear that market sentiment towards the bank had turned sharply negative and we would not be able to raise the amount of capital we would require. At that point Morgan Stanley advised us they would not be prepared to underwrite the issue of our bonds.'

'Do you think that was a fair assessment?'

'Yes, ma'am. I'm not blaming them. I likely would have made the same assessment had I been in their place.'

'Why did the stock price fall, Mr Custler?'

'That I couldn't say, Senator.'

'It fell before any of the losses you mentioned became public knowledge.'

'Yes. That's correct.'

'Are you aware that anyone was using inside information about the losses you had accrued?'

'No, ma'am.'

'So, it's a mystery?'

'Yes, ma'am.'

'A mystery about why your stock price falls just when it needs to stay up so you can recapitalize the business.'

Custler didn't reply. Whatever innuendo the senator thought she was making, he let it stand.

'I'd like to come back to these losses you referred to. When did you become aware of them?'

'Of the developing market losses? That's what you're referring to?'

'Yes, Mr Custler,' said the senator brusquely. 'That's what I'm referring to. When did you become aware of them?'

'That would have been over a period of time, ma'am, as the picture became clearer.'

'Were you aware of it when you became CEO of Fidelian?'

'No, ma'am. I was recruited from a competitor bank and would have had no knowledge of any internal matters at Fidelian.'

'Then when did you first become aware?'

'That would be after I joined.'

'When?'

Custler hesitated. He turned to his counsel, who covered the microphone in front of Custler and whispered in his ear. Bill Custler knew that a wave of law suits would likely arise out of the Fidelian failure – the first of which had already been filed – and that he himself would not be immune to prosecution.

Custler turned back to the congresswoman. 'Various problems became clear to me as time went on.'

'And yet you made no announcements about this to the public?'

Custler turned to his counsel again. This time there was a brief whispered conversation.

'Ma'am, I believe that all announcements were made in accordance with regulatory requirements.'

'Yet nothing was said until the day your bank went bankrupt?'

The lawyer whispered in his ear again.

'Ma'am, I can only repeat what I said. To the best of my knowledge – and I was very clear about this throughout my time there with our chief financial officer and our chief compliance officer – we complied one hundred per cent with the requirements of the relevant accounting rules and regulatory authorities. I think the paper trail will show clearly that this was the case and it was certainly my intention. I think that's all I can say on this.'

'I hope you're right about the paper trail, Mr Custler. I believe that's going to be examined in some detail.'

Custler was silent.

Senator Givens turned to Donald Goss, a big bear of a man from South Carolina.

'Mr Custler,' he began right away, 'let me explain why I'm confused. I don't understand why your bank went bankrupt. See, where I come from, if business ain't too good, well, you look around for someone who'll take it off your hands and you sell it to 'em. You don't just go belly up, not if you can help it. You don't just throw your employees out on the street, you try to do a little better for them. How many people did your bank employ? Can you remind us, Mr Custler?'

'Eighteen thousand, Senator. Slightly more.'

'And how many of them still have a job?'

'I don't have that exact number,' said Custler quietly.

'Can you estimate?'

'Not very many, sir.'

'I see. Not very many. Now, I understand there was someone who wanted to buy your bank. And I understand that you did not accept that offer. Now you told Senator Westheim that your objective as CEO – and I have to say, I agree with the senator that if you think you carried out those objectives, sir, you are sadly mistaken – now you told him that one of those objectives was to get the best value for your stockholders. So perhaps you would like to explain to this committee how the course of action you followed got the best value for them.'

'Sir, it is true that there was an offer for the bank.'

'Well, we all know there was an offer. What we don't know is why you said no to that offer.'

'Senator, it was not an acceptable offer.'

'Says who? Says you?'

'No, sir. That was not a decision for me. That was a decision that came from consultation with my board.'

'And who is your board, Mr Custler? Is that the People's Investment Corporation of China?'

'No, sir.'

'Is that Mr Hu of the People's Investment Corporation of China?'

'No, sir. The People's Investment Corporation does have two seats on the board of Fidelian Bank but that is far from constituting the entire board.'

'So I'm going to ask you, did the People's Investment Corporation of China tell you that you should not take this offer?'

'Senator, as I said, the People's Investment Corporation is not the only stockholder in Fidelian Bank.'

'I know that, Mr Custler. Let me ask you a question. How many times, in your experience as the Chief Executive Officer of Fidelian Bank, did the board agree to do something that the People's Investment Corporation of China did not want you to do?'

Custler looked at his lawyer, who whispered in his ear.

'Senator, I ...' Custler paused and looked at his lawyer again.

'Mr Custler, don't worry about that. Let us assume it is a very rare occurrence. I would assume it would be a very rare occurrence for a board to act against the wishes of such a large stockholder. Would you agree, without naming any names, that it would be a rare occurrence?'

'Yes, Senator. I think that's fair.'

'Thank you.' Goss smiled. 'Maybe it might happen once.'

Custler waited.

'As a matter of interest, how much Fidelian stock does the People's Investment Corporation of China hold?'

'I believe that would be fractionally over twenty-five per cent of the stock.'

'Mr Custler, how much does it *really* hold?'

'Senator, I don't believe I understand your question.'

'Is it possible that the People's Investment Corporation of China holds more that twenty-five per cent of Fidelian stock through its subsidiaries?'

'Technically I suppose that would be possible.' Custler paused as his lawyer covered the microphone and whispered in his ear. 'That would be speculation, sir.'

'Sure, I know. I know. Let's speculate a little further. If they did hold more stock through these subsidiaries, and if they did not declare that, given the level of stockholding that would amount to, would that be illegal?'

'I'm not a lawyer, sir.'

'I am. It would be illegal. Now, Mr Custler, do you know how much stock of Fidelian Bank in total the People's Investment Corporation of China holds through its subsidiaries?'

'Sir, as you said this is speculation.'

'I've heard it may be as high as forty per cent.'

Custler shrugged.

'So you don't know?'

Custler hesitated for a moment. 'No.'

Goss stared at him.

Custler stared back.

'Okay. That would be a hell of a loss if they held forty per cent of that bank.' Goss shook his head theatrically. 'They wouldn't be too happy with you, Mr Custler. I wouldn't be too happy if I owned a company and my CEO ran it into the ground, and someone came along with an offer and he didn't even take it. I'd wonder if that CEO didn't have a screw loose. Couple of screws. A whole boxful of screws. First he destroys my company and then he doesn't manage to get a dime for what's left. I wouldn't think much of that CEO, would you, Mr Custler?'

'I … don't know what I'd think.'

'I do. I'd think that was one hell of an excuse for a CEO.'

'That's your opinion, sir.'

'That's my opinion? What kind of a CEO is that, Mr Custler? Can you tell me? What kind of a CEO sees eighteen thousand people lose their jobs and can't so much as lift a finger to try to save them?'

Custler took a deep breath, trying not to let the senator's insults get to him, which was exactly what the senator wanted. 'Sir, whether or not to accept any offer was not my decision.'

'Of course not. Did you speak to anyone else on the board about this offer? Anyone outside of the board members of the People's Investment Corporation of China?'

'All the board members were consulted, sir.'

'And did any of them say they were in favor of accepting this offer?'

Custler's lawyer put his hand over the microphone and whispered in his ear.

Custler looked back at the senator. 'Senator, I'm required to decline to answer that.'

'You're required to decline?'

'Yes, sir.'

'*Required?*'

'Yes, sir.'

Goss smiled as if in complete disbelief. 'Mr Custler, let me remind you that you are seated before a committee of the United States Senate. Now, I am giving you the opportunity to tell the American people how it came to pass that a viable, commercial offer for Fidelian Bank was rejected by yourself. I don't know what *requirement* could be more important than the American people's requirement to know how that happened. Now, sir, I'm going to repeat a question I asked you before. Did the People's Investment Corporation of China instruct you to reject this offer? You have the opportunity to tell the American people what happened to your bank. Please answer this question.'

Custler listened to his lawyer whispering in his ear. He nodded grimly.

'Senator, I'm required to decline to answer.'

'Then I have to conclude that an agency of a foreign government led directly to the bankruptcy of this American institution. Now, Mr Custler, I am giving you the opportunity to tell me why I should not conclude that. If you will, Mr Custler, please tell me and tell this committee and tell the American people why we should not conclude that.'

Custler frowned. 'That's not how I would put it,' he said quietly.

'Then how would you put it?'

Custler's lawyer began to speak in his ear, but Custler shook his head.

'It was not an offer that my shareholders felt was acceptable. Senator, that is what happened. That is all I can say.'

'That's it? It was not an offer that my shareholders felt was acceptable.' Goss repeated the words sarcastically. 'That's all you have to say on the matter? To your eighteen thousand ex-employees. To your customers. To your stockholders. I'm talking about the stockholders who were not big enough to tell you what to do, not Mr Hu of the People's Investment Corporation of China, Mr Custler, but the honest stockholders who held the stocks of your bank, sir – *your* bank, sir – thinking they were going to help fund their retirement while all the time you knew you had these losses sitting on your books waiting to come out. Do you think they had a good Thanksgiving last week, Mr Custler? I don't think they had very much to give thanks to you about.'

Custler gazed at him.

The senator gazed back with a look of disgust. 'Well, I'm bound to tell you, I don't know how you sleep at night, Mr Custler.'

Bill Custler continued to stare at the senator. The truth was, he hadn't slept much at all recently.

'Mr Custler?'

Custler looked at the chairman of the committee, Bill Givens. In the wake of the election results, in which three Republican members of the House in Givens' home state of Louisiana had been deposed, the Senate Banking Committee chairman was toying with the idea of staging a run for the Republican nomination in two years' time. He had no interest in protecting the president. By inflicting some damage on him in this hearing, he had the opportunity to get his own run started.

'Did the president speak to you in the days before you declared bankruptcy?' Givens asked.

Custler shook his head. 'No, sir.'

'Did you speak to anyone in the administration?'

'Yes, sir. Naturally, I had a number of conversations and meetings with Secretary Opitz and Mr Rabin of the Federal Reserve and Mr O'Brien of the SEC and various of their officials.'

'But you didn't speak to the president?'

'No, sir.'

'Has he spoken to you since?'

'No, sir.'

'Has any member of the administration?'

'I've spoken to Secretary Opitz and Mr Rabin and various of their officials.'

'Have they suggested to you or intimated to you in any way what you should or should not say before this committee?'

'No, sir.'

'You say you spoke to Secretary Opitz and Mr Rabin in the days before the bankruptcy. Do you think it's feasible the president was not aware of what they were saying to you?'

'That would be–'

'Do you think it's feasible the president would not have approved of what they were saying to you?'

Custler waited to see if the senator had finished. 'That would be speculation, sir.'

'Would you care to speculate?'

'No, sir.'

Givens nodded. 'Are you aware if the president spoke to President Zhang of China during this period of time?'

'No, sir. I am not aware if the president spoke to President Zhang.'

'There are persistent reports that President Knowles spoke to President Zhang about your bank, Mr Custler, shortly before you filed for bankruptcy. I am going to ask you again whether you are aware if President Knowles did make such a call.'

'No, sir,' said Custler. 'I am not aware.'

Givens stared at him silently.

Custler stared back.

'Mr Custler, I want to ask you a question I asked before. Has any member of the administration, or anyone you have reason to think might be connected to the administration, suggested what you should or should not say before this committee?'

'No, Senator,' replied Custler firmly. 'And if such an approach had been made, it would not make any difference at all to the answers I'm giving. I'm not here to protect or defend President Knowles or any member of his administration.'

'What are you here to do?'

'I am here to tell the truth in response to the questions you ask.'

'Not to tell the truth about the way your bank collapsed?'

'Of course, Senator. If that's what you want to know.'

'To tell the truth about why a commercial offer was rejected for this bank? To tell the truth about why an offer that might have saved the jobs of eighteen thousand people was not taken up?'

'Yes, sir.'

'Then I invite you to answer the question Senator Goss asked you a short time ago. Did the People's Investment Corporation of China instruct you to reject this offer?'

Custler's lawyer put his hand over the microphone and whispered in his ear.

'I have already answered those questions to the best of my ability.'

'Mr Custler, you declined to answer.'

'Yes, sir.'

'And that's answering to the best of your ability? You just told me you came before this committee to tell the truth. If that's the way you do it, Mr Custler, I doubt very much the American people will believe you.'

They didn't seem to. Or at least the press didn't. Interpretation of Custler's performance in the media over the ensuing twenty-four hours was that his silence was admission, and that the People's Investment Corporation, backed by President Zhang, had been the prime mover behind the rejection of the offer for Fidelian.

The markets, which had been sitting nervously in limbo, began to falter. But the thing that really sent them into a new nosedive wasn't so much the remarks that Bill Custler made in front of the Senate Banking Committee as a statement that was issued from a foreign capital two days later.

But it wasn't from Beijing.

39

IT WAS A month since Ed Grey had found himself hundreds of millions up thanks to his early bet against Fidelian and the rest of the banking sector. It felt like a year. If he had held on to the short positions he had accumulated, he would have quadrupled the profit he realized on those trades. Instead, the man who prided himself on never closing a trade until it had run its full course had closed out too early. Way too early, leaving him exposed to huge losses on long positions he held before the crisis began.

Since then he had lived on his nerves as Fidelian went bankrupt and the markets plunged and then jack-knifed around driven by rumor and panic, selling stocks to meet margin calls by Red River's banks. The money raised by the Fidelian trade had disappeared almost quicker than it had materialized, barely a drop in the ocean of cash the banks demanded of him. Red River had had to shed a further eight billion of assets to meet margin calls, selling them into falling markets in which every other DIV on the planet was doing the same. He was struggling to hold off redemptions from his investors that would have forced him to sell even more. And still he didn't know if the market had bottomed. No one knew. If the market turned out to have been only pausing, if it was ready to take another slide, the banks would be scrambling for more cash and asset disposals would turn into a plummeting, self-fueling death spiral.

Ed Grey had always prided himself on his ability to leave work at work. Good days, bad days – and he had known them both at the extremes in his years as a trader – he had always been able to sleep nights. But not now. At night he lay awake, wondering what might be the trigger that would set off another slide. Whatever it was, he knew it would probably turn out to be something no one was expecting.

Another major bank failure was almost taken for granted. The markets might take it in their stride, might even show some relief when it finally happened. But something that wasn't expected, an event the markets weren't sure how to deal with – that was the danger.

As Ed looked at the CNBC screen in his office, he wondered if this was it.

The statement had been made shortly after 4.30pm in St Petersburg, 8.30am in New York. Within a half hour it was being replayed on just about every news and business website in the world.

The Russian prime minister was standing in a room with white, gilt-edged wall paneling behind him. Anatoly Peskarov was a thin, red-haired man in his forties, the latest of Putin's Puppets, as Russian leaders had come to be known. He had taken a question from one of the journalists at the press conference about how he thought Russia was going to be affected by the collapse in the US markets. Ed Grey listened to the voice of the translator as the prime minister made a brief comment about the strength of Russia's domestic market, which was almost fifty per cent bigger than at the time of the economic crisis in 2008. He said something about the way Russia was playing its role in the G22 Financial Stability Council to ensure the losses were contained. 'I can also add,' said the translator over the rumble of Anatoly Peskarov's voice, 'that in case anyone is wondering, the investment funds of the Russian state operate only on a commercial basis with the aim of achieving the best result for their ultimate owners – the Russian people. When one of our investments fails, that is a loss we do not want to see.' Ed Grey saw a slight smile steal across the Russian's face. 'That includes any businesses that may have failed recently. I can't speak for other governments, but the government of Russia has never and would never be tempted to use the people's investment funds for political purposes. That is a guarantee I can give. To prove this, I will instruct any fund of the Russian state to cooperate fully, to even open its books to the regulatory authorities of any market in which it operates. I invite other governments to do the same.'

The journalist asked if the prime minister could name any other government he had in mind.

Peskarov shrugged. 'I am not thinking of anyone.' That same hint of a smile was there again. 'You would have to ask them.'

Ed Grey felt a tingle down his spine. It wasn't a tingle of excitement. It was a tingle of fear.

Peskarov was as good as saying, we didn't fiddle Fidelian, but the Chinese did. If they didn't – let them say so.

And they hadn't said a thing.

Grey found a link on the CNBC website and watched the statement again. The fear in his belly was turning into a deep, deep sense of dread. He looked at the screens in his office. On the European bourses, the indices were turning red. Wall Street wasn't open yet. Another ten minutes. Ed Grey winced. When the bell went, blood was going to flow.

IN THE WHITE HOUSE, Tom Knowles was handed a note summarizing Peskarov's remarks soon after he started a morning-long meeting on the financial crisis with members of the National Economic Council and senior congressional leaders from both parties. He read it briefly, whispered in the ear of his personal aide to have a meeting set up for when the talks with the Congress people were done, and turned back to listen to a point one of the senators was making.

A lunch of sandwiches was waiting in the Oval Office when he finally got back there.

He stood and watched the footage of Peskarov's statement, munching on a chicken sandwich. Then he sat down in disgust.

'Well, that's great. What the hell does Peskarov think he's doing?'

'He enjoyed it,' said Dean Moss.

Knowles nodded, picking a couple more quarters of sandwich off the plate on the table. He had seen the smirk on Peskarov's weaselly face. 'What's happening on Wall Street?'

'Exactly what you'd think,' said Ed Abrahams, who had grabbed a plateful of sandwiches. It took a lot of fuel, he liked to say, to keep an Abrahams going, and he was never backward when the food arrived.

The market had been open three hours by now and there was no way of knowing where the drop, currently six per cent, would clunk to a halt.

'Zhang's got to say something,' said Knowles. 'He's got to say something now.'

'He won't say it today,' said Abrahams, his mouth half full of ham and cheese.

China was thirteen hours ahead of Eastern Time and it was now past midnight there. Even if Beijing was planning to issue a statement, it wasn't going to happen immediately. Realistically it would be another eight to ten hours – at the very earliest – before anything could be expected. That was the whole trading day on Wall Street.

They needed to be sure it happened. Unless a statement was rapidly forthcoming, Knowles would have to call Zhang again. That was obvious. Or he could call right now and wake the Chinese leader, but Zhang wouldn't do anything until morning in China anyway. By then the trading day in New York would be finished. If Knowles waited until morning Zhang's time, the Chinese would have all day in their time zone to issue a statement before New York opened again the next morning. All in all, they weren't going to get a statement out of the Chinese president while the US markets were open today, so there was no point waking him.

'Except it impresses him with the urgency of what's at stake,' said Gary Rose.

'Let's not treat him like an idiot,' said Abrahams. 'I'd assume he'll have worked out it's urgent for himself.'

'In which case, Ed, I don't need to call him,' said the president. He took a bite out of another piece of chicken sandwich and chewed it quickly. 'I called him once already so he knows it's important. If he's not an idiot he ought to have done something by now.'

Abrahams smiled. 'Fair enough.'

But Knowles didn't feel like smiling. He put down his sandwich in disgust. 'Makes me sick to call him again.'

'Maybe we should send him an email,' said Abrahams, only half jokingly.

In the aftermath of an unusually successful G20 meeting a few years previously, a network had been created of secure, direct email connections between the leaders. As far as Tom Knowles was aware, the US connection to the Chinese president had never been used.

'Yeah, right. I can definitely see him responding to that.' Knowles grimaced irritably. 'What about our guys in Sudan? What about them, huh? Kidnapped and taken into some godforsaken shithole of a foreign country with a government that thinks it's got us over a barrel. How long is it now? Two weeks! Why the hell can't Pressler find them? Maybe Mr Zhang would like to give us a little help to get them out. Maybe I should tell him that as well.'

'We need to separate the issues,' said Abrahams. The complexity of trying to link everything up together was mind-boggling. 'Let's focus on this. The message is clear. We have a full-blown crisis brewing on the markets here and it's going to hit there as well unless we get it under control. This is a shared crisis, not an American crisis. It's as much in his interest as ours to resolve it. So we need to work together. He needs to step forward like Peskarov and–'

'Peskarov! What the fuck does he think he's doing? Like it's some kind of joke! Saying he'll open his books. Like hell he will! Raises the stakes with no risk of having to execute.'

'Zhang needs to do his bit. He doesn't need to say he's going to open his books. Everyone knows that's just Peskarov trying to push it. But he does need to say there's nothing behind this other than what we can see on the surface. It's one bad bank going bust. That's all, nothing else. There's no political agenda behind it.'

'You think he's going to say that?'

'That's the message.'

'Ed, I know that's the message. That's the same message we gave to Bai, and where did that get us? You just said we should assume he isn't an idiot. He'll know that's the message.'

'Sir,' said Rose, 'you do need to call him.'

'Yeah,' said Knowles grudgingly. 'Let's wake him up. That'll make me feel a little better about it, at least.'

'I wouldn't do that.'

'I'm kidding,' growled the president.

40

FOR THREE WEEKS, Zhang had watched the movements on the American markets and tracked the impact in China. He had instructed Bai to do whatever was necessary to support the domestic economy and maintain order in the Chinese markets. Under command from the finance ministry, lending between banks was still strong. Intervention in Shanghai and Hong Kong through the PIC and other state investment funds had restricted falls in stock prices to under fifteen per cent. But there was a limit to the length of time such measures could continue. If they went on too long, the same kind of problems would be stored up as had burst out in 2014.

Zhang's faith in Bai was strong, but he was beginning to wonder whether the finance minister had been right in his advice. He hadn't said, as Qin had done, that the American president would certainly save Fidelian. But he had said that if Fidelian failed, there would be a panic that would last days. The panic had certainly come, but it hadn't lasted only days. By now it was three weeks. Was it a panic, or was it a crisis?

In one respect, at least, a crisis was not unwelcome to Zhang. Internationally China was heavily involved in the many discussions that were taking place on coordinated action to be taken should the crisis continue. Western finance ministers were nervously looking for commitments that China would stimulate its economy, and many European leaders had been on the phone to him asking for that assurance. Again China's strength was needed, as it had been needed in '08 and '09. In '08 and '09 there had been so much talk, so many promises about the role China would be given in the institutions managing the global economy. Perhaps this time a few of them would be kept.

But it was the excessive stimulus of the Chinese economy that had been required at that time that laid the seeds of the disturbances five years later and the near destruction of the Communist Party regime, which only the army had prevented. That was something Zhang would not risk again. This crisis could not be allowed to build to a point where such a stimulus was required. Bai continued to tell him there was no risk of that. As long as that was true, there was no need for him to do anything.

The finance minister had delivered the message that he had received from the American Treasury secretary. Until now, Zhang had chosen to remain silent.

It wasn't so easy for him to make a statement. People both in the party and the army were watching. He knew from various sources that the power he seemed to have exerted over the American economy had made a strong impression. If he made a statement, if he seemed to be trying to moderate what he had done, they would draw their own conclusions.

And yet if this ran out of control, if this turned from a panic to a crisis, it would present a pretext for Fan to step in.

But the statement from Peskarov changed everything. He had been told about it as soon as it was made. In the morning he met with Bai over a breakfast of rice congee. He also had Qin in the room.

Bai continued to maintain that the sense of panic would alleviate once there had been a few weeks without any more surprises. Peskarov's statement, he said, was the last twist in a story that was coming to an end. It was mischievous, but didn't change the economic fundamentals.

'What about the political fundamentals?' said Zhang sharply.

'I think the world will soon see that Peskarov is merely meddling. That is what he is like.'

Zhang grunted non-committally and took a spoonful of congee, adding a pickle to it with his chopsticks. He ate thoughtfully.

'Everyone now expects me to say something,' he said.

'You will look as if you are being forced to follow Peskarov,' said Qin. 'You will look as if you are forced to speak because of the Russians.'

'Yes, but what if I don't say it?' He looked at Bai. 'What then?'

'There is no cause for a crisis,' said Bai. 'Everyone knows Peskarov is just blowing on the fire. His suggestion to open books is ridiculous. Who would believe what they saw in such books, anyway? Yes, there is more panic now. In another few days, everyone will forget about it.'

'Won't everyone think we want them to believe we had a political reason for letting the Fidelian Bank fail?' said Zhang.

'That is not the only interpretation,' replied Qin.

Zhang took another spoonful of his congee. The influence that China's state control of companies in the American economy gave him was striking. He had not really been aware of it himself before, but now that the case of Fidelian Bank had demonstrated it, one could not help but be in awe of the effect. If he was in any doubt, the anxiety he could detect when he spoke with Knowles had shown him the strength of the power he had discovered. It wasn't even necessary to use it. Merely the awareness of it was sufficient to create an impact. It was like a military parade, or testing a bomb. Something to show that it was there. In the years of Chinese subjugation in the nineteenth century, when western powers had wanted to show their power over China, they had sent their naval vessels to sail up the Yangtze River to display their might. That was enough, they didn't need to shoot. Fidelian Bank was an equivalent for the twenty-first century. One bank, a foretaste of what could happen. This time it showed China's power over the west.

The weapon he had in his hands – which he had barely used even in the case of Fidelian Bank, and certainly not in any planned or coordinated way – seemed immensely powerful. But immensely powerful weapons, he knew, can be immensely dangerous, not only to the target, but to the one who uses them.

'Do you not think that if I say nothing, President Knowles will think that I really plan to try to manipulate his economy?'

'Who could imagine we would try to do that?' said Qin. 'It would be too dangerous. Anyway, to let a bank fail is not the same as to cause it to fail. Did you ask it to make so many bad loans? Did you tell the CEO to make such bad decisions?'

Zhang took a piece of pickled radish with his chopsticks and chewed it slowly. The situation was becoming extremely complicated. The further he had gone with this, the greater the stakes had become.

The showdown with Fan had been coming for some time, but he had not consciously chosen to precipitate it now. And yet it felt as if this matter of Fidelian that he had started had brought it to a head. His case had always been that it was economic power that would guarantee China's ascendancy. Now all the factions in the regime – and Xu's first amongst them – were watching to see if that was true and if he had the ability to wield it.

He was fearful of what would happen in Sudan. The situation there also had the potential to become very complicated. He did not think the American army would tolerate for long two of its soldiers being held hostage by a regime that many people in the United States would like to see removed. The president of Sudan had told him that his army was not aware of the Americans' location but was searching for them. Zhang did not believe that. He wondered whether the Chinese military in Sudan was involved. The truth was, Zhang himself did not know whether the Chinese army in Sudan was operating purely as advisors or took part in anti-insurgency operations. Fan had staffed the force there with loyalists and had tight control over the deployment, and Zhang did not trust what the general told him nor the reports that he saw. He wanted the two airmen released. He had told this to the Sudanese president and he had told it to Fan. The stronger he appeared in his ability to confront the US with economic power, the more likely it was that Fan would be forced to comply.

Zhang knew that he had backed himself into a corner, unable to make concessions in the outside world because of the need to shore up his power at home. But at some point, that was always going to be the case. A final reckoning with Fan was inevitable. Now it seemed to have begun, so he must take his chances. Half measures would be fatal. Whatever he did, he would have to do with all his conviction.

Appearances were crucial. It was no longer enough for China to look like the victim of American browbeating, the posture with which the Chinese government had so often been satisfied in the past. With all eyes in the regime on the developing confrontation between him and Fan, China under his leadership needed to show a new strength. The more President Knowles made demands on him, the more he would be forced to resist them. Only if Knowles backed down on something, then he would be able to help him.

Qin understood all of this well, more so than Bai, whose political cunning was only slowly emerging from under the weight of his technocratic training.

'Qin,' he said, 'let them give us something. Let them back down on South Africa. We must get something from this.'

Qin nodded.

'What if he calls you?' said Bai.

'He should stop these calls!' said Qin. 'He should understand this does not help. We look as if we must do what the American president says. Soon we will hear about this one in the press like we heard about the other one.'

'Then what should I do?'

'Perhaps he will not call.'

Zhang turned to Bai. 'You should be telling me to make the statement they want. You should be telling me to calm the markets.'

Bai nodded.

'Well?'

'I am also aware of all the other things, President Zhang.'

Zhang watched him. Bai, he knew, wanted to prove his political credentials. He wanted Zhang to see that he was more than an economist.

'You told me at the start it would be a panic of a few days. Now it is weeks. Then it will be more.'

'That is the price for showing our strength,' said Bai. 'Both outside and inside.'

Zhang shook his head. 'That is too high a price.'

'President Zhang, this is not like it was in 2008. The panic will go. We will not need to put in the stimulus we put in 2008. For a few more days, for a few weeks, perhaps, the panic will continue. But it will pass.'

'Are you sure of that?'

Bai nodded.

Zhang looked into his bowl. The congee was finished. He took a piece of pickle with his chopsticks.

There was a knock on the door. Zhang's private secretary entered.

'President Zhang, the office of President Knowles has rung to schedule a telephone conversation with you.'

41

HE HAD REFUSED to take the call. Twice. Roberta Devlin had contacted the Chinese president's office personally and both times she had been told that Zhang was unavailable.

So they waited on him to make a statement. But the silence out of Beijing was deafening. A week after Peskarov had stood up in St Petersburg and made his remarks, nothing had been heard. Everywhere else there was noise. The markets were sliding, the press was shouting and pressure groups all over the country were demanding action to protect their own pet interests. The White House was being assailed by foreign leaders wanting to talk with the president.

His approval ratings were in territory they had never been to before. Sandy Ruiz-Kellerman's latest numbers were truly awful and there were plenty of polls by other organizations to confirm them. A president whose approval hadn't been below fifty before, he was now struggling to hit forty.

It was four weeks to the day since Harley Gauss had died and Dewy and Montez were captured. It was supposed to be the holiday season. He had turned on the lights in the tree behind the White House with the press demanding to know if Dewy and Montez would be home for Christmas. Every time anyone in the administration remotely connected with security or defense spoke to the press, there was a journalist who asked that question. They talked as if he had promised it.

Things were slipping out of control. The markets were in a self-fueling cycle of panic where each fresh fall drove the next one. Ron Strickland and Susan Opitz announced one new measure after the next and each one just seemed to make things worse, driving the markets further into what appeared to be an unstoppable suicide dive.

He got together the people whose advice he valued most. Ed Abrahams, Roberta Devlin, Gary Rose, Marty Perez, John Oakley. He wanted to know how this could be controlled. The measures Strickland and Opitz had taken should have been more than enough to deal with the failure of one bad bank, including its secondary effects. It was irrational.

Marty Perez disagreed. 'What the markets are doing isn't irrational nor is it disproportionate. Mr President, we have a bank whose owner – a foreign government – let it fail. For no reason we can understand. With that, right now, no sense of panic in the market is disproportionate. They can't panic enough.'

'That was the case the day Fidelian failed,' said the president.

'Yes, and something's changed. The foreign owner refuses to exonerate himself. All he has to say is he didn't do it on purpose – and he won't. We've crossed a line with this.' Perez paused. 'The implication of the fact that Zhang refuses to talk – after everything that's happened – is that this *was* done on purpose, and the implications of that, of a foreign government manipulating the failure of a publicly held corporation – and a bank, at that – are incalculable.'

'Come on, Marty,' said Oakley. 'That's a little extreme, isn't it? Incalculable?'

Perez was almost tearing his hair out. All week long he had been fighting a battle against people in the White House who were telling the president that the markets were responding irrationally, that the actions taken by the Fed and the Treasury should have been enough whether Zhang had spoken or not. 'John, believe me, it's not extreme. Everyone knows that Chinese sovereign wealth funds and Russian sovereign wealth funds and Arab wealth funds and any other wealth fund out there are up to their necks in ownership of US stocks. Banking, mining, construction, utilities … You name it, they own it. Now, after Fidelian, everyone's looking around asking which is the next one that one of these funds is going to manipulate.'

'And which would that be?' said Oakley.

'I don't know! No one knows. That's exactly the point. People are looking around trying to figure out who owns what and dumping anything they think is in danger. And that is not disproportionate.' He turned back to Knowles. 'Mr President, the market is reacting exactly as it should. A market runs on the belief that participants will act rationally in an economic sense. It's an unwritten law that underlies everything that happens in our economy. I buy a stock or a bond a company issues because I believe the other people who are buying stocks and bonds and the people running the companies all want the same thing. Profit. Value. Now you get a bunch of owners who don't want those things, who aren't acting rationally in an economic sense – but they don't identify themselves, and they don't tell you what's driving their behavior – and that's not a market you want to be in. It's not a market – it's a casino. Invest in that and you're playing Russian roulette with your money.'

'Marty,' said Ed Abrahams, 'how long can this go on?'

'How long? Do you know what would happen if the PIC and a few other similar funds decided to dump *all* their stocks on the market tomorrow? Dump *all* their bonds? Those instruments wouldn't have a value.'

'But how much would they lose?'

'Trillions. But they don't have to do that. They don't have to take those losses. Even if they just *said* they were going to sell. It's the threat. It's not knowing where they're going to go next. It's like you've got a bunch of things in front of you and some of them have a bomb ticking inside them. Which of them do you want to own? None, because you don't know which ones have the bombs. None of them have to go off – you still don't want to hold them. And even if you knew which ones have the bombs, you don't want to own the others either, because if the one next to them blows up, chances are they're going to get damaged as well. Mr President, we've had this conversation already. We're looking at something unprecedented. This literally could bring our economy to a complete halt. No investment. No trust. The market's response is a hundred per cent rational. Anyone who's telling you that is wrong.'

'Okay, Marty,' said the president. 'You've made your point.'

'This crisis is not the same as the last. Last time, it was only our entire financial system that was about to fall over. This is way scarier. Our economic system has been infected by the political. That's not the American system. The fear we're seeing is because of a recognition that the two have become combined. You have that fear and there's *nothing* Ron and Susan can do to stop it.'

'Okay, Marty. I understand.'

No matter how stridently he said it, Perez felt, he couldn't say it strongly enough. 'This is the endgame. This is the door to Armageddon and it's starting to open.'

'Marty,' said Oakley, 'when I hear you put it like that, I think what you're describing is a form of war.'

'Yes! I think that's a perfectly legitimate comparison.'

'Well, if what you say is true, I don't know how else you could look at it. If an act of war is anything that strikes consciously and severely and with destructive intent at a vital interest of our country, then that's what this is. I can't think of anything more vital than our economy. And what you've just said here, Marty, is that these actions destroy our economy. That's as much a form of war as if they sent over a bunch of bombers and knocked out our electricity transmission grid. Except if they sent over a bunch of bombers we'd know it for what it is.'

'It's Pearl Harbor for the twenty-first century,' said Ed Abrahams.

'And cheap, too. How much did we spend in Iraq? Upwards of one and a half trillion before we made it out of there. How much did these guys lose on Fidelian? They only owned twenty-five per cent. A few tens of billions? And like you said, Marty, these guys hardly need to make any more losses. Just make the threat, and every so often maybe set off one of those bombs you were talking about.'

'And the only person who can tell us it's not what you're talking about, John, that it isn't some premeditated act of aggression, is Zhang.'

'Exactly. It's like I said to Livingstone. If they don't come out with a statement, then we'll know they've caused it.'

Gary Rose frowned. 'Let's not go too fast here. I don't know if I've ever heard of a country being accused of starting a war by failing to say something. Let's not talk ourselves into anything. We should be careful with the terminology.'

'Mr President,' said Devlin, 'can I play devil's advocate here? Like Gary said, we're talking ourselves into a position where we're seeing the Chinese silence as an act of aggression. I think we need to ask ourselves how they see it.'

Oakley laughed. 'Right. Bob may not be here, but Mrs Livingstone is in the building.'

'John, this is important. Go on, Roberta.'

'Let's say they didn't do anything,' said Devlin. 'Let's say there was no political interference in the process of Fidelian going bust.'

'Why not just say it?'

'Because why should they? I guess it is like Bob Livingstone said. It's our problem, not theirs.'

Knowles shook his head. That might have been acceptable first time around, but with what was happening in the markets, and after Peskarov's statement, that was no longer acceptable. 'I agree with John, it's an aggressive stance. And with due respect to what Gary said – because he's right, we need to be careful with the words – by an aggressive act I mean one that's not the act of a friendly nation. It's the act of a hostile nation. I'm saying not even neutral. Hostile.'

'What if it's an internal thing?' said Devlin. 'What if it's something we can't see that's motivating him?'

The president looked questioningly at Rose.

'It's always possible. When it comes to the big issues in the regime, you can never be sure if it's the party or the army that's in charge. Their head of the army holds as much implicit power as anyone in the regime. Could he have constrained Zhang from acting to save Fidelian? Depending on the dynamics of the day, and other events that were happening, you'd have to say yes.'

'So it could be the army driving this?' said Oakley. 'That makes it even more of a war.'

Rose didn't respond to that. But he repeated the argument he had made to the National Security Council almost a month earlier. 'The dynamics of what's happening within the Chinese regime, as far as this goes, are irrelevant. They have to be irrelevant. We can't ever get into a position where we tolerate this kind of action, with this kind of impact, for the domestic purposes of a foreign leader. Bottom line, whether it's Fan or whether it's Zhang, or someone else in there, they don't fight turf wars with our economy. Period.'

'So what do we do?' said the president.

'They need to understand that whatever they think, for whatever reason they're doing this, we're under attack here. They need to understand very clearly that whether intentionally or not, they're the ones who are attacking us. Now what they choose to do about that is up to them.'

'And by the way,' added Oakley, 'there are two of our guys in Sudan they'd better help us to get out.'

'If they've done this to send us a signal that they've got some kind of power over us because of their ownership of stock in our companies, then they need to understand this is not a form of power they can safely exercise. And if they haven't done it, and they just think they can make us twist a little by staying silent, then they need to understand that right there is a hostile act. And if they didn't do anything to Fidelian on purpose, but they've simply seen the effect now and they think they can use the threat whenever they want, then like Marty said, they've got to understand they can't do that either. They need to know they're playing with fire.'

'Roberta,' said the president, 'you were playing devil's advocate. Do you want to keep playing it or do you agree with that?'

Devlin shook her head. 'I'm with Gary. Whatever motivated Zhang at the start, I agree this has gone too far now for him to stay quiet.'

'We can't afford to show any weakness here,' said Rose. 'We can't give the slightest hint we're going to back down on anything because of this. We need to get a lot tougher. The world needs to see us coming right back at them so no one goes away with the idea that this is a trick they can pull on us again. Before you know it you'll get Peskarov turning around and doing the same kind of thing.'

'What do you propose?'

'First, there's Sudan. It's time to come out and announce publicly that we know our guys are in Sudan, who have no right to be holding them, and we expect the Chinese government to help get them released. We can't hold them technically accountable but in effect that's what we'll be doing. A friendly nation would exercise its influence in that regard. And then there's the South Africa resolution. The Brits are going to get that on the table before Christmas and we need to back it. If we don't, it's like we'll trade democracy in a country of fifty million people for our two guys.'

'That's what I've been saying all the time,' said Oakley. 'It's blackmail.'

'Exactly. We don't do that. We get our two guys *and* we back democracy in South Africa. Neither of those things is negotiable. Now, we do this publicly so we send a strong message to everyone who's watching that the United States won't back down on its people and on its principles. In private, we need a letter to Zhang. We state very clearly the gravity of what's happening and what we need from him, the kind of public statement that we need, and our expectation that he'll do it. This isn't a matter of negotiation. This is what has to happen.'

'I like that,' said the president, glancing at Ed Abrahams.

'This is straight down the line,' said Rose. 'You've brought us to the edge, here's what you've got to do to bring us back. We expect to see you do it. Period. Now, the other thing is, could we also talk about taking steps to restrict ownership by sovereign investment funds? Could we reclassify them as some kind of foreign-government-owned entities and put some kind of restrictions on them from a national security perspective?'

'I'd be very cautious before we do anything like that,' said Marty Perez.

'Well, Marty,' said the president, 'I think we need to think about things like that. What if we don't resolve this quickly? What if we can't take the political out of the economic as quick as we'd like, if that fear you're talking about continues? What measures do we take?'

Perez's expression was troubled. 'I don't know what that would look like. It would be extreme.'

'You're the one who said the market can't panic enough. If we're going to stop that, we may have to do things we've never thought about before. Talk to Susan and Ron. Figure it out.'

Perez nodded silently, his brow furrowed, his mind already working. The president watched him for a moment, then turned back to the others. 'Okay, so we make a public statement on Sudan and our expectations that our friends in Beijing are going to help us get our guys out. We give the go-ahead to the Brits on their resolution. And in private we send a letter to Zhang laying out what we're expecting in terms of calming the markets. Is that right?'

There were nods.

'And the statement, is that me? Do I make that statement myself?'

'Definitely,' said Abrahams.

'Why don't we see if we can get a bunch of other countries with sovereign investment funds to make a statement like Peskarov as well? The Saudis, the Qataris, whatever. Let's up the ante. Let's make sure Zhang sees how isolated he's going to be. Let's see if that'll get him talking.'

'That's a good idea.'

'Roberta, draw me up a list. I'll talk to the leaders of those countries.'

'Yes, sir.'

'So how does this work? Roberta, you set up the calls with those other leaders. Gary, you draft me the letter for Zhang and brief Josh on the statement?'

Rose nodded.

'When do we do it?'

'As soon as we can.'

42

ELLA AND BEN were asleep when Marion got home. She tried to remember how many nights in a row that had happened now. Was it three? She tried never to let it go past three. The worst thing about being UN ambassador wasn't exchanging body blows in the Security Council, it was the hospitality schedule that went with it. If she didn't make an effort, she knew, she could easily end up not seeing the kids all week.

'You okay?' said Dave.

She nodded.

'You want something?'

Marion thought about it. She wasn't hungry. A dinner for the Nato ambassadors had seen to that.

'A little decisiveness, please, Madam Ambassador.'

'You know, I might have a glass of white wine.'

Dave smiled. 'Go and make yourself comfortable and I'll see what I can do.'

Marion went into the living room and kicked off her shoes. She closed her eyes. A couple of minutes later Dave came in carrying a glass.

'Nothing for you?'

He shook his head and sat down beside her. She took a sip. 'Pinot gris,' he said, watching her. Dave was something of a wine buff. 'Californian. What do you think?'

'I like it.'

He took the glass from her for a second and tasted it. 'Yeah, I like it too. Crisp, but it's got a little pepper in it.'

She took another sip.

'I believe our net worth halved again today, by the way,' said Dave.

Marion looked at him.

'I just thought you might be interested. Not that I have any doubt in the administration in which my wife plays such a prominent role, but it would be nice if there was something to suggest they have any idea what they're doing right now.'

'Is that how it seems?'

'Umm … Yes. And I'm pretty sure I'm not the only one who thinks so.'

Marion savored the wine, closing her eyes again. 'I'm not on the financial side, by the way. Just in case you were wondering.' She took another sip. The wine was good and crisp, as Dave said. 'I did something a little naughty today.'

Dave looked at her with interest.

'TS. I had a talk with the British ambassador.'

'Sir Antony?'

'The same. I told him we didn't think it was the right moment to push the South Africa resolution.'

Dave laughed. 'Who did you say "we" was? Was that … you and me?'

'I suspect he might have inferred it was the government of the United States.'

'Would that have been a reasonable inference?'

'Yes.'

'And I'm assuming this isn't something you were asked to tell him.'

'Correct,' said Marion briskly, raising her glass to her lips again.

Dave laughed. 'Well, that's a hell of a thing to do.'

'Correct again.' Marion held the glass out. 'This is almost empty.'

'Are you trying to drink yourself into a stupor to forget what you said?'

'Possibly.'

Dave got up and came back with the bottle. 'Thought I might save myself another trip.'

'A little more will be enough.'

'We'll see,' murmured Dave. He poured.

'You sure you won't have one?'

'You know, why not?' He got himself a glass. He poured the wine and took a sip, working it around in his mouth. 'This is good. I'm going to get some more.'

Marion settled back on the sofa, legs folded, and gazed at him. 'What do you think?'

'Of what you did? What does it take to get the sack in your job?'

'I didn't plan it. It pretty much just came out.'

'Oh, that's much better. That's a good thing to happen for a diplomat.'

'Dave, the Brits are determined to bring this to a vote before Christmas. Seale was talking about who might vote with us and who might not and I said to him, you know, we're going to get vetoed on this. And he said, sure. And it didn't seem to worry him. He seemed to take our support for granted without having thought through any of the implications from our perspective. I think it was that, it was the way he just seemed to brush it aside in that flippant British way of his. So I said to him maybe the United Kingdom has nothing to lose by forcing a veto on this but the United States does. The United States has a lot to lose. And then I said we didn't think this was the time for it.'

'And his response?'

Marion smiled a little as she remembered his face. 'I think it would be fair to say he was startled.'

'Startled?'

'Alright, shocked.'

'What did he say then?'

Marion sighed. 'All this stuff about it's a point of principle, how this kind of thing is the thin edge of the wedge, as he likes to say. Then he talked about the way they'd supported us over Uganda and how we'd gone in there without even waiting for them to get a response together about whether they wanted to join us, how bad that made them look, blah blah blah. Other stuff they'd done for us, going all the way back to Iraq.' Marion smiled. 'I didn't tell him that maybe it would have turned out better for everyone if they hadn't supported us on that one.'

Dave laughed. 'So what did you say then?' He took another sip of the pinot gris.

'Nothing. I'm not in a position to start negotiating with him. What I'd already said isn't our government's position. I didn't want to compound it. I need a little deniability. A couple of remarks during a conversation – anyone can misinterpret that. A whole discussion about the pros and cons, a negotiation over the strategy, what we will support, what we won't support – that's a different story.'

'Honey, you know, this is how wars start. One little misunderstanding ...'

'Dave, I don't think we're going to war with Great Britain. At least I haven't heard of any planning for that contingency.'

Dave was serious again. 'So what happens now?'

'Well, I guess by now Sir Antony will have sent a report to London about this surprising change of direction by the US government and I would say in about ...' Marion paused and glanced at her watch, 'six hours from now somewhere in Whitehall there's going to be quite a lot of interest in this. A couple of hours after that, I suspect our ambassador in London is going to get a call. A couple of hours after that, I suspect Bob Livingstone is.'

'And a couple of hours after that ...'

Marion raised her glass. 'I'm waiting for it.'

'And you will say ...?'

'That's a very good question, Mr Bartok. I'm not sure. What if I were to say that I didn't say it – Seale misinterpreted or something like that – but actually, he has a very good point? A resolution wouldn't be helpful, and the Brits must know it themselves or they wouldn't have construed my perfectly innocent remarks in such a ridiculously slanted fashion. Obviously there's some kind of Freudian diplomatic slip going on and they know themselves they shouldn't be pushing the resolution.' Marion paused. 'What do you think?'

'I think ...' Dave paused, nodding, then he shook his head. 'No. That's not going to work.'

'No, I don't think so either.'

'Because we do want a resolution, don't we?'

'That's the problem. We do want a resolution.' Marion frowned. She put down her glass.

Dave watched her.

Her frown deepened. 'Dave, I just don't get what we're doing. This is going to be another kick in the teeth for China – which achieves absolutely nothing in South Africa apart from strengthening Mthwesa, who we want to weaken – and I just don't understand what the president thinks he's going to get out of doing that. We kicked them over Uganda. Now we're going to kick them over this. And we need them. We keep asking them for stuff and we keep kicking them.'

'What are we asking them for?'

'A statement over Fidelian and … there's other stuff.' Marion hadn't told Dave that Dewy and Montez were thought to be in the Sudan. 'There's a number of things. We keep going to them and asking them for stuff, and then we keep hammering them.'

'I'm not sure that getting rid of the LRA and calling for democracy in South Africa is hammering the Chinese,' said Dave. 'That's a partial way of seeing it, don't you think?'

Marion looked at him. 'You're right. It is. But right now, when we need their help – and believe me, we *need* their help – we have to see it like they do. Does it really matter if we don't put a resolution down on the ANC before Christmas?' Marion sighed. 'We need to give them space. We need them to do a couple of things for us and instead of going back and asking over and over again, at the same time as we're kicking them in the teeth, as they would see it, we need to step back and let them do it in their own way.'

'Is there time for that?'

'What's the alternative? We don't get anything if we don't give them the time. TS – Knowles wanted to talk to Zhang and Zhang said he wasn't available.'

Dave stared at her.

'I don't know what that means. No one knows what it means. But to me, it doesn't mean, yes, let's keep going harder. The White House perspective seems to be, if they won't do what we want, they're being obstructive. And if they're being obstructive, then we need to keep hammering at them. But I think the more we keep hammering them, the more obstructive they're going to be.' Marion threw up her hands. 'It's crazy. It's like two kids in a schoolyard. We need to change our way of doing things with them. The world's changed. We're not going to get what we want by confronting them. There are too many things we need from them. We need to start collaborating. Really. Not just with words.'

'Yeah, but honey, they're not a pleasant regime.'

'You're right. They're dictatorial, they oppress human rights, they don't have free speech.'

'Or rule of law.'

'Or rule of law.'

'Or habeas corpus.'

'Dave, we should have thought of that twenty years ago before we bound up our economy so tight with them. They're not just another country any more. They're part of us. We're part of them. We're like two …' Marion paused, searching for a way to express it. 'We're like a pair of conjoined twins, we share the same blood vessels. The same blood. And we're not going to get anywhere by hitting our conjoined twin on the head, because they're just going to hit us back, and neither of us can ever get away from each other. We've got to stop hitting.'

Dave smiled.

'What?'

'It's the image.'

'Yeah. It's like some kind of Greek tragedy. Two people tied eternally together but doomed to be always trying to get ahead of each other.'

'I like the conjoined twins hitting each other on the head better.'

Marion shook her head, smiling in despair.

'What if they don't want to stop hitting?' said Dave.

'Someone has to stop. Someone has to stop first.'

'What if I don't like my conjoined twin? What if I don't like the way he does things? Maybe if I keep hitting him a little longer he'll stop doing those things and then I can stop hitting him.'

'And maybe he'll keep doing them even more just to show he can. We need to ask ourselves, how are we going to help him change? Hitting him on the head day after day is unlikely to do it.'

'What if he won't change?'

'Something has to. Someone has to be first.'

Dave was silent.

Marion was reminded of what Joel Ehrenreich had said to her the last time he had been in this apartment. 'Is Tom Knowles the man to do it?' she asked rhetorically.

'Is Zhang?' said Dave.

'That's a fair question.' Marion was silent for a moment. 'You know, I'm starting to think what Joel said in his book is right.'

'He's got the diagnosis. I'm not sure he's got the solution. It's easy to say our global problems are shared problems. Easy to say we should share the problem-solving. I didn't see him describing the mechanism.'

'That's his point. If the mechanism isn't there, we have to create it. If you've got shared problems, you have to share the problem-solving. There's no alternative.' Marion picked up her glass and took a sip of the remaining wine. 'We have a president who's in the middle of a crisis that would test anyone – I'm not saying it's easy – but in terms of mobilizing the support of our greatest global rival, he just isn't doing it. Again, you know, I'm not saying it's easy, but if we don't change the way we go about it, we're in trouble.'

'So you think they did something with Fidelian?'

'I don't know. I honestly don't know.' Marion let out a long, weary sigh. 'My experience from working in two administrations and seeing how things work at this end is, who the hell knows? They may not know themselves. Sometimes things just happen. They think we won't let the bank fail, they think we will but it won't matter, they think their investment fund will make some money, they think they can show how strong they are ... who knows? All of the above and none of the above. Somehow they end up doing it.'

'Or they did it specifically to influence our elections.'

'That's possible as well.'

'And the implications of that are huge.'

'True. That's why we lost half our net worth today, remember? But they didn't *necessarily* do it to influence our elections. And the only voice in this administration who's trying to put a little moderation into the debate is Bob Livingstone. And Bob ...' Marion didn't need to say the words. Dave knew that she liked the secretary of state but that she had seen him progressively marginalized over the last two years by Gary Rose and John Oakley until he had lost any influence he might have started with. 'And Doug Havering,' she added, 'has turned into a kind of White House mouthpiece in the department because he figures Livingstone will go in the second term and he's jockeying for his own position. Everyone's jockeying for the second term but the way we're going I wouldn't be too sure we're going to get past the first.'

Dave was silent, watching her.

'And I don't count for anything, Dave.'

'Honey, that's not true.'

'It is. My position had cabinet status under Obama. Not under Tom Knowles. You know, I don't care about cabinet status. I knew from the start I wasn't going to have it. The point is the way this president governs and where the advice comes from that he values. I can't get anything to him without it going past Rose. Believe me, I've tried. Bob should be able to, but I don't know if even he can any more. And that's frightening, Dave. Right now that's a frightening situation.'

Dave watched her. 'What are you going to do?'

'I don't know. Whispering to Antony Seale like some schoolgirl isn't going to do it.' Marion shook her head. 'I just … This White House, every day now I wonder what the hell they're going to say next.'

43

'THANK YOU FOR coming today.'

The president was making the statement in the East Room, flanked by Defense Secretary Oakley and Treasury Secretary Opitz.

'I would like to make a few remarks concerning some of the key issues that are facing us. The last weeks have not been easy ones for the American economy and I think the time has come to set this clearly in perspective and show that in fact our economy remains sound and the American people can be confident as we enter the holiday season that there is no return on the horizon to the kind of experiences we went through ten years ago. I also have some news to give you on our two brave airmen who were shot down in Uganda a month ago. I would like to start with that.'

The reporters gazed at him expectantly, pens poised. They had been told that he would not be taking questions.

'As you know, we have been working constantly to locate our servicemen, Captains Pete Dewy and Phil Montez, utilizing all the intelligence capabilities at our disposal, and I would like to thank the many men and women in our military and intelligence services who have spent long hours in this quest. Their efforts have not been wasted. We now have what we consider to be incontrovertible evidence showing that Captains Dewy and Montez have been moved across the Ugandan border into Sudan and are now either in the control of the Sudanese army or at the very least that the Sudanese army is aware and permissive of their presence there.' He paused. 'This is a state of affairs that is not acceptable to the United States of America nor should it be acceptable to the government of any member state of the United Nations. I call on the Sudanese government to immediately release Captains Dewy and Montez, shot down and abducted while carrying out an operation sanctioned by the United Nations, who have been illegally conducted into Sudan and are being held either by an internationally proscribed terrorist group or by the Sudanese army itself. The Sudanese government should be aware that a failure to comply with this requirement at the earliest possible opportunity will be met with the severest response from the United States. Let me be clear on this – I take nothing off the table.

'To the Dewy and Montez families, I will say what I have said from the start: we will get your boys back. We will leave no stone unturned, no effort undone, until they are with us again. We will get them back.

'I would also like to take this opportunity to speak to the friends of Sudan within the international community. A true friend is one that tells its friend when it is in the wrong. So to the friends of Sudan: the United States expects you to use your good offices with Sudan to help achieve the immediate release of Captains Dewy and Montez, just as the United States would use its good offices with any of its allies, in the unlikely event that they would be so foolish as to engage in such an illegal act, to ensure that such an episode would be brought to a rapid conclusion. Any member of the international community that can use its relations with Sudan to help achieve this objective and chooses not to do so, will be seen by the United States for what it is – part of the problem and not part of the solution. Now let me say explicitly in this context, that the United States expects the government of the People's Republic of China, as a friend of Sudan, to play its role. I remind the Chinese government that Captains Dewy and Montez were shot down and abducted while in the execution of an operation sanctioned by the United Nations, and as such it is the obligation of every member of the United Nations to do what it can in order to ensure the return of these two brave men. I expect that the government of the People's Republic of China will comply with that obligation.'

He paused.

'Now, I turn to the economic situation. It's clear that we face a perfect storm of uncertainty that is creating widespread anxiety across the financial markets and the economy more broadly. I would like to step back and remind ourselves what has actually happened here. We have seen the bankruptcy of one bank resulting from a series of poor commercial decisions that were taken many years ago. This bank-ruptcy has created understandable caution on the part of other banks, for two reasons. First, they themselves have been exposed to losses from the failure of Fidelian. The Treasury Department, the Federal Reserve and the Federal Deposit Insurance Corporation have all worked closely with affected banks to understand the scale of these losses and at this point we do not believe that any other bank is in danger of failure as a result of Fidelian's bankruptcy. Where additional liquidity has been required, Chairman Strickland of the Federal Reserve has been quick to provide this. The second reason: banks are understandably concerned about the possibility of additional banks being found to be in difficulty. This saps confidence and reduces the willingness of banks to lend to each other, with the effect of further freezing the system. The measures already taken have provided crit-ical assistance and we believe that, as a result of this firm action, confidence is returning. Chairman Strickland and Secretary Opitz continue to monitor the situation on a daily basis and are ready to step in with further measures as needed. So let me be clear. There is no banking crisis in this country. There will be no banking crisis. Our banks are sound. Our regulatory authorities are closely monitoring the industry. The executive arm is ready to act.

'So where does the uncertainty come from? It's no secret that the collapse of Fidelian Bank took place in circumstances that were, to say the least, confusing. Inquiries are in train, both in Congress and within the Treasury Department, to understand the decisions that were taken by the Fidelian management in the days and weeks leading up to the collapse. The relevant law enforcement agencies are also looking into it. If there is even a hint of illegality in what was done, the full weight of the law will be brought against those responsible. But there is another question, and I want to openly acknowledge it. Were government-owned foreign investment funds involved in, or responsible in any way for, the decisions that were taken by the exec-utive management of Fidelian Bank? And if so, was this involvement motivated purely by financial considerations – as would legitimately be the case with any investor – or was this involvement guided in some way by the ultimate owners of these funds, the relevant foreign governments, with non-financial motives?

'Now, let me state this very clearly. The United States will not tolerate the manipulation of its markets for political purposes by any foreign government. We would view this with the utmost gravity as an attack on a vital interest of the United States. Now, let me also state this very clearly. I do not believe that this has happened. I do not believe that it will happen. We have already seen Prime Minister Peskarov of Russia state explicitly that in the case of Russian state investment funds, there is complete separation of the commercial management of the funds from the political process, and I thank him for his willingness to speak frankly on the matter and for his offer to cooperate with the Securities and Exchange Commission and other regulatory authorities should this be required. I am very confident that you will see over the coming days other governments whose countries also run large investment funds making the same commitment. I invite all countries whose state investment funds hold US assets to provide this assurance. Most importantly, I expect the countries with the largest such funds to take a lead in making their position clear.'

He paused to ensure the implication was noted.

'In case they do not – and I think they will, but in case they do not – I have asked Secretary Opitz and the relevant authorities to look at developing a set of regulations that can be enforced to ensure there is no manipulation of our markets. This is no different in principle from the many measures that already exist to prevent market manipulation. We have strong laws and we take firm action against individuals and institutions who engage in insider trading, propagation of rumor, and other manipulative practices. If there is the possibility of a new form of manipulative practice, in this case from foreign governments, we will introduce new measures to stop it. We will cut it off. States with funds that do not provide an assurance that they are acting purely on commercial grounds – and I hope there will be no such states – should expect to see these measures enforced rapidly and vigorously against them.

'Those are the remarks I wanted to make today. I will leave it to Secretary Opitz and Secretary Oakley to provide further clarification.

'Thank you. I wish you all happy holidays.'

44

OVERNIGHT, NINE COUNTRIES responded, as they had promised to do prior to the president's statement being made. Saudi Arabia, the United Arab Emirates, Kuwait, Norway, Singapore, Libya, Kazakhstan, Australia and South Korea, between them holding sovereign wealth funds ranging from as small as $40 million in value to as large as $1.6 trillion – made statements denying political involvement in the decisions of the funds and committing to refrain from any such involvement in the future.

The press wasn't impressed. A leader in the next day's *New York Times* was titled *The Genie is out of the Bottle*. It argued that once political manipulation of US markets was even considered to be possible, the rules of the game had changed. Or to put it another way, the game had changed, and right now there were no rules.

The financial press speculated ominously about the new regulations the administration might introduce and whether they were about to see the end, at least temporarily, of the free market model that had served the United States since the birth of the republic.

The markets seemed to think they might. The flow of money out of stocks and company debt and into cash, bonds and gold gushed further as rumors swept across the financial sector about the changes the Treasury secretary would be introducing and the prospect of economic conflict with China.

And that was before the Chinese government, seven days later, finally broke its silence.

EVERYONE SEES AN event from a different place. When the event is momentous, everyone has different memories of the instant they hear about it that will stay with them forever. For Ed Grey, the memory of this event would always be associated with the whirr of a running machine. As he did every day around 6am, on a cold, grey Monday morning in December, Ed Grey pounded the moving belt in his apartment, watching the Asian market report on CNBC.

His gaze became fixed. For a minute or so he kept pounding, and then his hand searched for the control, and he turned the machine off, still gazing at the screen. The whirring of the motor died away. The belt slowed and then stopped. Ed stood and stared.

Like just about every other Divvie in the past few days, he had chased the markets down, always looking for the floor that surely had to be there and always finding that it disappeared under his feet just as he put funds into the market again. Red River was down in just about every asset class it held. Securities, commodities, derivatives, developed markets and developing. Close on eight billion had disappeared, more than ten per cent of Red River's value at its height, before Peskarov opened his mouth. That had gone to ten, then fifteen, then twenty as asset prices fell and the banks called in margin on a daily basis and he was forced to try to sell into a market where it was almost impossible to find a buyer.

He didn't know where it was going to end. Unless the market turned around, the only thing that could save him would be a suspension of accounting rules, the mark-to-market requirement whereby the value of an asset portfolio was determined on a daily basis against current market prices. Just about every day there was a rumor that the Fed was about to announce it. Ed Grey didn't think it would happen. It would be too good to be true. They had talked about that in '08 but had never done it. He didn't believe in miracles.

In 2008 people had talked about the end of capitalism, but Ed knew all along it was only the hangover from a very good party, one which he had the luck to leave early, and that sooner or later the party would start up again. This was different. Like everyone else in the market, he agreed with the line taken by the *Times*. The genie was out of the bottle and it was going to take a new bottle to put him back in. No one knew what that new bottle was going to look like, but the president's statement left no doubt they were trying to design it. Would there be limits on stocks held by foreign investment funds? How would that be policed? What would the limit be? What was going to happen if a fund currently held stocks in excess of the limit? Would the funds abandon US markets entirely? What would it mean for liquidity if you took that amount of money out of the market? What would it mean for the prices of stocks you already held? Were the regulations going to be introduced at a stroke or were they going to be phased in? How would they be phased?

The questions were endless. Whatever the answers, they were going to be bad. At best they would represent a restriction of opportunity, at worst a horrendous degree of disruption which would take a lot of people down. Knowing the haste with which these measures were being put together, Grey had a hunch which end of the spectrum it was going to be. So did everyone else. People were getting out of stocks as fast as they could. There were sellers but no buyers, forcing prices down to ridiculous levels, forcing even more sales as people who hadn't sold marked to market and were forced to find margin cash for the banks. Meanwhile, bond prices were soaring as investors transferred the funds they had been able to salvage into government securities. Grey himself was doing that as fast as he could. But if something hit the bond markets, he was going to lose another shitload of cash and there was going to be nowhere left to hide.

He was living from minute to minute, data point to data point, in a way he had never lived, not in the darkest days of the crisis in '08 when even some of his own bets had gone south.

And now he stared at the screen, early on the cold, catastrophic morning of December 17, the December 17 that the markets – in the way of all great traumatic events since the World Trade Towers went down – would come to call 12/17, standing in his jogging shorts on a stationary running belt.

The report was coming from Shanghai. The remarks had apparently just been made by the Chinese premier, Liang Jianzhu, in a speech that he had given to a gathering of foreign business leaders.

The reporter was giving a summary of what Liang had said. Ed Grey couldn't believe it. Didn't want to believe it. He picked up the remote and went to another website, then another. It didn't take long to find the actual footage being played. Liang, a man with a high forehead and brushed-back, jet black hair, stood at a flower-festooned lectern. He was speaking in English.

'Now, let me refer to the speech that was made a few days ago by the president of the United States. It is clear that we are entering a new phase. The Chinese people have made investments globally with the proceeds of the people's hard work as any prudent people should. The United States was very glad to receive those investments when it had a need for them. We only need to think back ten years when the government of the United States was desperate for money to stimulate its economy and went to the market with its bonds. There were very few people to take up those bonds except the people of China. But we did it. We only have to think back six or eight years when the corporations of the United States required new capital to return to growth, and their shareholders could not provide it. We provided it. But it is clear we are entering a new phase. It seems that the United States is no longer happy to have the investment of the Chinese people. It talks about introducing new measures. If that is the case, the Chinese people will take its investment back. Others can have the bonds and the stocks. It is a free, global market. The president of the United States should remember one thing. China is not only able to buy, it can also sell.'

The words sent a shiver down Ed Grey's spine. An electric spasm of dread.

They echoed in his mind.

CHINA IS NOT ONLY ABLE TO BUY, IT CAN ALSO SELL.

Not only stocks, but bonds.

Feverishly Ed Grey clicked and clicked and clicked again. In front of him now were the latest prices from the bond markets. London, Paris and Frankfurt had been open for hours.

Down. Everything was down. Ten, fifteen, twenty per cent.

HE WATCHED IT through the day, as bonds and stocks and every other asset fell. There was nowhere, it seemed, that anyone felt their money was safe but under their bed. By the end of the day Red River's losses had extended from twenty billion to thirty. In ten short weeks since that cursed day when he listened to Boris Malevsky tell him that Fidelian Bank was going to raise some capital, the value of the Red River funds had halved.

His portfolio managers and analysts were disbelieving. They stared at their screens with wide eyes or furrowed, incredulous frowns. Apart from Tony Evangelou, not one had been in the business in the fall of 2008. Some of them hadn't even been in college. They had never seen a day like this.

The world was on the precipice of an abyss and no one knew what was down there. All through the day announcements came out of the world's central banks. It didn't matter. No one cared what the central bankers were saying, how much capital they were pumping into the system, what guarantees they were offering. If the Chinese government was going to dump its holdings of US bonds, there wasn't a single financial instrument in the world that would hold its value.

His people would be scarred by this, Grey knew. He had seen the effect last time around. No matter how tough they think they are, traders who have grown up in good times are never ready for their first big crash. Some would be no good for the business after this. Boris Malevsky sat silent, almost catatonic, barely responding to anything around him. Ed tried to keep up morale, the most important commodity at a DIV when the markets were tanking. Demoralized traders made bad decisions. He walked around the trading desk, put his hand on shoulders, pulled up a chair. 'At least you'll be able to tell your grandkids you lived through it,' he told them. He even forced a smile. 'The eye of the storm. We should get T shirts.'

There didn't seem to be many takers.

When they left, they drifted out like ghosts into the night. Sell orders were in place in the unlikely event that a buyer turned up somewhere in the east. A couple of the portfolio managers were staying back with the night analysts to monitor the Asian and then European markets as trading moved west overnight.

Ed went back to his office. Tony Evangelou followed him in. They didn't know what to expect the next day. All they knew was that they were going to keep bleeding, and the best they could hope was to staunch the flow wherever they saw it.

Red River was gone. Unless a miracle happened, Ed would have to sell anything he could just to pay the cash the banks would demand, wiping out not only what was left of six years' accumulated profits of his clients but the principal they had put in as well. And his own. And even that wouldn't be enough. When he had sold everything he could and the cash ran out, Red River would be bust.

Tony went. Ed stayed on, feet up on the desk in his office. Six years. Six years of tireless work to build Red River into what it was – and about six weeks to watch it disappear. It made him think of the stories you heard about the Great Crash, of people jumping out of windows. He glanced at his own window with a bitter smile. He went over things in his mind. Not just today, but the past weeks, the past couple of months. He didn't know if it was exactly guilt that he was feeling. No, not guilt. The markets were the markets. Everything he had done was legal, or almost legal. One piece of insider information, surely, shouldn't lead to this. The markets were in free fall, a stampede of utterly panicked beasts, and it seemed to have gone beyond them now. There was belligerent talk coming out of the White House, and the tone of the speech made by Liang – obviously deputed by President Zhang to deliver the message – had been equally hostile. During the day, a Chinese government spokesman was reported to have refused the opportunity to provide a less aggressive interpretation of the premier's words.

Whatever Grey had done, whatever he had started, the markets had overwhelmed him and swept him away. But something had had to set them off. He wondered – not for the first time – whether it really could have been him, whether the plot he plotted in this very office with Boris Malevsky and Tony Evangelou could have been responsible for events of this magnitude, whether, had he not plotted that plot, none of this would ever have happened.

He thought about it, staring at the darkness outside his window. Then he picked up the phone.

THE SECRETARY DIDN'T get back to him until after midnight. Ed was in his apartment. He had said to call any time she had the chance, it didn't matter how late.

'Ed, I've got a note-taker on the line,' said Opitz. 'And I don't have a lot of time. I'm sorry. You said you had something important to tell me. I assume this isn't some kind of attempt to find out about anything we might have under consideration.'

'Of course not,' he said. 'I know you wouldn't tell me.'

'Okay. It's been a long day.' Opitz paused and took a deep breath. 'What is it?'

'Susan, this is confidential, okay? I'm telling you this because I think as a good citizen I need to.'

'What is it?'

'It's confidential.'

'Alright, it's confidential. As long as it doesn't go against my legal duty as Treasury secretary to divulge what you tell me. What is it?'

Grey hesitated. 'I started it.'

'What?'

'This. Everything. The collapse.'

There was silence for a moment, then Opitz laughed. 'Ed, it's very kind of you to offer to take the blame, but I'm not sure–'

'Susan, we're the ones who started shorting Fidelian. And a bunch of other banks.'

Opitz's laughter had stopped. 'Why did you do that?'

'We had a hunch.'

'Were you passed any inside information?'

'Absolutely not.'

'Be honest with me.'

'We only knew what was publicly available.'

'Were you acting alone?'

'Of course.'

'You couldn't have had such a big effect by yourself.'

'It was a big position, Susan. The more they went down, the bigger I made it.'

'That's still not enough.'

'A bunch of other Divvies probably figured out what we were doing and joined in.'

'Was this a coordinated raid? Is that what you're telling me?'

'Absolutely not.'

'Did you start any rumors? Is that what you did?'

'No! Susan, I did nothing illegal. We just had a hunch. Call it a lucky hunch.'

'Then why are you telling me this? I'm not interested in your hunches.'

'Because the way the president's talking,' said Grey, 'the way you're talking when I see you on TV, it's like you think the Chinese started it. You think they had some kind of political plan. That's not what happened. I had a hunch and I shorted Fidelian.'

'Did you know it was on the brink of twenty-three billion in write-downs?'

'No.'

'Then what was the hunch, Ed?'

'It was … it was a hunch, Susan. We did some analysis. We had a hunch there were a bunch of banks that probably weren't as strong as they looked and were overpriced. I didn't expect any of them to go bankrupt.'

'Not even Fidelian?'

'No.'

'Do you know anything about the process by which Bill Custler decided not to take the rescue offer?'

'No. I've never spoken to Bill Custler in my life.'

'From some other source?'

'No.'

'So what you called to tell me,' said Opitz, 'is that the origin of this crisis doesn't lie with the PIC or the Chinese government, but with you. With a hunch you had that you could make some money by shorting Fidelian? Is that it, Ed?'

'That's right.'

'That's a hell of a story, Ed. Maybe one day you could write a book about it.'

'Susan, it's true.'

'I'm not saying it isn't. What does intrigue me, Ed, is why you thought you should tell me.'

'Because it shows it's not a political crisis. There isn't any big political conspiracy here. That's not how it started. It started with someone – me – taking a bet. It's what happens every day. It's the markets.'

There was silence for a moment, then Opitz started to laugh.

'What? You don't believe me?'

'No, I do, Ed. I do.'

'Then what's funny?'

'You are. Calling to tell me. Where have you been, Ed? Don't you know what happened today?'

'Of course I know what happened today! Hell, Susan, my fund's falling apart in front of my eyes.'

'I'm sorry, but–'

'Suspend mark to market! For Christ's sake, Susan, suspend mark to market and let some of us survive.'

'Is that what you rang to tell me?' demanded Opitz angrily.

'No! I rang to tell you that I started it. I rang to tell you it isn't political.'

'It is now. Ed, it doesn't matter how it started. Don't you get it? That doesn't matter any more.'

'Then what are you going to do?'

'Wait and see.'

'For God's sake, Susan, I'm telling you what to do. Suspend mark to market! Suspend it now!'

Grey was desperate. He was down on his knees. Literally, in his apartment, the phone shaking in his hand. This wasn't what he had rung to say but it burst out of him. It was his only chance of survival. 'Suspend it, Susan! Suspend mark to market!'

Opitz listened to him in distaste. Grey was sobbing.

'Suspend it. Please! Please! For God's sake–'

'We'll do what we have to do,' said Opitz, and she put down the phone.

45

LIU'S VOICE WAS agitated. There was no small talk or introduction. The first words out of his mouth after Ellman picked up the phone were an abrupt, direct question.

'Marion, why are you doing this?'

Ellman closed her eyes for a moment before replying. 'The US government believes this is the right thing to do.'

'The resolution won't pass.'

'Simon, that's up to you.'

'Not only us. There are others.'

That wasn't quite right. Marion knew that the UK had the votes to pass its South Africa resolution on the numbers. It was only a veto that would stop it.

The agitation in the Chinese ambassador's voice became greater. 'Marion, I don't understand what your president thinks he is doing. Do you understand? Can you explain to me?'

Ellman didn't respond.

'You need our help. You need our help on your economy. You need our help on your soldiers in Sudan. But all we get are demands. Is this the way one asks for help?'

There was no point telling him that she didn't think it was much of a way to ask for help either. The president wasn't going to change his approach.

'Simon, we see these issues as so clear cut. I don't think we see these as demands. We see these as what any member of the international community ought to do for the sake of any member it regards as a friend. Help get its soldiers who are being held illegally. Help restore confidence in its economy. Why wouldn't you do these things if you're our friend?'

'Do we not regard you as a friend? Show me what we have done that says we are not a friend.'

'These are the things. These things we've been asking about.'

'No, *you* are not a friend. A friend does not make demands in public without even giving the other the chance to act first. A friend waits. A friend trusts that the other one will act and lets him act without speaking in public.'

'Simon, come on. We asked privately. Secretary Opitz spoke to Minister Bai weeks ago. That wasn't public. That was private. Like friends. And nothing happened.'

Liu was silent for a moment. She could hear him draw a deep breath.

'Marion, I'm speaking personally. I shouldn't do this, but I will. This is not for your government now, this is for you. All we see are demands coming from your president. One demand after the other, in private, in public, everywhere. No one on your side seems to understand this. I'm telling you so you can understand. No one in Beijing can understand how another power can want for help and issue such demands.'

Ellman resisted the temptation to retort that these things only turned into demands because the Chinese government failed to act without being pushed. 'Simon,' she said, 'there's a simple way to deal with that, and that's to do what you should do, what any friendly country should do. Instead you threaten to dump our bonds.'

'Because you threaten to make restrictions. Who made the first threat?'

'It wasn't a threat, it's reality. What choice do we have?'

'And what choice do *we* have? If you say to someone who owns your assets, we will restrict you, he will sell them! He will sell them while he can!' Liu's voice had risen. 'And now this! This resolution. It will not pass. You know that. If you are in any doubt of it, let me assure you now. It will not pass. What do you think you will achieve?'

'Simon, it's a matter of principle. For the United States, democracy is a matter of principle.'

'And the principle for the United States seems to be, *hit* China whenever you can.'

'That's not what it is.'

'That's what it looks like. Marion, I am speaking to you out of friendship. I am not authorized to tell you this, but I am telling you. Do you understand, in Beijing, that's what it looks like? After such a speech from your president! We must lose face everywhere. With other countries. In our own party. With our army. President Zhang cannot lose face like this.'

Marion narrowed her eyes. 'Simon, what's going on?'

Liu was silent for a moment. 'I don't understand how your president doesn't see what he is doing. Does no one tell him? Does Secretary Livingstone not tell him?'

'Simon, if your government would just do the couple of things it needs to do ... If it would help get our men out, if it would just say it didn't manipulate Fidelian ... That's all you need to do. Things of simple decency. Your president could get our guys out of Sudan tomorrow.'

'Do you think so?' demanded Liu. 'Is it so simple?'

Marion was stumped at that, wondering if it was possible that the Sudanese government wouldn't respond to a demand from Zhang. They were almost entirely dependent on the Chinese for their foreign income.

'Why does he care about your men who you sent in without consultation?'

'Simon, come on, we passed a resolution–'

'Only because we let you!'

'He could get up and make a speech about Fidelian tonight. Just two minutes, that's all it would take.'

'Why should he do it?' There was incredulity in Liu's voice. 'Why should he? Marion, it is not so simple.'

'Simon, you keep saying that. What do you mean?'

'Why does he care about your bank if you can't manage your own system? Why should he help someone who makes such demands? And now someone who brings this vote.'

'We're not bringing it. The United Kingdom is bringing it.'

'You could have stopped them.'

'They're determined to bring it.'

'Then don't support it!'

Marion was silent for a moment. 'Simon, I still don't understand why you keep saying this isn't simple. Sure, it's complicated, but it can be done. What's going on?'

There was silence. Marion waited, frowning, to hear what the Chinese ambassador would reply.

'Where is this ending?' demanded Liu suddenly. 'Does your president know that? Tell me, Marion, before he began to escalate like this, does he know where the exit is?'

'There's no escalation intended.'

'No? Well, there is escalation. Let me say to you, the United States is not in the strong position. It is not China's men who are captured in Sudan. It is not China's economy that is in such trouble.'

'If it's our economy, it's yours. There's no separating them. You know that. If we suffer, you'll suffer.'

'Yes, but who will last the longer? Who will suffer the more? Is that what President Knowles wants to find out?'

'Simon, this is not the way we should be talking. No one wants any suffering. This is not the way the president's thinking.'

'Good. Then do not support this resolution.'

'Liu, there's only so much I can do.'

'You still have time. Speak to your president.'

'Simon, I can't—'

'Marion, do not do this. Do not do it.'

'Simon, is that you speaking, or your government?'

'Listen to me,' said Liu. 'I have rung you to tell you this. Just listen to what I have said to you.'

There was silence for a moment, then the phone went dead.

Marion put it down slowly.

She sat back in her chair, a frown on her face. She brought her hands together under her chin. The frown deepened.

Liu could have been trying to manipulate her. When a diplomat said he was speaking personally, or confidentially, or on his own initiative, you always had to be wary. When he said he was speaking out of friendship, you had to be even warier.

It was possible that China didn't want to be seen vetoing the South Africa resolution that the UK was about to bring to the Security Council. This could have been a last attempt on his part to prevent it reaching the chamber. And it had struck her the way Liu's voice rose a notch when he talked about his government having no choice but to sell their assets once the US government talked about restricting ownership. Maybe that was what they were really worried about, having to sell assets that were plummeting in value. Maybe, if they got the US to back down on the South Africa vote, they could claim it as a victory and magnanimously – condescendingly – agree not to sell their assets as a favor to the US.

Or maybe he wasn't manipulating her. Maybe he was genuine. Marion didn't know him well enough to tell. And the part about Zhang losing face with the army and the party, and things not being simple … He must have been referring to internal tensions. Marion ran the words again in her mind, trying to be sure she had really heard Liu say what she thought she had heard. What was going on inside the regime that the US didn't know about? A conflict like this would always be likely to bring tensions out. But was there anything new? Was Zhang in trouble?

Marion feared for the effect this vote would have. Liu could have been trying to manipulate her or not – it didn't really matter. What mattered was that she agreed with him.

The first thing she would do would be to send an urgent report of this conversation to Bob Livingstone, Gary Rose, Director of National Intelligence Ryan Ferris and the president, highlighting Liu's hints that Zhang was under pressure and her belief that the US position on the resolution should be reconsidered before the vote on the following day. Yet she knew there were no ears in the White House for that message or pretty much anything else that came from the State Department.

Ellman didn't like the way this administration had begun to act over the past few months and the way Bob Livingstone and State were being shut out. She was a moderate Republican, at best, and she had the feeling that she was increasingly out of step with the forces driving policy inside the White House. There were too many compromises and she could only see them getting worse. Marion knew she would have to raise her hand in support of that vote tomorrow, despite the fact that she firmly believed the United States should have acted to prevent it being brought to the Council. That happened. Any diplomat has to expect to put arguments she doesn't believe in from time to time. But as UN ambassador, she expected at the least to have a say in the debate. If there had been a debate, she hadn't been part of it.

In the past few days, Marion Ellman had begun to wonder whether she should resign.

She knew that she was tired and overworked. She knew her state of mind might be influenced by that. It had been an intense and difficult fall. Christmas was only a week away and psychologically that had become a kind of target for her. She was hanging on for Christmas, and then, with a week off and some time with Dave and the kids, she hoped things would be clearer.

THE NEXT DAY, Marion Ellman entered the Security Council chamber and took her seat. Antony Seale, already present in the chair beside her, leaned over and welcomed her.

Her intervention in the debate was short. Seale had already made a long speech setting out the reasons for bringing a Chapter VII resolution calling for the immediate restoration of constitutional rule in South Africa and the holding of free and fair elections within three months, with the threat of sanctions if the ANC government failed to comply. There was little more for her to say than to set out the United States' support for the British position.

Liu watched her. Every minute of the debate, she could feel his eyes boring into her.

When Mohammed Razak, the Malaysian ambassador who was serving as the Council's president for the month, called for those who were voting in favor, she raised her hand. Liu shook his head and closed his eyes in despair.

A moment later Razak called for those voting no. Immediately Liu's hand was in the air.

46

FOR TWO DAYS, officials from the Fed, Treasury and SEC had worked around the clock to finalize the necessary measures. While they did, the Chinese threat to dump US stocks and bonds had led to a final collapse in market confidence. The financial system was breaking down. Margin calls were going unpaid as collateral was seized but couldn't be sold, leaving a multitude of investment funds technically bankrupt at the whim of the banks who held their debt. US government securities already in existence were trading – when they did trade – at discounts of sixty or seventy per cent, reflecting a fear that interest rates would have to skyrocket in order for the US to finance its borrowings. Bonds with redemption dates within the next year were virtually unsaleable at any price, reflecting a fear that the US might be forced into default. Ron Strickland had taken the decision to cancel the Treasury Bill sale for that week, the last before Christmas, after it became obvious there would be no buyers. The holiday break was going to offer temporary respite but they needed an announcement. If the situation remained unresolved for any length of time into the new year the government would be unable to raise debt. The United States would be insolvent.

At midday, the president met in the Oval Office with his key advisors to review the final package of measures. Opitz led him through it. The measures were extreme. First, on the stock markets, stock holdings by a defined list of named entities, their subsidiaries, agents and representatives would be frozen for an initial three-month period while an investigation was carried out into market manipulation by those entities. If manipulation was found likely to have taken place, a process would be formulated for the recovery and offering to the market of those stocks at a price not lower than the price at the close of the market on the last session prior to the announcement, December 20. Second, on the bond markets, the same named entities and their representatives would be barred from participating in Treasury bond sales for an initial three-month period. In both cases, the idea was to ringfence and remove toxic participants from the market.

The named entities were all known Chinese sovereign investment funds and their subsidiaries. The list of subsidiaries ran into the hundreds and, as Treasury officials worked around the clock to track ownership structures, was likely to continue to rise.

The hope was that the measures on the stock markets would put a floor under the price of stocks – guaranteeing that the Chinese investment funds couldn't dump their huge holdings and, if the stocks did eventually come to the market, they would be priced no lower than the price they held immediately prior to the announcement. On the bond markets, by excluding the Chinese investment funds from upcoming Treasury sales, it ringfenced the new bonds from those already in the market, which were close to valueless, and created the hope that buyers would be found for them when the next Treasury Bill sale took place. As far as the collapse in the value of existing bonds was concerned, no one was selling because it was impossible to find buyers, but on paper the banks and other holders of those bonds had taken enormous losses to add to their losses in other assets. Therefore they were also going to announce a third measure: a three-month suspension of mark-to-market accounting.

They hadn't yet worked out what method they were going to accept to replace mark to market. Suspending the accounting method was an extreme step and no one liked it, but there was no choice if the country was to avoid a catastrophic flood of bankruptcies amongst insurance companies, investment funds, banks and even industrial corporations because of the paper losses incurred through artificially depressed asset prices. Hopefully, when all this was over, bond and stock values would recover and mark-to-market accounting could be restored with assets valued at more sensible levels.

Each of these was an unprecedented measure. They didn't require congressional approval, since they dealt with regulatory and market issues that came under the remit of the SEC and the Federal Reserve, but that didn't diminish the extreme sweep of their intent. Together, they created a package of radical constraints such as had never before been seen in the previously free American markets. They weren't intended to be permanent. And they wouldn't restore the markets to normal. At best, they would stabilize the markets at current prices and at an extremely low level of activity while people watched to see what would happen next, giving time for the political crisis underlying the collapse to be resolved. Their ability to do even that, even for a period of a few days, would depend crucially on whether the markets believed the authorities could implement the measures they had announced. Market participants would be watching intently for any evidence of stocks being dumped or new bonds being discounted after the sales. At the first hint of that, any fragile stability that had been achieved would be fractured and the markets would be in freefall again.

The principal risk would come from an inability to enforce the exclusions. The Treasury knew there must be entities related to Chinese investment funds that they didn't know about and would never know about, no matter how much work was done to identify them. They knew that much of the activity of those funds was carried out by chains of agents and representatives who often didn't know the ultimate client, who might be two or three or ten links away in the chain. For that reason, they were announcing a fourth measure aimed at brokers who might, wittingly or unwittingly, break the embargo. Emergency legislation would be introduced to make it a federal felony, punishable by a minimum of two years' imprisonment and a $100,000 fine, to deal on behalf of the named entities – even indirectly. Strickland and Opitz had already warned congressional leaders that this legislation was on its way. Roberta Devlin had started applying pressure. In the country's current mood, and before the new Congress took office, they believed they would have the numbers to pass the measure, despite resistance in some parts of the Republican Party. To the inevitable protest that brokers often didn't know the identity of the ultimate customer, the answer would be: find out, and if you can't find out, don't do the trade. The idea wasn't to encourage activity on the markets, it was to shut it down.

Finally there was a question of legality over what they were doing under international law, and specifically World Trade Organization regulations. Advice had been sought from a number of experts and opinion was divided. There was an argument that the US had the right to introduce these measures as a national emergency derogation under WTO rules. Another view held that even under the emergency derogation these actions could be regarded as discriminatory in that they singled out Chinese entities, although a third opinion offered that the charge of discrimination might be found baseless since the action was aimed not against Chinese entities, but against entities that merely happened to be Chinese. Opitz had considered applying the restrictions to every foreign government-owned investment fund, but had rejected the idea because it was likely to make the US a lot of enemies just when it needed a lot of friends. China could and almost certainly would bring a complaint to the WTO but it would take a minimum of one year to be heard, and with careful maneuvering would more likely take three. The markets were trading today. That was their mentality. If you were lucky they looked maybe three months ahead. What the WTO was going to say in three years' time couldn't have concerned them less.

A briefing paper in the file that was in the president's hands outlined the likely reaction. Outrage was expected from many quarters at this interference with the markets, not least from within the Republican Party. Following on from the meetings Strickland, Opitz and Devlin had been having with congressional leaders over the past two days, the president would need to weigh in heavily, starting as soon as this meeting was over. As for the markets themselves, certain participants who had made money on the way down would squeal, but there were vanishingly few of them. Although others would object on principle – and possibly loudly – the devastation had been so extreme that at this stage most would seek some kind of stability, any kind of stability, with private relief. At this point survival, not profit, was their objective. Opitz pointed out that the suspension of mark-to-market accounting rules, however distasteful it might seem, would remove the specter of bankruptcy from many of them and would garner their support.

After the initial shock of the plan's announcement, success would come down to the question of whether brokers seriously believed they would go to jail if they traded for the wrong people, even if they had no way of knowing who the ultimate client was. The administration had to be insistent that that would be the case. There could be no ambiguity in the legislation. There were certain to be people who would test the new regulations. Those people had to be quickly identified and shut down.

At last Opitz was finished.

There was silence in the Oval Office.

Knowles leafed through the pages in the file, conscious of everyone's eyes on him. Nothing in here was new to him. Over the past two days he had been kept up to date as the measures were developed. Yet seeing them like this for the first time, together, as a final broad package of proposals that he was going to have to stand up and introduce, he couldn't help but be awed by the sheer scale of the intervention that was being proposed. If that was the effect on someone who already knew what was under consideration, he didn't want to imagine the effect it would have on others.

It had to be done before Christmas. Opitz and Strickland were in firm agreement on that. There was a psychological element, arbitrary as it might seem, that said a line had to be drawn and it had to be drawn before the holidays. The markets had to believe there was something to come back to. The outgoing Congress was also a lot more likely to pass the required legislation in its final days of session than the new Congress that would take its place in the new year. The president agreed. There was already one thing that looked like it was going to hang unfinished over the holiday. Dewy and Montez were still in Sudan. Admiral Pressler had a set of rescue plans ready for various scenarios, and every element of US intelligence capability was being strained to locate the men, but they hadn't been able to pin them down with sufficient certainty to launch a mission. Twice already they thought they had a fix but had had to call off the operation before it was launched. If he could get them back before Christmas, Knowles knew, it would feel as if it had been a short period. If it dragged beyond that, if it went into a new year, it would start to feel like a saga. Like a Jimmy Carter, Teheran-style saga.

With every day that passed, it seemed less likely. He kept telling himself there were still x days, or y days, or z days, for them to be found. But each day that number dwindled. Now there were only five days left. It just didn't feel as if it was going to happen.

The president brought his thoughts back to the matter in hand.

He didn't like what he had to do. It ran against everything he believed in, acting as some kind of policeman to say who could and couldn't trade and what price they could trade at. Putting people in jail for executing orders in good faith for their clients. But he had to do it. Opitz said it was the bare minimum that had to be done. Marty Perez talked about Armageddon if they failed to act.

'The upside,' said Gary Rose, who had sat silently through the discussion, 'is that the Chinese are probably going to like this.'

The president would have laughed if the situation wasn't so grotesque.

But Rose was serious. 'They'll make their complaint to the WTO, of course, but secretly, they'll be grateful. If I understand the numbers correctly, put their funds and their foreign reserve together and they're holding north of three trillion in US stock, bonds and cash. They don't want to actually dump this stuff – that's their threat. They want a floor and this gives it to them. This way they don't look like they're chickening out. They look like the victim. They look like we're beating up on them again. They love that. This is perfect for them.'

The president gazed at the national security advisor, still trying to detect if this wasn't some kind of uncharacteristic joke.

'From a strategic perspective,' said Rose, 'this is a circuit breaker. They understand we have to do something. They know we can't allow a situation to develop where we can't sell our government bonds. They must want a halt as much as we do, because what's happening here doesn't do any good for anyone. This gives them the halt and we look like the bad guys. It's win win.'

Tom Knowles thought about it. Maybe Gary Rose was right. Maybe Zhang secretly would be relieved that the US had found a way to break the circuit and let him look like the victim.

It didn't matter, anyway. It had to be done.

'So we announce it today?' he said.

Opitz nodded. 'After the markets close.'

AT 6PM WASHINGTON time, Tom Knowles stood at the lectern in the Press Room in the West Wing with Opitz, Strickland and O'Brien, the head of the SEC, flanking him. He announced that he was taking immediate measures to restore confidence in the markets and ensure a return to fairness and transparency. He listed the measures succinctly. Afterwards, the three officials gave a more detailed briefing to the journalists.

He went to bed that night wondering if the measures would work when the markets opened the next day. By the time he got up, the Chinese government had attacked him for discriminatory action in contravention of WTO regulations and announced they would be bringing a case at the world body against the United States.

That was exactly what everyone had predicted, and no one was too worried about it.

But two days later, on the Sunday two days before Christmas, the Chinese government did something else. Saying that China wasn't prepared to await the outcome of an interminable WTO process, they imposed a stinging set of tariffs, quotas and exclusions on US trade with the People's Republic. To be enforced immediately.

Knowles felt as if he was locked in a struggle with an opponent who wouldn't pause, wouldn't stop, wouldn't back off, but would escalate and simply hit and hit and hit until ... he didn't know. He felt as if he was suffocating. He couldn't see an end.

This wasn't working. Nothing was working.

He called a meeting of the National Security Council for the next day. That would be Christmas Eve and most of the council members had already left Washington over the weekend to head wherever they were going for the holiday. Knowles didn't give a damn. They could get on a plane and come back.

Over the two years since he had become president, Tom Knowles thought he had put together a pretty good team. Now he was wondering if any of them had the slightest idea of what they were doing.

47

KNOWLES WENT QUICKLY to the Situation Room. He had just got off an early morning call with the director-general of the WTO, who had pressed him to revoke the measures he had announced, to which the Chinese measures were a response. The director-general assured him that the Chinese would revoke their actions if the US acted first. But he didn't have answers to the questions Knowles asked him directly. As president, what was he supposed to do as the underpinnings of the American economy were torn out from under it? How else was he supposed to stabilize a market that was sliding into quicksand? The director-general assured him that he was certain the Chinese government had intended no such thing. Tom Knowles assured him the Chinese government had had plenty of opportunity to say so, both in private and public.

The other members of the National Security Council were waiting.

'I'm sorry to be getting you in here on Christmas Eve,' he said as he sat down. 'Wasn't exactly what I would have planned.'

There were a few rueful smiles in response.

'Okay,' he said. 'Let's get down to business. Everyone here knows what the Chinese government announced, right?'

Marty Perez had circulated a summary.

'Gary thought they'd secretly want us to do what we did, didn't you, Gary? I think you said it was going to be win win.'

'It was,' said Rose. 'This isn't rational.'

Bob Livingstone, who hadn't had a conversation with the president in a week, rolled his eyes. 'Of course it's rational,' he murmured. 'It's always rational.'

'What's that, Bob?'

'It's always rational, Mr President. Anything anyone does, *they* see as rational. You just have to understand how they see it.'

'And how do they see it?' said Gary Rose.

'I would say they think we're attacking them. Over Uganda, over South Africa, over this, over–'

'Attacking them?' demanded Oakley. 'Hell, Bob! We're the ones under attack here. We're the ones facing a foreign power that's infiltrated our markets and our economic institutions and has spent the last two months showing just how much damage they can do. What have we done to them? Huh? What? Gone into some godforsaken jungle to help innocent people who are being killed by the most evil bunch of killers on the planet. Jeez, Bob. Honestly! Whose side are you on?'

'Whose do you think?'

'Hold up!' said the president. 'We're on the same side. I won't have that kind of talk. No one's saying anyone's not on the same side.' He looked around the table. There was an enormous amount of tension in the room and they had barely started. 'Okay, John? Alright?'

'Yes, sir,' murmured Oakley.

'Okay. We need to figure out what we're going to do here and I'm not going to let us start squabbling like a bunch of kids. Now, I'm stumped by the sheer aggressiveness of Zhang's action. It's everything at once. What else have they got to throw at us?'

'Very little,' said Perez.

Gary Rose nodded. 'It's like saying, whatever you do, however you try to get yourself up off the floor, we're going to hit you hard. We're going to hit you right back down.'

'And see if you're prepared to hit us again,' said Oakley. 'It's like saying, do you dare? Are you going to do it or not?'

'Or they're hitting out blindly,' said Livingstone. 'They feel they're attacked. What do you do when you're attacked? You hit out. It doesn't necessarily mean you think too hard about it before–'

'Jesus,' groaned Oakley. 'More of this under attack stuff. Who's under attack here, Bob? Don't you get it?'

'I'm not saying we're not. I'm saying–'

'I think you are. I think you're saying we're the ones doing the attacking. I think you're saying we're the ones at fault.'

'I haven't even talked about fault.'

'But it won't be long, will it?'

Livingstone shook his head in exasperation. He took a deep breath, trying to keep his emotions under control. He was at breaking point. The president had ignored him over the last week during the biggest crisis of their political lives and it couldn't go on. He had come prepared to speak out today, as much as it took. He was going to confront Gary Rose and even John Oakley if necessary. He had no choice. If he didn't do it today, he felt, he never would.

'Look,' he said. 'We have a difference of opinion here in the way we see this. We all agree that we feel we've been attacked. Okay, John? I agree with that. But what I don't agree with is what you're saying when we look at how they feel. You're painting them as if everything they're doing is to attack us.'

'Isn't it?'

'Let me finish! You're painting them as if they're on this premeditated kind of campaign. And I'm saying, they might be thinking the same thing about us. Everything we do that we see as defensive, they might see as offensive.'

'They'd be wrong,' muttered Oakley.

'Doesn't matter if they're wrong! Jesus Christ, what matters is what they think! Can't you see that?'

'Calm down, Bob,' said Walt Stephenson, the vice-president, beside him. He chuckled. 'You'll have a heart attack.'

Livingstone took another deep breath. 'Mr President, what matters is what they think. Maybe they think they're being attacked. Maybe they think the rest of the world thinks that as well. If that's the case, they'll do anything not to look weak. Maybe that's why they announced these measures. They don't want to do it, but they have to, because otherwise they think everyone else is going to look at them and think they're backing down. Isn't that a possibility?'

'Well, if it's a possibility,' said Oakley, 'we need to teach them you don't do that kind of thing. They need to learn a lesson.'

Livingstone closed his eyes for a second. 'Right,' he said. 'They need to learn a lesson. Absolutely, John. And I guess now, when we're in a position of *such* strength, is the time for us to teach them.'

The president watched him closely. 'Bob, do you have any evidence for this?'

'Marion Ellman had a conversation with the Chinese ambassador at the UN. He was talking to her personally. Her feeling is that Zhang's under internal pressure over this.' He looked at Ryan Ferris. 'Have you followed that up?'

Ferris shrugged. 'We've got nothing from our sources.'

'Ambassador Ellman's view is interpretation,' said Gary Rose. 'There's nothing more to it than her interpretation of what she heard in a single conversation. Are we really going to make decisions on the basis of that?'

'Show me something better,' said Livingstone impatiently. 'Gary, you ask for the evidence and you sit there rolling your eyes and you don't want to listen to it. Then you say it's interpretation. And in the meantime, what have we been doing? That hasn't been based on inter-pretation? Everything we've done so far has been on the basis of the interpretation that the Chinese are trying to smash us, and if you ask me, on the face of it, what we've done hasn't worked. Maybe you think it has, but I don't. So if you ask me, maybe it's time to stop making the same mistake over and over and start thinking about an alternative interpretation.'

'I wouldn't have asked you,' muttered Oakley.

'Well, the president did, John!' Livingstone stopped. His heart was thumping so hard he almost felt ill.

'Okay, guys,' said Knowles, 'this isn't getting us anywhere.'

There was a tense, angry silence.

'Sir,' said General Hale. 'As a military man, I would have to say that the actions of the Chinese are a typical strategy to keep your opponent off balance. In terms of a military campaign, to harry him, if you will, so you knock him off balance and he can't regain stability.'

'This isn't a military campaign, General,' said Livingstone curtly. 'Perhaps that's escaped your notice.'

'This is not constructive,' said the president. 'Bob, let's try and make some progress.' The president looked at the Treasury secretary. 'What's the damage here?'

'Once they implement these measures?' said Opitz. 'We're still working on that but ball park, it's serious. It's big.'

'What about them?'

'It'll have an effect. I don't think there's any doubt about that. How big it'll be … that's harder to say. It also depends on how we respond.'

'Their press has been loud on the measures once they were announced,' said Ryan Ferris. 'They're saying the Chinese economy is a lot more independent of ours this time round and they don't think there'll be an effect at all.'

'That's the line for domestic consumption. It's got to have an effect.'

'They're saying they're going to boost the domestic economy, fiscal stimulus, etc., etc. They're also saying a lot of the slack will be taken up by exports to Europe and other economies.'

'That depends on what the Europeans do.'

'What are they going to do?' said Rose. 'This is a WTO dispute between us and them. The Europeans aren't getting involved.'

'So bottom line,' said Knowles, 'we take a hit. What happens to them?'

'They'll take a hit,' said Opitz. 'How big it'll be, we need to work on that.'

'No way Zhang would take a risk of a serious hit,' said Rose. 'No way he's putting Chinese workers out of jobs.'

'No way he's going to put a huge stimulus in, not after what happened last time.'

'He'll crack down hard. He'll crack down hard and early.'

'Gary, that doesn't change the fact that they'll take a hit. They have to. That's *if* they implement the measures they announced against us. Mr President, that's not a given, by any means, certainly not in full. They've got a track record of talking louder than they act.'

'Let's call their bluff,' said Oakley.

The president looked around the table. 'Do we agree on that?'

'What exactly does that mean?' said Livingstone. 'Calling their bluff. What are you trying to say?'

'I'm saying let's match them,' retorted Oakley.

'You mean we take those kind of measures as well?'

'Absolutely. What we've done to protect our markets isn't illegal. It doesn't contravene any rules.'

'Well, I think you might find that–'

'National emergency. Isn't that what Susan's told us, we have a national emergency derogation under WTO rules? I don't know what we've got here if we haven't got a national emergency so that gives us the right to do what we're doing.'

'I don't think they see it–'

'They're the ones in breach! There's a process in the WTO for complaint if they have a complaint and they've chosen to circumvent that and take the law into their own hands. Well, fine. You want to do that, we can do it too.'

Livingstone stared at the defense secretary. He felt faint. He pulled at his necktie.

'I'm not sure about that, John,' said the president. 'Let's take it one step at a time. One thing that's certain is we can't step back from what we've done.'

'But if what we've done is right,' said Rose, 'if we really believe we're justified in doing it, then I think John has a point. We've done something we have a right to do and now we've been attacked. Not through due process, but by a kind of wildcat action. What's our response?'

Walt Stephenson, who had made no contribution since the discussion began, cleared his throat. 'I don't claim to know too much about finance and foreign affairs, but this thing the Chinese have done does sound awful aggressive.' He glanced at Bob Livingstone, who was sitting beside him. 'Bob, you okay?'

Livingstone nodded. He felt clammy and nauseated.

'You look like hell. You want some water?'

Livingstone shook his head.

'Okay, well, this does sound awful aggressive. I'm not sure we should take it lying down.'

Tom Knowles thought about it. There was a logic to what Oakley and Rose had suggested. Accepting the Chinese actions without some kind of retaliation would make it look as if the United States accepted that China was justified in doing what it had done. And yet the idea of taking another step, so soon, so belligerently, seemed too much. Rose and Oakley were both strongly in favor of it, but his faith in them had taken a hit in the last few days. And it was clear that Bob Livingstone had a different view, although it wasn't clear how he would act on it. Stay silent, perhaps.

He glanced at Livingstone. The secretary of state's head was bowed, as if he was studying one of the papers in front of him.

'I'm not sure where this goes,' said Knowles.

'Mr President,' replied Oakley, 'we've got to come back at them. We let this pass, we look weak.'

The president glanced at Marty Perez. 'I assume we have plans for something like this.'

Perez nodded, looking pained at the thought. 'We have a set of measures we can activate. In principle it's the mirror image of what they've done to us.'

Knowles felt pained as well. He didn't want to announce anything now, not on Christmas Eve. Whatever effect the new market measures had had in restoring a sense of hope – whatever was left after Zhang's response – would evaporate utterly. If he could somehow get to the holidays, he felt, there would be time to … He didn't know what. Think it through. Or for something to happen. Something to lessen the tension.

'Sir, I think we should issue a statement,' said Roberta Devlin. 'We condemn the measures taken by China and say we're considering our response. That might be a complaint to the WTO or it might be something considerably more immediate. We could make that sound quite threatening. And reiterate our right to do what we've already done, of course.'

Out of the corner of his eye, the president noticed Ed Abrahams nodding.

'You could also say it's the holiday season and a time for people to try to step back and find ways to heal their differences. Give it a tone of magnanimity. Put a little statesmanship in there. It might even give them a way to back out.'

'Just puts the whole thing off,' said Oakley.

'I'm inclined to agree with John,' said Rose. 'We can put it off for a few days, but we're going to have to take some action, and it's going to need to be more than bringing a case to the WTO. I doubt they're going to back out, as Roberta says. Whether it's better to have it hanging over us or get it done right away, that's largely a political consideration.'

Knowles looked at Livingstone. 'Bob, what do you think?'

Livingstone nodded quickly. 'That's fine,' he murmured.

'What's fine? What Roberta said?'

Livingstone nodded again. He had lost track of the discussion. He was finding it hard to breathe.

The president watched him. The secretary of state didn't say anything else.

'Walt,' said Knowles to the vice-president, 'do you want to say anything?'

Stephenson raised an eyebrow. 'Well, it's a tough one.' He toyed with a pen, getting ready to deliver his opinion. 'We're going to have to face them down on this, but maybe Roberta's right. A little magnanimity the day before Christmas puts us on the moral high ground. On the other hand, if we're going to have to match them in the end, do we lose anything by waiting? Maybe we do. I don't see there's a right and a wrong answer here.'

The president watched him for a moment. 'Thanks,' he said eventually.

He considered the problem a little longer.

'Okay, here's what we'll do. I'm going to go with Roberta's idea. I'll make a statement along the lines Roberta suggested.'

'And then what?' said Oakley.

'Then … we'll see what comes back. Like Marty says, what else can they throw at us? Let them chew on it for a few days. Maybe then we try to make contact and see if they want to talk about it privately. We can still take action if we need to, but this gives us time to think it through a little more. Marty and Susan, you want to work up a plan for that? And let's have the full numbers for the impact on us and the impact on them. All that stuff. We need to know it. I'm sorry to be asking you to get this done over the holiday. I guess you're going to have a few people who won't get much of a Christmas. Tell them I appreciate it.'

They nodded.

Rose and Oakley glanced at each other.

There was silence. One other thing was on the president's mind. It was still early on Christmas Eve. Dewy and Montez were still somewhere in Sudan. Time was running out, but it wasn't impossible. He turned to Hale. 'Any chance of anything happening with our guys, General?'

'It could happen any time, sir. It just takes one sighting, one loose piece of communication, and we'll find them.'

'Admiral Pressler will let me know as soon as he thinks there's a chance to go in and get them, right? Any time, night or day.'

'Yes, sir. As soon as he thinks there's a situation that meets the operational requirements, it'll be your call.'

'Okay. It's just if we could somehow manage to–'

There was a thud. The president looked around. Bob Livingstone's head had hit the table and he was in the process of sliding off his chair. He fell sideways against the vice-president.

The vice-president stared at him. For an instant no one moved. Then General Hale jumped up and hauled the secretary of state down on the floor and thumped his chest with a fist. Roberta Devlin grabbed a phone and called for the duty physician from the White House Medical Unit. Three minutes later a doctor and a nurse ran in carrying a portable defibrillator and a bag of drugs. They tore open Livingstone's shirt and shocked him three times on the floor of the Situation Room, pumping on his chest until a stretcher arrived.

They were still pumping on his chest as the secretary of state was wheeled out.

48

IT WAS A dark, sobering Christmas. Tom Knowles couldn't remember one like it.

Bob Livingstone had been pronounced dead in the emergency room of George Washington University Hospital, where he had been taken from the White House. Tom phoned Alicia Livingstone when he heard. Sarah phoned her as well. That afternoon Tom and Sarah flew to Camp David. Tom gazed at the bleak, bare Maryland country-side below him. The landscape matched his thoughts. He thought of Harley Gauss's widow. It seemed a long time ago now that the airman had died and he had promised to bring his remains home. He hadn't done it. He thought of that poor young woman in Jacksonville facing up to her first Christmas without her husband. He thought of Pete Dewy and Phil Montez, the two men who were somewhere in Sudan, and what their families must be feeling.

At Camp David, Steve and his family were there to meet them. He gave Steve a good long hug. He put his arms around the twins and hugged them both at once. Tom felt a tear in his eye and struggled to keep it back.

By Christmas Day, the date of the funeral had been fixed for the 28th at the National Cemetery in Jefferson City, Missouri. Tom and Sarah had been planning to fly to Nevada on the 27th to spend New Year at their ranch in Elko, but decided to stay on at Camp David before heading to Missouri for the funeral and go to Nevada from there.

They were dark days. Reflective. The daily CIA briefing continued to take place. The Chinese government hadn't responded to the statement that Dean Moss had issued in Knowles' name late in the afternoon of the 24th. Knowles spoke to Gary Rose a couple of times, to Ed Abrahams, to Susan Opitz. Not much. The bare minimum. He spoke with the British prime minister, who called him Christmas Day to offer his condolences over Bob Livingstone's death and to discuss the statement the president had released. Knowles kept the conversation short. After that he made himself unavailable for any other foreign leader unless President Zhang decided to call up.

He read. He had hardly got a chance to do that for months. He played grandpa with the twins. He went for walks through the icy grounds of Camp David and did a lot of thinking.

He called up Dale Lambert, the ex-Idaho senator and presidential candidate who had been a formative influence in his political development. They had a good discussion about all kinds of things, including China. Dale said that he had to do what he had to do to protect American interests. If it meant facing China down, then that's what it meant. It wasn't going to be easy, but then that wasn't what he had been elected for, to do the easy things.

He felt that with those few quiet days he was able to gain some distance, to step back from the madness and the frenzy that had engulfed him over the last few weeks in Washington. Soon, he knew, they would engulf him again, which made these days all the more precious. The things that Bob Livingstone had said in that last meeting in the Situation Room stayed with him. In two years, he had barely once rung Bob for advice. Yet now that Livingstone was dead, he found himself wishing he could call him up and hear what he had to say.

Tom Knowles had doubts. He was deep in confrontation with China, and that was the last thing he wanted. Yet all anyone around him seemed to be able to do was take him further in. Those quiet days, those long walks, seemed to make that clear. Tit for tat didn't work, he knew that. Tit for tat had to end somewhere. But now you were in, how did you get out without looking weak? No one seemed to be able to tell him that.

He wondered if President Zhang was wondering the same thing.

The next time he sat down with Gary Rose and his other advisors, he decided, that was the question he was going to ask. How could he stop the tit for tat? How could he bring it to an end without looking as if he had backed down?

He had three full days in Camp David. Then early on the 28th he and Sarah were taken back to Washington and flew out to Missouri for Bob Livingstone's funeral.

IN MANHATTAN, MARION ELLMAN had spent Christmas thinking as well. Livingstone's death had put a lot of things in perspective. As had spending time with two young children for what seemed like the first time in months.

She reread Joel Ehrenreich's book. It impressed her even more the second time around. She thought a lot about what Liu had said to her. Neither side, the American or the Chinese, was better than the other, she thought. Neither side, she believed, wanted to be in the position in which they found themselves, and yet here they were. No better than two screaming, grasping children. She watched her own two children, and she found herself, for the first time, fearing for them. Really fearing for them. Not the familiar, quotidian fear that every mother feels for her child when they're out of her sight, when any of the things that can happen every day in this world could happen to them, but fear for the kind of world they were going to inherit.

Who was going to stop it? Bob Livingstone hadn't been able to. Doug Havering, acting secretary of state while the president sought another nominee, toed the White House line. Inside the White House, as far as she knew, no one was in opposition to the president's thinking. Certainly not Gary Rose, and she doubted anyone else was. They were all egging each other on in there, she knew. They had to be.

She spent a lot of time thinking about her position. Every spare minute, it seemed, when Ella and Ben weren't grabbing her attention. Late at night, she talked to Dave. There was nothing much he could say apart from the obvious. He listened over long glasses of wine and helped her say it for herself.

She would probably have to resign. She wasn't sure about the timing. Resigning in the middle of a crisis never looked good. But what did it matter? It would be the end of her public career. She wouldn't come back from that.

But how could she continue to serve when she felt the president was so wrong? He had cocooned himself away from anything that challenged his thinking, and there was no one who had both the will and the opportunity to put that right.

For three days, she mulled things over. By the 28th, she had made up her mind. Only the question of the timing remained.

That morning, in the frigid air before dawn, she boarded a plane. She was going to Bob Livingstone's funeral as well.

49

IT WAS A raw, unyielding day. Snow lay on the ground. The air was a cold, bone-chilling mist. Rows of headstones ran down a slope under the silhouettes of leafless trees.

The chapel was crowded. A marquee had been set up in front of it to take the overflow. Family, friends, former associates from Bob's days as a lawyer, senatorial colleagues and State Department officials had come to pay their last respects. The marquee was underheated in the freezing air and people shivered. The president gave a eulogy in the chapel. So did Alvin Burr, Bob Livingstone's closest friend in the Senate. Bob's eldest, Robert junior, had spoken first. He was Robert junior no longer, he said. He wished he still was.

Then they all came out into the mist and walked over the snowy ground, through the headstones, to the open mouth of the waiting grave.

The president and first lady stood alongside Alicia Livingstone and her three sons. Bob's casket rested on the ground as the last words were said. Tom Knowles' Secret Service detail tried to look inconspicuous. Two stood immediately behind the president, others in the crowd, others off amongst the headstones, constantly scanning the cemetery.

Marion Ellman gazed at Bob's casket. Slowly it was lowered.

She glanced at the president. He stood with hands clasped, a grim frown on his face.

Alicia and the three boys stepped forward and each dropped a lily into the grave. The gentle tap of each one as it hit the top of the coffin was audible in the stillness.

Alicia stood over the casket for a last moment, then turned away.

The president took her arm, and said something, and Alicia nodded, wiping with a tissue at her tears. The first lady said something to her as well while the president spoke with each of the sons, solemnly shaking their hands in turn.

Others waited to say a word to the widow. For a couple of minutes the president shook hands with the mourners nearby. As Marion waited her turn to speak with Alicia, she saw Knowles turn. His security detail closed up around him and the first lady. The crowd made way as they began to move off.

Marion watched him for a moment. Suddenly she stepped out of the crowd and called out.

The sound of her own voice startled her. In the frigid air, it sounded too loud.

The president looked around. Everyone was watching. He smiled when he saw who it was. His security detail didn't. Two of them were coming towards her.

He told them who she was. The two men backed away, still eyeing her suspiciously.

Marion went closer. 'Sir, I need to speak with you.'

'Now?'

Marion nodded.

'Go ahead.'

'It's sensitive, sir.'

The president glanced around. 'Let's go over there.'

They headed out into the snow amongst the gravestones. Marion was conscious of the crowd of mourners still watching them.

Knowles stopped. He looked at her expectantly.

Now that she was at the point, she hesitated. She hadn't even imagined doing this. It hadn't been rehearsed, not even in her head. She was shaking.

'Cold, huh?' said the president, noticing her trembling. 'Hell of a day. My God, one hell of a day.'

'There's something I have to tell you.'

'About Bob. He was a good guy, wasn't he?'

Marion nodded. Bob Livingstone had told her that you couldn't just *tell* Tom Knowles anything. But Bob was dead.

She drew a deep breath. It came out freezing in front of her.

'Mr President, what you're doing is wrong. Your approach, your strategy. They're wrong.'

Knowles looked at her in bemusement. 'What I'm doing about what?'

'About what's happening. About China.'

'You think so, do you?'

'Mr President, maybe it's not my place but someone has to tell you. You're taking us into confrontation with that country and it is not a confrontation either side is going to win. Not us, not them. You've misjudged them. You're giving them no option but to come back at us every time you say something. You're escalating this and you're leading us and them into a trap and if you keep going pretty soon there's going to be no way out.'

The president stared at her.

'You can ask for my resignation. I don't care. I'm going to resign anyway.'

'Whoa! Hold up. Let's not make any hasty decision.'

'It's not a hasty decision. Someone has to tell you, sir. Someone has to make you listen.'

'And you think resigning's going to do that?'

'No, resigning's going to stop me having to act in a way that I think is the exact opposite of this country's best interests. Resigning is going to allow me to speak publicly. We're in a lose-lose situation. We have to get out of it.'

The president folded his arms. 'What would you do if you were me?'

'We need to be actively seeking collaboration. We need a different approach. We could have done that over South Africa but we didn't.'

'So could they.'

'True. I'm not saying they're better. They're as bad as us, sir.'

'As bad as us?'

'This isn't a temporary, tactical situation we're in. Things have changed in our world, Mr President. We're going to keep beating each other up unless we change as well.'

'Do you think that's what they think?'

'I don't know.'

'Bob said you'd had a conversation with the Chinese ambassador.'

'That's true. I sent you my report. My impression is that Zhang's under pressure.'

'What kind of pressure?'

'I don't know.'

'You're not afraid to admit when you don't know, are you?'

'Do you prefer people who are?'

The president smiled for a second. 'No. I don't.'

'Sir, there's someone I think you should meet. His name's Joel Ehrenreich. He's just written a book that is one of the best analyses of US–China relations that I've read in the last several years.'

The president frowned. 'Not sure I recognize the name.'

'He's at Yale.'

The president looked at Ellman thoughtfully. 'Marion, no one's telling me I'm wrong.'

'I am.'

'But no one else is.'

'And that's your problem, sir. That, in a nutshell, is your problem.'

Knowles looked away over the headstones. 'Why haven't I heard any of this from you before?'

'Ask Gary Rose. It's not for want of trying.'

Knowles was silent.

'Mr President, you should meet Joel Ehrenreich. You should listen to what he has to say. Now. Today. Before you do anything else.'

The president glanced at his security detail. They were watching him. He looked back at Ellman. 'Marion, I don't think this is the time to be talking to academics. You can send me the book.'

'No, sir. Normally I'd agree with you. But there are times when someone who's outside the fray – someone whose perspective isn't over the course of a year or an election cycle but takes a generational view of things – sometimes there are times when that's a good perspective.'

The president gazed at Ellman. 'Send me the book,' he said, and turned and walked away.

'Mr President!'

He stopped and looked back at her.

Marion Ellman had nothing to lose. The timing, she realized, had decided itself.

She came closer to him. 'You asked me what I would do. I haven't been involved in your discussions. But if I had to guess, I'd guess you've spent an awful lot of time talking about what we want the Chinese to do.'

The president nodded.

She pointed at him, right at the chest, like a teacher to a pupil. 'You need to spend some time thinking about what the Chinese want from us.'

THERE WAS SILENCE in the car on the ride back to the airport. Sarah gazed out the window. The president pondered the conversation he had just had with the UN ambassador. It had reared up out of nowhere and kicked him in the teeth.

But he didn't have time to reflect on it. The ride to Air Force One was a short one. Almost as soon as he had boarded the plane for the flight to Nevada a call came through from General Hale.

'Mr President,' said the general, 'we know where they are.'

50

THE HELICOPTERS WERE in the air by the time Air Force One touched down in Nevada. At five in the afternoon Pacific Time it would be 4am in Sudan.

Hale had told the president not to expect to hear anything until around 6pm Pacific at the earliest. The attack team would maintain radio silence until they were off the ground and back out of Sudanese air space.

The plan was one of three that had been drawn up by Pressler's team. The president had seen the details days earlier and had approved it subject to key operational conditions being met. It called for a night-time raid by five Chinooks flying out of the US base at Lodwar in Kenya, cutting north across Uganda and into southern Sudan at almost the limit of their range. Each of the Chinooks would carry twenty-four marines and their weaponry, and the group would be under escort of a half dozen Apache attack helicopters.

By six the president and Sarah had arrived at their ranch north of Elko. Friends were due for dinner at 6.30. Knowles waited in his study, flicking through a bunch of papers that he was supposed to read. He couldn't concentrate, kept glancing at the phone.

One of the security guys knocked on his door to tell him his guests had arrived. He didn't get up right away. Sarah was out there to look after them, he knew. He couldn't tear himself away from the phone.

Finally, at around seven, he got up and went out.

The Maises and the Dickinsons were local Elko couples, good friends going back years. Sarah had already seen to their drinks. Tom poured himself a bourbon. The talk stayed clear of politics. Dick Maise was president of the local country club and was always good for a bunch of stories about the goings-on down there. Ed Dickinson was a more quiet kind of guy, almost morose. His wife Hilary was a hoot.

At around seven-thirty Tom excused himself. He went back to the study and had the White House operator get Mortlock Hale on the phone.

'There's no news, sir,' said the general.

'What does that mean?'

'It means they're not out of Sudan.'

'They definitely went in?'

'Yes, sir. They shut down communication at eighteen thirty-two eastern. That would be around four-thirty your time, sir.'

'That's three hours ago. You told me they'd be out by six.'

'Mr President, I said that would be the earliest possible time. That would be the time if Dewy and Montez were waiting with their bags packed.'

'But they should be out by now, right?'

'They'll be out, sir.'

'When?'

'When they're done, Mr President. Sir, I'll call you as soon as I hear anything. If I may … I've been through a number of these scenarios. They're nerve-wracking at the best of times. Right now, I've got five guys here with me and I think we've got about two whole fingernails between us. But nine times out of ten, when you think something's gone wrong, it hasn't. You've got to trust the guys on the ground. These are good guys Pressler sent in. Top notch. They'll do the job.'

Knowles didn't say anything.

'Sir?'

'I heard you, General.'

'Mr President, you'll hear as soon as we have any information whatsoever.'

'Okay. Thank you.'

Knowles put down the phone. If Dewy and Montez weren't waiting with their bags packed, as the general put it, then what kind of battle would the rescue force have to fight to extract them? One of the operational Go conditions for the rescue was that the forces holding the two airmen had to be lightly armed, either LRA or Sudanese army. A lightly armed, poorly trained group of soldiers would disintegrate into a panicked rabble firing wildly at anything that twitched – mostly each other – when a force of Apaches came out

of the night sky at them with their guns blazing. Pressler had estimated that the marines who would pour out of the Chinooks that
followed would eliminate them as a fighting force almost instanta-
neously, taking minimum or zero casualties.

They couldn't afford a screw-up. Knowles feared to think what the
press would do to him if some kind of helicopter rescue debacle was
taking place right now somewhere in Sudan. It would be his second
step to Carterdom. He didn't know what had done Jimmy Carter
more damage – the taking of the hostages at the American embassy in
Teheran or the failed attempt to rescue them that had ended with
stories of US helicopters choked in the desert dust. The first was
tragedy, the second farce. Nothing hurts a politician more.

There was a knock on the door. Sarah looked in.

'We're waiting to sit down, Tom.'

He nodded.

'You coming?'

'Sure.' He got up and forced himself to walk away from the phone.

They had big juicy steaks and fries and salad. Dick and Hilary and
Sarah carried the conversation. He found it a little hard to get
involved. He tried. He laughed at the appropriate times. Told a story
about some amusing incident that had happened early in their time at
the White House when they still didn't know how the place ran. Then
his thoughts drifted away again.

'You're quiet today, Tom,' said Hilary.

Tom looked at her.

'Everything okay?' She laughed. 'No national emergencies we
should know about?'

Tom smiled.

'The funeral was somewhat of an ordeal,' said Sarah.

Knowles nodded. 'Yeah. That was a hell of a funeral. And cold, too.
Jesus, it was cold out there.'

'That was the secretary of state, right?' said Dick.

'Were you close to him?' asked Hilary.

'Well, you know, you work with someone, you spend a couple of
years working with someone pretty intensely on some pretty
important stuff, and then he's …' Tom shrugged, sighing. 'Then he's
gone.'

Ed Dickinson nodded knowingly. Ed didn't say much but always perked up when talk turned to the morbid side of life. 'It was a sudden death, wasn't it? See, we're not accustomed to sudden death any more. What was it? A heart attack?'

'Right in front of Tom,' said Sarah. 'Isn't that right, Tom?'

'That's right. Right in front of me in the Situation Room.'

Everyone had stopped eating. They stared at him.

'In the Situation Room?' said Dick. 'Hell, that's dramatic.'

'Was there some kind of emergency going on?' asked Hilary.

'No. We have all kinds of meetings down there.' Knowles smiled. 'Only place you can get any peace and quiet.'

They laughed.

'Sometimes I go down there just for the hell of it. You know, just to–' Knowles stopped. His personal aide had come quietly into the room.

'Mr President,' he said, 'there's a call for you.'

KNOWLES LISTENED, TRYING to comprehend what he was being told.

'Four of the Apaches got out. Two of the Chinooks. The others were damaged to varying degrees and unable to exit.'

'Any dead?' he asked.

'We think we lost the pilots in the two Apaches that went down,' said Hale. His voice was somber. 'That's four. There's another eight dead that we know of, plus a bunch of injured.'

'And everyone else got back into those two Chinooks?'

'No, sir. They're still on the ground.'

'Wait, you told me we got two Chinooks out. We still have men on the ground?'

'Mr President, we think we've got about eighty men on the ground.'

The number exploded in his head like a gunshot. '*Eighty men on the ground*?'

There was silence on the line for a moment, then Knowles heard Hale's voice. 'Yes, sir.'

'We left *eighty* men behind?'

'Approximately, sir. At this stage it's an approximate number.'

The president threw his head back and stared at the ceiling. For a moment he could hardly breathe.

'Mr President?'

'I'm sorry, General. I'm just trying to understand how that can happen. Eighty men? Eighty of our highest trained marines! What are they doing? Are they still fighting?'

'Apparently not. They've taken over the facility where we thought Dewy and Montez were being held. It's moderately fortified.'

'Hold on.' Knowles tried to figure out what he was being told. Or not being told. 'What's the sequence here, General?'

'We're still trying to–'

'They landed. They got out. They took over the facility. And *then* they couldn't get out again?'

There was silence for a moment. 'Something like that. Apparently the Chinooks were destroyed after our men were out. Pressler's in contact. They say the firing's stopped. They could break out, but there's nowhere to break out to.'

'Let me get this straight. They're in this place, and now they're surrounded by Sudanese troops. Is that what you're saying? General, it seems to me this isn't exactly the rabble you told me was going to be down there. What were your words again? I seem to recall you telling me they were going to be shooting each other in the ass the minute they heard our choppers coming.'

'That's the other thing, sir. Our intelligence led us to believe the troops on the site lacked the weapons to inflict this kind of damage. It takes something to shoot down an Apache helicopter. It takes a certain amount of training, as well. And discipline. So these are either elite Sudanese troops that were brought down there, or they're elite Chinese.'

'Why didn't we know about that?'

'Intelligence is imperfect.'

'To hell with that! This is a set-up, General! This is a fucking set-up.'

'It could well be the case that there was–'

'You're damn right it could well be! These guys have outsmarted you. It's as simple as that, isn't it?'

'I think it's clear at the very least this was a well-armed, well-prepared defensive unit, sir.'

'Don't give me that. This is a fucking ambush and we were dumb enough to walk right into it. Let 'em come, wait till they're down, knock out their escape, pick 'em off. You don't need to go to West Point to figure that out. No wonder they kept Dewy and Montez within range. How the hell did we fall for something like this?'

Hale was silent.

'They make us think they've got two goons and a gun, they wait until we're on the ground, they come out with their weapons and their elite troops and blow the hell out of our helicopters and now they've got us locked in. How the fuck … How the *fuck* could this have happened?'

'It's very poor, sir.'

Knowles almost laughed.

'What about Dewy and Montez?'

'They weren't there.'

Of course not, thought Knowles. 'Why am I not surprised? Why am I not surprised you got that wrong as well?'

Knowles closed his eyes. He was overwhelmed with anger.

'Mr President, I know this doesn't look good.'

This time Knowles did laugh.

'Admiral Pressler– '

'Admiral Pressler's working on another plan, is he? Does Admiral Pressler have any idea how he's going to get our guys back? Perhaps he's going to send in another bunch of helicopters and see if they can do any better.'

'At this point, I think that would be unwise.'

'Yeah! I think it would be.'

'He has, however, taken steps to protect the men on the ground.'

'What steps?'

'Sir, throughout the course of the Jungle Peace deployment the *Abraham Lincoln* strike group, which is Admiral Pressler's command post, has been shadowed by a pair of Chinese destroyers.'

'Yes, General. I'm aware of that.'

'Admiral Pressler has deployed the strike group around them.'

The frown on the president's face grew deeper. 'I'm sorry, General. I don't understand. What does that mean? He has deployed his strike group …'

'It means he's in a position to destroy the Chinese vessels at will, sir.'

'This is in international waters?'

'He's also informed the commanders of the two vessels that he will sink them if any attack is launched on our men in Sudan.'

'Do they know about our men, these commanders?'

'The message was relayed to Beijing, Mr President. We listened in on it.'

'General, who gave Admiral Pressler the order to do that? Did you give him that order?'

'No, sir.'

'Is he empowered to take a decision like that?'

'The theater commander is responsible for operational decisions, sir, within the rules of engagement.'

'And this is within the rules of engagement?'

'I'm not sure that our rules of engagement covered this eventuality.'

Knowles took a deep breath. Only now, he thought, had he managed to extract from the general the whole, convoluted picture. He gazed around the wood-paneled walls of his study. Between his time as Nevada governor and as president, this room had seen its fair share of difficult situations. But none of them, he guessed, was as difficult as this was going to be.

'Let me understand this,' said the president slowly. 'What we have is eighty of our men in Sudan surrounded by a force of Chinese ...'

'Or elite Sudanese.'

'Or elite Sudanese soldiers, and two Chinese destroyers surrounded by our strike group off the coast of Kenya.'

'Yes, sir.'

The image that flashed into the president's mind was of a film he had seen years earlier. 'This is like *Reservoir Dogs*.'

'I don't think I follow, sir.'

The president didn't explain. He shook his head disbelievingly. It was like a giant Mexican standoff, stretching from a jungle in Sudan to the ocean east of Kenya.

'Does anyone know about this?'

'Only the militaries involved. We haven't said anything. Neither has China.'

'What happens next?'

'That's what we have to work out.'

51

THE SITUATION ROOM was crowded with military and intelligence officers. Just about the whole of the most senior level of the military in Washington were in the room.

A map on the screen showed the location of the *Abraham Lincoln* strike group off Lamu Bay on the north Kenyan coast.

'The two Chinese ships are destroyers built within the last six years,' said the officer who was presenting, Admiral Bob Tovey. A pair of pictures replaced the map on the screen. 'That one on the left is the *Changchun*, which is a Luhai II class. The other one is the *Kunming*, which is a Luyang III class and is the most advanced destroyer type in the Chinese navy. If you're interested in the specifications in detail, Mr President, they're in the briefing paper or I could go through them for you now.'

Knowles shook his head

It was eighteen hours since the rescue force had been ambushed in Sudan, sixteen hours since the two Chinese destroyers had been detained. In the interim the president had flown back to Washington.

'So, to move away from the theater, we're tracking two of their aircraft carriers, the *Mao Zedong* and the *Chou Enlai*, which are now under way across the Indian Ocean together with their strike groups. They were on station here ...' Tovey brought up another map and clicked with his laser pointer at an area of ocean southwest of India and north of the Maldives, leaving an X on the screen. 'They left their station around three hours after we took action against their ships and we now have them roughly ... here ...' He pointed a little further to the left across the expanse of emptiness that separated them from the Kenyan coast and clicked again.

Knowles tried to evaluate the distance. It was just a big gap on a map. He had no idea what it meant in reality.

'From our understanding of their operational capabilities, we would put them off the Kenyan coast in not less than sixty-six hours.'

'Mr President,' said the head of defense intelligence, 'these are two of the four carriers they commissioned two years ago. We don't consider them a match for our carrier groups but that doesn't mean there won't be serious impact if we come to grips.'

Tovey nodded. 'Our closest carrier on that trajectory is the *John F Kennedy*, which is ... here. We're sending the *Kennedy* with its strike group to support the *Lincoln*. We estimate it at seventy-eight hours away.'

'How come we're not in a position to get there first?' said Knowles.

'Sir, we were not anticipating to have to support the *Lincoln*. The sixty-six hours I've mentioned for the Chinese ships also assumes they'll perform to the maximum of their specifications.'

'I assume that goes for the *Kennedy*'s seventy-eight hours as well,' said Gary Rose.

'Theirs are largely untested ships, Dr Rose, which have never been in a genuine operational situation. I wouldn't say the same for the *John F Kennedy*.'

'Is it normal for two of their carrier strike groups to be in the same location?'

'No, sir.'

'Did we know about this?' demanded the president.

'We track all enemy ships, Mr President.'

'How long have they been there?'

'They joined up eight days ago, I believe.'

'And you *knew*?'

Mortlock Hale intervened. 'Mr President, the *Lincoln* is engaged in a UN-sanctioned intervention. We had no reason to anticipate that another UN member would attack it.'

'I don't care what you anticipated. If you know there are two foreign carriers close enough to gang up on one of our ships don't you think you should do something about it?' The president shook his head in exasperation and glanced angrily at Gary Rose.

Tovey waited a moment, then continued. 'We're also bringing the *George HW Bush* and its strike group from here ...' He indicated a point off the western coast of southern Africa. 'That will bring the *Bush* into Lamu Bay two days after the Chinese arrive and will create an overwhelming superiority of force. To be clear, sir, the *Kennedy* already creates a superiority of force but the *Bush* makes it overwhelming.'

'Admiral,' said Rose, 'if I was the Chinese and looking at the picture you're showing us here – the *Kennedy* and its strike force arriving twelve hours after I get there, the *Bush* coming in forty-eight hours later – I'm going to attack as soon as I get there. That's my best shot. Would you disagree with that?'

'As I said, sir, the seventy-eight hours is an estimate. So is their sixty-six. Depending on operational performance and conditions at sea, you could easily reverse the numbers.'

'Or not. And if not, would you disagree with me?'

'You're also assuming they want to attack,' said Hale.

'No, I'm not, General. That's the point. What I'm saying is they're going to have to make a quick decision because they'll only have a short window of opportunity to succeed. They've got twelve hours of superiority of force and after that the attack option's pretty much gone, whether they want to use it or not.' Rose paused. 'That's going to force them to make a very quick decision.'

The president nodded. He gazed at the screen and looked at the X's marked on the map, separated by the expanse of the Indian Ocean. But they were getting closer, he knew. Hour by hour, they were coming together.

'I don't see what the alternative is,' said Hale. 'We don't bring these forces up, they have unlimited superiority of force.'

'Admiral Tovey,' said the president, 'can you give me some idea of what this actually looks like? How many ships are we talking about?'

'We have fifteen in the *Abraham Lincoln* strike group, sir. They have forty-four under way. Once the *Kennedy* and *Bush* arrive, we'll have fifty-eight.'

'So that's ...'

'A hundred and two vessels if they all arrive. And a hell of a lot of aircraft. If it happens, it'll be one hell of a show. By the time the

Kennedy gets there, there'll be more ships on one patch of sea than any time since Midway, and that's going back to World War Two.'

The president took a deep breath and let it out slowly, contemplating the numbers.

The silence grew heavy.

Knowles looked at Hale. 'What about our guys in Sudan?'

'We've resupplied them. We've taken out the injured.'

'No problems?'

Hale shook his head. As the president knew, the general had personally given a message to the senior military attaché at China's Washington embassy that at noon local time the US was going to send in two Chinooks to deliver supplies to the men on the ground and take out the wounded, and if there was any fire on those helicopters one of the Chinese destroyers would be fired upon in turn. The message must have made its way back to Beijing and on to Sudan, because the mission had been completed, and apart from a couple of stray shots fired at the Chinooks as they landed, there was no attempt to stop them.

'How many do we still have down there?'

'Seventy-three, sir.'

'And that's without Dewy and Montez?'

'That's right, Mr President.'

'So that's seventy-five in all.' Knowles thought about it. 'Why haven't they made any of this public? We send a force into a foreign country, we hijack two of their ships on the high seas … That's piracy. Why are they keeping it quiet?'

'They've always denied having military in Sudan,' said Rose. 'They've admitted advisors, nothing more.'

'And we led them to believe we had proof that they were involved,' said Hale. 'We said we'd brought back a couple of their wounded men.'

'And had we?'

'We have now.'

The president shrugged. 'So, they have troops there. Big deal. Every intelligence agency in the world knows they have, right? It's not a crime if Sudan's invited them in.'

'They're sensitive about it.'

'And those troops were involved in resisting a rescue of two men abducted while executing a UN resolution,' added the director of the CIA.

'Our rescue operation was in contravention of that resolution,' said Rose. 'Technically Sudan had a right to resist.'

'But it doesn't do them any favors with the rest of the world. They should be pressuring Sudan to hand our men back. Instead, they end up fighting a pitched battle to hold on to them.'

'There's a lot of countries that would be very happy to see them doing that. Any kind of opposition to us is good opposition, regardless of whether it's legal.'

'To hell with that,' said John Oakley. 'They're spoiling for a fight. They've got those aircraft carriers that have never seen a gnat's ass in action and they want to use them. They want to show us they're a power. They've wanted to show it for years.'

'Then they're going to get blown out of the water,' said Hale.

'Mort, maybe they don't think so. They may be dumb enough to believe their own PR about those ships.'

'You really think they think they can beat us?'

'No,' said Oakley, 'I think they think they're going to steam on in there and we're going to get out of the way. I think they think they're going to pick up their ships and head on out. We're going to back down. And once we do, they're going to tell everyone about it.'

'That's not going to happen,' said Hale.

'Well, that's the question.' Oakley looked at the president. 'Are we bluffing or are we for real?'

That was the question. Knowles looked at Gary Rose. 'What do we think our Nato allies would do?'

'If we were attacked?'

'I've had a call from Admiral Rogers in London,' said Tovey. 'They know something's going on.'

'Of course they do,' said Oakley. 'And they'll be ready to help just as soon as it's finished.'

'John,' said Rose, 'if this blows up, it's not going to be restricted to East Africa.'

'Of course not. But what can we do? They're coming, Gary.' He pointed at the map on the screen. 'They're on their way. They're going to get there. The question is, what are we going to do when they arrive?'

'We don't give way,' said the president. 'That's for sure.'

'Exactly. And they're going to have twelve hours to make up their mind and do something or lose their ability to do it. They'll know that just like we do. And they're still coming. So when we don't give way, what happens in those twelve hours?'

'Mr President,' said Tovey, 'there's a good chance that if it does get to that point, something will happen whether anyone wants it to or not. It will be an extremely fragile situation. You get that many ships and aircraft together on one piece of real estate, it only takes one thing to go wrong, one misinterpretation, and the fireworks start.' The admiral paused. 'Sir, there hasn't been a set-piece battle between two carrier strike groups – let alone four – since World War Two. And you look at the ships we're talking about now, and the aircraft, you look at their firepower … Those World War Two battles aren't in the same league. The world hasn't seen a naval battle like this.'

The president looked at the CIA director. 'They've let absolutely nothing about this slip?'

She shook her head. 'Nothing. We're monitoring every channel and website we know of.'

'What if we tell them we won't make anything public either?' said the president. 'They can turn around and it's finished.'

'Would you believe us?' said Oakley.

'What if we let their ships go?'

'What do they do to our guys? We're going to turn what was a two-man hostage situation into a seventy-five-man hostage situation.'

'That's better than having a war,' said Rose.

'That is better than having a war,' said Oakley. 'Only problem is, if that happens, they've projected force and we've backed down. The United States doesn't do that. The United States has *never* done that. And for good reason. We do that, everyone's going to find out about it, you can bet your bottom dollar. We might stay silent but they won't. Every two-bit dictator in the world is going to think all he has to do is hold a couple of Americans hostage to get whatever he wants. *Then* we'll have to start a war to show the world we're still in business. And by the way, can you imagine what the reaction will be here at home when people find out we let their two ships go because we were scared of what they might do, and left our own guys hostage in Sudan?'

The president nodded. 'You're right, John. They have to turn around. They have to turn around and not get in that situation where they've got twelve hours to decide what to do.'

'That's the only way out.'

'They turn around, release our guys, and then we let the ships go and we agree not to say anything about it, on either side.'

'And the threat if they don't agree is …?' said Rose.

'The threat is they end up with a hundred and two ships in a very small area of real estate, like the admiral said.'

'Which is what they already think is going to happen.'

'Which they need to *believe* is going to happen,' said Oakley. 'That's the difference. They really, really need to believe it. And they need to believe what's going to happen after that.'

'How do we know they don't want that?'

The president turned. It was Admiral Tovey who had asked the question.

'What do you mean by that, Admiral?'

'Tactically, when I look at the situation, the question for me is, why haven't they already called our bluff? Why haven't they tried to sail their ships out of there? What would we do?'

'What *would* we do?' asked the president.

'What I outlined to you last night, Mr President,' said Hale. 'In the first instance, Admiral Pressler would fire across their bows.'

'And if they kept going?'

'We'd speak to you, sir,' said Tovey. 'We have various options. We could fire in warning again. Or we could fire to damage, or to inca-pacitate, or to sink. It would be your choice. But they haven't tested us at all to see if we're bluffing. They haven't even looked for the shot across their bows. Which means they either believe we'd take them out first up if they tried to get away, which is good, or … if we're bluffing, they don't want to know it.'

52

THIS TIME, ZHANG agreed to take a call.

It was 9pm on December 29 in the Oval Office, 10 in the morning of December 30 in Beijing, when the two men spoke. Neither of them had much stomach for pleasantries. After about a minute Knowles got down to business.

'President Zhang,' he said, as his interpreter spoke beside him, 'we're in a very serious situation. If our forces come together I am concerned that something will happen that neither of us wants.'

'China wants no conflict with the United States,' replied Zhang through the voice of his interpreter.

'President Zhang, let me be frank. That isn't how it looks.'

'I repeat, President Knowles, China wants no conflict with the United States.'

'Then turn your ships around, sir.'

'Release the *Kunming* and the *Changchun*, President Knowles.'

'Return Captains Dewy and Montez and let our men go in Sudan.'

'I do not govern Sudan, President Knowles.'

'Your forces are responsible for what's happening there.'

'So you say.'

'We have proof.'

'So you say, President Knowles.'

There was silence. Knowles hated having to call the Chinese president. They were both in an equally dangerous situation, but the fact that he was the one who had called made it seem as if he was asking for help. Again. And yet it had been clear from the beginning that the call had to be made. If there was even the slightest chance that what was happening might be the result of a misinterpretation, or miscalculation, the error had to be exposed. But Knowles was determined

337

not to say a thing that would put him in the position of the supplicant. Zhang must be just as uncertain about what was about to happen as he was. The Chinese leader's monosyllabic style, stiff and emotionless at the best of times, would help him hide it. Knowles was resolved to appear just as unyielding.

'This is a situation that will require both of us to act,' said Knowles. 'You must use your influence with Sudan to help settle this.'

There was no reply from Zhang.

Ed Abrahams, who was listening in to the call along with Gary Rose, scribbled a note. He handed it to the president. *Set out the steps to resolve this.*

'President Zhang, I suggest that the following things happen. Return Captains Dewy and Montez and allow our men to leave. Once the helicopters carrying them are out of Sudanese airspace we will allow the *Kunming* and the *Changchun* to set sail. Once the *Kunming* and the *Changchun* are out of range of our fleet, turn your ships around. We can have this whole thing done in six hours.'

'The *Kunming* and the *Changchun* have been forcibly detained in international waters,' came Zhang's reply. 'This is an act of piracy, President Knowles, by the United States. China does not negotiate over acts of piracy. Release the *Kunming* and *Changchun*.'

'What about our men?'

'That has nothing to do with the Chinese government. Your argument is with Sudan, not with China. You will need to address your concerns to the government of Sudan.'

'We have done that.'

'Then I'm sure the government of Sudan will respond reasonably.'

Knowles threw back his head in exasperation. Then he sat forward again. 'What if we do the two things together? We agree a time. We send our helicopters in to get our men, and we release the *Kunming* and *Changchun* at the same time. We'll show you that trust.'

'President Knowles, there is nothing to discuss about your men. If that is what you have called to discuss, you have rung the wrong phone. You should have rung the phone of the Sudan government. You should address–'

'We know Chinese troops were involved. We know they were there. We have three of your injured men under our care.'

'... the Sudan government.' Zhang stopped. Knowles waited. A moment later he started up again. 'To me, you can speak about the *Kunming* and the *Changchun*. President Knowles, your navy must release those ships. Believe me when I tell you this. You must release those ships. There is no other way.'

'President Zhang, do you have any idea what will happen if our forces come together?'

'China has no desire for a conflict with the United States. If a conflict occurs it is because Chinese vessels have been detained in international waters. You can bring this to an end very quickly. President Knowles, I am asking you to release those ships. That is the necessary step. There is no need for conflict.'

'And I am asking you to release our men. *That* is the necessary step.'

'Release the *Kunming* and *Changchun*, President Knowles. You must release those ships.'

Knowles shook his head. He didn't know what to say. He looked at Abrahams and Rose. They gazed back at him.

Knowles turned back to the phone. 'President Zhang, let's talk about something else. Let's talk about the economic situation. We seem to be in an awful state.'

'You have taken unlawful steps, President Knowles.'

'Steps to protect our markets. Steps to protect our economy. Steps you could have helped us avoid if you had come out and said what we asked you to.'

'Unlawful steps.'

'Which you could have helped us avoid!' Knowles restrained himself. It wouldn't help to show anger. 'How do we de-escalate this?'

'The one who has escalated, must de-escalate.'

'You announced sanctions, President Zhang. Many sanctions, all of which are unlawful.'

'Because of your unlawful measures, President Knowles. Retract those measures and we will retract ours.'

'I can't retract them!' Knowles took a breath. 'These are not measures of retaliation. Your measures are measures of retaliation. Mine are measures of protection. Our markets cannot function at this moment unless these measures are in place. Your markets can function perfectly well without the measures you have announced – in fact, your measures will damage them.'

'Then retract your measures and I will retract mine.'

'I can't retract them, President Zhang, unless we have assurance that your funds won't manipulate the markets.'

'The funds did not manipulate the markets.'

'Then where's the problem?'

'I do not deal with these funds. These funds are separate.'

'You own them. Mr Hu, the head of the PIC, is a member of your finance ministry.'

'They have their own remit. They are commercial funds. You must police your own markets, President Knowles. I do not expect you to police China's markets.'

'We do police our markets.'

'Then you do not need China to do it.'

'I'm not asking you to do it!'

Knowles saw Ed Abrahams lower his hands a couple of times, telling him to keep it calm. He was on the verge of shouting.

'President Zhang, let's come back to the measures you've announced. They're going to hurt China as much as the US. They hurt everybody.'

'That is what you say.'

'You know they will.'

'That is what you say. The measures are in place. President Knowles, understand, the measures are in place and when you retract the measures you have imposed I will retract mine.'

Abrahams scribbled a note.

'President Zhang, let's go back to the ships. I think that's the immediate problem.'

'I agree. That is a good idea. Release the *Kunming* and the *Changchun* and do not let the United States look like a pirate in the sea.'

Knowles could have beaten his head against the table.

'China does not want conflict with the United States.'

'Then let us both act to prevent it. What about this? You release our men, we'll release your ships at the same time. We'll show you that trust.'

'China does not hold your men, President Knowles.'

'Sudan holds them. And you have–'

'That's correct, President Knowles. Sudan holds them.'

'And you have enough influence with Sudan to make them release them.'

'So you say.'

'Your troops were on the ground! We have proof. We have three of them.'

'So you say.'

Knowles looked at Rose and Abrahams in exasperation. The two men, by their expressions, had no idea how to break the deadlock.

'President Zhang, if our ships come together, I fear greatly there will be conflict. I fear that we will see a terrible battle. We shouldn't take such a risk. Turn your ships around. Release our men and we will release your ships.'

'Release our ships. Believe me, President Knowles, you must release those ships. There is no other way.'

'President Zhang, please do not mistake what I'm saying. There will be conflict. If we do not find the way out of this, I fear greatly that there will be conflict.'

'There is a way out. You must release those ships.'

'The way out is for you to release our men.'

'Our ships, President Knowles.'

Knowles took a deep breath. 'Okay. President Zhang, it doesn't look like we're getting anywhere.'

'I have told you what you must do. You must release those ships.'

Knowles paused. He didn't know what else to say. 'I think we should stay in touch on this.'

'Yes,' said the Chinese president.

Knowles hesitated for a moment. 'Good day.'

'Good night, President Knowles.'

Knowles put the phone down. He glanced at the interpreter and thanked him. The young man gathered up the notes he had taken and left the office.

Knowles was silent. That was an awful conversation. It had been like butting heads. Just butting heads.

'He's going to take it to the wire,' murmured Abrahams.

The president looked at him.

'If he wanted to get out of this, you just gave him a way.'

'Do you think he got the message?'

'How could he not? You said it ten times. He lets our men go, everyone goes home.'

'If it comes to the point,' said Rose, 'they'll lose half their carrier fleet.'

'Might be a price they're prepared to pay,' said Abrahams. 'No one has stood up to US military power in a set-piece battle since World War Two. Just the act of standing up to us, in their eyes, in the eyes of lots of countries, that would be something.'

'Even if they get smashed?' said Rose skeptically.

'This time. In ten years they'll be the biggest economy in the world. Ten years after that ...' Abrahams shrugged.

'That still doesn't mean they're prepared to–'

'I don't want to smash anyone,' said the president curtly. He shook his head in frustration. 'You know, the thing I don't understand is, what's this about? It's not about those damn ships. We took those ships because they took our men. Why do they want our men? What do they get out of it?' He turned to Rose. 'We're sure it's them, right? We're sure it's not the Sudanese by themselves?'

'Absolutely. When Hale told the Chinese military we were coming in to get out the wounded, they let us do it, clean as a whistle. We told the Chinese, not the Sudanese. China's in control.'

'So what do they want with seventy-five US soldiers? What good does it do them? He must know we need our guys back. He must know we can't just leave them. It's a damn dangerous thing to do. It just complicates the hell out of everything.' Knowles frowned, trying to understand it. 'And he must know I had to take action on the economy. He must know we can't allow our markets to be manipulated or even look like they're being manipulated. What the hell do they *want*?'

'Whatever it is,' said Gary Rose, 'we can't let them have it.'

Suddenly Knowles remembered the conversation with Marion Ellman in the graveyard at Jefferson City. It was only yesterday, but Bob Livingstone's funeral seemed a long time ago. The president hadn't had a minute to think about it since he had got news of the operation in Sudan. It had gone clear out of his mind.

That was the last thing she had said to him. She stood there and pointed her finger and said: You'd better figure out what the Chinese want. But not, Knowles knew, so as to avoid giving it to them. That was the opposite of what she had meant.

'Mr President,' said Rose, 'General Hale is going to present a range of operational plans for what we might need to do. We need to decide how we contain this and be aware of the possible scenarios for how it might develop. If it comes to the point, we can be fairly certain it won't stay confined to the Indian Ocean.'

The president nodded. He was only half listening, still pondering that conversation in the graveyard.

Rose continued. 'We have a meeting set for nine tomorrow morning to go through the options with the Joint Chiefs.'

IN BEIJING, ZHANG watched his interpreter leave the room.

'They have three of our men,' he said to Qin.

His advisor nodded. 'Apparently.'

General Fan hadn't told him that. Zhang wasn't particularly surprised to discover that he hadn't. He was sure there was a lot more that Fan hadn't told him as well. If it had been up to him, he would never have allowed the Americans to be attacked. There was nothing he wanted more than to give them back now.

'Do you think President Knowles got the message?'

'You said it many times.'

Zhang nodded. He had said it as often as he could. There was only one way that Fan might be persuaded to hand back the men, and that was if he had his victory, if the Americans looked as if they had backed down under the threat of the Chinese strike groups. That would also hand Fan a victory against him – but that was preferable to a major battle with the Americans. If such a battle happened, there was no telling what the army would do.

But Zhang couldn't say any of that out loud to the American president. He couldn't reveal his weakness. He had said as much as he dared.

'What do you think they will do if our ships arrive?'

Qin shook his head. 'If our ships arrive, it means they will not have released the *Kunming* and *Changchun*. After your message, if they have not released the *Kunming* and *Changchun*, it means they are ready to fight.'

'Will we fight?'

Qin didn't reply. He had no better idea than Zhang. The aircraft carrier fleets were loyal to Xu. The defense minister was playing his usual game, going along with both sides for as long as he could. He was keeping Fan happy by sending the fleets to Kenya. What he would do when they got there would depend on what he thought the carrier fleet admirals were prepared to do and what would be in his own interest at the time.

There was a knock on the door. One of Zhang's aides came in.

'President Zhang,' he said, 'it is time to leave for the meeting of the Central Military Commission.'

53

THE MORNING DAWNED misty and grey in Washington. At 8am a feeble light was filtering in through the windows of the White House. In southern Sudan, it was four in the afternoon of a hot, tense day. The American marines holed up in the compound gazed out at the remains of three blackened Chinooks in a clearing outside and looked for signs of the forces encircling them beyond. Five hundred miles away, off Lamu Bay, a swell had risen and a squall was approaching from the southeast. The two Chinese destroyers rode the waves, surrounded by four of the ships from the *Abraham Lincoln* strike group. Through binoculars, far off, the Chinese captains could see the long, grey bulk of the carrier itself. Further distant, across hundreds of miles of open ocean, the carrier strike groups of the *Mao Zedong* and *Chou Enlai* and the *John F Kennedy* and *George HW Bush* were converging.

In the Situation Room, Admiral Tovey projected charts to show their positions. Running slightly slower than projected, but with calm conditions predicted for the route, the arrival of the Chinese carriers off the coast of Kenya was now estimated to coincide roughly with that of the *Kennedy*, in approximately fifty hours. The head of defense intelligence gave an update. He showed images taken from drones above the compound in Sudan to demonstrate the disposition of forces, highlighting features that appeared to be emplacements of surface to air missiles and concentrations of military vehicles. The wider world was still unaware of what was happening but military intelligence communities in a number of countries had detected the movements of the Chinese and American carriers through their own satellite surveillance. The Russians had started to move a carrier strike group that was at sea off Kamchatka southwards east of Japan. In an apparent response, the Chinese had sent one of their remaining two carrier groups north. The Japanese Maritime Self Defense Force, as the Japanese navy was called, had mobilized two groups of destroyers and destroyer escorts. If the Russians and Chinese kept moving, the Sea of Japan was set to get uncomfortably crowded. The small but efficient Taiwanese navy was fully mobilized around Taiwan. The Japanese and Taiwanese had been told there were US maneuvers taking place in the Indian Ocean. The same message had been given to other Nato allies who had become aware of the movements of the US fleets. The British and French, with their own satellite imagery, must have realized that something more was happening.

General Hale outlined four plans for the president to consider. The going-in assumption was that, in the event of a major Chinese defeat, action by the Chinese military would likely be initiated elsewhere against the US or its allies and that action against China might be initiated by Russia or India in disputed border areas.

The first plan was for an immediate repulse by the *Lincoln* strike group as soon as the Chinese carrier groups were within range, preceded by the pre-emptive neutralization of the *Kunming* and *Changchun*. The logic was that an aggressive posture and early hits would strike a psychological victory. The second plan, a variant of the first, was for a repulse by the combined *Lincoln* and *Kennedy* strike groups once the *John F Kennedy* arrived. In the event that the Chinese forces arrived before the *Kennedy*, Pressler would hold off on action unless the Chinese admirals chose to try to take advantage of their temporary superiority in numbers and he was forced to defend. The third plan called for the US force to adopt a watchful posture with an overwhelming response if the enemy opened hostilities. The risk in this plan was the high probability of an incident setting off a confrontation at a time and disposition not of US choosing. The fourth plan, and the most aggressive, was a pre-emptive aerial attack on the Chinese strike groups while en route in the Indian Ocean, delivered by stealth B3 bombers out of Diego Garcia.

'If we take that course of action,' said John Oakley, who had scrutinized the plans in detail with the Joint Chiefs before the meeting, 'we would need to issue an ultimatum and define the no go line at which we will take action. This would be in international waters. We would have to say that crossing that longitude towards a US force of lesser capability with belligerent intent would constitute a hostile act and would justify our pre-emptive action in self defense.'

'We'd need to get legal advice on that,' said Rose.

Hale nodded. 'It's clean operationally but that's when the complications start. In our opinion, Mr President, this is the course of action most likely to lead to a widening of the conflict. We would anticipate retaliation by the Chinese against our forces anywhere they could reach them, which is principally the East Pacific area. Attacks by submarine on our navy in international waters should also be expected. We see a good chance of an escalation to a short but vicious naval war fought anywhere our forces are in contact. We should remember also that China has the capability to go nonconventional. It could strike at our satellites, with a probability we estimate of thirty to fifty per cent of taking one or more out. It could also launch a nuclear strike against us. The Chinese military know that a nonconventional attack would lead us to retaliate in massive force. We don't think they'd be that dumb.'

'We can't be sure though,' said the president. 'That's right, isn't it?'

Hale didn't reply.

There was silence.

'In a naval war, sir,' Hale continued, 'Taiwan would be a likely target for Chinese aggression and they would be able to mobilize an overwhelming superiority of force in that theater. We would likely lose Taiwan.'

The president nodded.

'Coming back to our plans, from the military perspective, focusing narrowly on this one engagement off Lamu Bay, a pre-emptive aerial attack is the most attractive in the sense that it deals with the threat to the *Abraham Lincoln* before the enemy gets anywhere near our ships. In relation to the wider picture, however, in that it's most likely to lead to a scenario where there's an immediate widening of the conflict, it clearly has drawbacks. Mr President, we should talk through the follow-on scenarios in more detail.'

Hale went through them. The scenarios didn't vary greatly from one plan to the next. The differences were largely in the probabilities, with the last plan, as the general had explained, creating the greatest risk of a wider conflagration. But apart from the varying details of the local battle off Kenya, each plan involved scenarios with escalation spreading to other potential fronts of confrontation, involving the US, Taiwan, Japan and Nato allies, as well as the risk of opportunistic action by China's regional rivals at a moment when they considered China to be vulnerable. The greater the scale of the defeat imposed on China, the more likely, it was assumed, that China would retaliate elsewhere and the more likely would be its rivals to try to exploit the opportunity. There was also the risk of internal unrest in China caused by military failure and dramatic loss of prestige to the regime. Zhang's instinct would be to launch a severe pre-emptive crackdown. Paradoxically, if this failed to eliminate the opposition at the first sweep, it might worsen the unrest, which would provoke further repression and possibly a military takeover, which was only narrowly avoided in 2014.

The president listened silently.

'As you can see, sir,' said General Hale when he had covered the scenarios, 'there are a large number of military implications here and we're working to develop plans to deal with each of them, both in terms of pre-emption and retaliation. These will have implications for the disposition of our forces in various theaters and if I could I would like to discuss those with you this afternoon after we've had time to do a little more work.'

'As far as your four options for the immediate situation are concerned, what's your recommendation, General?'

'Militarily, sir, I would opt to hit them early.'

'That's with the bombers out of Diego Garcia?'

'No, sir. I wouldn't use aerial power to interdict them because, as I've said, the risk of an escalation in that instance is extreme. We would hope we can get this done by knocking out one or two of their ships when they arrive in theater and making them think again. So we would launch early and aggressively when they come within range to take out a couple of ships in an exemplary fashion and stop them in their tracks. If we can bring it to an end by taking out just a couple of their ships, they may be less likely to widen the conflict.'

'Admiral Tovey? Is that realistic, to expect to be able to knock out a couple of their ships in an early attack?'

'If they arrive expecting us to watch and wait, yes. There will certainly be a psychological effect. If they arrive expecting to fight, then we're in a fight.'

'Psychology wins battles,' said one of the military men in the room.

'And if the psychological effect isn't as powerful as we think?'

Tovey shrugged. 'We're in a battle, just like we would be anyway. But we have superior operational capability and should realistically expect to prevail.'

'But not without taking some hits?'

'No, sir. I don't think we could guarantee that.'

'Do we know anything about who's commanding their strike groups?' asked Gary Rose.

Tovey nodded. 'We know something about the individuals. We're trying to get better insight into the psychologies.'

'Who'll make the operational decisions? Will it be them or Beijing?'

'Beijing,' said General Hale, 'to the extent that they can. They have a rigid control structure. If the fleet comes under immediate attack the commanders in theater will take action while involving a higher commander in Beijing who'll be working with an operational staff. We believe that makes them vulnerable. If we go in hard and hit them, that exploits the rigidity. Any ambiguity or confusion in the orders coming back from Beijing will reduce their effectiveness.'

'And who makes the overall decisions about their strategic objectives?' asked the president. He had been briefed on this at some point, but he wanted to be sure he understood.

'That would be the Central Military Commission,' replied the head of defense intelligence. 'It's a combined army and party body consisting of thirteen members. In a situation like this they'll be meeting daily. President Zhang chairs the commission. Defense Minister Xu sits on it as well. General Fan is the leading military figure. The rest just make up the numbers.'

'To what extent does Zhang control it?'

'We can't be sure. In principle he does. In reality ...'

'Whatever happens,' said Tovey, 'we've got to be prepared to find ourselves in a shoot-out. I know Pete Pressler. That happens, we've got a good guy out there.'

'General Hale,' said the president, 'you said the plan you recommended was the right choice militarily. What did you mean by that?'

'Sir, you want to win a battle here, this is the best way to do it. Go hard and achieve an immediate impact with a robust assault by the US navy. If we adopt a watchful attitude, which is one of the alternatives, that takes the initiative away from us. Chances are some incident will start the shooting when neither side is ready and once it goes from there it'll be a free for all, and when a free for all starts, it's almost impossible to shut it down before a whole lot of damage is done. I don't want to have a hundred some ships milling around in a few square miles of water, I really don't.' The general paused. 'Now, that's militarily. For political reasons you may want to take the chance on a battle not breaking out and being able to resolve this thing without a shot being fired. So there's a non-military judgment here, sir. And if you say to me, General, I want to hold the military option back while I see if I can settle this, that's a judgment. If I thought we couldn't win the confrontation in those circumstances then I'd be saying, militarily, as your military advisor, that's not an option. But we will win it. The issue is it'll cost more American lives and more American hardware. So the question, I guess politically, is how do you weigh those lives, and that hardware, against the chance that you can talk this thing down? Which is not a question for me to answer.'

'Admiral Tovey, do you agree with that? As a naval officer? Do you agree we'd win the battle if it broke out in earnest?'

'Yes, sir. I do. But it would be a fearsome battle. In naval terms, it would be an era-defining battle, sir. I'm a navy man, and I have my share of interest in naval history, but I don't look forward to having Lamu Bay in that particular record.'

There was silence.

Rose spoke. 'Can I ask what we do about the men in Sudan?'

'We go in and get them,' said John Oakley.

'Once our ships start firing,' said Hale, 'their lives aren't worth anything. I'd rather go in there with as much force as we can and see if we can get any of them out.'

'When would we launch this attack?' asked the president.

'We want to be in there at the same moment we open fire on their ships. That's our best chance to get anyone out of there alive. To be honest, I don't think it'll be many, but it's our best chance.'

The president nodded.

'I'd like to brief you later today, Mr President, on the plans for dealing with the escalations we envisage. We'll need to make some decisions on force dispositions.'

The president nodded again.

There was silence.

Tom Knowles stood up. 'Thank you,' he said, and walked out.

KNOWLES SAT IN the Oval Office, contemplating what he had heard.

Every one of the plans Mortlock Hale had presented to him led to more confrontation. Now the military men were working away at plans to deal with counter-plans for escalation. And this was against a nuclear-armed state.

They were military men. Ask them for a plan and they'd come back with a battle. But Knowles didn't want to know how to fight this thing. He wanted to know how to shut it down.

He could ring Zhang again, but what would he say? What had changed in the past twelve hours? Nothing except that their ships had got closer. Maybe Zhang was bluffing. Maybe not. He was probably surrounded by people who were telling him that he, Knowles, was bluffing. If he rang him again, they'd just say that was extra proof that he was. If he and Zhang weren't careful, they'd bluff each other so well they'd end up fighting a war that would rage across three continents.

But he couldn't back down. He couldn't leave seventy-five men in Sudan. If he didn't get them back soon – and soon meant days, not weeks – he'd be Jimmy Carter. That was it. He'd be Carter.

Knowles gazed at the rug.

What did Zhang *want*?

His ships. That's what he had said, about a dozen times. But his ships were in danger only because he was allowing seventy-five US servicemen to be held in Sudan. What possible good did that do him? He couldn't use it as a bargaining chip over, say, South Africa. It was too crude, even for him. You couldn't hold a bunch of guys to ransom like that and expect the US government to give you what you wanted.

But surely Zhang realized that. So that left the same question: what did he want?

Knowles mind went back to the conversation in the Jefferson City graveyard, to the words Marion Ellman had thrown at him in that cold, bone-chilling mist. She had asked that question. She had said a lot of other things besides.

He glanced at his watch. Then he picked up the phone to his chief of staff.

'Roberta, did Hale say what time he wanted to talk to me about the other plans he has for this world war he's about to start?'

'I'll find out,' said Devlin.

Tom Knowles didn't know if he was clutching at straws, if he was going to make a world-class fool of himself in the process. He hesitated a moment longer. 'Roberta, before he does, there's a couple of people I want to see.'

54

THE WHITE HOUSE steward poured coffee. There were cookies on the table and a bowl of fruit.

'Cream?' said the president.

Joel Ehrenreich shook his head. It felt utterly surreal. Four hours earlier, he had been at home in Connecticut, looking forward to a Sunday afternoon with a book in his hand in front of the fire. Then came a phone call, a car from his house to a local heliport, a helicopter to La Guardia, a plane that was waiting to fly him and Marion Ellman to the National Airport in Washington, and a car to the White House. Now he found himself sitting in the Oval Office with Ellman, the national security advisor, the president's chief of staff and his closest political advisor, being offered cream by the president.

The steward withdrew. Knowles had already thanked Ehrenreich for coming, but he thanked him again.

'Pretty short notice,' he said. 'I appreciate it, Professor Ehrenreich.'

'It's an honor,' said Ehrenreich for the second time, although it also felt a little imperious, being summoned like that. The rebel-for-its-own-sake in Joel Ehrenreich, never far from the surface, was already battling with the part of him that was flattered by the president's call.

'I guess you're wondering what the big rush is.'

'I wasn't doing anything that couldn't wait.'

The president smiled. He took a sip of his coffee. 'You don't want to eat anything?'

'I'm fine, sir.'

'You don't want to wait. You never know if anything'll be left once Ed here gets started.'

Ed Abrahams grinned. He had already put a couple of cookies on his plate.

'I'm fine,' said Ehrenreich again.

'Okay. Don't be shy.' The president paused. 'So Marion here tells me she thinks a hell of a lot of what you have to say.'

Ehrenreich glanced at Ellman. 'That's kind of her.'

'She also tells me you probably voted for my opponent in 2016.'

'Well ... what can I say?'

'Nothing wrong with that. Fine man.' Knowles chuckled. 'Almost would have voted for him myself but Ed thought it would be inadvisable, didn't you, Ed?'

Abrahams nodded.

'Anyway,' said the president, turning back to Ehrenreich, 'I'd like to hear a little more about what you have to say.'

'What in particular, Mr President? I've got a lot to say about a lot of things.'

Knowles nodded, as if that was what he'd heard. 'You published a book recently. *Switch*, right? I like the title.'

'It was the best I could think of.'

'I haven't had a chance to see it but I understand it's very insightful. I'd like to hear a little more.'

The president waited for Ehrenreich to speak. Roberta Devlin had had a staffer do a speed-read of Ehrenreich's book and the president had been handed a summary fifteen minutes before Ehrenreich arrived, but he had no real idea of what to expect now that Ehrenreich was sitting in front of him. Getting an academic down here in the midst of a crisis with the only rival superpower to the US was an eccentric thing to do, as Ed Abrahams had put it when he heard who the president wanted to see. But Tom Knowles was desperate enough now to try just about anything, eccentric or otherwise, and Abrahams didn't seem to have any better ideas. If it meant there was a chance he was going to waste an hour of his life with this professor, it was a chance he was prepared to take.

'I'm guessing this relates to our current standoff with China,' said Ehrenreich eventually.

'The economic standoff, you mean?' said the president.

'Is there another one?'

For a moment Tom Knowles stared. 'No,' he said. 'That's the one.'

'Well, it's not an economic standoff, is it, Mr President? It's a political standoff. The economic element is the instrument. It's not the cause.'

'That's one way of looking at it.'

'That's how I do look at it. It's an example of what we're going to face more and more often. At an international level today, we're in a mismatch. We have a set of global problems – but we deal with them through national governments. Every government – including ours, if you'll allow me to say so – is perfectly unashamed about saying it puts the interests of its people first. And it has to. Any government that didn't wouldn't last very long. But the global problems can only be solved by global, coordinated action. Yet national governments want different actions because their national interests are different. Some want vigorous action. Some don't want any action. Some have an election and change their government and want the opposite of what they wanted two weeks before. What we end up getting is either nothing, or only the most diluted, uncontroversial elements that everyone supports. But those are never enough to deal with the problem. At best, they deal with the immediate effect and leave the root cause to fester.'

'Sounds like you think we need some kind of world government,' said Gary Rose.

'Dr Rose, it's easy to ridicule what I'm saying, but I'm not saying that. Although whether we will eventually see a world government – or world governance, I should say – at some time in the future, in a hundred or two hundred years, say, I wouldn't be surprised. With the level of globalization and interconnectedness we have even today, who could possibly be so naïve to imagine that the governance of our planet is going to look the same in a couple of hundred years? And why should it? If you'd asked the Native American tribes the day before the pilgrims landed at Plymouth Rock whether there'd ever be a pan-continental government in what is today the United States, they would have laughed in your face.'

Marion Ellman winced. This was exactly the kind of big, sweeping historical sense of context that Joel loved to project, which would go down in the White House right now about as well as a Chinese fund manager. She also didn't think it was such a great idea to tell Gary Rose he was naïve as soon as you opened your mouth.

'In principle,' continued Ehrenreich, oblivious to the glances Rose and Abrahams were giving the president, 'I don't know why something that works for a continent can't work for a planet. What that might look like is something we can debate. I don't think it looks like our federal government. It might look like a council that has the right to deal with certain issues – a defined set of truly global questions – in a way that is genuinely binding on everyone. Is that council elected through direct representation, nominated by national governments…?' Ehrenreich shrugged. 'The answers are a long way off. But our global problems aren't. They're here now. They're not waiting, they're growing. And if we don't deal with them in a global fashion, if we continue to deal with them competitively like a bunch of schoolkids trying to guard their piece of the pie, I'm not sure that anyone's going to be around in a hundred or two hundred years to even laugh at people who suggest we may end up with some kind of global government.'

'What are these global problems?' asked Knowles.

'I'm sure you know them as well as I do, sir.'

'I'm interested in your thoughts.'

'I count six.' Ehrenreich numbered them off on his fingers. 'Climate change and other environmental constraints; allocation of natural resources, especially water but also arable land and of course industrial commodities; financial regulation; communications; epidemic disease; terrorism, organized crime and corruption. There's more, but at a high level those are the flashpoints. There are no borders for these things, Mr President. Every country's interests in them extends around the world, because every country is affected by what every other country does. Those are the ones over which we'll go to war.'

'That's a big statement,' said Rose.

'Dr Rose, you're a student of politics like me. When the interests of human societies conflict, they fight. They might talk a lot first, they might try to find a way out, but when they genuinely conflict, in the end we return to our primitive instincts and fight.'

'Our interests conflicted with the Soviet Union and we didn't fight them.'

'We did. We fought them in the Middle East, we fought them in Afghanistan, we fought them in Africa, we fought them all over the world. Through proxies, I grant you, but we fought them. And in fact, our interests didn't even conflict. Our interests were the same, which is why in the end that empire dissolved.'

'That's not how I'd put it,' said Rose.

'Who will we fight?' asked the president, who was a lot less interested in the last war than in the next.

'Us?' said Ehrenreich. 'The United States? China.'

'No one else? Not India? Not Brazil? Russia?'

Ehrenreich shook his head. 'China.'

The president glanced briefly at Abrahams, then looked back at Ehrenreich. 'Why? Neither of us wants to fight.'

'But we will. The global problems I talked about, we can't solve them by ourselves and nor can they. But together, no one in the world can stand against us. Forget India, forget Brazil. Forget Russia. Forget the EU, which breaks down into its individual states as soon as a serious problem is on the table. No solution to any global problem will work unless both the US and China are signed up to it. You can call it a bipolar world, you can call it a G2, you can call it whatever you like. It may not be the way the UN likes to see it but that's tough. Only two facts matter. One, any solution to a global problem that isn't solidly backed by the US and China won't work. Two, any solution to a global problem that is solidly backed by the US and China – and which they're prepared to put their economic weight behind – can't be resisted by anybody else.'

'And why do we fight?'

'Because we don't agree on the solutions. In fact, most of the time we don't even agree on the problem. So long as we persist in trying to deal with global issues through a competitive lens of national sovereignty, we'll eventually come to blows. It might happen through proxies, but it'll be over one of these issues. Take what we've got going on right now, this economic crisis. It is a crisis, a historic crisis that has arisen because we insist on forcing our interconnected, single, global economy into a framework of separate national sovereignties rather than managing it through an integrated set of common laws and regulations. Foreign state ownership of our corporations has enabled elements of our economy to become a weapon through which those tensions can be expressed. So now we have a crisis and potentially this crisis undermines the entire market system on which our economy is based. So what do we do? We take certain measures that we think will protect our economy, and they retaliate with others. We're already fighting, aren't we?'

'That's not exactly a war,' said Gary Rose.

'I'm not saying we go to war directly over this. I'm not saying we fire missiles at Beijing because Beijing brought down Fidelian Bank. But effectively, indirectly, that's what will happen, because it creates the context. We're in this crisis, and we're trading economic blows, so we start to flex other muscles. Incidents happen. Where are we in proximity? Uganda. They have troops in Sudan, as we all know. We're right across the border from each other. Now two of our men have been taken into Sudan. You ask me, we have a hell of trigger for a conflict right there.'

There was utter silence around the table.

'No? Alright, say the South China Sea. Say they go after one of our planes. They say it was in their airspace, we say it was in international airspace. That happens all the time but normally we shrug it off. This time we respond. They do something to Taiwan, maybe some incident that results in a few Taiwanese soldiers getting killed. Things escalate. Normally they wouldn't, but because we're in conflict over this economic thing, they do. No one feels they can back down because the perception of weakness will translate itself into the financial arena and reduce their ability to get what they want. Or the arena of climate change, or epidemic disease control, or control of the blogosphere, or whatever the real issue of the moment is. So we do something, they do something, we do something, they do something – then we're at war, or our proxies are. You've got what you wanted, Dr Rose.' Ehrenreich paused. 'If you ask me, Mr President, if I had to bet on a scenario, that's how it'll happen. Something like that.'

The president glanced at Gary Rose. Almost imperceptibly, Rose raised an eyebrow.

'Marion,' asked the president, 'do you agree with this?'

'I think there's a lot of plausibility in it,' said Ellman. 'I do see us trading blows, sir. I said that to you before. If we continue to trade blows then I think at some point the blows are likely to leave the diplomatic arena and the financial arena and get to something more physical. I think Joel's articulated a somewhat more pessimistic view of human nature than I hold but I do agree with him that there's a route to that scenario that's very plausible.'

Ehrenreich shrugged. 'Human beings fight when they're in conflict. We like to think they don't, but they do. You look at every century, including our own. The way to prevent fighting isn't to pretend that we don't, but to admit that we do and deal with it by removing the cause of the conflict.'

'As I said,' said Marion, 'Joel's a little more pessimistic than me.'

'Mr President,' said Ehrenreich, 'you may disagree with me that the issues I mentioned are intrinsically global in scope.'

'No, Professor, I don't disagree with you on that.'

'Then if you don't, it follows from that – it *absolutely*, one hundred per cent follows, inevitably, logically – that we have to deal with them globally. As one, single, global community. Otherwise, it's like saying that here in the United States, state governments with conflicting interests can come up with whatever solution they want to a shared problem. That doesn't work, which is why we have a federal government. At the global level, we need one coordinated, clear, explicit, shared set of objectives that everyone supports through actions everyone is prepared to take. Until we do that, we're kidding ourselves. Take climate change. If this was a local problem, if one country alone could deal with it, don't you think it would have been dealt with by now? Years ago, without any of the damage that we all know is inevitably going to happen? Of course it would. Well, if you accept that, you can't accept that our system of decision-making at a global level is right.'

'That's a big thing to ask a politician to accept.'

'I agree. And it'll take a big politician to change it. Not just one big politician. A generation of big politicians.'

'Professor Ehrenreich,' said Ed Abrahams, 'you obviously take the long view of things. I can't remember the last time anyone asked me what the Native American tribes would have thought before the pilgrims arrived.' He paused and smiled for a moment. 'Let's say we agree with you. What you've given us is a diagnosis, not a solution. It tells us what's wrong, not what we should do. It's fine to say we need a single, shared set of objectives, but how do we get them? You're in the White House. This is the place for decisions, not theories. Put yourself in our shoes. What are you suggesting we do?'

Ehrenreich wondered, again, why he had been called down here in such a hurry. He doubted the president had suddenly decided that the one thing he craved for entertainment on the second-last day of the year was an urgent seminar in international relations from someone who wasn't exactly known as his biggest supporter. Something must be going on. For all his intellectual confidence, it suddenly scared the hell out of Joel Ehrenreich to think that something he said might actually have an influence on a real, practical decision that the president needed to take.

'I can't tell you what to do,' he said carefully. 'But I can tell you what you shouldn't be doing, at least in my opinion. We shouldn't be trying to deal with these things by ourselves. We don't have the power to do that – not economically, not militarily. We did once, and when we did have it, we used it. The international system that we set up after World War Two was a US-inspired international system. We designed it, we implemented it. The UN, the IMF … That was us. Effectively, for a space of three to four years in the mid-1940s, when the rest of the world had been pretty much destroyed by war, the US was a de facto global government on the few genuinely global issues of the day. We had the power and no one else did. Now, we lost that relative advantage in power once the Soviets developed the bomb–'

'Professor Ehrenreich,' said Abrahams, 'can we skip the history lesson?'

'The point,' said Ehrenreich curtly, giving Abrahams a dismissive glance, 'is that during the Cold War there were very few genuinely shared global issues. Climate change and the environment weren't on the agenda. Financial integration wasn't an issue. Mr President, let me put it this way. During the Cold War, you could have dug a trench along the land borders of the Soviet Union, blown the whole thing up and let it sink into the sea, and life for us would have gone on just like before. Better than before. But think about China. If we could sink China tomorrow, our economy would be down the tube as quick as theirs. We're no longer separable. So, here's the problem. Fundamentally, give or take a few tweaks over the years, the system we have is still the one we designed after World War Two, when the Soviet Union could have disappeared into a hole. It's a system for nation states where nation states are pretty much independent. But the world's changed. The big problems aren't national any more.'

'Professor,' said the president, 'I'm not sure you've answered Mr Abrahams' question. The question was what should I do?'

Ehrenreich nodded. 'With respect, Mr President, I did answer it. I said I didn't know.'

'With respect, Professor, that's not good enough. I'm going to ask you for more. Let's say I agree with you. I can't change the world's global system overnight, even if I wanted to.'

'No, sir.'

'So let's say I want to take these global issues and share them. You say China's the one to watch. Let's say I agree with you again. Here's my problem. I look at China, and I see an autocratic regime that systematically abuses human rights and acts on global issues in a way which pretty much ignores what the rest of the world requires. It's only worried about its own growth. So how do I–'

'Mr President, may I interrupt you?'

Knowles stopped. 'Go ahead.'

'Let me replay what you've said in a slightly different way. I look at China and I see a country that only thirty years ago came out of an almost unimaginably horrible period of revolutionary communism that choked its development and put a large part of the country a good way back towards the Stone Age, a country that's eager to improve the standard of living for its people and that is utterly bemused by the insistence of other countries – and chiefly the United States – that it should replicate foreign political practices, while those same countries are trying to constrain its carbon emissions and its growth so they can boost their already exceptional standards of living.'

The president gazed at Ehrenreich.

'I hate authoritarianism and suppression of civil rights as much as anyone, but there is another way of looking at it.'

'I guess you can look at it that way,' said Knowles, 'but I don't know how that helps me. I don't know how I go along and say, let's drop everything and pretend like we don't have national interests and work this stuff out together. How do I give them more say in the IMF, more say over international financial regulation, more say over all that kind of stuff after what they've just done? Why should I have any confidence they'll use that power for our mutual benefit? Everything I've seen tells me the opposite.'

'Can I replay that again for you, sir? I'm China and I'm looking at you, and I'm saying, why should I work with him when he doesn't want to give us anywhere near the influence we should have in the IMF and in international regulation in proportion to our size and importance in the global economy, when there was all this talk in 2008 and 2009 about giving us a meaningful voice at the top and it didn't happen? Where's the evidence that he's got any interest at all in mutual benefit or that's he's doing anything more than simply looking after America?'

The president shook his head. 'I don't know where we go if we start talking like that.'

'Exactly. Where *do* we go?' Ehrenreich sat forward in his chair. 'Mr President, I don't mean to speak out of turn, and I sense I take a little more historical a view than Mr Abrahams is comfortable with, but ... I'm going to say it anyway. You're a pawn in this process. You're a tiny little piece in the middle of a big historical process, as the peoples of this planet become so integrated that a bunch of interests have to be balanced against each other for the good of all peoples as a whole. Because if they're not – everyone suffers. Not just them, but us. It's impossible to overstate how new, how utterly new, this situation is for our civilization. That's why it's so hard for us. But Mr President, here's the thing. It's going to happen whether you want it to or not. You, and the United States, are not powerful enough to stop that. The only question is, how much pain is it going to take as this historical process plays out? Is it going to be excruciating, are we going to fight war after war as a way of balancing those interests, and perhaps destroy ourselves entirely? Or is it going to be peaceful? Disorienting, but peaceful? Are we going to be able to live with the ambiguity long enough to construct a way to do it without violence? That's the choice. You do not have the power to take that choice away. No one does. But in your position, you do, sir, have the ability to influence the choice that we make. It could be that this financial crisis is the chance you have to start exerting that influence. It could be that it isn't. But what it definitely isn't – what I can guarantee you, absolutely, one hundred per cent guarantee you that it isn't – is an opportunity to make that choice disappear. The process is in place and has been for decades. It can't be stopped, sir. Whatever you do, please don't mistake it for an opportunity to hold it back. There is no such thing.'

The president was silent for a moment. 'You put that forcefully,' he said.

'Marion should have warned you what I'm like.'

'You make it sound like we're in some kind of global endgame.'

Ehrenreich shrugged. 'Maybe we are. A long one. If that's what this is, we're at the very start of it, but how we start might make a big difference to how we end and how long it takes us to get there. You know, there's a saying attributed to Bismarck about what makes a great statesman. Do you know it, Mr President?'

Knowles shook his head.

'Bismarck said, the truly great statesman is the one who hears the distant hoofbeat of the horse of history, and through an extraordinary effort manages to leap and catch the horseman by the coat-tails and be carried along for as far as he can be. Not ride the horse, Mr President, not replace the horseman, but just to catch him by his coat-tails is a great feat. Sir, most statesmen who think they're great – who their own times think are great – when the horse has gone by, and the horseman looks around behind him, it turns out they actually just stood in the way and got trampled into the dust.'

'And you hear the hoofbeats?' said the president quietly.

'I do, sir. They're loud.'

'Then what would you do to catch on to the horseman?'

Ehrenreich smiled. 'I'm not a great statesman.'

'Pretend you are.'

Ehrenreich shrugged. 'I don't know. I'd make a start.'

'How?'

'However it looks like.'

'Do something in the G22? The UN?'

'No. That's not going do it.'

'Then what?'

'I don't know. Call a summit with Zhang? Get him involved. Make him part of the solution, not part of the problem. Throw open the question of regulation of funds. Their funds, other funds. Make some changes that suit them.'

'Roll over, you mean?' said Rose.

'No. We have to stand firm as well. It's not one way. Whatever else it is, it can't be that. It's give and take.'

'What if he refuses to get involved?' said Abrahams.

'I don't know. Ask again? And again? I said it'll take more than one big politician. This isn't all our fault, Mr Abrahams. I'm not saying it is, and we have to remember that.' Ehrenreich looked back at the president.

'You know what my fear is? That it will take some kind of massive catastrophe, some kind of horrible and bloody confrontation, before we get enough big politicians to realize what has to be done. Historically that's how it's always been. The tragedy of our species is that we can react to a catastrophe that we've actually experienced and yet we seem consistently unable to react ahead of time when it's obvious we're heading towards a new one. Somehow we can never really believe it's going to happen.' Ehrenreich paused. 'If we do start on that road towards a new way of doing things, no one will know what the end will look like. It's a transitional process. We'll have to live with uncertainty for a good long while. Not just our generation, but generations after us. It doesn't happen all at once. You're changing the governance of the world. We've had presidents who have tried to do that before. Woodrow Wilson tried and failed. FDR arguably succeeded because of the unique moment of power he enjoyed, which gives us the system we have to change today. George W Bush, you could argue, was the last one who tried, even on a relatively limited scale, and he failed miserably because he completely misunderstood how much our military power could really be expected to achieve. But the change needs to happen. With every year that goes by it needs to happen more. Someone's got to start. We've got to get them in the tent. We've got to have them in the tent pissing out. But that does mean, and we have to accept, the tent's going to look different after a while.'

'Wet,' said Abrahams. 'And smelly.'

Ehrenreich smiled. 'Maybe. So we have to live with a wet, smelly tent for a while. At least we've still got a tent. That's the road we have to take. I'm not pretending I can see where it goes. I can see the start but I can't see the end. That's a difficult thing. But then I look at the alternative, the road we're on, and I can see the end. And you know what?' Joel Ehrenreich took off his glasses and gazed at the president with his myopic eyes. 'I may not have the best eyesight in the world, but I can tell a dead end when I see one.'

'That's well put,' said the president.

Ehrenreich put his glasses back on. 'You can use it if you like. Be my guest. Keep taking us down that road, Mr President, take us down that road until we slam into the dead end, and I fear for my children. Not my grandchildren, sir. My children.'

55

JOEL EHRENREICH HAD been shown out. Only the president and Marion remained in the Oval Office.

'He's big on the history stuff, your professor.'

Marion nodded.

'That kind of talk can sound a little delusional.'

Marion smiled. 'On the other hand, it can be right. Once in every five hundred years.'

'You think it is?'

'Broadly. Not every word, not every implication, but a lot of it. The gist of it.'

'And that bit about making a start and seeing where it goes?'

'After two years on the Security Council, Mr President, I'm with Joel a hundred per cent on that.'

Knowles was silent for a moment. 'Marion, last time we met you told me you were thinking of resigning.'

Marion nodded. Until she got to La Guardia that afternoon and discovered that Joel Ehrenreich was with her on the plane to the White House, she had thought the president had asked her down to fire her.

'I want to tell you about something that's happening right now but I can't do that unless I know you're not resigning. Not yet anyway. I need you to stick around a little longer. Are you prepared to do that?'

Marion frowned.

'I need to know you're going to do that, Marion.'

The president was almost imploring her. She nodded. 'Okay.'

'Thank you. I want to tell you something.'

Marion listened as Knowles told her about the events of the past two days and the clash that was coming as the Chinese and American strike groups converged across the Indian Ocean.

'We would have about forty-four hours now until they get to Lamu Bay,' he said, glancing at his watch. 'Call it forty hours. The navy boys can't be sure exactly how quick they'll get there.'

Marion was silent, trying to take it all in.

'What do you think Professor Ehrenreich would say if he knew about it? You think this is the war he was talking about?'

'It could be,' said Marion. 'One of the battles, at least. I think he'd say if it wasn't this it would soon be something else.'

'He has a damn pessimistic outlook, doesn't he?'

'Actually, he can be quite a humorous guy. He does quite a good Eddie Murphy impression.'

'You're kidding me.'

'It's true.'

The president shook his head, laughing. Then he was serious again. Ehrenreich had talked about an awful confrontation, a massive catastrophe that would have to happen before things changed. 'What do you think he would say if I told him what I just told you?'

'I think Joel would say now's the time. Now's the time to do something different.'

'Now? With everything that's happening?'

'Extraordinary events make for extraordinary opportunities. He'd say something like that.'

The president's eyes narrowed slightly.

'But as you've seen, Joel takes a long, historic view of things. If I can be frank, sir. If I can be completely frank ...'

'He doesn't think I'm the guy to grab on to the coat-tails. That's what you're about to say, isn't it?'

Marion nodded. 'He's never been one of your fans. I think Joel would say you're not big enough to do it.'

Knowles took that on the chin. 'General Hale and the Joint Chiefs have developed four plans,' he said. He outlined them.

'What happens afterwards?' asked Marion.

'The military boys have got plans for that as well. They're anticipating an escalation. They're briefing me as soon as I'm finished with you.'

'What if we lose this engagement? The plans all seem to envisage us winning.'

'We will. On a military level, we will.'

'Then we create an enemy that's going to come back for more.'

'You don't think they'll learn a lesson?'

'No, sir. They'll be back for more. And in the meantime, whatever happens militarily, we're going to have the biggest economic war we've ever seen.'

'So which of those four plans would you choose?'

Marion thought for a moment. Then she looked back at the president. 'None.'

56

THE MEETING WITH the Joint Chiefs took hours. The president saw plans for the defense of Taiwan, the abandonment of Taiwan, the defense of Japan, response to Russian aggression against China on its northern border, Indian aggression against China on its southern border, Chinese aggression against India and Russia on both borders, attacks on US facilities in east Asia, submarine-launched attacks on the US west coast, a crackdown by the Chinese regime and collapse of the Chinese regime. But none of these was likely to take place in isolation. The more plans he saw, the more Tom Knowles realized that only one thing was certain: when shots were fired, the first casualties would be the very plans he had just seen.

In Sudan and off Lamu Bay, the standoff continued. The situation was exactly as it had been that morning, except the strike groups were now ten hours closer to each other.

He went up to the residence floor and took some time out in his study. As far as he was concerned, each of the military plans was as bad as the next. He didn't want to get there. He thought over the discussion with Joel Ehrenreich. He didn't know quite what to make of what the professor had to say. It was appealing to think you could change everything with good will and a couple of smart decisions. But the world didn't work like that.

And yet Ehrenreich's logic was obvious. Blindingly simple, which was what made it so hard to dismiss. And maybe extraordinary moments do create the opportunity to do extraordinary things. Not to change the world, perhaps, but to nudge it in a different direction.

But was he the man to do it? And more importantly, was Zhang? What if neither of them were the men to catch the horseman's coat-tails, as Ehrenreich had put it? Maybe they were going to be merely two more that the horse left trampled in the road – together with all the men and women whose lives might be lost because of their miscalculation.

At about nine o'clock he called down and asked Roberta Devlin to get everyone into the Oval Office. No military men. Just his closest advisors. And Marion Ellman. He had asked her to stay after Joel Ehrenreich was flown home.

No one had gone far. By nine-ten, everyone was there.

'I know we're all tired,' he said. 'Let me explain where I'm at.' He frowned for a moment, gathering his thoughts. 'We're in a multi-front confrontation with China. The truth is, I don't know why. Couple of months back, everything seemed fine. Now it looks like we've got a financial crisis, we're starting up a trade war and we've got a full-blown military confrontation going on. And every time I try to get some kind of a compromise and try to find a way out, it just gets escalated. And within the next thirty-six hours, when those ships get together, it's either going to get very, very escalated or something else is going to have to happen first. And the hell of it is, apart from us backing away and leaving our guys in Sudan – which just isn't acceptable – I don't know what that something else is. I can't see it.'

He paused again. Everyone in the room continued to watch him.

'Now, as most of you know, I had a meeting today with someone who told me he thought war with China some time in the not too distant future was inevitable unless we start to do business in a radically different way. By the way, he didn't know about what's happening out there in the Indian Ocean, so it was kind of eerie to hear him say that. His view is that we share certain global problems but we deal with them through the prism of national interests, and that means by definition we can't solve them. And eventually, when nations can't solve their problems, they fight. That's why he said at some stage we or our proxies are going to have a war – unless we find a way of dealing with these problems through a global prism. It sounds logical but it also sounds theoretical and I don't know how you do what he's talking about. I don't think he does either. Marion, is that a fair summary of what he said?'

Ellman nodded. Oakley gazed at her. Gary Rose had told the defense secretary about the meeting with Ehrenreich. The defense secretary thought it had about as much relevance to the crisis they faced as a seminar on quantum physics.

'So I don't know what to do. I do know that I don't want to fight a pitched battle with a hundred-odd ships out there on the Indian Ocean. I'll do it if I have to, I'm not saying I won't. It's my role as commander in chief to make that call and I'll make it if I judge it's in the best interests of this country. And if I thought it would put an end to this, I'd certainly do it. But I don't see how it does put an end to it. It seems to start a whole bunch of other things, and to be honest, I'm damn scared those other things will get out of hand and anything can happen. On the other hand, if I don't do it, I don't see how that puts an end to it either, and it just raises the prospect of a whole bunch of other things that might happen.' He paused. 'In all honesty I don't see the way out. And that makes me think, maybe we are in this historic confrontation between two powers, and maybe there is no choice and it's going to end up in a fight. But that's a damn depressing thing if you can see the fight coming and you can't do anything to stop it. It puts us back into the way World War One started. It means we haven't learned a thing in all the years and all the wars that have happened since then. And I know if something like this starts it's going to be a long fight and a hard one and I don't know that anyone's going to win, but I do know we're all going to suffer. Economically, militarily, in every damn way.' He shook his head, then threw up his hands. 'So that's where I am. I'll fight them there on Tuesday if I have to, but I don't want to do it. I don't know if history would look on that as a good judgment or a bad one. So that's it. Now I want to know what you all think.'

There was silence.

'Mr President,' said Oakley, 'I think you can get completely lost in trying to figure out where things will go over time and what history's going to say when what you've got to do is deal with a real, live situation in front of you. We need to deal with that first and let the historians write their books later. There's a military situation right now and we have to resolve it. That's the first thing. And if you do want to consider some new way of doing business with China, you have to do it from a position of strength. So in resolving this military situation it's all the more important to do it strongly, decisively, to win it clean, so they know who's boss. Let's win the battle, then start talking about the war.'

'We might lose the war,' said Abrahams.

'We don't have a war yet, all we have is a battle. Do the battle right and we may not have a war.'

'Mr Secretary,' said Ellman, 'I would argue that the war, if we're going to talk in those terms, has already started. The conditions for it started years ago when China overtook us as the biggest emitter of carbon, when it became the biggest holder of our government debt. When its interests and our interests became inextricably entwined and we didn't develop a new way of solving our problems.'

'Ambassador, that's your view and you're entitled to it. Personally I haven't noticed too many battles being fought since those things happened.' Oakley turned to the president. 'Mr President, let's deal with this first, show how strong we are, then you can start addressing these other things.'

'Hold on, John,' said the president. 'Let's back up. You said you hadn't noticed too many battles being fought in the past few years, so why are they doing this now?'

'That's a good question. We're in Uganda, that's one thing.'

'That's a sideshow,' said Gary Rose. 'They chose to escalate there. If they didn't want to escalate, they would have handed our boys back the minute the LRA took them across the border into Sudan.'

'It depends on what really happened with Fidelian,' said Roberta Devlin. 'We pretty much assume the political leadership gave orders to the PIC to bring Fidelian down. They may not have originally planned to.'

'But by the end they knew they had to take action.'

'And the fact they didn't may well have been opportunistic.'

Marion agreed. In her view that was the most likely way it developed. But if it was a matter of opportunity, then it would only have been a matter of time. 'If it hadn't been Fidelian,' she said, 'sooner or later it would have been something else.'

'Is this relevant?' demanded Oakley impatiently. 'It's here. It's now. We have to deal with it.'

'So you would go an immediate repulse when their carriers arrive?' said the president.

'I'd even consider an aerial attack out of Diego Garcia. I know we've taken that off the table but maybe we should put it back on.'

'John, that's unbelievably aggressive,' said Rose.

'So is shooting the hell out of a bunch of guys who were only trying to rescue their buddies. So is sending two carrier strike groups across the Indian Ocean to attack a force carrying out a UN-sponsored mission. And by the way, what were they doing waiting in such close range? Two of them? We can have our bombers out of Diego Garcia over their ships in six hours. Six hours and it's done. No one will even know about it.'

'John, I don't think we're going to destroy a bunch of ships out there and no one's going to find out.'

'Whatever. We issue the ultimatum, they might turn them around. In that case, we don't destroy them and they back down. That's good enough.'

'They'll be back for more,' said Ellman.

'That's your assessment, Ambassador. What's the intelligence you base it on?'

'Nothing we know suggests they'd be prepared to slink away and forget.'

'Nothing we know suggests they won't.'

'Zhang is under some kind of internal pressure over this. He can't just back down and pretend it never happened.'

'Or so you think on the basis of a single conversation with one of their ambassadors, if I recall correctly. A conversation that may well have been staged precisely to lead you to that conclusion.'

'Secretary, is there some reason you want to go to war with them?'

'We need a fact-based discussion here, Ambassador. If you've got facts rather than conjecture to present I'd be keen to hear them.'

'John, all of this is subjective,' said Abrahams. 'Let's not pretend otherwise. Mr President, let's step back and look at the options in broad terms. We can drive for a naval victory at Lamu Bay, whatever plan we use, and we can win it. Fine. Do we create an enemy that's going to look for another pretext or do we put them back in their box? That's a judgment and frankly I don't think anyone in this room has the answer. If we choose to go that way, time will tell. Second, we can look for a non-military solution. We can try to negotiate, but so far that hasn't worked. There's still time to try that again. Or we can call their bluff, and if it turns out it isn't a bluff we can back down then. Release their ships, try to work through some kind of deal over our men. Okay, that could take months and personally, in terms of your standing with the American people, you would take a terrible hit. More importantly, does that give them the sense they can do anything they want if they show a little military force? Do they progress to something else? Will we have to do something even more drastic next time to prove we won't be pushed around?'

'Ed,' said Rose, 'all you're saying is what the president said at the start. Whichever way you look at it, there's a risk this escalates. Whether we stand up and fight or back down, whichever way we do it, the risk is there.'

'And I would say,' said Devlin, 'that the fact that we can't get a negotiation going suggests we're on the path to an escalation. This military situation is all around a pretext. If they didn't want it, Dewy and Montez would have been returned to us at the very beginning. And that doesn't even begin to deal with the economic issue.'

'Let's not forget that we're the ones who created the naval standoff,' said Ellman. 'If I understand it, we did that, right?'

'In response to their ambush.'

'But that's an escalation. Is it proportionate? Two destroyers against seventy-three men? Why didn't we take one?'

'Does it make a difference?' demanded Oakley.

'It may to them.'

'Jesus Christ!'

'Okay,' said the president. 'Stop. This isn't helping right now. I've got to make a decision.' He paused. 'I think from what I'm hearing, on balance, is that I'm with John. We have to look at what's in front of us. If they're set on using this as an opportunity to prove something, that they can either beat us or they can stare us down, then the only thing we can realistically do is not allow them to prove whatever point they want to prove. And that means beating them.'

'Beating the crap out of them,' said Oakley. 'Then they can go back to Beijing and figure out some other point to make.'

'I disagree,' said Ellman. 'I think that's the wrong conclusion.'

Oakley snorted.

The president looked at her. 'Tell me why.'

'Listen to us. We're not looking more than an inch in front of our nose. We're saying, they want to prove this point, we won't let them. How do we know what point they want to prove? And by the way, what's the point *we* want to make?'

Oakley rolled his eyes. 'I think we know what point we want to make.'

'Then articulate it!' Ellman looked at Oakley angrily. She was getting more than a little irritated with his air of superiority. Besides, she had spent the last two days thinking she had resigned and she still believed that she was going to, so her mindset was that she had nothing to lose. 'Mr Secretary, I believe the way you put it was "we want to beat the crap out of them". Personally, I'm not sure that's quite a sufficiently well-developed analysis, but perhaps the president will think it's okay when he stands up to explain it in front of Congress.'

Roberta Devlin suppressed a smile.

Ellman turned to the president. 'Sir, we need to be thinking way broader here. What do they want? Not in terms of whether they want to blow up three ships or four ships, but what do they want from this whole situation they've created, the economic as well as the military, which I suspect very much they feel has got just as much out of control as we do?'

'I suspect it's turned out exactly like they planned,' said Oakley.

'Well, if I can use your own words, Mr Secretary, that's your view and you're entitled to it. We need to ask, what do they want out of this? What do we want? Where's the overlap? Or if there isn't any, where could we create an overlap if we're both prepared to move a little?'

'They're not prepared to move,' said Rose. 'We know that.'

'That's what they say.'

'They want to prove a point, and beating us, or even standing up to us and getting beaten, allows them to do that. The point they want to make is they're not intimidated by us.'

'That they have military power,' added Abrahams, 'to put alongside the economic power they're already exerting.'

'Probably,' said Ellman. 'If they could make those points, they'd love to.'

'Well, great,' said Oakley. 'Isn't that just a convoluted way of saying what I already said?'

'No. Because the question is why? Why make these points about your power? Why now? And what are you going to do with them once you've made them?' She paused. 'Mr President, we know they want greater say in international institutions. We know they feel they were short changed after 2008. We know they want to be seen as a partner in world leadership.'

'Then they need to learn to act like one,' said Oakley.

'Exactly. That's what *we* want. We want them to act like a responsible leader in the world. A responsible leader that doesn't destroy the financial markets of a friendly country just for the hell of it. That doesn't imprison its servicemen. That works with us on climate change instead of rejecting every proposal because it isn't enough. But to paraphrase Joel Ehrenreich, they'll be looking at us and saying similar things about what we should be doing in relation to them. Now, somehow getting those things together, that's our objective. To come out the other end of this process – and it's a long process, it's not one month or one year – as partners solving global issues from one perspective. So the question is, how can this situation help us get there? How do we take this crisis and use it? Not how do we use it to slap them down as hard as we can, but how do we use it to start turning them into a partner? How do we use the fact that they want to make some kind of a point about their power or about their lack of intimidation – whatever it is – to help us advance *our* agenda, to help start making them behave in the way we want them to?'

'We beat the crap out of them,' said Oakley, 'so they'll listen next time when we start talking.'

'And that's exactly the wrong attitude.'

'And what we have exactly from you, Ambassador, is a whole bunch of fine-sounding theory, and back down here in the real world, meanwhile, we have two aircraft strike groups bearing down and a bunch of guys surrounded in Sudan, and if you think backing down is going to get those guys out then, I'm sorry, but that's just not the world anyone else lives in. It's sure as hell not the world President Zhang lives in.'

'Secretary Oakley, don't twist my words. I never said we should back down. They have to be accountable. They absolutely have to be accountable.'

'Well, you don't want to back down and you don't want to hit them, so I'd like to hear what you *do* want to do.'

'I want to give them a way out.'

Oakley laughed.

'If there's going to be a way out of this, they can't lose face. Zhang is facing pressure over this and he can't lose face.'

'To hell with his face.'

'You can say that, but if we're asking him to lose too much face, he just won't do it. That's the reality. He can't do it.'

'Can't he? Zhang chose to start this thing and it's about time he learned what that means. I say we make him lose so much of his goddamn face he won't dare ever come back for more.'

'And our economy?'

'The here and now is the military issue. We make them lose so much face they don't dare touch our economy either.'

Ellman stared at him for a moment, then turned to Knowles. 'Mr President, this is a historic moment. Whether it developed opportunistically or in some other way, it's here and now. The United States is being challenged in a way it has never been challenged before, not even in the Cold War. The challenge in the Cold War was military. This is way bigger. Take away all the weapons, take away the guys in Sudan and those strike groups, and it's still there. We respond to this as if it's a military challenge, and we miss the point. We miss the opportunity.'

The president frowned. There was something about the way Ellman had put that. Take away the military challenge, and the underlying challenge was still there. That was true. That was an important point, one that seemed to have been lost sight of in the rush to a military response.

'I'm intrigued,' said Ed Abrahams. 'Ambassador, what's your idea for letting them get a way out?'

'It means taking a chance.'

Oakley snorted. 'Backing down, you mean.'

'No, sir. Not backing down. I said it means taking a chance.'

'We're going to take a chance with them? That's great. Let's not worry about what they've already done. Let's not worry about the eleven men they killed when we went in to get our boys back. Let's give them a chance to screw us over again.'

'John,' said Rose, 'you haven't even heard what she's got to say yet.'

'We need to give them a way out of this,' said Marion. 'To paraphrase Mr Abrahams earlier today, we need to invite them into the tent and hope they piss out. I suggest that–'

'Mr President,' snapped Oakley. 'Ambassador Ellman in her ivory tower can hope all she likes. I can tell you what's really going to happen. If we invite them into the tent, they're going to piss all over us.'

The president ignored him. He looked at Ellman. 'Tell me what you mean.'

57

PRESIDENT ZHANG SAT at the head of the table at the daily meeting of the Central Military Commission. On one side of him was Defense Minister Xu Changjiang and on the other side General Fan Keming. In theory, as chairman of the commission, Zhang was the most senior figure in the military chain of command.

One of the two admirals on the commission was giving an outline of the battle plan for the *Mao Zedong* and *Chou Enlai* strike groups against the American forces. He expected forward elements of the *Kennedy* strike group to be in position to join battle off Lamu Bay in support of the *Abraham Lincoln* within two hours of the arrival of the Chinese ships. The objective of the plan was the recovery of the *Kunming* and *Changchun*. Should the two ships or any others be destroyed during the fighting, the objective would be continuation of the battle until a surrender of the American forces on terms providing compensation for the losses suffered by the Chinese forces.

'And you believe our forces will be capable of bringing the American fleet to surrender.'

The admiral glanced at Xu, then back at the president. 'Yes, President Zhang.'

From the looks that he could see around the table, Zhang doubted it. He doubted that any of the other twelve men shared the admiral's faith, including the admiral himself. But standing up to the American fleet and inflicting at least some losses on them could be portrayed as a victory. He knew the way the Chinese press would be ordered to present it.

He looked at Xu. A couple of years previously the defense minister had developed a twitch that made his left eye blink frequently. He was blinking now, more often than normal.

'Thank you, Admiral,' said Zhang.

The admiral nodded.

Fan gave an overview of other developments. He described the current deployments of the Russian, Japanese and Taiwanese navies and the deployment of land forces on the Indian and Russian borders. People's Liberation Army troops had been dispatched to reinforce both sectors. After a Chinese victory, action by the United States could be anticipated in a number of sectors including punitive strikes on mainland army installations. The commission staff had drawn up plans for a series of pre-emptive strikes on US military facilities in the East Asia region to prevent this, as well as having a number of pre-selected targets in Hawaii and the west coast of the United States for immediate retaliation if US forces responded. Submarines would be in position to launch missile strikes at the naval bases in Pearl Harbor, San Diego, China Lake and Puget Sound.

Zhang listened with a growing sense of unease. 'When will you launch the pre-emptive strikes in our region?' he asked.

'As soon as battle commences between the ships,' replied the general.

'And the retaliatory strikes?'

'If the Americans respond with any other action.'

'Do you think the Americans will be able *not* to take action if we launch these pre-emptive strikes?'

'They may retaliate,' said Fan calmly. 'But they should not. The strikes will be in our region. Their defensive intent will be clear.'

'But if they did take action, we would retaliate on their west coast?'

'Yes. But if we do not launch the pre-emptive strikes, we do not protect ourselves. We must launch them. If the Americans are wise, they will not retaliate. They will see that the pre-emptive strikes are defensive.'

'The strikes will be forceful,' said another general. 'They will see that we will defend China with every means we have available.'

Zhang glanced at Xu. The defense minister blinked.

Zhang turned back to Fan. 'What will the Americans do after we retaliate for their retaliation?'

'After these strikes are launched, it will take them some days to put in place new deployments.'

'And then?'

'That will be a new phase, if they wish to open it.'

Zhang nodded. 'General Fan, these pre-emptive strikes do not sound defensive.'

'We are defending ourselves. The aggressive action was the hijacking of the two ships. Everything we do now is defensive.'

'Maybe we should not do the pre-emptive strikes.'

'Then we will be hit.'

'Maybe not.'

'We will be hit and the people will see that we are hit,' said Fan pointedly.

Zhang was silent. He envisaged a terrible series of escalatory actions. But he was not in control of the situation. It was unclear to him to what extent Fan had engineered it. Before President Knowles had made his public demand that China force Sudan to release the two American airmen, he had told Fan that he wanted the airmen released. He had told the Sudanese president as well. The American president's demand had made it easier for Fan to keep helping the Sudanese army hold them, if that was what he was doing. Zhang had not authorized that, much less had he authorized a Chinese-led ambush of an American rescue force to be planned, although it was clear from the military reports he had seen, and from what President Knowles had told him, that this is what had happened. By then, the *Chou Enlai* and *Mao Zedong* were under way towards the Kenyan coast. They must have been placed on station to be ready to intervene. He had not been consulted prior to their departure. From the beginning, therefore, the order that would have been required from him was not to let the carriers go, but to turn them around.

All of this had changed the balance of power in the crisis. While it had been economic, he had held the levers. Once it became military, it was Fan who had the initiative.

Zhang couldn't be sure what would happen if he made the demand for the ships to turn around. He could not be sure it would be obeyed. If that happened, if he gave the order to turn the ships around and it was not obeyed, he would be facing a coup. He would have to finish Fan or he would be finished himself.

Those ships would not be sailing without Xu's agreement. Zhang knew that didn't mean Xu had put his support definitively behind Fan, but it did mean he had put himself in a position to do that. If Zhang demanded that the ships turn around, Xu would have to decide. The question was whether this was the right moment to put the defense minister in a position where he would be forced to make that decision.

Zhang was certain that Fan would not move against him if Xu's support was not assured. To do that would run the risk of provoking a civil war with roughly equal military factions confronting each other on either side. He, Zhang, would be supported by the security forces, and Xu would have the leadership of the air force and key naval units. Fan would have the hardline wing of the army, which believed after 2014 that the military, as the guarantor of the state, should hold open political power. Fan would not want to see the Chinese air force, on Xu's orders, bombing army barracks. On the other hand, if Fan believed that he had Xu behind him, or if he believed the defense minister had been abandoned by his supporters, he might move. The internal security forces alone would be no match for the army. The fight would be bloody, but the army would prevail.

Zhang glanced at the defense minister. Xu was blinking furiously. He must know, thought Zhang, that if he brought Fan to power, he would not last long. That was what had kept the balance of power between the three of them for the past four years. Even now, if he lost his support, he would become irrelevant. So the question Xu must be asking himself, thought Zhang, was what would cause his support to drain away? What would cause the admirals and air force generals to abandon him? Being ordered to go into battle with the Americans – or being ordered to turn around? If that was the most important question for Xu, Zhang knew, it was the most important question for him too.

Zhang did not believe the admirals really wanted to fight the Americans. For all the talk he had just heard, he didn't believe they thought they would win and he didn't believe they would want to see two of their precious new carrier forces destroyed. But if the only way to avoid this was to back down, would they accept it? If he gave the order in the commission to turn the *Chou Enlai* and *Mao Zedong* around, and if Xu stood with him, would they feel that the Chinese military would lose so much face against the Americans that they would nonetheless support Fan in opposing it? Actually the question was not whether they would – but whether Xu believed that they would. It was not reality that mattered now, but perception. If Xu believed that his supporters would desert him if he agreed to back down, he would countermand the order. If he countermanded the order, then Xu would have definitively joined Fan, and the general would have won.

Yet if Zhang did not give the order, there would be a battle off Lamu Bay that would escalate on the other side of the world even before it was finished.

He had told the American president that the ships must be released. He had told him again and again. The only other thing he could have said was that Knowles must release the ships because he did not feel strong enough to give the order to turn the *Chou Enlai* and *Mao Zedong* around, but he could not say such a thing to the American president. Even if Knowles complied, the damage to China would be incalculable.

Zhang did not know what he would do. There was little time left now. The Americans had to back down. If they did not, he didn't know whether he would risk the coup or the confrontation. The confrontation, he felt sure, would escalate, but he did not know how far, and if he cracked down immediately on the opposition, domestic unrest might be contained. The coup, if he gave the order, might not happen, but if it did, the violence in China would be terrible, and the country's enemies, inside its borders and out, would seize the opportunity to seek their own goals.

Fan was watching him.

'How long is it until the carriers arrive?' he asked.

'Thirty-six hours.'

58

TOM KNOWLES HAD slept very little. He got up on this last day of the year and met with Gary Rose and Marion Ellman in the Oval Office to look at the note they had drafted. Then they went to the Situation Room.

Overnight, the Chinese and American strike groups had continued to make progress. Estimates now had them converging on Lamu Bay in around twenty-two hours. Russian naval movements had ceased and a Russian strike group and a Chinese group were holding position at a distance apart of around a thousand nautical miles, fifteen hours' sailing time if both groups closed. On the ground in Sudan there had been sporadic exchange of small arms fire but with no casualties. Drones had visualized the arrival of further reinforcements to the troops surrounding the American soldiers. Seventy-three Americans waited in the compound, in radio communication with Pressler's command center but unaware of developments at sea. They had seen two American drones shot down but others continued to operate above them.

The news silence was increasingly fragile. A reporter had surfaced on a Japanese TV station with a report of Chinese naval maneuvers taking place in the Indian Ocean. Intelligence sources surmised that there had been a leak on the Chinese side about large-scale ship movements and the Chinese had had to come up with a reason and had planted the story. Defense intelligence was also aware of rumors circulating within the US military of some kind of an operation related to Jungle Peace that had gone wrong. There was strong conjecture that the operation was related to Dewy and Montez but no one yet had any details of the action. Once those rumors started it was only a matter of time before they made it out of the military and into the media. The communication ban imposed on the servicemen within the *Kennedy* and *Bush* strike groups hadn't yet been breached but had been noticed by others in the services. No one was yet connecting them with the Jungle Peace rumor, but that was only a matter of time as well. Whether the communication blackout would hold until the strike groups met off Kenya was impossible to say.

A screen on the wall of the Situation Room showed the updated positions of the *Abraham Lincoln*, the *John F Kennedy* and the two Chinese carriers. The triangle of ocean between them, which had been so vast when this first began, now looked disturbingly small.

Hale briefly set out the military options again. This time a decision was needed.

The president looked around the table. It was a meeting of the entire National Security Council. He had taken advice the previous day from the White House counsel, who advised him that the full complement of the council should be involved. Overnight, Gary Rose had briefed Susan Opitz, Marty Perez and Doug Havering, the acting Secretary of State, about the events that had been unfolding in East Africa over the previous three days. Marion Ellman was in attendance as well as all six of the Joint Chiefs of Staff.

'Susan, Doug, Marty,' he said. 'Anything you want to ask?'

Doug Havering wanted more detail about the conversation the president had had with President Zhang. Marion knew he was probably doing that to put some kind of stamp on the fact that he was there. He had been throwing glances in her direction since the meeting started and they weren't friendly. Havering didn't know where Bob Livingstone's death left him and he was less than pleased to turn up and discover that they were three days into a major crisis and that Marion Ellman, of all people, was here before him.

Opitz had a couple of questions as well.

'Okay,' said the president after he had answered them, 'I've decided what I want to do and I want to run you through it.'

John Oakley stared at him.

'Once we're finished here, I'm going to send a note to President Zhang. In that note I'm going to say that we're going to release the *Kunming* and *Changchun* in twelve hours' time. An hour after that–

Hold on, John, just let me finish. An hour after that, we're going to send a force into Sudan to take out our men. I'm going to tell him that we expect to do that peacefully. We're going to go in, pick them up, take them out.'

'I can't believe she's actually persuaded you to do this.' Oakley shook his head in disgust. 'What if Zhang says no?'

'I'm not asking him, John. I'm telling him.'

'And he's just going to do what you say?'

'I hope so.'

Oakley gazed at the president for a moment, then shot a glance at Marion. 'Do you really think they'd believe that once we've backed down and given their ships back, we would fight them over seventy-five guys in Sudan? Are you really so naïve you think they'll believe that, Ambassador?'

Ellman didn't respond. The idea for this course of action was hers, and she and Gary Rose had drafted the note overnight. It hadn't been much fun. After long discussion on the details with her and the president, Rose had accepted there was a chance that her proposal might offer a way out of the impasse, but it was clear he didn't like the way she suddenly seemed to have become part of the core team on this crisis.

'They'd better believe it,' said Knowles. 'If they want to try to stop us, if they want to fight a war, we'll fight them. But over our guys. Over something that matters, John. Not over a couple of ships.'

'Mr President?' said General Hale.

'Yes, General?'

'You said twelve hours. Is that twelve hours from now?'

'That's twelve hours from 11am our time. I make that seven in the morning in Kenya.'

'So that makes it eight in the morning when our guys go in?'

The president nodded. 'We need to do this in daylight, General. I'll take your advice on that but I want to minimize the chance of something going wrong through a misunderstanding.'

'Daylight would be best to minimize that risk, that's true, sir. It does, however, expose our forces to significantly greater risk if the enemy chooses to fire on us.'

'I understand.'

'If we were going to plan this as an attack, sir, we would do it under cover of darkness. The equipment and training we have would give us a significant advantage.'

'General, we're not planning this as an attack.'

'Then that's trap number two we're walking into,' said Oakley.

'The fact that we're doing it in daylight,' said Ellman, 'is a clear signal that we're not attacking them.'

'Clear signal that they can fire at will.'

'Can we do it?' said the president to Hale, ignoring Oakley. 'Can we have a force ready in time?'

Hale nodded. 'Admiral Pressler has a force ready to go. But as your military advisor, I do need to point out the greater risk that our men will face by choosing to do this in daylight.'

'Understood, General. I take that responsibility.'

'I also should point out – although I assume you've already considered this – that once we release the *Kunming* and *Changchun* we lose the leverage we have established to protect our men from attack in Sudan. This puts them in a situation of maximum vulnerability and I can only stress–'

'I understand your point, General.'

'Without leverage, sir, strategically we have no–'

'General, I said I understand your point. I didn't order this leverage, remember? That was a decision taken by Admiral Pressler.'

'Who's the operational commander in theater.'

'Yes. In theater. And the implications now go a lot wider than the theater that he commands. According to your own plans, this precious leverage of his has put us twenty-two hours away from what might be the start of a global war. I understand the point. I've taken account of it.'

'We'll need clear rules of engagement,' said Hale, as if it was some kind of threat. 'When the forces going in can shoot, what weaponry they can use. How much provocation they'll be expected to put up with before they're allowed to defend themselves.'

'Dr Rose will discuss that with you.'

'Mr President,' said Admiral Tovey, who had been doing some calculations on a piece of paper, 'without reopening the question of your decision, operationally, if we were to release the *Kunming* and *Changchun* and then for one reason or another an hour to two hours later we made the choice to recapture them, perhaps because of the outcome of the mission you're talking about, given the positions of where our respective fleets would be at that point, realistically we wouldn't be able to recover them before we ourselves came in range of the enemy fleet. Even before that we would risk aerial engagement with aircraft from the Chinese carriers. I guess what I'm saying, sir, is once we let them go, they're gone.'

The president nodded. 'That was my assumption. I also assume the Chinese will work that out as well.' He turned back to Hale. 'General, are there any other considerations from an operational perspective?' He waited. 'General?'

'No, Mr President.'

'Then you'll speak to Dr Rose about the rules of engagement after this meeting and I'll approve them when they've been drafted. I assume Admiral Pressler will be developing the operational plan to get our men. I'll also approve that and speak with him when it's done. General, let's make sure everything in the plan is very clear. I don't want to provoke a misunderstanding in what I am sure is a very tense situation. Please make sure Admiral Pressler understands that. If there's anything in the plan that looks like it might lead to a misunderstanding, I will hold the admiral personally accountable.'

'Mr President, are we forgetting something here?' said Oakley. 'What about Dewy and Montez?'

'My understanding is that they're not at that location. Is that correct?'

'At the moment we don't have a fix on their location,' said one of the officers.

Oakley shook his head.

'What do you suggest, John?'

'They were the reason we went in.'

'We went in on the basis of poor information.'

'John, we got suckered,' said Rose. 'That's obvious.'

'Yeah, and who suckered us?'

'What is it, John?' said the president impatiently. 'Say it. Say it now and let's have it on the table.'

'We're in the endgame here. We've taken it *this* far, and now, when it comes to the crunch, we're going to back down and take an indefensible chance. There's no other word for it. It's indefensible. You may like the sound of what the ambassador said, but to me it's fantasy.'

'What?' said Doug Havering quickly. 'What did the ambassador say?'

'And we're betting a hell of a lot of lives on it,' continued Oakley, ignoring him. 'Seventy-three men on the ground plus Dewy and Montez plus the guys who'll be going in there to get them. And I wouldn't stake the life of *one* of them,' he said, stabbing a finger hard on the table, 'on Zhang taking your note and saying, sounds good to me, let's let those men go. Not one.'

'John,' said the president slowly, 'I have as much care and concern for the lives of each one of those men as you do. I'm conscious that I'm the one sending them in, just like I sent Harley Gauss and Jack Duffey. Don't think there's a day I'm not conscious of that.'

'Tom, I'm not saying you aren't. But I think your judgment is wrong. I think it's dead wrong. And as Secretary of Defense I have a responsibility to tell you. The ambassador has got some rosy-eyed view of what's going to happen if we're nice to Mr Zhang and now is not the time for rosy-eyed views. Mr Zhang doesn't respond to nice. He responds to reality.'

'We're not being nice. We're being firm.'

'Well, that's the problem, isn't it? On the one hand the ambassador would like us to believe we're going to be seen as being tough by telling Zhang what's going to happen. But the reality is, what's going to happen is we're going to back down. And that ain't tough. And it's pretty clear what interpretation Zhang's going to put on it. So we've got this ambiguous message here and either side can interpret it like they want and the only thing you can be sure of is they'll interpret it differently.'

'Mr Secretary,' said Ellman, 'in a situation like this, that's a strength.'

'Yeah. It's about as strong as General Hale here giving Pressler an order to attack and Pressler reading it as an order to retreat.'

'No, sir. This is not a battle. Not yet. If we want to avoid that, it's useful to have something both sides can interpret in the way they want. To one party it looks firm, to another it looks weak. Yes, there's ambiguity, but that gives both sides what they need. That's how you get yourself out of these situations, Mr Secretary. You can argue over the interpretations later when tempers have cooled.'

'Ambassador, it's arguing over the interpretations later that gets you into a war. All this is going to do is–'

'John,' said the president. 'You can stop talking to Ambassador Ellman, because it's not her decision, it's mine. Now, I've heard what you've had to say. Thank you. I've made the call. This meeting isn't to reopen the debate over the decision, it's to discuss what we do to implement it.'

Tom Knowles was conscious of the way the defense secretary was looking at him. He respected the passion in Oakley's commitment to his point of view. And he wasn't at all certain that the other man's judgment was mistaken. There was a risk, a very real risk, that this would go wrong and that many lives would be lost, both amongst those on the ground in Sudan and those who would be going in to recover them. And yet Tom Knowles had found himself having to balance those lives against those that might be saved, not only by avoidance of the sea battle – which would recur at some point, at some time, if the underlying causes that had brought the confrontation to a head weren't resolved – but by the possibility of creating a new way of doing business with China. And the only way, he had decided, to create it, was to do it, even though that required a leap of faith so big that he himself found it hard to contemplate.

He knew that it was possible his entire presidency would come to be judged on this decision. And in the end he had made his choice. He had barely slept all night for thinking about it, but he had made it. Perhaps it was the words Joel Ehrenreich had spoken to him, the gauntlet the bald academic had laid down. Or perhaps it was some instinct deep within him, an instinct to do the challenging thing, the striking thing, that had taken him out of a commercial law practice in Reno twenty years earlier and propelled him all the way to the White House, an instinct that had been stifled over years of campaigning and calculating and choosing what to do on the basis of what pollsters told him, but which now, at the last gasp, reasserted itself.

If history was going to judge him on one decision, on the direction he chose to take at Lamu Bay, then let it be a bold one. That was the choice he had made. Let it be a brave choice. Let it be a decision that broke the mold – or at least tried to – not one that cowered in fear of the consequences if anything changed.

'Tom,' said Oakley, pleading now, 'at least, at least, do them at the same time. Tell them we're going in to get our men at the same moment we release their ships. At least that way you don't look like you're backing down.'

'I'm not trying to give the impression that we're backing down.'

'But that's what it looks like!'

'Then that's unfortunate. But they have to know their ships are gone. Now if we go in at the same time, they don't have any guarantee of that. That's why we figured–'

'And if their ships are gone we have no guarantee our guys are coming home!'

'That's why we figured,' said the president firmly, 'that we'd need to leave an hour, so they could be sure their ships really are released, like Admiral Tovey said. Is an hour enough, Admiral?'

Tovey nodded.

The president looked back at Oakley. 'John, I've thought long and hard about this. In some ways, it would be easier to do what you say. But I'm going to go with this. I'm going to take this chance.'

'Then at least put some kind of threat in the note! For God's sake, Tom, we have no leverage once those ships go and if he chooses to shoot our guys down in Sudan he just shoots them down. At least put something in the note about what we'll do if he does that.'

'Mr Secretary,' said Ellman, 'the whole point is that we don't put a threat in the note.'

'And what do we do if it happens, Ambassador? Maybe you might want to start thinking two steps ahead. What do we do if they shoot our guys?'

Ellman was silent.

'You've got no answer, have you? No answer at all!'

'That's something we'll deal with if we have to,' said the president.

Oakley shook his head in anger. 'Let's just hope it never gets out, Tom. When our guys are dead, and the Chinese are crowing to the world how they made us stand down, let's just hope no one ever finds out it was because Ambassador Ellman thought we should take a chance on President Zhang.'

'It's not the ambassador's decision, John. It's mine.' Knowles paused. 'The debate's done. President Zhang's going to get the note. It tells him what we're going to do, then he's got twelve hours to decide how he's going to deal with it. If he wants to call me, he can call.' The president looked around the table. 'If anyone else has a reason I shouldn't send it – something that overrides everything we've thought of – now's the time to tell me.'

Looks were exchanged around the table.

'This sounds too sensitive for a note that other officials might see,' said Susan Opitz.

Knowles nodded.

'Shouldn't you call him?'

'I don't want to have a discussion. I don't want an argument. I just want to lay down what's going to happen.'

'How do you know no one else is going to see it?'

'We've got a way.'

59

PRESIDENT ZHANG OPENED the bedroom door in his pajamas. It was 11.30pm in Beijing. In front of him stood his personal secretary. His knocking had woken Zhang's wife. The Chinese president himself had not been asleep.

'President Zhang, there is an email,' said the man.

Zhang didn't understand. He followed him out. The secretary had been alerted that an email had come to the secure account that was linked to the president of the United States.

They had never used it. It took ten minutes of both of them looking in cupboards and files before they found the password for the account.

Zhang opened the message, triggering the receipt function that alerted the other side to the fact that it had been accessed. He scanned the note quickly. Then he pressed to print it. The secretary opened a door to go and retrieve it from the printer.

'No!' said Zhang quickly. He closed the email account and went to get the paper himself.

'Do you want it translated, President Zhang?'

Zhang shook his head. The secretary watched as the Chinese president took the note to his study. 'Wait here,' he said, and closed the door.

He sat down and read the text. No translation was required. It had been sent not only in English but in Mandarin, as if it was understood that Zhang might choose to read it without involving an interpreter. It laid out the actions the United States was going to take over the next fourteen hours. The tone of the note was firm. It said Knowles would be happy to take a call for clarification if there was anything that required explanation.

It wasn't intended as a backdown, Zhang knew. He was being told what would happen. If anything, it could be interpreted as an act of humiliation towards him, like the note a parent would send to a child who couldn't manage his own affairs.

But Zhang wasn't looking for such interpretations. He was looking for something, anything that would enable him to give the order to turn the *Chou Enlai* and *Mao Zedong* around with confidence that it would be obeyed.

He studied the note. There would be an hour between the release of the ships and the rescue of the American soldiers. His mind fixed on that, toyed with it, turned it around. An hour. That was the thing this note gave him. What possibilities did it create?

An idea began to form in his mind. One hour was very little. Two would be good. Four would be better. But if he rang Knowles and asked for four, he would need to explain why. If he didn't explain why, the American leader would think he was prevaricating. And he could not divulge the reason.

So it was one hour. That was what he would have. But that was something. It might be sufficient.

In his mind he inspected it from every side, this one hour that he would have, like a precious piece of treasure that had suddenly appeared from nowhere and that might – or might not – be enough.

Zhang read the note one last time. No one but his private secretary knew the note existed, and not even he knew what was in it. The Chinese president began to tear it up. Tear after tear, until it was in little pieces. He put the pieces in an ashtray and set a match to them.

He watched them burn.

The note changed the entire balance of the situation. When the *Kunming* and *Changchun* were released, there would be no reason for the carrier groups to keep approaching. Xu could tell them to stop, even if Fan wanted them to proceed. Would he? What would happen, he wondered, if he spoke to Xu and said he had spoken with the American president and that Knowles was going to back down and release the ships? What if he said the American president was doing this in order to get China's help to solve America's economic problems?

That would turn the situation on its head. That would show his version of China's true power, its economic strength, trumping Fan's military muscle.

Where would Xu stand then? Would he turn the ships around? Would he believe that his admirals would agree to do so? As far as they were aware, they would have won. The Americans would have backed down.

Then there would be one hour before the Americans went in to get their men. Where would Xu stand if he, Zhang, went to Fan during that hour and gave him a choice?

60

TOM KNOWLES SAT in the Oval Office and wondered what was happening in Beijing. Were orders being given? If so, what for? Time ticked by. It was the early hours of the morning in China, he knew. He wasn't sure if he had really expected a call from Zhang. No call came.

The *Mao Zedong* and *Chou Enlai* carrier strike groups continued their progress. The last satellite sighting before nightfall in the area, at 10.40am Washington time, showed them closing from the east on the Kenyan coast. The *John F Kennedy* was approaching from the south. In Sudan, the standoff continued. A heavily reinforced ring of troops surrounded the compound and the burnt-out Chinooks outside it. From the other side of the world there were reports of Chinese mobilization. Troops had deployed at key points on the Russian and Indian borders. Additional naval forces had put to sea. US defense intelligence was tracking them. They were moving to positions from which they could threaten US military assets in the region, which included the US presence in Okinawa and elements of the *William J Clinton* strike group, which were in the South China Sea. US forces in the region were on combat alert. Air support out of Diego Garcia was being readied.

Through the afternoon Knowles had meetings on the economic situation with his officials and congressional leaders. He tried to keep his mind on the issues, keep it from thinking about what might or might not be happening in Beijing. But in the back of his mind he kept wondering. Had he made the right decision? Was John Oakley right after all? Of the people he was meeting, only Susan Opitz was aware of events in the Indian Ocean. From time to time she glanced at him and he could tell she knew what he was really thinking about. As for the measures they had introduced to put a floor under the markets, they hadn't been truly tested yet. Everyone agreed the real test would come in two days' time, when the markets reopened after the New Year's Day holiday. But by then, Knowles knew, the world might have been plunged into an entirely new era. If that happened, there were no measures that would be enough to hold the markets back from a last, massive dive. But that would be the least of his worries.

By five o'clock in Washington it was dark. Sunrise over Kenya, and the first satellite view of the ships, wouldn't come for almost another six hours.

It was early morning now in Beijing. Still no call from Zhang.

He had finished his meetings on the economy. There was nothing now to take his mind off it.

'We got the receipt message,' Abrahams reminded him. 'There's only one way that can happen. He definitely got the email.'

Knowles nodded.

Ed Abrahams smiled. 'Hell of a New Year's, isn't it?'

'You going somewhere?'

Ed shook his head. 'Best party in town's right here.'

The president had originally planned to be in Nevada for New Year's. A bunch of people were going to be at the ranch. He had called Sarah to tell her he wouldn't make it. Sarah knew something must be going on but didn't ask.

'You want to watch the football?'

Ed grinned. 'I thought you'd never ask.'

Time crawled. At eight-thirty he turned on Monday Night Football. Last MNF of the year, Buffalo Bills and the New England Patriots. Not a game that was going to make a difference to anything. Ed had brought Gary Rose and Roberta Devlin with him to the president's sitting room on the residence floor, as well as Marion Ellman. The president had asked her to stay at the White House as the day unfolded. He ordered up pizzas and beers and Cokes.

A little after ten-thirty a call came through from General Hale to say that daybreak over East Africa had shown the carrier groups still approaching the *Abraham Lincoln*.

'I guess they're not going to turn around until they're sure we've let them go,' said Rose.

Knowles nodded. He turned back to the television and took a swig of his beer.

The game was drawing to a close with a score of fourteen to ten in favor of the Bills. But Knowles didn't have his mind on the action that was winding down in the Ralph Wilson Stadium in Buffalo. Halfway across the world, a new year was dawning, and the action there was just beginning.

At a couple of minutes past eleven Hale called to say that the *Kunming* and *Changchun* had been released. The commanders on both ships had acknowledged the communication from Pressler informing them they were free to go. Twenty minutes later Hale rang again to say they were on their way.

It was done now. The leverage, as Hale called it, was gone.

On the TV some kind of New Year's program reviewing the previous year had come on. Clips and commentary. Knowles saw footage of himself. The five people in the room watched, but their minds were elsewhere.

Soon the TV was counting down the New Year.

'I should have got some champagne up,' said the president.

'Let's just hold on a little for that,' said Abrahams.

The phone rang. Hale said that the helicopters out of Lodwar had just lifted off.

IN BEIJING, PRESIDENT ZHANG and Defense Minister Xu walked into General Fan's office. Fan was having a lunch meeting with four of his senior officers. They sat at a conference table covered with maps. Zhang gazed at the general. Fan told the officers to leave. They got up and walked out, taking their time in a show of arrogance towards the president. Fan stayed seated.

'The *Kunming* and *Changchun* have been released,' said Zhang. 'The *Chou Enlai* and *Mao Zedong* have been stopped.'

Fan's glance went quickly to Xu, whose eye was twitching.

'I spoke with President Knowles. He agreed to release these ships in exchange for help with his economic problems.'

Fan watched him suspiciously.

'I have told him we will allow his men to be removed.'

Fan jumped up. 'That will not happen without my order.'

'The victor should be magnanimous. To let him take these men is another victory for us.'

'If that is what you call a victory,' Fan retorted sarcastically, 'what is a defeat?'

'The Americans are moving immediately. Their men are already in the air.'

'Then we will deal with them.'

'You will not. They will not be molested.'

Fan smiled.

'What?'

'We'll see.'

'There will be no battle in Africa today, Fan. If there is a battle in Africa, there will be a battle here. Look out the window.'

Fan looked. Internal security forces ringed the building.

Fan reached into his pocket. He pulled out a cell phone. 'With one call, those men out there will be lying dead.'

Zhang took out a cell phone from his own pocket. He glanced at Xu. The defense minister hesitated, then pulled out a phone as well.

The three men stood around the table, phones in hand.

Zhang had never visualized in his mind what it would look like when it came, the final moment of confrontation with Fan. Now it was here.

'You need to make a call,' said Zhang. 'You can give the order to our men in Sudan to allow the Americans in, or you can unleash a war here in China. Look at Xu and ask yourself if you think you will win. Think about it carefully, Fan. You only have a couple of minutes. You need to decide which call to make.'

Fan's eyes narrowed. He looked at Xu. The defense minister stood behind Zhang, his eye blinking furiously.

ON THE TV, the program had changed. Some kind of entertainment show had come on.

It was a distance of almost a hundred fifty miles from Lodwar to the target in Sudan, Knowles knew, but the helicopters would be over Sudan when they were about halfway there. He watched the time ticking by. Half past midnight. They would be over Sudan by now. They might already be under attack.

He glanced at the others. Roberta Devlin had fallen into an exhausted sleep. Ellman was gazing at the rug, thinking about something. Rose was watching the TV. So was Ed Abrahams. Ed looked at him and smiled ruefully.

Every couple of minutes he glanced at his watch. He kept telling himself he wouldn't, but he did. Quarter of one. Twelve of one. Eight of one. The watch hands slowly moved. One o'clock. He closed his eyes. One o'clock. They'd be on the ground now, or just about. He could almost see it in his mind like a movie, the helicopters coming in over the clearing he'd seen in so many reconnaissance photos, hovering, setting down beside the blackened Chinooks outside the compound. The dust rising, their rotors slowing.

And then what? Gunfire? Missiles? Perhaps before they'd even come down. Perhaps they were in flames.

Second thoughts swarmed through his mind, as they had in every spare moment of the day. What John Oakley had said that morning was true. If it failed, and if the story got out about how it happened – and it would get out – it would be the end of him. No one would care about the fact that he had averted a global war, all they would care about would be the men he sent in to die. He may as well hand over to Walt Stephenson right now because for the next two years he would be the greatest lame duck in history. Compared to him, Jimmy Carter with his Teheran rescue farce would be a tactical genius.

Suddenly he wished he hadn't done it. He looked at his watch. Ten past one. It was too late. They were on the ground. They had to be.

'Tom?' said Ed Abrahams.

He looked up.

'You okay?'

He frowned. 'Yeah.'

Ellman and Rose were watching him.

'It's too early to have heard anything,' said Rose.

'I know.' He took a deep breath. Too early to have heard anything, and too late to change it.

They waited.

'Anyone hungry?' said Abrahams.

There were shakes of heads.

'Well, I am.' He ordered up nachos and sodas.

One-thirty came and went.

One forty-five.

Two.

An hour there, an hour back. How long on the ground to load everyone up if things had gone smoothly?

Nothing happened. Marion was struggling to stay awake. Beside her, Roberta Devlin snored gently.

Two-thirty.

Two-forty.

The phone rang. They jumped.

The president picked up the receiver. He hesitated for a moment. 'Yeah?' he said.

The others looked at him expectantly. Hale had rung him to say there was no news yet.

Ten minutes later the phone rang again.

He picked it up. 'Yeah?' His face changed. Suddenly he was deep in concentration. 'Yeah … Yeah … All of them … Yes …' There was a long silence as the president listened. 'Really? I didn't expect that.' Another pause. 'Okay, thank you, General. And pass on my thanks to Admiral Pressler. I'll speak with him shortly.'

He put down the phone.

The others were watching him.

'Well?' said Abrahams.

The president was silent for a moment. Then he nodded. 'Happy New Year.'

They burst into grins.

'We got a bonus. Dewy and Montez were there as well.'

'*Yes!*' said Rose, clenching a fist.

The president allowed himself a smile, savoring the moment. Then he looked at Marion Ellman. He nodded slightly.

She smiled.

'I guess all we have to do now,' said Knowles, 'is figure out what we do next.'

61

A WEEK AFTER Dewy and Montez were brought out of Sudan, the two airmen stood beside the president at the White House. Colonel Ron Dagovich, commander of the rescue force, stood with them as well. The East Room was filled with reporters and camera crews. The president introduced the servicemen and then each said a few words. Behind the president, John Oakley, Marion Ellman and Susan Opitz watched on.

Dewy and Montez had rested and received treatment for the injuries sustained during their capture and captivity. Each had superficial wounds. Montez also had a broken arm which had been splinted with a stick in the jungle and required operative correction. The arm was in a sling. They had been debriefed and helped by Defense Intelligence staff to articulate the words they would deliver to the world's media. During their captivity they had seen Chinese soldiers operating alongside the Sudanese troops to whom they had been handed over. They and Dagovich were firmly instructed to avoid talking about that and other operational details.

In the White House, the week had been filled with intense discussions. If this confrontation wasn't to happen again, its resolution needed to be the start of something new. What? The points of view clashed and clashed again. Marion Ellman found herself within the circle of the president's closest advisors. Long meetings were held by the president with her, Oakley, Devlin, Perez, Opitz and Rose, with intelligence and State Department China experts participating as needed. Knowles had had two conversations with Zhang, to each of which Ellman listened. They detected hints of accommodation in his voice. Was he as shaken by the confrontation that had nearly taken place as Knowles was? Had he been strengthened by it within the regime, or weakened? Intelligence reported that General Fan had not been seen in public since the event and there were rumors that he was no longer in Beijing. It was unclear what, if anything, this meant. In the second conversation, when Knowles broached the subject of a meeting to resolve the economic conflict, Zhang gave what seemed to be a strong signal that he would welcome the idea. Knowles still didn't like talking to him, and probably never would. But it seemed possible that the Chinese leader might be open to something more.

The draft of the remarks the president was now about to make in the East Room had gone around and around that tight circle of his advisors.

'First,' he said, after the servicemen had spoken, 'I'd like to pay tribute to the bravery of these two men, Captain Pete Dewy and Captain Phil Montez.' Knowles turned to face them. 'We've heard in your words something of what you went through but, gentlemen, I'm sure it doesn't approach the experiences you actually endured. I think that very few of us in this room today can truly understand what that involved. And I would also like to thank you, Colonel Dagovich, for bringing these men home. Your leadership and strength of purpose brought your men through a difficult time until success was achieved. And we should remember this. The cause in which you were fighting, all three of you and every other man with you, is a just one. Let us also pause to remember those who paid the ultimate sacrifice in this cause. They were brave men and their families and their country are rightly proud of them. They fought to liberate people from a tyranny of evil. Their comrades continue this fight. It's a cause that does justice to this great country. If the day ever comes when the United States doesn't feel it can pick up its arms in such a cause, then I would fear for what we will have become. Gentlemen, your country thanks you.'

The president turned back to the reporters and paused. There was applause for the servicemen. Tom Knowles nodded.

'Now, in case anyone is wondering, I would like to affirm that the United States is going to continue Operation Jungle Peace until we achieve what we set out to achieve. I've said before, Jungle Peace is a good cause, it's a just cause and I am proud to lead that fight. If anyone thinks the United States is going to back away from it because of one episode like this, then they are wrong. If anyone in the Lord's

Resistance Army is seeing this message, then I have some words for you: give up now and face fair justice. Surrender now because the United States is coming and we *will* get you.'

The president paused. The three servicemen, under the impression that applause must be normal at presidential press conferences, clapped. A few of the journalists joined in, to the amusement of their colleagues.

'Now, it seems to me that this is a good opportunity to make some other remarks. We're at the start of a new year. I don't think the last year ended too well.' Knowles smiled self-deprecatingly, then the smile went. 'This new year is not going to be like the last.' He paused, gazing at the audience, to make sure they knew this was where the serious part of the message started. 'I know we all say that every year, and by about the end of January things are looking very similar to the way they always were. Not this year.

'The fact that Pete Dewy and Phil Montez are able to stand here with me today and aren't imprisoned somewhere in Sudan is because of the way we worked with the government of China. Naturally there are details I can't talk about in public. I'm not saying it was a completely smooth process. I'm not saying we didn't have our moments. But we do have these two fine men and Colonel Dagovich here with us today and what I can say is that without the cooperation of the government of China they would not be here. That's an important fact. I have already expressed my thanks privately to President Zhang, but I would like to repeat my appreciation publicly here today. President Zhang: Thank you.'

Knowles stopped to give the thank-you emphasis. Details had been released of the mission to rescue Dewy and Montez, of a firefight followed by a standoff with Sudanese troops that had taken place while the United States was enjoying its holiday week, and of the successful resolution of the siege. Word of the confrontation that had loomed with China at sea had not been released. Information pertaining to that was classified at the highest level and not even the commanders of the *John F Kennedy* and *George HW Bush* strike groups had been given the full details of the situation off the Kenyan coast as they headed towards it. How long the secrecy would hold, it was impossible to say. One way or the other, participants in the drama would start to talk, but few of them knew the whole story, and hopefully it would be historians in ten, or twenty, or thirty years who would piece together the full picture of what had almost taken place off Lamu Bay in the holiday week of 2018. Not now. If the reporters in front of him had been aware of that, Knowles knew, the demand for a confrontationist attitude to China would have been almost impossible to resist, not least from his own support base in the Republican Party. And that attitude was the opposite of what he was about to express in the words that came next.

These words were for President Zhang.

'That cooperation is a good thing. It's an important thing. The United States and the People's Republic of China can no longer pretend they can do something that helps themselves if it hurts the other. This goes for each of us – it goes for both of us. We're too close for that. Our global system is too entwined. The problems we face, we have to face together. That doesn't mean telling each other what we're going to do without any room for discussion – it means working out what we're going to do together. Like we did for Captain Dewy and Montez. That worked. If it worked for one thing, I don't see why it can't work for another. If it worked for Captain Dewy and Montez, I can't see why it can't work for everything else.

'So let me go back to what I was saying about the way last year ended. It ended badly because we were not cooperating. I'm not placing blame. It takes two not to cooperate. But I think the position in which we find ourselves today – the market measures and the trade barriers and the painful economic effects we're all going to feel unless we can quickly find a way out of this – shows just how bad things get when cooperation isn't there. I don't want the American people to feel those effects. They're not abstract. They're not ideas in a book or numbers on a page. They're people, they're lives, they're dreams and aspirations that have every right to be fulfilled. And it's my responsibility to spend every minute of my time and every ounce of my energy to make sure that happens. And I believe that President Zhang feels the same about his responsibility to the Chinese people, and I respect that.

'I'm not making any demands. I'm not calling today on President Zhang to revoke the sanctions his government announced, because I know he'll do that when he feels there's no reason for those sanctions to be applied. Those sanctions don't help him and they don't help us, and I know he doesn't want to use them. And I'm not saying that I'm revoking the measures we announced to protect the integrity of our markets. I don't like those measures. I don't want to have them in place. They go against every instinct and belief I have in the power of fairly regulated, freely operating markets to help drive our economy and make our lives better. The sooner I can revoke them, the happier I'll be. But I think the last few days have shown that they've brought back stability to our markets. I know President Zhang understands I can't revoke them until I'm convinced that our markets are protected in other ways.

'So we need to find a way to get these measures and sanctions removed, and we need to do it quickly. Here's what I'm proposing. I'm proposing that President Zhang and I sit down together with our respective officials and talk about this. I'm not talking about next year, or next month. I'm talking about next week. I'm talking about tomorrow. My diary's free. I ask President Zhang to join me. Let's talk about how we can work together to make sure that everyone can be satisfied that sovereign investment funds act in the markets as truly commercial participants without a hidden political agenda. There's no reason they shouldn't be in the market. The market needs them. How do we make that happen? I don't know. I don't mean to speak for President Zhang, but I suspect he doesn't know either. But we do have some very smart people in Washington and Beijing who can help us figure it out.

'Let's talk about that for a start. Then maybe we can talk about other things. Let's talk about China's role at the IMF. Let's talk about carbon dioxide emissions. Let's talk about what's happening in South Africa. I'll talk for as long as it takes. My diary's free. Let's talk about the things we need to solve, but can't solve alone.

'Now, I know this isn't the way summits between leaders are done. I know we're supposed to have the agreements in place before we even sit down. Well, I've got news for you. This time we don't. But we still need to sit down. And yes, this is the start of something that goes on and on. I don't know exactly what it looks like, I don't know exactly where it leads, but I do know we need to make a start, because the alternative just won't work. A wise man said to me a little while back that he couldn't always necessarily see to the end of the road, but he could tell a dead end when he saw one. If I had to choose between the two, I'd rather be on a road that leads somewhere, even if it's going to take us a little while to find out where it goes, even if there's going to be a little uncertainty, than heading into the dead end we're all familiar with. As president of the United States, I owe it to the American people to take us on a road that leads us somewhere. As president of the People's Republic of China, I'm sure that President Zhang feels that he owes that same thing to the Chinese people. So I'm saying to you, President Zhang, let's take that first step together.

'This is a new year. Let's make sure that at the end of it, it doesn't look like the last.'

The president paused. He surveyed the journalists sitting in front of him. Some were writing in their notebooks or tapping on tablets, others were watching him.

'Now,' he said, and he glanced briefly over his shoulder towards the back of the room, 'before I conclude, I have one more announcement to make.'

62

ED GREY HAD missed the start of the White House press conference, caught up on the phone with a client who was trying to get his money out of Red River. Grey had been forced to shut down redemptions from the fund and was spending half his days cajoling clients who swore they would take out every last cent of their investments the minute redemptions opened again. They might do it, they might not. When the dust settled they might realize they would be hard put to find another fund manager who hadn't done the same thing. Either way he had no choice but to stop them now.

When he finally managed to get off the phone and come out into the trading room, the president was talking about the importance of cooperation with China. All eyes in the room were on a screen showing the press conference. The only sound was the president's voice.

The trading room wasn't the same as it had been before the crisis. Somehow it was a sadder, smaller place. A couple of faces were missing, people who had gone home for Christmas and decided they didn't want to come back. There would be more, Ed knew. He could see four or five who would drop away over the next few weeks. You could tell by their faces, by the look in their eyes. Something had gone. The fire was extinguished.

Boris Malevsky was going to be one of them. He was listless, mechanical. Fidelian had burned him up.

Grey turned his attention back to the screen. The president made his appeal to Zhang to join him in a summit to solve the economic crisis, then said he had one more announcement to make.

Grey folded his arms as the president continued speaking. It was a bold step, he thought, to call for a summit. Or a desperate one.

The president didn't look desperate, thought Grey, watching him carefully. What was Knowles expecting Zhang to say to the idea of a summit? He must have had an expectation of Zhang's response to make that suggestion. More than just an expectation.

On the screen, a tall woman in a blue pant suit was coming forward from the group of officials who had been standing behind the president.

Grey had been momentarily lost in his thoughts. 'Who's that?' he asked.

'Marion Ellman,' replied one of the portfolio managers. 'She's the UN ambassador. Knowles just said he's naming her as his nominee to be the new secretary of state.'

The president shook her hand and stepped away from the lectern. Ed Grey listened as she began to speak.

'Mr President, I'd like to thank you for this great honor. Before I say anything else, I'd like to pay tribute to my predecessor, Bob Livingstone. Bob was a truly ...'

Grey grunted. One secretary of state was bound to be much like another. The president's choice was going to make no difference to his life.

There were more important things for him to think about. He went back to his office.

Tony Evangelou followed him in.

'Interesting, huh?' said Grey.

Evangelou nodded. He took a seat.

Grey pulled up some market indices on a screen. There was a slight bounce going on.

'You think this might be the start of something?' said Evangelou.

'You want to be careful of wishful thinking in these situations.'

'I know. Still, if they get something together ...'

Grey nodded. The response from the Chinese president would be the thing that really moved the market. If he was negative – if he was even only lukewarm – the market would be right back where it had started. If he was positive, there'd be a kick.

'Ed, do you think we really started it?'

It was a question Ed Grey had been asking himself for weeks. Was he a pawn or was he a player? The idea that this whole crisis was the result of his decision to short Fidelian was somehow unbelievable and yet there was nothing to say that it was impossible. If he hadn't started shorting Fidelian, would the market have stumped up the twenty-three billion when Fidelian came looking for cash? Maybe it would have. Was it conceivable that one fund, with one well-timed set of trades, had triggered a series of events that had sent the world's markets from New York to Tokyo plunging in panic? The possibility was both terrifying and awe-inspiring. Ed Grey didn't know if he even wanted it to be true. Part of him did for the sheer rush of being able to boast – or even merely to know – that he was the man who had moved the markets. Part of him feared it for the vulnerability it revealed of how the markets could be moved by the right set of trades at the right psychological moment.

'I don't know.' He shrugged. 'Who cares, right?'

None of that really mattered. It was twelve weeks since Ed Grey had made the decision to short the stock of Fidelian Bank, and in that twelve weeks he had seen the value of Red River fall by twenty-four billion. The fund would have collapsed entirely under the margin calls of the banks if the accounting rules hadn't been suspended. All that mattered to him now was what position the fund was going to be in when the accounting rules were reimposed, and how he was going to make that twenty-four billion dollars back. And then some.

You could lose money fast. But get in ahead of the market, make the right set of bets, and you could make it back again just as fast.

If the Chinese president said yes to Knowles' suggestion, bond prices were going to rocket. Equities too.

Ed Grey thought about what Knowles had said. Whatever the president claimed, he couldn't possibly make a public proposal for a summit without knowing that Zhang would agree. There must have been a deal. In Ed Grey's mind, an idea rapidly formed of what that deal looked like. Zhang must have agreed to get the Sudanese to hand over the helicopter pilots in return for having Knowles ask him to a summit. It made perfect sense. A deal like that would play to the constant Chinese gripe that they didn't have enough say in international financial affairs.

And whatever Knowles said, however tentatively he presented it, neither man, thought Grey, would go to a summit if there wasn't at least the outline of an agreement already worked out. That wasn't how politics worked.

Tony Evangelou was thinking exactly the same thing.

As was every trader in every DIV, bank and brokerage around the world.

Evangelou raised an eyebrow questioningly.

'We still got that cash?' asked Grey.

Evangelou nodded. Red River had close to a billion in cash from assets they had liquidated in the last hours before the mark-to-market rules were suspended. The money had been destined for their banks to meet margin calls, but with the suspension of the rules, the margin calls had been suspended as well.

Evangelou was still watching him.

Ed Grey looked at the screen for a moment. Then he turned back to Tony Evangelou.

For the first time in weeks, he had a smile on his face. He was about to say something he had thought, in the darkest of the dark days in the past few weeks, that he might never say again.

'Let's get in there and buy.'